EIRINI PRESS

CW00422273

The House Martin

BY WILLIAM PARKER

EIRINI PRESS

Eirini Press (Eirinipress.com)
510 Long Hill Rd.
Guilford, CT 06437

Eirini Press—exploring reawakenings to wholeness
© 2010: William Parker

Cover design: Tarol Samuelson

Library of Congress Control Number: 2010921543
The House Martin/William Parker

ISBN: 978-0-9799989-2-8
    1. Parker, William—Author
    2. The House Martin—Title
    3. Recovery—Fiction
    4. English—Fiction

For George, and for Ma and Pa,
who are not the people in this book.

Special thanks to my sisters Viv Parker and Stella Parker-Bowden for their constant encouragement and suggestions, and my brother Bruce for helping to keep distant memories alive. I'm very grateful to the following who took the trouble to read my first clumsy drafts and came up with a stream of helpful comments: Matthew Barry, Gilly Brennan, Jamie Crichton, Jan Eade, Sue Drummond Haley, Helenka Fuglewicz, Peggy Kirby, Elizabeth Lewis, Edie Reilly, Sally Scott, Rose Shepherd, Baillie Walsh, and Sue Williamson.

Also many thanks to Anna Brickles, Richard Gates, Deri Lindsay, Sarah Lowry, Steve Mackay, Pauline Mosesson, Helen Owen, Amy Prior, Gillian Rowe, Tim and Karen Rowe, Carla Sever, Helen Sterling, Doremy Vernon, Stella Walker, Patti Webb, and Sam Woods.

I'm greatly indebted to Denise Meyer who edited my pages across the Atlantic so skillfully, patiently, and with such sensitivity. Lastly, but by no means least, a huge thank you to Nina Hopkins Deerfield and Katherine Deerfield who were so determined to see this book published.

I.

Oh *fuckandbolloxandpissandshit!* My trousers—they're ruined, totally ruined. There's a bloody great hole in the knee. I can't believe
I've just done that; brand new suit, too—first time I've bloody well
worn it. We're not talking Tom Ford here, or even Hugo Boss—
Marks and Spencer's Italian Collection actually, and the cost hadn't
exactly broken the bank, but I fancied I looked the business in it.

How the bloody hell did it happen? Well, I know the answer to
that, of course. I'm monumentally drunk, that's how.

One moment I was at the top of the stairs outside Charing Cross
Station, and the next I'm flying down them like a tap-dancer on
acid, trying to stop myself from going into a dive; halfway down, I
had one of those life-flashing-before-my-eyes moments. Just when I
thought I might be winning, down I went, my arse rat-a-tat-tatting
on the stairs, hurling my briefcase into the air at the same time.
Anyway, I ended up stretched out along Villiers Street with the back
of my jacket flipped over the top of my head and my lips French
kissing the tarmac—and the tinkling sound I could hear from far
away was various bits of my mobile scurrying down towards the
Embankment.

I lost it for a bit, and when I came to, I was being propped up
into a sitting position against a wall by three bright eyed young lads.
Eastern Europeans—all high cheek bones, crew cuts and Primark
jackets. One of them was making an attempt to dust me down,
flicking at me with great big hands, while the other two went about
collecting fragments of my mobile before putting them in the pocket of the jacket they'd just removed from the top of my head. My
briefcase was fetched from the cobblestones above the stairs, and
before I could say anything to stop them, my head was being tipped
back and my new friends were administering a shot of tepid lager
from a half empty can straight into my mouth—as though I needed
any more, for Christ sake.

'Is okay? Is okay?' They were all patting my back at the same time.

'Yes, yes. Is okay. Thank you so much. Thank you, thank you… Very sweet of you.'

I couldn't wait for them to leave me alone, and they did quite soon, after pulling me to my feet and more patting on the back. Just for a tiny while, with the shock, I felt completely sober, and then horribly embarrassed, of course, with half of London looking on, including a whole load of laughing kids who were staring out at me from the windows of Pizza Hut. I'd put on a hell of a show for the end of their school outing. 'Go to London early to see the Changing of the Guard, then on to a matinee of Chitty Chitty Bang Bang for your first visit to a West End Theatre; afterwards sit in your favourite pizza restaurant and watch a drunk geezer rolling down a flight of stairs outside.'

—⁕—

I've managed to make my way down here to the closed up flower stall outside Embankment Station, trying not to limp while looking for a semidark place where I can sit down and survey the damage. There's a lot of acting going on because what I really want to do is have a bloody good rub of my elbow and give in a little to my quivering chin. Very gingerly, lowering my very sore bum onto an iron bollard, I prepare myself for the worst.

There's no future in the trousers, I can see that immediately, so I'm delving around in the pocket of my jacket for my mobile, doing a breathy little whistle that is meant to convey a nonchalant attitude to whoever might be listening. I'm just praying that all the parts that have broken off might just click back together again like a kid's Lego set, but now I've opened my hand, I can see an empty casing, a smashed screen, and a disconnected something that might be the battery. That means I'm going to be joining the queue at the Carphone Warehouse tomorrow morning.

I can't bear that—the bloody pointless waste of time. Waiting in line and very ill-at-ease anyway because it's just the sort of situation that makes me feel so inadequate—all those questions being fired at me that I really should know the answer to, about 'SIM' cards, 'minutes carried over', 'predictive text' and insurance policies I've not taken out because I was sure they were a bit of a con. It's the same feeling of being out of my depth that I get around macho mechanics when taking the car in for a service, or those cocky lads that serve you at New Covent Garden. Last time I was there I caught sight of myself in a mirror performing a ludicrously unbelievable swagger holding a tray of geraniums. Didn't fool anyone. Middle-class, middle-aged poof buying his bedding plants.

It's not only the trousers—I've trashed the jacket as well. Two of the buttons on the right cuff have disappeared, the third's hanging by a thread, and the lining inside the arm has been ripped to pieces and is hanging out the end of the sleeve. I'm already busy working out a little scheme in my head to take the whole suit back to M&S in Oxford Street to complain about the quality and insist on a refund.

'This garment has developed a fault, I'm afraid.'

'Where, Sir?'

'The buttons on the cuff have dropped off, and there's a hole in the trousers.'

'Ah yes, Sir, I see it. A big hole at the knee encrusted with dried blood, a bit of gravel and an old cigarette butt.'

Oh bugger and balls, that's not going to work.

—m—

Until the stranger appeared, it could have been just any one of hundreds of identical evenings at The Rainbow. I'd taken up my usual position in the downstairs bar, leaning against the wall at the far end, briefcase between my feet and jacket over my arm. I would have been holding not the first in a succession of enormous glasses of white wine in one hand while the fingers of the other fiddled with the change in my trouser pocket that was to provide me with the next. Two barely pubescent barmen with acres of Calvin Klein underpant showing above their jeans were manning the bar at the far end, failing to notice thirsty punters because they were too busy flirting with each other and jigging around to the Kylie and Madonna concert videos on the big screen in front of them.

Standing right next to me, Willy Whitehall—my name for him because he shrieks 'civil servant' in his pin-stripe suit, leather attaché case and tight black brogues—was already about to treat himself to what was probably his fourth or fifth glass of wine, the point in the evening at which he's liable to launch into a serious discussion with the non-existent person standing next to him. Nick and Gerard, two laymen from Westminster Abbey, were at their allotted places at the bar, balancing their huge frames on the narrow stools, flirting with a young oriental guy with long black hair and a shirt knotted above his belly-button. The gents were already well into their second bottle of Chablis when I arrived. I'd given them a quick nod of acknowledgement—my way of saying 'I'm not coming over this evening for a gossip about the dean...' and then I'd settled down for a good long drinking session with no interruptions, lost in my own little dream world. Just the way I like it.

'Ben? Ben Teasdale?'

Shit. Unsolicited company. The grinning face in front of me was only very vaguely familiar, and a name was absolutely out of the question.

'Hello, there...' I said, embarking on a desperate mental search through the alcoholic haze, whilst trying to organize my features into a look that might imply recognition. 'Well I never! Fancy seeing you! How on earth are things?'

Bloody well caught out. I hate that.

My position in the downstairs bar at The Rainbow gives me a clear view of anyone coming down the stairs, and if it's ever someone I know, their temporary disorientation in the dark usually allows me time to escape. It isn't that I particularly mind being caught in alcoholic 'flagrante delicto'—it's just that drinking has recently become an intensely solitary pleasure. One's company, two's a crowd. So my concentration had slipped this evening. My eye was off the ball. However many I'd had was nicely hitting the spot, and the smiling face was bearing down on me before I had any chance of avoidance.

'It's Val,' the stranger said, giving the lie to my facial efforts. A hand was extended.

'Val Lorrimer?'

A great hurricane of names and faces blew past me as I tried to place his face in various parts of my life, starting in the recent past, before I was forced to delve farther and farther back into the mists of time. An acquaintance from another office? Someone who used to train at the YMCA? The former partner of an old friend? Christ, a dodgy one night stand from the early days? Even farther back, for God's sake—University halls of residence? And then at last, memories stirring from about as far back as it's possible to go...

'My goodness,' I said, 'What an extraordinary memory you have!'

'You haven't changed!' He was nodding his head in surprise as he pumped my hand slowly and deliberately, a huge grin on his face, 'Totally recognisable!'

It was the name that had made sense to me first, followed by his features—first the dimple at the chin, then the two slightly wonky front teeth and the lopsided smile—pieces of a jigsaw being moved around before slipping into place, then the puzzle suddenly complete under the heavy disguise of the now receding hairline and furrowed laughter lines round the eyes.

'But it's incredible that you remember me, Val,' I'd shouted into his ear above the Justin Timberlake soundtrack, 'We were just kids.'

'Yea, but you were exceptional, Ben. Who the fuck wouldn't remember you! You were everyone's hero after what happened!'

I got away as soon as I could without being impolite—thirty

minutes or so, but I can't be sure. Time's one of the first things to go wonky when you drink like I do. Before managing to leave, I'd earnestly asked him, while stealing impatient glances at my watch, all the right questions about how he'd spent his life. He'd told me of his childless marriage and the ten years passed as a solicitor in an old family practise in Tewkesbury, followed by a tortuous coming to terms with gayness, a difficult divorce, and the epiphany of a new life after flight to London. I'd placed my hand on his shoulder and squeezed empathetically at the story of his first adored lover who'd died in the epidemic of AIDS at the end of the eighties. He'd not been able to adjust to a lone gay life in the city and had returned to his roots and the very same job he'd left behind a few years before.

'I pop back up to the bright lights every now and again just to remind myself that I'm still a sexual being, Ben. Nothing doing at all in Tewkesbury. They like to think they're absolutely cool about it all at work—as long as there's no mention. They don't mind me being a poof as long as they think of me as being interested in nothing more threatening than the odd glass of sherry.'

Of course I remembered him. After a few minutes, it was as though his face hadn't changed at all in forty years. In fact, as we were talking, the image of every one of those six boys that shared the dorm with me that extraordinary summer term began to knock at my consciousness. Closing my eyes now, I can see not only their individual faces and the beds they slept in, but also the colours in the tartan rugs we all unpacked from our trunks and laid across our beds at the beginning of every term. That last look over the shoulder back into the dorm as I left it early in the morning all those years ago is an indelible stain on my retina—like a press photographer's flash that never stops blinding.

A gay Val Lorrimer makes perfect sense to me in hindsight, of course. Lanky, pigeon-chested Val, shy of the shower, terrified of games, adoring of Julie Andrews and preferring the company of his mother to that of his father. Not totally unlike yours truly, actually.

Just typical of me, though, that when he mentioned that it might be an idea to leave the bar and pop out to find somewhere quieter for a bite to eat and a 'real chinwag' about 'that funny little school', I bestowed upon him my usual well rehearsed lie which implied the existence of a brooding presence awaiting my return, somewhere south of the river, rolling pin in hand and finger pointing at the clock.

'You've a lover, Ben?' he said.

I nodded solemnly, half kidding myself that the absence of a spoken reply somehow diluted the falsehood.

It's totally barmy that I do that. I don't know why I always need to get away. I don't know why I didn't want to stay and explore further his proposition of casting me as a schoolboy hero. Why couldn't I have invested just a little more of my time in little Val Lorrimer?

Except not so little Val Lorrimer these days. The puny figure of the boy has given way to one with a princely girth. As I'd lowered my ear to his mouth to catch an anecdote about coming out to his aged father, I'd noticed the suede jacket flapping open to reveal shirt buttons straining to hold a bulging waistline in check.

Perhaps that was it. Perhaps I feared the invite for a bite might lead to a suggestion of something a little stronger, and the idea of having to deliver an embarrassed rejection was just too much to bear. A deeply unappetizing image of two portly gentlemen rolling around on top of each other 'for old time's sake' had sprung to mind—not the sort of fantasy I'd set out to enjoy at the beginning of my evening. In the cold reality of a sober morning, I'm going to be asking myself why on earth I flatter myself that 'Lucky' Lorrimer from school would have the slightest interest in flinging himself around with an ageing schoolmate, especially since, from the quickest of updates of his life, he seems to have a particular interest in—and to have enjoyed a modicum of success with—the much younger man.

Perhaps I wanted to protect the image he had of me as a young schoolboy hero and felt it was necessary to make a rapid exit to cut short his exposure to the reality of me as a tipsy lone drunk?

But I'm not being totally honest here, because it was probably nothing more than the need to protect my drinking time, not wanting to slow down and wait for a companion sipping at half the rate I'm used to when alone.

As soon as we'd properly completed our reintroduction, I'd insisted on buying a celebratory drink—and then another when my glass had idled empty far too long while I waited for him to catch up. Within a few minutes I was clocking his slight confusion as he noticed my glass was empty yet again, while the ice in his first gin and tonic—I'd insisted, against his protests, on getting him a double rather than the half pint he'd asked for—clinked impatiently in the tumbler in his hand and another, double again, sat on the ledge behind us, awaiting his attention.

'Er, white wine, isn't it?' He'd hurried over to the bar and come back with a lone refill for me.

'Not joining me?' I said.

'Christ, no, Ben. Actually, I'm not that big a drinker,' he said, raising his tumbler to his lips and taking an unpractised gulp.

'Your mobile, Ben. Give me your number. We simply must meet again soon,' he responded when I finally managed to make it clear that I was right out of time and heading for deep trouble with someone at home who must have come across as having all the allure of a possessive Widow Twanky.

I changed the penultimate digit. Made it a 'naught' instead of an 'eight', slurring a vowel sound and sliding it to an end with an emphatic 't'. Eleven numbers, but useless with just the one out of place. An easy mistake for him to make, I assured myself, as he typed it into the mobile held close to his face, the blue-green light shining up into his eager eyes.

I gave him a bear hug. Quite genuine, too, with my hands moving up his back to stroke and pat not only in acknowledgement of our school days and shared sexuality, but also because I was smitten with a real sense of sadness for him. It seemed to me he'd struggled to put a brave face on a lonely and rather unfulfilled sort of a life.

I winked at him and gave him a nudge in the direction of a blond college boy type who'd come into the bar while we'd been talking, implying that yes, indeed, it was time for me to be off but that I was also standing in the way of the real purpose of his visit and must therefore hurry along and leave him alone to get on with it.

'He's looking at you,' I lied. 'He's definitely looking at you...'

A common ruse of mine to allow for an exit. I can't count the times when I've interrupted a lagging conversation to point out with an envious gleam that some drop dead gorgeous young thing was trying to catch an eye.

'Are you sure?' he said slowly, staring unashamedly and wide eyed in the young man's direction.

'Absolutely bloody certain. Two's company, three's a crowd! I'm off!'

'Go get!' I mouthed pantomimically as I reached the bottom of the stairs, 'He's waiting.'

'You funny fucked up old bastard,' I said aloud to myself as I stopped halfway down the street. 'What the bloody hell's up with you?'

I nearly went back to say I did have my mobile on me after all so I'd better take his number too, and 'I've phoned my better half to say I'll be late—fuck the consequences—let's catch that bite to eat after all.' But I didn't. The idea had been overridden, and I'd carried on down towards the Embankment to prepare for my impromptu circus act on the stairs.

I don't suppose it mattered to Val Lorrimer one way or the other, though. Typical of me to invest him with a sense of rejection that I don't suppose for a minute he was feeling. No doubt he stayed at the bar, battling with the unwanted gin and tonics and risking a smile or two at Blondie before deciding that Ben Teasdale was quite wrong and that the young chap wasn't the slightest bit interested, but anyway, there were plenty more fish in the sea. Then he'd no doubt remind himself that he was up from Tewkesbury for the night to misbehave, and misbehave he bloody well would—after all, he hadn't travelled over a hundred miles to spend the entire evening reminiscing with a barmy old school friend, however nice the re-making of an ancient acquaintance might be. And wasn't it just great that Ben Teasdale had had the sense to know when to fuck off and leave him to it?

Perhaps he was already filing the meeting with me into his portfolio of anecdotes.

'Guess what happened to me last night? Bumped into—and recognised, would you believe—someone I was at prep school with nearly forty years ago. Forty years ago! Knew him instantly!' And how would the description go on from there?

'He was a real nutcase, was Ben Teasdale. Totally, absolutely flipped out one summer term... Bit of a broken down sort of a character now. Quite obviously over-fond of a drink. Couldn't quite put my finger on it, but I felt really rather sorry for him. Think he's probably led a lonely and rather unfulfilled sort of a life.'

—⁂—

My new suit's ruined, and I don't have a mobile any longer. My knee's bleeding, I've twisted my ankle, and I must have bashed my head as well because it's pounding like fuck. There's a bit of a gooey mess somewhere near the crown; I can't quite see it but something's oozing down onto my shirt.

I'm not 'monumentally' drunk—typical bit of Teasdale exaggeration there. I'm no more than a bit tiddly, actually. I might have had about five glasses, I suppose, but these days, that's just the very start of an evening. If I hadn't crashed down that flight of stairs, I'd already be another two glasses down the line by now.

This is bad, though. It's not alright, this crazy drinking alone behaviour. I'm just a bit short of fifty years old and I'm going on nightly benders, drinking like a student at his twenty-first. But this is how it is now. This is what I do, with terrible hangovers in the mornings as though I've been out to some fantastic party, when in fact I'm opening bottle after bottle at home, alone, and falling asleep on the sofa with my clothes on and waking up to bright eyed people being interviewed on the telly that's been on all night.

I don't know how it's happened; it's just sort of crept up on me. Perhaps it's a family thing. Perhaps it's because I'm like my poor old mum. But this is really frightening now, and it's going to get worse if I don't do something about it. Game's up with this drinking malarkey, Ben. Game's got to be up.

And I've let something precious slip through my hands this evening, too. I could have stayed to ask Val to tell me everything he remembered about what happened that night in the dormitory. He could have filled in some of the gaps. He was there, right there, and I've passed it all up just because for some mad reason I need even more white wine than I've already had. I must be fucking mad.

II.

Courtlands School, May, 1968

I'm waiting for her.

I hate waiting more than anything. Even if she was going to be here on time I wouldn't like the waiting, but with Mummy you just never know. She could be early or late. It's even possible that she won't come at all. And then if she does come, I don't know how she'll be. It might be one of her bad days. I don't know why she's coming. She's never been by herself before. Anyway, I'm sitting here all ready to go. I'm wearing my blazer and my boater's on my lap.

Mr. Burston—that's the Headmaster—came into history class just as we sat down and took me into the corridor. It must have looked to the others as if I'd done something wrong, or something terrible had happened, like when Granddad died.

'Teasdale, your mother has phoned and asked if she might take you out to lunch, and just this once, as a special concession, I'm going to allow it.' It's a special concession because I don't see my mum and dad as often as the other boys. We live near London, and it's just too far away for them to come and collect me and take me home for the weekend and then bring me back. It's one hundred and ten miles from our front door to the school front door. My dad measured it in the car once. Some of the other boys from London go home at half term, but my dad's a very busy man. He often travels abroad and can't spare the time to come and get me. I could go home by train, but it's an expensive business and my dad would still have to take me across London on the tube, though actually I think I'm old enough to do that by myself.

She said she was coming between twelve o'clock and one o'clock. That's what she said, but she must be coming by train to Chepstow, and then she'll have to get a taxi all the way to Saxham, and sometimes it's very difficult to find one at that station. I know that because once Mummy got the dates wrong and sent me back to school a whole day late, and I had to get a taxi from the station. It took ages for it to come, and in the end I didn't get to school till after high tea was finished.

If I'm still sitting here by the end of lunch hour, perhaps Mr. Burston will change his mind about the special concession and tell me to go back into class. Perhaps he'll have another phone call in a minute, and Mummy will say she's missed the train. But she can't do that because she must be on the train at the moment, and if she'd missed it she would have phoned by now to say she wasn't coming. Unless she's very bad today.

It's not free time, though, because I'm learning my dates while I'm sitting here waiting. Mrs. Marston came out of the class to give me my copybook. 'Don't think you're getting away with just sitting there doing nothing when you've got work to catch up on,' she said. I'm doing all the dates from the Battle of Hastings to the Battle of Bosworth Field. History's my very best and favourite subject, but it's not sinking in at the moment because nothing sinks in while I'm waiting.

I'm sitting in the big leather chair in the entrance hall. It's really huge, with sides that go up and then out at the top like an elephant's ears. I think it was to stop your head getting into a draught in the olden days. I saw a picture of King James I sitting in one just like this when he came down from Edinburgh to be the King of England as well as being the King of Scotland. It's not that I'm small for my age—I'm going to be eleven next birthday—but it's so big that my feet only just touch the ground, even with my bottom right on the edge of it. It's a horrid slippery chair and there's horse hair coming out of tears in the arm and the seat. It's more like wire than hair. It's scratching my elbow and the back of my legs. It wouldn't do that if I was wearing long trousers. I've told my dad that I'm just about the oldest boy wearing short trousers, but he hasn't bought me long ones yet. He says they're too expensive, but he'd change his mind if he knew how upset I get about the teasing.

I've just pulled out a whole clump of the horse hair by accident. I try to stuff it back in but I can't, so I've pushed it down the back to hide what I've done, but they'll know it was me on account of the fact that I was the last one to sit here. That's another thing to worry about.

We're not usually allowed in the entrance hall. It's strictly for the staff and when we're arriving and leaving with our parents. The floor's very shiny because Mrs. Morgan, the cleaner, polishes it every day and is very proud of it. Worgan's mother slipped on it once and fell over with a bang when she was bringing him back from a weekend exeat—that's what they call the day when we're allowed out with our parents. It's Latin for 'go out', I think. Anyway, Heath, who's one of the prefects, giggled about Mrs. Worgan being flat out on the floor that day and was straightaway given a detention and nearly demoted, but after that they put an old Persian carpet down which is just as bad because it moves around if you're in a hurry on it. It's very dangerous if you ask me.

It feels funny to sit on this big old chair, because no one ever does, but Mr. Burston told me to while I'm waiting. But actually, the really good thing is that when everyone passes by on the way to lunch, if I'm still here, I'll be invisible. I don't want anybody to see me waiting. They'd be able to if I was right underneath the grandfather clock which is where we usually are if we're ever in the hall. We have to stand underneath it when we're waiting to go into the Headmaster's study for the slipper or even worse, the cane. I've never been slippered or caned.

I'm sitting so close to the clock that I can actually see the big hand moving round, and the tick-tock is really loud. There's another sound that comes out when you're this close to it. A sort of swooshing. It must be the pediment swinging back and forward inside.

This hall's the smartest part of the school. There are mezzotints on the walls—so many they're nearly touching each other. Mezzotints are prints that were made on copper plates hundreds of years ago. They show all the kings and princes and generals who beat Napoleon. I counted them once, and there are thirty-two altogether.

They've been here since before the school was a school. In the olden days it was a big house built by twin brothers who liked each other so much they lived together for the whole of their lives. They had two of everything put in—two sitting rooms with big windows overlooking the river, two studies, two bathrooms, two lawns and four huge bedrooms each for their friends who came to visit. But there's only one front door and hall, one kitchen and one dining room because they liked to have their dinner together. It's funny that they forgot to take their mezzotints with them when they left. Perhaps they moved out in a hurry.

I'm very worried about Mummy coming. It might be that my dad doesn't know she's on the train. Perhaps he's gone away for a bit and she's very bad at the moment. Perhaps she's got in a muddle and that's why she's coming.

I don't want anyone to know about Mummy. I worry that people at school might start talking about it, especially the matrons and the teachers, though I know, in fact, that they do talk about her. I don't want them to feel sorry for me, but mostly I don't want anybody at all to say nasty things about her.

It's my number one secret. Nobody must know about it, and if I think they're beginning to know, I have to show them that they've got it all wrong. But it's getting more and more difficult, because Mummy's actually getting worse and worse, and one day the whole secret's going to come tumbling out, and I won't be able to do anything about it.

It's not the only secret that I've got. There are two more. One's a brand new secret from last term that I've got to keep for someone else forever and ever, and that person doesn't even know that I know about it. And the third secret is the oldest one of all and especially bad because if the other boys find out about it they'll bully me forever, and probably all the boys in the next school I go to—if I pass my common entrance exam—will know about it too, and perhaps even at university.

I hope Mummy doesn't get here while everyone's going past into lunch. I don't want anyone to see her, even if she isn't very bad. When she came to the Carol Concert at Christmas, Redmond asked me if she was a gypsy. I don't even think he was teasing me. Mummy doesn't look like the other mothers really. She has very long dark red hair and wears big earrings and lots of jangly bracelets and she used to wear fishnet stockings, though now she's become a hippie, which is even more embarrassing. My dad said that they might be coming to Sports Day at the end of term. I was thinking of writing a letter to say please don't wear the earrings from Christmas, but anyway, now she's coming today, and all I can do is wait.

I hate waiting so much. It feels as though something dreadful is going to happen.

The term starts off with me waiting—sitting on the sofa in the drawing room at home waiting for the taxi. This last time I'd been waiting for such a long time, I think longer than usual. You'd think that I'd be getting more used to it by now, but I'm just not. The funny thing is that I really wanted the taxi to come, and I really didn't all at the same time. I hate to go away from home at the beginning of term more than anything, but I really didn't want to miss the train either. It's just the sort of thing to get me worried.

Then I thought I heard a car, so I stood up and looked through the window at that gap in the hedge where a bit of it has died and saw the lights go on when the man put the brakes on. I'd told Mummy it should come for us at half past ten if the train was at eleven, but it was only quarter past ten. I expected him to turn the engine off and wait for a bit, but he tooted the horn straightaway and drummed his fingers on the steering wheel as though we were late rather than him being early.

I pretended not to notice him. I didn't want to leave yet, and Mummy wasn't ready anyway. She was in the kitchen listening to the radio like she normally does in the mornings. I could just about hear that song about going to San Francisco with flowers in your hair, which is one of Mummy's absolute favourites. She was singing along quite loudly. The radio was making a funny noise though, because ever since it stopped being the Light Service and became Radio 1, she's often not been able to tune it in properly, even though I've explained to her about FM and medium wave a hundred times. She turns it up really loud as if that's going to make it clearer. Now when I hear it sounding as though the hoover's been left on, I know it's going to be a bad day.

Even though the taxi driver couldn't see my face, I put on a bored expression to show that there was more waiting to do before I was ready to go. For all he knew I might have had my own radio on too loud to hear him. It wasn't my fault that he was early. I picked up the little glass of sherry that Mummy had given me—she always gives me one on the day I go back to school—and took a big swig. Sometimes it makes me feel less worried, but it wasn't working that day. It was the only thing I'd had to eat or drink all morning because on the day that I go back to school my mouth always goes very dry, and my throat feels as though it's too small to let anything at all go down, even something slippery like a banana.

My blue bag was all packed and zipped up, and my boater was on top of it. It was how it usually is when I'm waiting for the taxi at the beginning of every term. I sit on the sofa with the bag by my feet, and I wait and wait and wait. I'd got my blazer on for the first time since the last day of summer term last year, and it smelt of the downstairs cupboard where it had been hanging for a whole year long. I've had to have three new white shirts for this term, and there's a whole lot of the sleeve showing because now the blazer is far too small. My shoulders feel all tight inside. Perhaps if I keep tugging the sleeves down every now and then it will stretch as time goes along. So now I have a small blazer and I'm still in short trousers. It's another thing to worry about.

I was hoping I'd remembered to pack everything. It had taken me ages the night before, and even after I'd turned off my little light by the side of my bed, I suddenly remembered I wanted the tee shirt that Granny gave me last summer. That's really silly, I know, because I can't wear it at school, but I just wanted it with me for remembrance sake. Anyway, I had to put the light back on and get out of bed to put it in the bag. It's not such a big bag, and I can't take everything I want with me. All night I was worried I'd left something essential out, and there's always something missing when I get back to school. It's an unavoidable mistake, really.

At the bottom was my stamp collection, and straight on top of it I put Jollo, who's going to have to stay at the very bottom all term long. He's my furry lion that I've had since I was a baby, and I've never been anywhere without him. None of the boys know about him because he never ever comes out of the blue bag. I'm not the only boy who takes a teddy bear back to school, but I just don't want the others to know about him. Both his ears have gone missing, he's only got one eye, and the fur is all prickly since I gave him a bath when I was small. I think he smells of wee a bit too, though I have sprinkled him with talcum powder and given him a spray of Mummy's perfume. I'd really hate for the others to see him and make fun of him. The blue bag stays under my bed in the dorm, and sometimes if I'm feeling bad I put my hand into it and hold Jollo's paw for a bit. He's quite happy living there as long as I'm close by.

I'd packed my fountain pen—which I only use for special occasions—that Godmother Lynne gave me at Christmas and the lemon drops that Mrs. Hamilton from next door gave me 'for the journey.' I had my wash bag with the new toothbrush and toothpaste and flannel and shampoo, and my alarm clock that was bought with my pocket money at Rome airport years and years ago when we were first going to live in Beirut. I'd folded it in tissue paper and put it in between Jollo's front paws before wrapping them both in an old towel I found in the garage that Mummy had put in the bag for when the charity collecting people come. I love my clock. I think it's Jollo's best friend, and it never comes out of the bag either. I wind it up and set the right time before I pack it, and then I try to make sure that it never stops ticking for a single second during the term. Then I can say to myself that its ticking started in my bedroom, and it's a little sound of home that has come away with me. I'd taken one of Mummy's silk scarves from her wardrobe, too. It smells of her. I don't think she'll miss it because she's got lots of them. I'd put my little transistor radio in as well. We're not meant to have radios in our bags—and it would be confiscated if it was found— but sometimes when I can't sleep I take the risk and listen to Radio Luxembourg under the blankets. Lastly, right at the top so I could get it easily if I had to, I'd put in my Ventolin inhaler because now and again I get a bit of asthma, especially if I'm worried.

When I woke up that morning, just for a second I'd forgotten that I was going back to school. I thought I was going to be sick, but I lay very still till the sweat on my forehead went cool and I felt a bit better. I don't really enjoy my holidays because all I do is dread the beginning of term—right from the moment I get back home on the first day. So perhaps there isn't any point in having a holiday at all.

It was still quite dark outside, so I knew it was too early to get dressed even though I couldn't see my clock because I'd packed it away. I think it was the middle of the night. I got up anyway and went downstairs and cut a piece of the honey spice cake that Mummy had made the day before because it was one of her good days. I wrapped it in some silver foil from the second drawer down and put it in a brown paper bag with two bananas and pushed it carefully down the side of the bag trying not to squash it all too much. I usually like to have some food from home with me, though mostly I forget that I've got it and have to throw it all away after a few days when it begins to smell, though once, at the very end of term when I was packing to go home, I found a hard black shrunk thing at the bottom, and guess what? It was a very old banana!

'All set, Darling? The taxi'll be here in a minute, I think.' Mummy was standing at the door to the drawing room holding the handle with both hands and she was swaying as though she was caught in a gust of wind. I could tell she couldn't see me properly although

I was sitting straight in front of her on the sofa. That's when I knew it was going to be one of her very bad days.

'Horrid, horrid, horrid. I hate you going away, Ben. I just can't bear it. I hate it like you do, My Only,' she said. She calls me 'My Only' because I'm the only child she has, and she says she won't ever have another one now. Just me.

Then she leant against the door and it swung wide open and knocked into the chair behind it, which then bumped the tall lamp so hard I thought it was going to fall over. That funny smile she does with half her mouth on her bad days came for a while. I thought she was going to cry which is another thing that happens when she's not so good, so I looked out of the window for a second and hoped that everything would just be alright, which was plain silly really.

'The taxi's here already, Mummy,' I said. 'It's outside. I'm ready to go, actually—I'm all ready. You don't have to come with me. I can easily get to the station by myself; I just need the taxi money.'

'Of course not. I'm coming to the station with you. I'm going to wave to you till the train has completely disappeared! I just need to find my bag and my ciggies and then we'll...'

'Please, please, Mummy—I can manage, I really can. I'd much prefer to go by myself, really I would...'

The taxi driver tooted the horn again. He could see us through the window, and he was getting even more impatient. I don't know why he was in such a hurry, especially when he wasn't even meant to be there yet. I started to rub my eyes, and my chest was hurting.

'I need a wee before we go, Mummy.' She'd sat down on the arm of the chair by the door, but even then she was a bit wobbly. I ran past her and up the stairs to my room and closed the door.

Then I lay down on my bed and put my face right in the pillow. Sometimes if I squeeze my eyes closed hard enough I think that I'm somewhere else just for a second, and it makes things easier. Then I got up and straightened the bedcover so that my room would still look nice, even though I'm not going to be in it for a long time, and went back downstairs.

Just before leaving, I tuned the radio properly so that Mummy would have it nice to come back to, though I knew it wouldn't be long before she twiddled it, and it went all blurred again. She had it turned up so loud that just for a minute, when I put it right, it seemed as though Pete Murray was shouting the whole place down with one of his silly jokes. The house went completely silent when I turned it off, just as though it was lonely and about to start missing me as much as I was going to miss it. For a long time, there'll just be Mummy here alone with me at school and my dad out at work all day.

When I was closing the front door, the blossom from the wisteria that grows up the side of the house was beginning to fly away in the wind and cover the front steps. It was like the confetti that everyone was throwing at Sandra from next door's wedding, but this wasn't a happy occasion like that. Already I was too hot in my blazer although there was a breeze, and I had my boater on because it was easier than carrying it and one less thing to remember.

Mummy was looking in the bottom of her handbag for her keys. She can never find them, but they're always there in the end.

'I'm sure I had them, Ben. I'm sure they're here…' There was a bottle in her bag. She never goes out without one in her bag, but this one must have been half empty, because I could hear the sherry sloshing up and down.

'Let me lock it, Mummy,' I said to her when she found the keys. 'It doesn't fit in very easily, and I know just how to do it.' I took them out of her hand and locked the front door. I put the keys back in the bag, though I could tell she didn't want me to, because she doesn't like me to see the bottle. I took out a packet of her mints. She always has mints in her bag—lots of half packets of extra strong ones. I don't know why she starts a new packet when the old one isn't finished, but she likes to have them all around her so that her breath smells nice instead of sherry.

By the time we got to the station, Mummy was getting to be very vague, and she was trying to open her bag and hold a cigarette at the same time. Her fingers got all glued up, so I took her bag from her to get out the purse to pay for the taxi. I was very worried the money that my dad had given her for my ticket and the taxi wouldn't be there because I know for a fact that sometimes she loses money; I heard them arguing about it once. Money's always a problem, and it's been much worse since my dad was sent a bill from the wine stores after Christmas for £100. £100! Imagine that—that's as much as it costs to send me to school for a whole term! But, the money was in her bag, thank goodness, so I paid the grumpy old taxi driver, and then I didn't put the purse back because I had to buy my ticket to Chepstow at the ticket office. After I'd bought it, I tried to buy Mummy's platform ticket from the guard at the barrier, but he stared at her for a while with his mouth a bit open and then said 'That's alright, Sonny; that's alright,' and let her in free.

It wasn't busy at the station. All the people who work in London had already gone, and there was only me and Mummy on the platform, apart from a smart old lady with shiny black shoes and white gloves and a man in a suit with a briefcase who kept looking at his watch. I thought that he might know something about the train being late that I hadn't been told about.

There was a girl with her mother on the opposite platform, and I could see she was going back to school like me. She was pretty with blonde hair, and she was wearing a red check dress. She had a blazer like mine on the bench beside her, and her boater was on top of it. I felt a bit silly wearing mine when I saw her. At school everyone tries to wear their boaters as little as possible because they look so stupid, and it's a major thing to get teased about if people ever see you wearing it when you don't absolutely have to. I took it off and put it on top of my blue bag. The girl had a tennis racket over her lap and she was fiddling with its strings and the handle was banging against her mother's knees. She didn't seem to notice. They didn't look at all worried. I think she was just going along to Guildford or Godalming, and if that's where her school is, she probably goes home nearly every weekend so there was nothing for her to be homesick about.

Then I heard the bell in the distance that means the train's about to arrive, and straight after that the announcer came on the loud-speaker above my head. 'The train approaching platform two is the fast service to London Waterloo. Waterloo only, platform two…'

It was gently rocking from side to side and the steam from the engine was swirling all around it in the breeze. I like the steam engines. Quite soon there's only going to be electric ones, which is a bit of a shame if you ask me. This one was just like an African elephant I'd seen on a wildlife telly programme at school last term, lumbering out of the misty forest. And just like the taxi, I was pleased to see it, and at the same time, I wasn't.

'My bag, my boater, my ticket,' I said to myself. Granny taught me that. Count how many things you're starting your journey with and keep repeating it to yourself as you go along. Three things. 'Bag, boater, ticket.' That's why I had my blazer on even though it was too hot. So's not to have four things. I stood up and decided to put the boater on however silly it looks because it could so easily have been forgotten in the train. There was no one from school to see it. Then I squeezed the top pocket of my blazer and felt the stiff-ness of the ticket inside. The schoolgirl on the other platform looked up and smiled at me just as the engine passed so that I couldn't see her anymore. I didn't have time to smile back.

'Bye bye, Mummy. I'll write to you on Sunday before church. See you at the end of term…'

'Oh Darling, I can't bear it,' she said, standing up and looking sort of surprised. She put both her arms around me, but she forgot she had her bag in her hand. It swung round and banged into my back, and I could hear the sherry inside again.

'I'm going to come and see you, My Only. All by myself. No Daddy. Just me and my lovely boy.'

'Okay, Mummy. I'll see you then.' She was holding me so tight I couldn't move. I wondered what I would do if she didn't let me go, and the train went without me. I could hear the doors slamming closed as some people got off and the smart old lady and the man in the suit got on. Then for a little while there was just silence as Mummy stood there with her arms around me. She had started crying silently, and I could feel some warm tears on my ear and my neck.

'I've got to go, Mummy...' I pushed her away then. I tried to do it as gently as possible but she still wouldn't let go. 'Please, Mummy...'

Then she put her arms down to her sides, and I ran to the carriage door and tried to open it. But I just couldn't because it was too stiff. I could see the guard had his whistle in his mouth. He was waving his flag, and I thought I was going to be left behind. Luckily he saw me and quick as a flash came over and opened it.

'In you get my old mate!' He took my bag and just about threw it into the carriage, and I climbed in while he was blowing his whistle! I put it on the seat, and then I turned back to the window. It was all smoggy with dirt and when I tried to open it so that I could see Mummy properly, it was stuck as well. But I pushed it as hard as I could and it opened a bit at the top, so that when I went up on tiptoes I could just about put my chin on the ledge and see out. The train started to move. Mummy was staring at the door, and tears were running down her cheeks.

'Don't cry, Mummy. It'll go very quickly, you know. The summer term always does...' It's not true, that. It's the longest term of them all, but I wanted to say something to cheer her up.

She was telling me something, but I couldn't hear it because we were quite close to the engine. Then I tried to push the window down again, and suddenly it opened all the way with a clang.

'Daddy'll be waiting for you under the clock, Ben,' she said.

'I know, Mummy, like he usually does...'

'I'm coming to see you, Ben. Very soon...'

'Bye bye, Mummy.'

I watched her growing smaller and smaller in the distance. I put my hand out of the window and waved as hard as I could, and she waved back with one hand and clutched her handbag against herself with the other. Soon she was as small as an ant and then she disappeared, but I carried on waving in case she could still see me.

I tried to close the window, but it wouldn't budge. I was the only person in the compartment, so it really didn't matter. The window was open on the other side too, so there was a rush of air as the train got faster and faster. It was one of those carriages that doesn't have a passageway that you can walk along—just two doors on either side. They only use them for short journeys when people are going to work in London and coming home again. You couldn't go for a long journey in a train like that because there's no way to go to the lavatory or get something to eat.

An empty crisp packet swirled round and round in the breeze as though it was a bird, like when that robin flew down the chimney at home and couldn't get out even when we opened the windows. The packet stopped for a moment by a poster on the compartment wall that said 'Welcome to Bournemouth' and then went on travelling again till it finally stopped on the luggage rack above my head. I'd love to go to the seaside at Bournemouth one day, but my dad says it's not really our sort of place.

'Boater, bag, ticket,' I said to myself very loudly. It didn't matter because there was no one to hear me and make fun. Boater on my head, bag by my side on the seat, and the ticket safely in my pocket. I could have a bit of a relax. Actually, I never mind that bit of the journey when I'm going to meet my dad at Waterloo. I quite like being by myself for a little while, and it's not like the term has already started.

Mummy probably went to The Two Brewers after she left the station. She would have had even more sherry there, and I don't know how she would have got home. But I was on the train, and there was nothing I could do about it.

Mummy's favourite drink used to be tea, and I know exactly how to make it just right for her. You've got to warm the teapot with hot water first and then just before the kettle boils you pour the water over two teaspoonfuls of tea leaves. Then you have to leave it for a minute or two before you put a little milk into the bottom of the cup and pour the tea in after. 'M.I.F. Ben...' That's what she used to say to me when I brought the tray in. It stands for 'milk in first'. She says I'm the best tea maker in the entire world. But she only has it in the mornings these days, and she's told me that she really prefers a drop of sherry now. Some mornings when my dad's away and her new friends have been around for the evening, she stays in bed very late, and then I still make her a cup of tea to help her get up.

The Two Brewers is her favourite place now, and she's met lots of new friends in there. That's where she met Trotsky John. He wears a dirty duffle coat and a blue beret even when it's really hot and his beard is yellow and stinky from all the smoking he does. He comes to the house when my dad's away and sometimes in the afternoon before he arrives back from work. He sits for hours and never says anything, just drinking beer and smoking. Then he sort of loses his temper and starts going on about Stalin and Khrushchev and state capitalism and Che Guevara. Mummy says Trotsky John is teaching her all about injustice, and she says Che Guevara was like 'a light unto the world'—a bit like Jesus—and has given his life in the fight against American imperialism. There was a picture of him in my dad's paper few months ago, dead on a table with his eyes open. Mummy and Trotsky John were going to demonstrate at the American Embassy last month to protest about the war in Vietnam, but they sat in the sitting room all morning and then it was too late to bother to go. I was glad they missed it because I saw on the news later that some people had been hurt when the police horses charged into the crowd, and I just know my Mum. She would have been one of the people to get hurt.

Mummy recites her favourite poetry to Trotsky John, like The Ballad of Reading Gaol and Under Milk Wood. Once, when I was in the study, waiting for Children's Hour to start, I heard Trotsky John shouting at her. He said 'fucking bourgeois bitch' over and over again, but I don't think he was really cross because they were both laughing at the same time. My dad doesn't like him, and Mummy's asked me not to say when he's been in our house. After he goes, she opens all the windows in the sitting room to let out the smokiness. Mummy smokes lots too, but his cigarettes are really smelly. My dad doesn't know he's at the house so much.

The train to Waterloo whizzed along and never slowed down once, even when we went through all the stations on the way. There was a crowd of school children with their teacher on the platform at West Byfleet, and they all had to hold onto their caps as we passed. It made me laugh, and I thought to myself that I was feeling quite happy, all alone like a grown-up on the train. But then quite suddenly we were in London and started to pass all the big offices along the side of the river Thames that look as though they're made of glass. In between them on the other side of the river I could see the Houses of Parliament with the massive flag flying over the top, and when you see that you know you're just about arriving at Waterloo. It went really dark for a minute when the roof of the station blocked out the sun, and by the time I got used to it and could see clearly again, the worry had come back.

My dad was waiting for me under the big clock as usual. He didn't have his briefcase with him because he was going straight back to the office after taking me to Paddington. It must be a nuisance for him to come and get me because he's a very busy man and doesn't have much time to spare.

'Ah! There you are Ben. All ready for the off, then?'

It's always really funny to see my dad when we're not at home or not with Mummy. When I saw him standing there with his hands behind his back, I thought for a little second that if he hadn't been waiting where he usually does under the clock, perhaps I wouldn't have recognised him. Then he smiled at me, and I felt a bit stupid. It was one of his funny smiles that means he's in a hurry. I got a little embarrassed and couldn't think of anything to say and did that thing where I wiggle my head from side to side and smile with my mouth closed. I'm not used to being with him without Mummy, and I worry about interrupting something important he has to think about in the quiet.

When we were going down into the underground on the escalator, he put his hand on my shoulder. I thought he was going to say something about me not standing properly, so very, very slowly I tried to straighten up without him noticing.

The last time I'd been alone with my dad was when he had to take me to the doctor at Christmas because my asthma got so bad I couldn't eat anything. I was getting skinnier and skinnier and could only sleep if there were three pillows propping me up. Mummy got so worried she thought I wouldn't be able to go back to school, and then I hoped that my asthma would be bad forever, so I'd have to become a day boy and go to the Grammar School in Guildford.

Fat old Dr. Scott listened to my chest with his stethoscope. He was wearing a big bow tie, and the hanky in his top pocket tickled my nose. He smelt of cigars and coughing. Then he pushed his hand into the middle of my back and said. 'Of course the boy can't breathe. Look at his posture! The young man's got to learn to stand up straight, hasn't he? Straighter! Come on—move that back!' I looked at my dad while the rubbishy old doctor carried on, and he was putting his eyebrows together in the way that means he's angry. 'More PT and cross country running's the answer if you ask me—not nearly enough of it at schools these days.' I actually started to cry a little, but they didn't see it because I was able to wipe the tears away very quickly on my vest because luckily, just then I was putting it back on.

When I was sitting on the tube with my dad, he started to talk about my schoolwork, like he always does on that journey. It's something for him to talk about, at least.

'Now I want you to think very hard about what I was saying to you before the weekend, Ben. Remember—hard play after hard work and not before. We've really got to see a marked improvement in your next exams because we just cannot have a repeat of the sort of results you turned in last term...'

It was the same old lecture that I always get a few days before the end of the holidays in the study at home, but he wasn't being quite so cross with me because I was after all going back to school. In the study he always sounds angry and on the tube he always sounds nicer, but his voice is still doing disappointment.

'...and if you don't understand the first time, then don't be frightened to ask again. The great thing to remember is that geometry and algebra both follow the elementary rules of mathematics that you've been learning for years now.' I looked at him now and again as he carried on, nodding my head as though I'd never heard the lecture before, and thinking that this term I really would try and work harder so he'd be more pleased, and there would be no need for the shouting in the study at the end of the summer holidays.

'...and the thing is to learn all the kings' dates so you've got a context—a frame—in which to put the events, starting with the Conqueror in 1066...'

I was staring at a piece of bright pink bubble gum stuck in the wooden floor of the carriage while my dad went on and on. It had probably been spat out after the flavour had been chewed out of it by a boy on his way to his school that morning. I started to think about him, although I was making a face for my dad as though I was listening. Probably he was going to go home on this very same tube train to have tea with his Mum and then watch the telly till his dad came in from work. Then he would do a reasonable amount of homework like they do in most ordinary schools, not like the hours we do every single day, except Sundays. After that he was going to watch a bit more telly, including 'Top of the Pops' which everyone at prep school misses.

'...and then pass the ball—don't hold onto it if someone farther back has a better chance of scoring a try than you. What I'm saying is don't be selfish with your possession of the ball...' My dad was talking about rugby, and I hate that game. It's typical of him to be talking about it when we don't even have rugby in the summer term; we play cricket which is even more boring. Sometimes it seems as though he doesn't know anything. I didn't say, though, because he was at least talking in a quite nice voice. He knows I don't like games, and I know he's sad about it. But it's better than when he's talking about my maths.

He was staring straight ahead as though he was talking to another boy altogether and not to me, right by his side. His mouth was moving very slowly like when he talked to Suzette, the French au pair, who only stayed for two weeks. His hands were flying up and down which only happens when he's trying to make a point. I know he thinks I'm not very clever; perhaps he thinks if he moves them around there might be more of a chance I'll understand.

Then he went quiet for a bit because there wasn't anything more for him to say.

'Good looking beggar, your father.' That's what Netty, one of Mummy's new drinking friends, but quite nice, said about him when she picked up the wedding photo on the sideboard in the dining room.

'That's a very old photograph,' I said to her, 'from when they just got married.'

'Not so long ago, Ben, and he's still a very handsome man.'

He's got blond hair which is combed back flat against his head, a high forehead, light blue eyes and cheekbones that make me think of a picture of some warriors I once saw in a book about Genghis Khan. I wouldn't be surprised if my dad told me he was descended from some of those people.

Last week in one of Mummy's magazines, I read a letter from a lady who was worried that her little boy didn't look like her husband. The doctor said that very often boys look like their mothers first, and then begin to grow more like their fathers just as their voices begin to break. But then after my bath, when I wiped the steam away from the mirror to look at myself, even with my wet hair flat against my head, I could see I don't look like my dad, and I'm sure I never will. I look like Mummy, with dark red hair and brown eyes.

My dad was walking toward the ticket office at Paddington, and I had to remind him that I'd bought the ticket already with the money he'd left for me in Mummy's purse. He slapped his big black leather wallet shut and put it back in his jacket.

'…of course, of course. I left it with Mama, didn't I? Now, which platform is it we want?'

It was platform four; I'd seen it up on the board already. It was funny that he'd forgotten about the money for the ticket because he's always saying how careful we have to be, but it was probably because he was in the middle of a work day, and his mind was wandering a bit.

Now I started worrying because when you see the first people from school, it's like the term is beginning and there is no turning back. We walked along the side of the train past a trolley selling sandwiches and chocolate, passing by the first class carriages where some women were still sweeping inside to get it ready for the passengers. The buffet carriage had smart tablecloths and silver knives and forks and red curtains at the windows and a waiter with a white jacket and gold buttons.

One day, when I can do what I like because I'm not at school anymore, I'll travel to Scotland all by myself in a train like that, and go to the dining car as it gets dark. The train will slow down for the soup course so as not to spill it, which is a thing that I know that they do. After I've finished my dinner, I'll have a cigarette and some coffee, and then I'll go to bed in my own compartment and wake up in Edinburgh. Then I'll go to a business meeting which will be part of my job. When my meeting's finished, I'll have a lunch and then some brandy and another cigarette and after, I'll go and see the room in Holyroodhouse Palace where Mary Queen of Scots' boyfriend was stabbed and the floorboards are still stained with his blood.

The other boys were standing in the distance along the platform. I knew it was them by the colour of their blazers. They were at the far end by the engine, and the sun was shining on them. There were three of them. We're called 'the London Boys' by the teachers, because nearly all the other boys come from Wales and around Gloucester and the Forest of Dean. It's not always the same amount of boys at Paddington because sometimes their dads drive them back.

When I was walking along the platform it was like I was getting deeper and deeper into how I am at school, and by the time I reached the others, the term had started except that my dad was still there.

I'm not the same person when I'm at school. You have to learn to be different from how you are at home. The most important thing when you get to about ten years old is not to show that you're missing your mum and dad. It's alright for some of the very young ones, like Spencer and Perrington who are only six, but you are expected to be less and less homesick as you get older. It's best to try never to look sad or worried, although I think it's okay to look angry about upsetting things. When Granny was coming to take me out for Sunday exeat a few weeks ago, she crashed her car backing out of her driveway and phoned the school to say she wouldn't be coming. I got really worried and upset about it. I cried for a bit in secret when I came out of Mr. Burston's study, but afterwards I pretended to be just really angry about it by saying 'typical, typical' over and over again with a fed up expression on my face.

Nick Gower was the first boy to see me, and he put out his hand for me to shake. He's funny like that. Sometimes he shakes your hand in the middle of term for no reason at all except for it's a new day!

'Hi, Ben—nice hols?' he said. He's very tall and he has a lump of hair that hangs over his forehead. I don't know how it is that the school barber doesn't cut it off, but he never does. He's got goofy teeth which you would think that he would be teased about, but no one teases Nick. I don't know why, but they just don't. I don't think he does homesickness, either, though he doesn't see his mum and dad much more than I do. Usually boys like us who don't have any brothers and sisters seem to be more homesick.

'Hello, Nick,' I said, 'how was your skiing holiday?'

'Not enough snow. Next time we're going to go at Christmas. It's really boring there when there's no snow. We went on long walks instead.'

There are just one or two boys in the school I call by their first names, and Nick is one of them. That's because I've seen him outside of school where it's silly to use surnames. His dad has sometimes given me a lift at the end of term. He came to get us for the Christmas holidays when the train wasn't running because of a strike that day. He was in his grey Jaguar which was all splattered with mud because he'd been clay pigeon shooting in the country on the way. I was already worried about being sick and wanting a wee during the journey. The inside of his car smelt of leather and cigars, which I knew would make things worse. He drives really fast, especially round corners, and when it started to get dark and I couldn't see out, I felt very woozy. Then, of course, I did want a wee, which is a certain thing to happen when I'm at all worried, but I was determined not to ask to stop because Major Gower likes to be on time or a little bit early. It was such a long way to Heathrow Airport where we were meeting my dad, but I did manage to hold on. When we got to the pub which was the rendezvous point, Nick and I both jumped out of the car and dashed to the loo. He was as desperate as me and hadn't wanted to say anything either! We didn't talk about it, but while we were peeing he looked at me, and we had a giggle about it.

Steven Latymer gets the train at Paddington, and he's always the first one to arrive. He had a new pair of glasses that made his eyes look even bigger and more watery than they did before. His mother was bending down and whispering in his ear and stroking the back of his head, and his dad was smoking a pipe and looking up the platform as though he had just seen someone who was a friend. I think Latymer had been crying. It was strange to see him with his mum and dad because usually his aunty brings him to the station. It was really weird that he was upset, because at school he never seems to be bothered about anything, even when he's a bit bullied. He's not a main person for bullying, but sometimes they pick on him because of his funny eyes. He's called 'Fisheye'. He usually keeps to himself, and actually I'd never thought about him with a mum and a dad.

He's just someone who's always reading or revising for exams and coming top of the class. Seeing him so upset changes things, though. It's like I've got a secret with him, and I like that. I pretended that I hadn't seen him and made up my mind not to speak to him until we were safely on our way and he'd started to cheer up. Not that I'd have much to say to him actually, because once he was on the train he'd be busy reading.

My dad was talking to Major Gower and calling him 'old chap', which means that he couldn't remember his name, and he was looking around to see who else was there to talk to. He doesn't like Nick's dad very much. Whenever he talks about him at home he says the word 'Major' louder than the word 'Gower', and once I heard him say to Mummy he was a 'Golf club bore and about as much of a bloody major as I am.'

'Good morning, Benjamin. How are you?' Miss Newman, who is our under-matron, was standing in the doorway of the carriage with an extremely elegant lady who I'd never seen before. In front of them was a very small boy with big blue eyes and blond curly hair. For a second, I didn't recognise Miss Newman. She used my Christian name because my dad was there, and she wasn't wearing her white matron's coat. Also, she'd never come to London to meet us before.

'Hello, Miss Newman—isn't Mr. England here today?'

'No, he's meeting us at Chepstow. I was in London visiting my sister for the weekend, so we decided it would be a good idea for me to guide you all back this time.' Mr. England is our Latin, Scripture and English teacher, and he usually comes to get us. Once or twice Mr. Burston the Headmaster has come, which no one likes because everyone's a bit frightened of him, and we don't know what we're meant to say to him.

'Has your trunk been sent on alright?'

'Yes, Miss Newman. It went on Friday.' I blushed a bit, because last term Mummy forgot to send my trunk in time. For three days I didn't have all my things with me. When I was lying in bed in the dorm on the first night, with Mr. Burston about to switch off the lights, Miss Carson, the matron, and Miss Newman came in to find out what had happened. They looked at each other and then at the Headmaster without saying anything. This term, not only had I made sure that Mummy phoned the station people to order the Passenger's Luggage in Advance collection, but I'd helped her pack my trunk too, just to make sure nothing was left behind. Just as well I did, otherwise she would have forgotten my white cricket trousers that we had to wash in a hurry to get last year's grass smudges out.

'Benjamin, this is Giles Webster, our new boy. He'll need a little bit of guidance for a few days, and I thought that you might like to show him the ropes.'

'Yes, Miss Newman. Hello, Webster.' I shook the hand of the little boy, though I couldn't see it at first because his blazer was so huge that his hand was nearly completely hidden by the sleeve. That was the first thing he was going to be teased about. In his other hand he was holding a massive cricket bat, all new and white. It was so big and he was so small that the handle nearly came up to his chin. That was going to be the second thing he was going to be teased about. Then I noticed the knot of his tie was as big as a fat juicy orange. That was going to be the third thing they would tease him about, because everyone at school tries to make the knot as small as they possibly can. He's going to be the only 'nip' this term—that's what we call the new boys. He's lucky though, because he'll only be a nip for this one term. Being a nip is horrid because everyone's allowed to boss you around, and the prefects make sure you're given lots of jobs to do that no one else does—like cleaning the outside lavatories and checking that there's toilet paper in there.

'Hello, Benjamin, I'm Angela Webster, Giles's mother,' the beautiful lady said. 'Miss Newman's told me all about you. She says you'll keep an eye on my young man for me. I'd be ever so grateful.'

She put a white hand out to me which felt cool and soft when I shook it, and she had red nail varnish that was the same colour as her lipstick. She smelt of lovely perfume that reminded me of the air hostesses that looked after me when we flew on long journeys before my dad started to work in London. I'm pretty sure that Webster's mother must be an air hostess, or a model, or something like that. She wore a hat with a little bit of a blue veil on it that covered the top half of her face and made her eyes look a bit misty and far away. I could tell by looking at them that she was worried about leaving her son.

'I'll look after him, of course. Everything will be alright, Mrs. Webster. Don't worry about him.' She looked at me, and I could see her eyes changing. Then she put her hand gently on my cheek for a bit and smiled at me. She was the most beautiful lady I'd ever seen and I will do my best to look after her little boy and stick up for him even if he turns out to be a bit of a weed and everyone teases him, which I think they will.

'Right, my old chum,' my dad said then, 'I'm going to leave you in Miss Morley's capable hands and shoot off back to work.'

'Miss Newman, Dad...'

'Oh, silly me! I do beg your pardon—Miss Newman, of course.' He smiled at her and she looked at the ground as she smiled back. Then he leaned towards me, and I thought he was going to forget and kiss me, which is quite ridiculous because he never ever kisses me. I moved away from him a bit, and then he put his hand out and ruffled my hair which he does sometimes. It's not so bad as him kissing me, but I wish he wouldn't do that.

'Now chin up, and we'll be seeing you for the summer holidays.' He did a funny little wave to everybody and then some backward steps. I wish he wouldn't do that either. I don't think anybody noticed very much, but it's the sort of thing that worries me a bit. He walked away down the platform so quickly I knew that he was glad to get away. Perhaps it's because Major Gower was talking to him. I watched him going in and out of the crowd when he got to the main bit of the station. It was easy to follow him because his hair's so blond, and I know what he looks like when he's in a hurry. With one hand he was holding the front of his jacket, and when he got to the entrance of the tube, I saw his other hand come out and his legs begin to move down the steps as though he was doing a tap dance like Fred Astaire in one of those films you see on the telly on Sunday afternoons.

I'm sure he was happy that he was going back to his office. I have a picture of it in my mind. It's right in the middle of the city of London. I think he spends hours and hours on the phone to people in places like Beirut, Athens and Geneva, arranging for things to be sent everywhere on ships and airplanes. He takes his jacket off when he arrives and hangs it on the back of his chair; then he puts his feet up on the big desk in front of him with his hands behind his head and his secretary comes in to tidy up. When she's finished, she sits down with her back all straight and does some shorthand on a chair with no arms on it, and after that she brings him coffee and chocolate digestive biscuits, and she probably thinks he's very handsome like everybody else does.

Suddenly I was alone on the platform, and Miss Newman asked me if I was alright. Perhaps I was looking a bit sad or something, but really I was just hoping that no one would ask me why my dad had gone. I told her that I was feeling fine and that my dad was a very busy man and had to dash straight back to the office for an important phone call—which was very probably true, actually.

I stood there all by myself for a bit while everyone else was chatting away and then I saw a note on the window of the compartment which said 'Reserved for Courtlands Preparatory School.' There were some bags and boaters on the seats, but nobody was inside yet, so I decided to settle myself in while the other boys were busy saying goodbye to their parents. That meant I was able to bag the best seat—the one right by the window and facing the direction that the train was going in. I put my blue bag right beside me, then suddenly remembered that I was wearing my boater and Fisheye and Nick Gower had seen me with it on, which is quite a big mistake. I took it off and put it on my lap. Perhaps in all the kafuffle they hadn't noticed. I didn't take my blazer off though because that would be four things to remember. Then I checked that my ticket was still in the inside pocket. 'Boater, bag, ticket', I said out loud to myself, just to be sure.

When I looked out of the window at the others, it seemed to me that they might be about to miss the train because I could see the clock on the platform said seven minutes till half past twelve—the time the train was leaving. Nick was playing boxing matches with his dad, which I've seen them doing before when the term is starting and Major Gower is about to go. They do it all in slow motion, and Nick has a queer smile on his face that I've only ever seen just before his dad says goodbye. Latymer's back was being rubbed very hard by his dad as though someone had hit him, and his mum was picking bits of fluff off his blazer and had a wobbly chin like when you're trying not to cry, so that means it's not just Mummy who doesn't like the start of school.

I was getting more and more worried about what I would do if they missed the train and what I would say to Mr. England at Chepstow about it, but then they started coming into the compartment. Fisheye Latymer sat down opposite me and opened a big red book even though his mum and dad were standing outside looking at him. He is a bit weird, really—one minute upset and the next minute reading his book. Nick came in with his dad and sat beside Fisheye. Nick doesn't care about looking out of the window and going backwards. Major Gower started putting all the bags and boaters and blazers up on the racks, and Miss Newman looked a bit angry about it, actually. There was plenty of room on the seats because there were only four boys and one matron in one big compartment, but she didn't say anything. I put my arm round my blue bag but Major Gower suddenly said, 'Let's get rid of that for you, old boy,' and he just about threw it up onto the luggage rack. Then he took my boater from my lap and threw that up as well. I could see it perched on top of my bag and wobbling a bit, and I knew perfectly well that it was going to fall down when the train started. I wasn't very worried about Jollo because he's quite squidgy and has had a lot worse things happen, but I did wonder what might have happened to my clock with such a big jolt. Just as well I'd been careful to wrap it in the tissue paper and the towel. I was worried about my Ventolin inhaler and what I would do if I needed it because Miss Newman's not nearly tall enough to reach right up to a luggage rack. I was thinking it was quite possible that when we arrived at Chepstow, we'd have to tell the station people to stop the train for a bit longer and help us get the things down. Perhaps if Nick and I were very careful and stood on the seats we might be able to drag the bags to the edge of the rack and catch them when they fell down, but that would be another jolt for my alarm clock.

I didn't say anything to Major Gower because there was probably going to be time on the journey to work things out. Perhaps the ticket collector would be able to take everything down when he came round to see our tickets. Thank heavens I kept my blazer on because otherwise that would be up on the rack as well—with my ticket inside it!

The new boy came in with his mother. She smiled and sat him down right by my side. Major Gower had thrown his bag up too, but when he tried to take away the cricket bat, Webster wouldn't let go and his mother said 'Probably best to leave it with him, don't you think?' Then she kissed him and said in a shaky voice, 'Bye bye, Darling; see you in three weeks,' and quickly went out of the carriage and back to the platform where she could see him through the window. When Major Gower said goodbye to everyone, he went out and slid the door of the compartment shut so hard by mistake that I thought it was going to break all the glass.

Miss Newman took off her jacket and brushed it down using her fingers. She very carefully folded it up and put it on the seat beside her and undid the front of her cardigan. She was wearing a nice white blouse underneath which was very tight on her. The older boys at school always talk about how big her bosoms are, but her matron's uniform makes it very difficult to see them. I could see them really well when she undid her buttons, though. I smiled at her then, but she didn't smile back.

Giles Webster, the new boy, got up from his seat and pressed his forehead and hands against the window to look at his mother. She was fiddling with a brooch on the scarf round her neck and her hand shook a little. Her lips moved very slowly trying to talk to him, but he wasn't able to understand because the glass was too thick. She kept looking towards the engine to see if it was ready to go, and I thought that if it didn't move soon she might start to cry. It was a bit like me waiting for the taxi at home. She wanted the train to go, and she didn't want the train to go—all at the same time.

The whistle blew, all the doors started slamming shut, and some soldiers with great big rucksacks on their backs ran past in a hurry. When the train's really big like this one, it starts moving so slowly that there's a tiny moment when you're not quite sure whether it's going or not. Fisheye's parents started to wave at him though Major Gower was telling them something and didn't seem to notice we were about to go. Mrs. Webster began to walk along the side of the train as it started to go faster. I could read her lips, and she was saying 'Ben will look after you.' She was pointing to me and waving at the same time. I gave her a little bit of a wave back, but I felt a bit funny about it because I thought I was getting in the way of them saying goodbye.

'Bye bye, Mummy.' The boy was whispering so quietly that I could only just hear him. I wasn't sure what I was going to do if he started crying, but Miss Newman was there and she would have to look after him if that happened. He was still pressing his forehead against the window. She walked very quickly to keep up until eventually she blew one last kiss and stopped just before the platform came to an end. He didn't move from the window for ever such a long time, and in the end I took his elbow and said, 'Sit down, Webster.' He picked up the bat that was on the seat and put it between his knees and held tight onto the handle. The cricket bat is the same thing for him that Jollo and the alarm clock are for me—a little bit of home that is going to school with you. But it's sad for him that it's the wrong type of thing to have. People will make fun of him because of it. He's far too young to be any good at cricket, and the bigger boys will be jealous of such a posh new bat. There's nothing I can do about it, though.

I don't read on the train like Latymer. I never do. I don't even have a book in my bag. I want to see the world going by and watch it changing. I love the rumbling sound of the wheels crisscrossing the tracks when we leave the station. It's as though the train is searching for its way out of London, and you know it's found the right course when the rhythm becomes all steady. It made the train jiggle around even more than usual, and my boater fell down from the rack like I thought it would; Miss Newman smiled at me as I put it back on my lap.

We passed offices and blocks of flats with windows dirtied up by the railway and tall old houses with flat roofs and clothes hanging out to dry so close you could just about grab them. Quite quickly there were rows and rows of smaller houses with long gardens down to the railway. Later there were parks and playing fields with white clouds above and bigger houses with huge trees in between. Soon we were whizzing along by the River Thames with Windsor Castle in the distance and then out into the countryside with the train going as fast as fast can be.

Luckily, the ticket collector came round very soon after we were outside London and Miss Newman asked him if he would help get our bags down because it would soon be time for us to have our lunch. He was a tall man, and he lifted everything down for us with no bother at all in just a few seconds. Miss Newman took her knitting out of her bag and clickety-clacked away with a happy expression on her face. I think she'd been worried too about how we would get the bags down. I was very pleased to have mine back, especially when I pushed my ear against it and could hear my clock ticking away.

Then I started to think about Miss Newman saying to the ticket inspector that it would soon be time for our lunch. That's when I remembered about the sandwiches. I was supposed to have my own and Mummy was meant to have made them for me, but it was my fault because it was up to me to remember and remind her of those sorts of things. I started to worry about what Miss Newman was going to say and what sort of excuses I could make, and I stopped looking out of the window.

Just a little while before we got to Swindon when the train was slowing down, she said, 'Right everybody—I think it's time you had your lunch. We're not having high tea till six o'clock tonight, so I do want you to eat now, please.' Fisheye opened his case and took out a brown paper bag and Nick took a package of silver foil from his. Miss Newman opened Webster's bag and took out a small lunch tin with a picture of Noddy on the front which had some sandwiches wrapped in grease-proof paper, an apple, a Milky Way bar and a small thermos flask in it.

'Get your lunch out, Teasdale,' she said to me.

'I'm not hungry, Miss Newman...'

'Come on—I want you to eat, please.'

'I really couldn't, Miss Newman. I'm not hungry.'

She looked at me for a long time and then said very slowly, 'You haven't got any sandwiches with you, have you, Teasdale? Your mother hasn't given you any for the journey, has she?'

'Yes, she has, Miss Newman—it's just that I'm not hungry, that's all.'

'Show them to me.'

I didn't know what to do so I unzipped the bag and I put my hand in as though I was searching for the sandwiches. Then I remembered the cake and the bananas that I'd packed in the morning and I tried to feel around for the paper bag I'd put them in. My face was getting hotter and hotter and the others were looking at me, and I knew I might start to cry. I found the bag and took one of the bananas out of it.

'Perhaps I'll just have a banana for now,' I said.

'I told you to show me your sandwiches, Teasdale.'

I looked at her for what seemed an awfully long time and my hand was still in my bag. I didn't know what else to say and then I started talking to myself to try and stop from crying. I started to shout to myself in my head. 'Please, please don't start crying in front of Nick and Fisheye and especially the new boy that I'm meant to be looking after.' But it was too late because suddenly I could feel my face was getting wet although I wasn't making a crying noise. There was nothing I could do about it. And then Miss Newman was looking at me with a shocked expression.

'It's alright, Teasdale, there's no need to get upset. You don't have to eat your sandwiches if you really don't want to. Try and eat your banana when you've calmed down a little.' I think she was really surprised to see that I was crying. I put the banana on my lap with the boater on top of it and couldn't eat any of it.

I hate to cry in front of people. I can't remember the last time anybody saw me crying. Although I didn't make any noise when I was doing it, the others saw I had tears on my face. I'm sure they're all going to talk about it.

We stopped for a bit at Swindon, but I had my eyes closed and didn't see any of it. When the train started moving again, I opened them and Miss Newman was looking at me with a concerned expression on her face.

'Alright, Teasdale?'

'Yes, thank you, Miss Newman,' I said. But I wasn't really, because I knew that she'd tell Miss Carson that I didn't have any sandwiches with me on the train, and then they would talk about Mummy.

When we got to the big tunnel that goes under the river to Wales, Nick Gower told Webster to get ready for when we came up on the other side because the Welsh police would be coming along the train to see everyone's passports. It wasn't really big teasing. It was meant to be just a bit of a joke but Webster's face went all red, and he said, 'My mummy didn't give me a passport. Will the police take me to prison?' I don't think Miss Newman heard Nick because after she'd had her sandwich, she'd started clickety-clacking away at her knitting again.

'It's alright, Webster—Gower was only kidding you,' I said. 'You don't need to have a passport to go to Wales. It's the same country as England, really.'

The train always slows down to go through the big tunnel under the river, which is very wide at Bristol. I think it must be incredibly deep because I've noticed that sometimes your ears go pop when you're halfway through—like when you're in an aeroplane and the stewardesses have to come round with a tray of sweets. Webster looked frightened again, and I told him not to worry and that just on the other side we would be at Chepstow Station where we were getting off. I said it in a low voice though, because I was beginning to see that he might need quite a lot of looking after, and I didn't want to make it look too obvious that I was the one who would be doing it. It really was beginning to look like I was lumbered with quite a weedy boy.

'How old are you, Webster?'

'Six and a half,' he said. That means he's one of the four youngest boys in the school. There's him and Spencer and Perrington who are six, and Norton who's only five and whose mother died when he was four. His father couldn't cope by himself in Swaziland, so he sends him all the way to England and only sees him for the summer holidays. Everyone at school says his father doesn't care about him, but I'm not so sure because last Sports Day he came thousands of miles to fetch him. When he saw Norton by the cricket pavilion he picked him up in his arms and kissed him in front of everyone!

Just as we came out on the other side of the tunnel I asked Webster why he had changed schools and was starting a new one in the summer term instead of in the winter term, like most people. He didn't seem to know what I was talking about at first but then he said, 'My mummy works in shows in the evenings and my daddy doesn't live with us anymore, so she said it was for the best if I went to boarding school for a little while. But she says I don't have to stay if I don't like it.' I wanted to ask him more questions about it, but there wasn't time because we were coming into the station at Chepstow.

I always worry about getting out of the train in time. It doesn't seem to wait for very long before it starts off again, but this time we all got off quite easily. I knew I didn't have to worry about my ticket because the inspector had seen it on the train and had punctured a hole in it, and I hadn't taken my blazer off for the journey. So all I had to remember was my blue bag and my boater, which I was holding in my hand because of the not wearing it unless you are ordered to.

Mr. England was waiting for us just on the other side of the ticket barrier. The guard let him through, and he came towards us with a big smile on his face.

'Hello, everybody. Nice journey?' He went straight up to Miss Newman and took her bag from her. 'Oh thank you, Stuart,' she said. It wasn't a very heavy one, but she liked being treated like a lady. Mr. England and Miss Newman are quite good friends, actually; very often you can hear them talking in the Matron's surgery after lights out. Then he went up to Webster and said, 'Hello, young Mr. Webster. My name's Mr. England, and you're going to be in my class for Latin, Scripture and English.' He put his hand out to him, and after a bit of a pause, Webster shook it and gave him a rather shy smile. I don't think he's used to having his hand shaken. I was pleased about it, though, because I suddenly remembered how good Mr. England is at looking after upset boys, and I thought that I would have some help with Webster if it got a bit too difficult.

'Hello, Ben—how are you? Nice hols?' He smiled and winked at me and ruffled my hair a bit which usually I don't like but it's alright when he does it.

Actually, one of the things that's not so terribly bad about coming back to school is Mr. England being there. He's by far the best master in the school, and everybody really likes him. He only punishes you if you've been incredibly naughty, and then only with things like setting you an essay about manners or a detention or standing in the corner for a few minutes. He makes sure never to send anyone to Mr. Burston because he doesn't like people getting slippered and caned. Another thing about him that's really different is that he knows when anybody is unhappy—like when you're having a bad homesickness day or properly upset about something and not wanting to talk about it. When my granddad died, everyone at school was quite nice to me for a bit, but for a long time after, Mr. England was especially kind. Sometimes when I was sitting all by myself on the bench at the very end of the tennis courts thinking about it all, he'd come and sit with me and cheer me up with a bit of talking about my stamp collection and stuff.

When we got to the little car park outside the station I was looking round for Mr. England's car but couldn't see it anywhere. 'I've got Mr. Burston's car with me—my Mini's far too small for all of us,' he said before I could ask him about it.

I'd been wondering how we were all going to fit into Mr. England's Mini. Four boys, and a matron, and Mr. England! Even when he's in it by himself, Mr. England looks a bit funny. He's very tall and skinny so his head nearly touches the ceiling, his knees poke up on either side of the steering wheel and his elbows are halfway out of the windows. It's a funny sight really. There's no room for anything in that car especially with all the mess in the back like records, essays for marking, and books about archaeology, music, and churches. He just loves churches; I know for a fact he's got hundreds of books about them—and cathedrals and abbeys. That's partly because he likes old buildings and the history of it all, and partly because, actually, he is really quite religious. He's not at all stuffy about it, though. Last term I had a big row with Macer-Wright, our class monitor, after he said I'd been cheating in a history dates test, when in fact I never did. I got so angry I actually punched him in the chest—which is something I never do—and just as he punched me back, Mr. England came in and stopped it becoming a big fight. We both had to go and see him after prep that evening, and he made us apologise to each other. Macer-Wright said he was sorry he'd called me a cheat and said it was only teasing really, since everyone knows I'm good at history dates. I said I was sorry for punching him. I felt very ashamed about it all actually, because I'm really not a fighting person. Then Mr. England talked to us about forgiveness, which he says is just the most important thing ever and that if you're truly sorry for something bad that you've done, you'll always, always be forgiven. The next day after the lesson in Assembly, just when I was about to go upstairs to make my bed, he gave me a piece of folded paper.

'This is from the Book of Common Prayer, Ben,' he said. 'Just say it to yourself under your breath when you're sorry about something you think you've done wrong.' I waited till I got upstairs and had made my bed, and then I sat down and read it. This is what it said: *'Remember not the sins and offences of my youth; but according to thy mercy, think thou upon me, Oh Lord, for thy forgiveness...'*

I folded it back up, and when I went downstairs I put it into the Bible that Granny gave me when I first came to Courtlands; I'm going to keep it there forever and ever.

I've been in his car once or twice before. Sometimes when we've gone to a concert and there weren't enough of us for the school to order a minibus, we've been given lifts in the teachers' cars. The last time was at the end of last term when we went to the Colston Hall in Bristol to see the Vienna Boys' Choir. Three of us went in the Mini with Mr. England, and four others went with the Headmaster. It was quite a special occasion because the tickets were difficult to get, so only the boys who are the most interested in music were chosen to go. Not only was I one of the chosen ones, but Mr. England chose me to sit in the front with him. There was so much clutter in there that before I could get in, I had to take some stuff off the seat and put it on the floor. Then it was all in the way and my knee kept banging up against the gear stick, and I had to keep saying sorry because of it.

That was the day that my second secret started. And that's why I was glad that we were going back to school from Chepstow Station in Mr. Burston's dusty old Rover car, so I wouldn't have to think about the nasty secret in Mr. England's Mini.

We piled our luggage into the boot and then started to put more stuff on the back seats. I thought that even in a big car like that there might not be enough room. But then the four of us climbed in, all scrunched up together on the back seat while Miss Newman and Mr. England got in the front. Webster was still holding on tight to his bat, but I didn't say anything about it although it really was rather in the way.

I was getting worried on the journey. It's not a very long way, only about twenty minutes, and I just didn't want it ever to end. Looking out of the window, I began to see things that meant we were getting closer and closer to school. Fisheye was sitting beside me, and of course, he read his book all the way. I think he was doing it to take his mind off the fact that it was the beginning of term. Perhaps if you're always reading a book, you're half in the real world and half in the book world, so then you're only half upset. I wouldn't be able to read in a car, though. It would make me feel sick very quickly.

There was a lumpy thing in my back, and when I put my hand round to see what it was I pulled out a baby's bottle. Luckily it was empty. Mr. and Mrs. Burston have got a quite new baby called Mark who's very cute, who's just on the edge of learning how to walk.

Mr. England and Miss Newman were talking away. They were both at Oxford University, though not at quite the same time. Miss Newman isn't a real full time matron; she's just doing it for a bit to help out before she looks for a better job at the end of term. She was studying Russian at her college, and I think she's probably nearly as clever as Mr. England, who did classics. They've got a lot in common. Miss Newman had just been to see a show in the West End of London with her sister. It was called Cabaret and was made out of a book written by one of Mr. England's favourite authors. Then they were having a laugh about a new show that's opening right now in New York called Hair where everybody takes their clothes off and stands on the stage completely naked. Can you imagine how embarrassing that is—standing in front of all those people and singing songs without even your underpants on? They were talking about it rather quietly, and I don't think we were meant to completely hear, but I managed to catch all of it. After they finished on the naked people, they talked very seriously about a Cardinal Newman who lived in the last century and might have been a relation of Miss Newman's but probably wasn't.

Then we were there, outside the big green double front doors of the school. I was at the moment I'd been most worried about. It was horrid to be back, just as it always is. It's like you have to jump into a freezing swimming pool, so you take a big breath and just get on with it.

There was a bit of a queue of cars with parents bringing boys back and unloading bags and tennis rackets and things. The street outside school is very narrow, but Mr. England went past the other cars and up onto the pavement opposite. It felt like we'd jumped the queue, but we were with a teacher and matron after all, so it was a bit like being slightly more important than the other boys.

We went into the front hall, which was dark after the sunshine outside, and Miss Carson was there in her shiny white matron's coat waiting for us. A whole line of parents waited to say hello to her with a terrible din of mothers talking too loudly, and it all echoed round the hall. Webster was in front of me with his boater on—he didn't know yet about not wearing it, of course—and loaded down with his bag and the big white bat.

'Hello, Webster. I'm Miss Carson, the Matron...' She held her hand out to him and for a little while he stood there not knowing what to do because his hands were full. Then he dropped his bat, which made an awful clatter on the wooden floor, and shook Miss Carson's hand.

'My name's Giles, in fact...' he said in a very quiet voice.

'That may well be, but at school we use surnames, so you'll be known as Webster by everyone here. Teasdale, I believe you're going to be looking after this young chap? He's in Surrey dorm, and his trunk's on his bed. I'd be grateful if you'd help him unpack, please.'

'Yes, Miss Carson.'

'...and you're on the top floor, in Dorset dorm. I'm glad to say that this term your trunk has arrived before you and is on your bed waiting for you.'

'Thank you, Miss Carson.'

Then I heard Smythson giggling and pointing to Webster's bat on the floor. He's famous in the school for being so good at batting. Last summer term Mr. Burston took him to Gloucester and bought him a cricket bat as a special prize. One day he might be the head boy on account of being so good at cricket, which I think is very stupid because he's not particularly good at anything else, and actually, isn't a very nice person. I could see that the teasing was going to start on Webster already.

Smythson said 'Bat boy!' in a loud voice and pointed at Webster. Then Hapgood, who was standing next to him, started to laugh.

'Oh give him a break, Smythers, you spastic,' Nick Gower said from behind me. That's typical of Nick. Smythson's bigger than him, and he's got his silly little gang of people who suck up to him. He thinks he's the most popular boy in the school, but Nick just ignores all that. That's probably why it's not possible to bully him. He just doesn't care.

There wasn't tea and cakes in the hall like they do at the beginning of the winter term for all the new boys and their parents. Webster was the only new boy this term. I can remember my very first day here with Mummy and my dad. The window shutters in the hall were wide open, and the sun was coming in. There was a table with a white cloth on it with loads of chocolate biscuits, and cakes, and orange squash for boys, and tea for the grown-ups. It looked really lovely and homely. I was still too young to know what homesickness was, and I just thought I was on a big adventure. It's funny when I think back to that now, because it seems like it was a different room then, not this dark hall we all hate because it's where the term starts.

—✺—

Mummy's going to be ever so late; I know she is. She's never on time for anything, and she's getting worse and worse. I'll still be sitting here when they all come out of lunch, and the other boys will laugh at me. Then Miss Newman and Miss Carson will give each other looks and start feeling sorry for me. I don't want them to feel sorry for me, and I don't want them talking about Mummy.

Perhaps they'll forget that I'm here. They can't see me round the corner from the corridor, after all. When they come out of lunch I'll hold my breath so they can't hear the slightest bit of me. But then I might be here right until teatime, unless baby Mark crawls along the corridor. If he sees me he'll want to get up on my lap. He always does, because whenever I see him I like to have a bit of a play with him, and so he knows me better than all the other boys. When Mrs. Burston comes looking for him and finds him with me, I'll have to tell her that I've been waiting all this time, and she'll start to feel sorry for me.

The clock says nearly half past twelve. I've heard some cars go by, and I keep thinking it must be her in the taxi, but I can't see the road out of the windows because the bottom part of the shutters is closed. Any minute, lessons are going to finish, and everyone will be assembling in school hall waiting to go into lunch. Any minute now.

Suppose that Mummy doesn't come by herself? Suppose she comes with one of her new drinking friends from the pub? She might bring Trotsky John with her. She might come with Anna Maria. What would I do if the people from school saw her? She looks so horrible. She'll be wearing her black coat even though it's the summer. It's got a fur collar that's greasy from her hair which is all matted with white bits on her skull because she hasn't remembered to dye it. She's got horrid tiny brown teeth and purple lips with white hairs at the side, and when she comes near me I try to be breathing out in case a bit of her breath goes inside me. I hate her more than all the others. She smells. I don't know why Mummy likes her so much. She hardly speaks at all—especially to me—and when she does she's got a foreign accent though she's been here for thirty years. It's quite difficult to understand her, actually. Mummy says she feels sorry for her because she had to run away from General Franco, who killed all her relatives and still hasn't been punished for it. She used to be a nurse at St. James Hospital until there was some mistake about the key to the cupboard where they keep the drugs that she was in charge of. Mummy told me that 'Very unfairly, they had to let her go…' If I was sick in hospital and she was my nurse, I'd climb out of the window in the middle of the night and run away.

Sometimes during the holidays when I've been to the library on the bus to look at the new Gibbons stamp catalogue, I've seen her with some of the other people who like to have a drink, sitting on the steps of the War Memorial with her dirty white tights all wrinkled round her knees and a bottle wrapped in a white napkin poking out of her black bag. Please let it be that Mummy doesn't come with Anna Maria…

I can hear them all getting ready to go into lunch now, and here I am still. The talking's getting louder and louder, and Mrs. Marston's telling everyone to be quiet and get into line.

Oh heck! I was chosen to say grace today, but I'm not going to be in the dining room. Perhaps they'll come out and get me.

Now the gong's gone, and they're walking along the corridor in silence. It's one of the strictest school rules to go into lunch in complete silence. If you're caught talking on the way in, or before grace is said, you're sure to get the slipper. I'm pushing myself back into the chair to make myself as invisible as possible, but really I'm quite safe from being seen. It seems like they're taking an awfully long time to get there, as though there's more boys than there actually are.

Now in the dining room, there's an awfully long silence. I think everyone is wondering who's going to say grace. It has to be said when the clock strikes one. That's another thing that is a very strict rule. Grace when the clock strikes one. I don't want to be fetched to do it and then have to come back to the hall to carry on waiting with everyone knowing that Mummy's not arrived yet. Please make it that someone else says grace.

There goes the clock. It's one o'clock. They've all gone quiet. And now there's lots of noise so someone else must have said grace, thank goodness, and everyone has sat down for their lunch. That means that everybody thinks that I've gone out.

I wonder what's for lunch. It's Wednesday, so it will be mince. Horrid watery mince; I don't mind missing that. If Mummy does come, I'll be having lunch with her, anyway.

But she's meant to be here by now. She said between twelve and one o'clock so that means from now on she's properly late. I'm getting more and more worried.

———

That first day of term we had lots of time before high tea for unpacking, so before I did mine, I took Giles Webster up to Surrey dorm and unpacked his stuff for him. I was trying to tell him all the things that he needs to remember, like where the Matron's surgery is, where the big wardrobes for all the pants, and vests, and socks, and pajamas are, which washstand and jug he was going to have to use, and where to keep his wash bag. But he was just sitting on the chair next to his bed staring out of the window, and I could see he wasn't paying any attention to what I was saying. He's such a small boy that his feet weren't even touching the ground. He was holding a teddy bear in one hand and the silly big bat in the other.

'You don't have to hold onto it all the time, you know, Webster.' It was beginning to annoy me, especially since he wasn't listening to what I was trying to teach him. Then his face slowly started to go all crumply, and I could see he was going to cry. He said something in that very very quiet voice he's got.

'What did you say?'

'I want my Mummy...' Then I felt really horrible because there was no point getting angry with such a new boy who was feeling so homesick. There wasn't anybody else in the dorm to see so I put my arm round him and said, 'It's alright, Giles. You'll be seeing her again very soon, and you'll soon get used to all these new things. Everything will be fine in one or two days when you've made some friends...'

Surrey dorm is for the youngest boys, so it's right next to Matron's surgery. There are quite a lot of teddy bears and stuff on the beds. Sometimes when the fifth form and seniors go in there they have a bit of a laugh about it all. Perrington has eleven teddy bears, all with different names, and once I heard Miss Carson saying in the staff room that she often heard him talking to them all under the covers when she was doing her last round in the middle of the night. I don't think she tells him to stop talking to them, even when it's very late. That's quite a nice thing about her, actually. I bet Perrington doesn't ever do homesickness though, because all of his friends come with him to school in his trunk!

It's a funny thing, but when I was unpacking for Webster and trying to cheer him up, I forgot that I was homesick too. The feeling of it all came back once we went into high tea, though. It was sardines, and there's nothing I hate more in the whole world than sardines, apart from kippers. I hate those even more, and everyone knows how much they make me feel sick. Once at breakfast when I wasn't looking, Smythson took the eyes out of his kipper and put them in my tea, and I drank them down and nearly choked. He had a big laugh about that. When no one's looking, I try to give my kipper to Nick if he's on my table, because he loves them. But if he's not, they make me stay in the dining room and eat the horrid thing after everyone has gone up to make their beds and get ready for classes. Sometimes Worgan is there with me. If Mrs. Ridgeley isn't the cook for the day, the assistant cook does the porridge. She makes it lumpy, and he can't eat lumpy porridge. So I'm sitting there staring out of the window at the river, and he's there rubbing his knee with one hand and his throat with the other, trying to make the porridge go down. I just hate it that the kipper still has its head on and its eyes in. Sometimes I've been at the table right up to the start of Assembly before Miss Carson has come in and said, 'Okay, Teasdale, you can leave it this once...'

What a terrible start to the term. Sardines for high tea, with their innards still in and everything!

Afterwards, just before the bell rang for bedtime, everyone was outside enjoying a bit of the sunshine. That's one good thing about the summer term. We can play around for a bit outside after prep before we go upstairs. Clarkson was showing off his new model aeroplane that he got for his birthday. It has a proper engine and can really fly. He was putting some petrol in it and trying to start it up, but it would go for a few seconds and then stop. I thought that when he did get it to work it would probably fly straight into the river, and that would just serve him right for being a show-off about his present. I would really love to see it going, though. The engine makes a terrible noise, and I knew that as soon as Mr. Tulley, who's the science master, saw it, he would stop him from having a go with it, because what with the petrol and it being big and heavy, it's most probably quite dangerous. That's exactly what's happened, of course. It's confiscated till the end of term on account of being 'highly inflammable'.

Webster sat on a bench all by himself after we'd done his unpacking. He was looking at Smythson practising his batting in the nets that are always put up on the number two play lawn for the summer term. Silly old Smythson showing off. He loves the summer term when he becomes all famous and the Headmaster spoils him.

'Okay, Giles?' I said.

'Yes, thank you, Benjamin.'

'That's good. You'll soon be making friends with lots of other boys in form two... Listen, Giles, I know it's a silly rule, but you mustn't call me Benjamin. Sometimes it would be alright if we were in the same form but you're a nip—that means you're a new boy. You'll only be a nip until next term when you go up a form. I'm just going to call you Giles for today, and you must call me Teasdale from now on, but that doesn't mean that I'm not your friend. Do you understand?'

'Yes, Benjamin.'

This term I'm in Dorset dorm. It's high up at the very top of the school with a sloping ceiling because it's under the roof, and it has three huge dormer windows. That's the name you give to a window that pokes out of the roof, and it doesn't have anything to do with the fact that they're in a dormitory.

From two of the windows, you can see the river ever so clearly. It's so close that you would think you could jump out straight into the water. It's very wide with England far away on the other side across the sand banks that you can see if the tide's not up. When it comes in, there's a great wave they call the Severn bore which rushes up the river and causes great lapping brown waves that smell of mud and salt and bash against the banks. If you didn't know better, you'd think that the school was in danger of being washed away. The other window, which is above the washstands at the end of the room, looks out on three massive trees growing in the school grounds. There are hundreds of rooks in them, which sit cawing all day long and squirrels who live even higher up than we are in the dorm. Sometimes I dream about what it would be like to live all snuggled up in one of their cosy nests made out of twigs.

There are only seven of us in the dorm—it's one of the smallest, and when I went up before high tea and unpacked, I was happy about that, though it worries me when I think about who might be in there with me, and wonder whether they're good at keeping secrets or not. It's the very first thing that I have to worry and concentrate about at the beginning of a new term. Not the secret about Mummy that I think only the matrons and Mr. and Mrs. Burston know about, or the secret in Mr. England's car that no one knows except for me, but the one that I have to make sure doesn't ever get out of the dormitory. If there's going to be just seven boys it makes it much easier to stop things spreading.

Henry Pugh is my dorm prefect. He was last term, too, but then we were downstairs in Northumberland, which is one of the very biggest dorms. He's a very fair person but last term he started coming over to my bed after lights out and trying to put his hand in my pajamas. He's a very big boy with ginger hair and strong arms, and it took all of my strength to stop him. I just wouldn't let him, though, and I thought he might get annoyed and tell everyone my secret, but he didn't. Now I think he knows that I don't want him to do that to me, and I think he's not going to try again. The good thing is that he hasn't got angry about it.

My bed is underneath one of the windows. In the early morning if I'm awake before the bell goes, which is very often, I can hear the house martins who live under the eaves getting their nests ready to lay their eggs. I love to think about what they are all doing only a few inches away from my pillow. Just a few weeks ago, they were far away in Africa where they go for the winter. Now they've flown all the way back and are settling down for the summer, almost in the dorm and so close that if the wall wasn't in the way, I could reach out and touch them! I like to stand up on my bed and lean on the windowsill to watch them busily flying around, catching insects and diving down to the riverbanks to collect the mud to build their nests with. I don't think they ever stop to rest unless they're sitting in their nests. Sometimes I've watched them flying about for such a long time that without realising it, the sun has come up over the far away Cotswold Hills and has changed the river from murky grey to blue.

I've got the best bed in the dorm, and when I saw it on the first day of term I really felt quite happy, like when you get on an aeroplane and find out you're sitting next to the window and can look out.

I couldn't wait for the lights to be turned out that first night. After saying goodbye to Mummy, the journey, and the shock of suddenly being back at school, all I want is to be by myself in the dark and have a think about things. But it takes a bit of time because Miss Carson has to come in to check we've unpacked properly and put everything away in the wardrobes. Then she looks into our wash bags to make certain that we've got all those things we need like toothpaste and shampoo. I had everything this time, because I'd made sure of it before leaving home.

'Good, good,' she said when she looked into my wash bag on the washstand. That made me pleased and a bit unhappy all at the same time, because I know that really they're checking to see if Mummy's remembered or not. But I've got everything this term. The only big mistake was not having the sandwiches for the train journey.

Then Mr. Burston came round to say goodnight. He always does that at the beginning of term, to tell you what he expects of you. It's called a pep talk, like a little school report before you even start, and he goes round the whole dorm and talks to us one at a time while the others listen.

First he talked to Henry Pugh and told him to keep up with the good work he was doing with the younger boys. He uses a different sound in his voice when he's talking to the senior boys. It's not so loud as the one he uses if you're not a prefect. I think he said something to him about his maths having to be worked on before his common entrance exam, which he's taking this term. If he passes it, he's going to go to a school called Shrewsbury. His father's a Headmaster, and I always think how silly it is that he and his brother have to come away to this horrid boarding school instead of going to their own dad's grammar school.

Then he went to the end of Jonathan Theodorakis's bed and congratulated him on playing the piano at the service in the church at the end of last term. He can play the whole of Men of Harlech without once having to look at the music book. The funny thing about Theodorakis is that he can play without any stops, but he has a terrible stutter, which makes it very difficult to follow what he's saying because he's always stopping and starting. His mouth gets stuck, but when he's playing the piano, his fingers don't. I'm not sure how much he really likes music, though. Theodorakis and Jenkins were two of the boys that were chosen to go to see The Vienna Boys' Choir in Bristol the day that the secret of Mr. England's car started. They fell asleep in the middle of the concert and had to be woken up. It was really quite shameful, actually, especially since it was meant to be such a special occasion. This is the third dormitory that Theo—that's what everyone calls him for short—and I have been in together.

When he went over to Lucky Lorrimer's bed, Mr. Burston called him by his Christian name, which is Val. I think that was because his mum and dad have just decided to divorce each other, and every-one's trying to be as kind as possible to him; though actually, I don't think he minds very much. When he talks about the new house that he's going to be living in with his mother, he just sounds ex-cited about it. He told me last term that his dad's got a mistress who lives in a flat called a 'love nest' in Cyncoed, which is a posh part of Cardiff, and after the divorce he's going to marry her. I think that Lorrimer's glad that his dad won't be living with them anymore. Trenton in the sixth form started calling him 'Lucky' when he was a nip. He said it was because Lorrimer had skinny, weedy legs, and he was lucky that they didn't snap off. I know it's not very nice, but he doesn't seem to mind it very much.

'Where's Simon Chirl?' Mr. Burston said when he saw one of the beds was empty.

'He's in surgery with Matron, Sir, because of his collarbone and knee,' Pugh said. Chirl's from a farm near Ross-on-Wye, and he'd fallen off his horse the day before the beginning of term.

'Yes, and we're expecting young Mr. Whickham back at any mo-ment, I think,' he said when he saw another empty bed.

Mr. Burston's a very tall man; so tall that he nearly doesn't fit in the dorm because of the sloping ceiling. He walks very slowly sway-ing from side to side with his hands behind his back. Sometimes he sways so much I think he's going to fall over, and once, when we were in class he swayed into the blackboard, and it fell over. I thought that perhaps he was like Mummy and had had too much sherry, but really he's just very awkward and clumsy on account of being too tall. While he talks to us in the dorm he bangs his knees up against the end of the beds. He always does that, and sometimes when we're in class we pretend that we're him and do it to the desks. Reynolds is very tall and is always imitating him—he's quite a good actor and can do his voice as well. Everyone falls about—it makes us laugh so much.

When Mr. Burston got to Nick Earl, who's in the bed next to me, I could see that every bang against the end of the bed made Earl's head move, and for a terrible moment, I thought that I was going to start laughing and get myself into trouble. I was relieved when he got to Earl, though, because after him, there was only me to talk to and then the lights would go out, and I'd be by myself.

'Nick Earl, Nick Earl, Nick Earl… What on earth are we going to do about you, eh?' Mr. Burston said to him, 'Laziest boy in the school. I don't know, I really don't. You drive us all to despair.'

He is lazy, Earl. He's always in trouble for it. He gets detention after detention on account of his laziness, but it never makes any difference. It's like he's purposely decided not to learn anything at all. In prep he usually just stares out of the window. In class when he's asked a question and he doesn't know the answer, he moves his fingers through the air as though they're crab's claws looking for an invisible bit of the right answer that he might be able to catch. Everybody has a giggle whenever he does that.

But the thing is he's very clever. He can make radios after lights out with his torch on under the blankets; he knows the names of all the stars, how the combustible engine works, and why feathers on birds make it possible for them to fly—in other words all sort of things that we haven't got to in class yet and probably never will. He can tell you things that I bet some of the teachers don't know.

'What to do with you? What to do?' the Headmaster said to him. He was nodding his head and staring at him and then after a long silence he said, 'You know, Earl—Ben Teasdale here'—and he nodded at me then—'would give his right arm to have half your intelligence. Isn't that so, Teasdale?'

'Yes, Sir,' I said.

Just as the Headmaster was beginning to bang his knees up against the end of my bed to start my pep talk, Simon Chirl came in from surgery with his arm all wrapped up in a big white bandage with a huge bow behind his neck and a sulky look on his face. Mr. Burston started making fun of him falling off his horse and saying stuff about the Lone Ranger falling off Silver and best to leave the hard work to Tonto. I think Chirl expected him to say those things, which is why he looked so fed up. Actually, he's a very good rider and doesn't fall off much. I know that for a fact because I've been home twice with him for weekend exeat, and I've seen him racing around on his huge horse, whose name is Stevie, as though he really is a genuine cowboy. Mr. Burston doesn't know anything about it, so it's completely silly if he's teasing Chirl. Everybody who rides a horse falls off now and again. It's a natural thing. Anyway, the teasing meant that Mr. Burston forgot to give me my pep talk, which was jolly good and a relief.

When he said goodnight and turned the lights out, it went quiet very quickly. Of course there's meant to be absolute silence—you can get the slipper for talking after lights out—but actually it usually takes a few minutes and sometimes a warning from Matron before it is completely quiet. Usually, once there's been dead silence for about five minutes, everyone falls asleep quite quickly. This was the beginning of term, and everyone was actually quite pleased about the very quick silence. It wasn't dark in the room being that it's the summer now, and the curtains were letting in the light from outside. I could see everyone in their beds. Henry Pugh was sitting up writing his diary which is a thing I remember him doing last term, holding the edge of the pillow up so that if Matron comes in he can hide it quickly. Simon Chirl was staring straight out with a funny expression on his face. I think his arm was really hurting him.

Lucky Lorrimer had turned over and was facing the wall; he was already halfway to being asleep, I think. I couldn't see Theodorakis because Earl had his hands in the way. He was making funny shapes with them in the air as though he was trying to count something— probably reminding himself about how many seas with no water are on the moon, or something like that.

Very soon after, while Pugh was still writing his diary and Lorrimer was just beginning to snore, Tom Whickham came in. He'd been driven from London airport in a taxi all by himself. Imagine how much money that cost! His dad's in the RAF, and he'd come from his home in Hong Kong.

Pugh said, 'Straight to bed, Whickham—you can sort out your stuff in the morning.'

'Yes, Sir!' he said and then he did a sort of funny salute. Pugh didn't seem to mind because I think they're a bit friendly already because of playing each other in the finals of the table tennis last term. Whickham won although he's younger, but Pugh was very sportsmanlike about it, and Mrs. Marston had said that he'd accepted defeat 'gracefully'.

'Hi Teasdale—nice hols?' he whispered to me. I put my thumb up to him so as not to break the silence, and watched him get ready for bed. He was in Northumberland with me and Pugh last term, and I remembered him coming in late at the beginning of term then too.

When he comes from Hong Kong he doesn't wear school uniform, like the rest of us, though he's really meant to. He was wearing light brown trousers with a crease down the front of each leg, brown tie-up shoes, a blue shirt which is called 'drip-dry' and doesn't need ironing, and a pink tie which shines like silk and has a pattern of wings on it. He's got a beautiful top called a 'sports jacket' which has leather patches at the elbows to make it last longer. After he'd changed into his pajamas he tiptoed to the big wardrobe at the other end of the dorm and got a hanger which he very carefully put all the clothes on as neatly as can be. Then he zipped up his travel bag, which is brown and smells of leather, even from the other side of the dorm. Its tag says 'BOAC'. That stands for 'British Overseas Airways Corporation' and means he comes from a family that travels a very long way. The people at the airport stick that label on your luggage if you're going very far away. If you're not going so far they stick on a label that says BEA, which means 'British European Airways'. Our luggage at home in the attic has BOAC labels on it. That's something about Thomas Whickham which is the same as me.

When he was ready, he slid the bag under his bed with his foot before he carefully untucked a flap on one side of his bed and got in. He does everything so neatly—he's got beautiful italic writing that Mrs. Marston taught him and he was able to do straightaway. His desk is always tidy, so is the locker in the basement changing room with his game kit in it. I think it's just a natural thing with him; even the parting in his hair is always straight and tidy.

It was just light enough for me to see that he winked at me and smiled before he settled his head down onto the pillow after he'd patted it with his hand. I nodded at him and smiled back.

He's the smartest, handsomest boy in the school, even when he's wearing school uniform. His grey windcheater—that we all have to wear for everyday when we're not in class—never gets dirty like everybody else's. Last term I tried my best to keep mine clean. I made a firm resolution not to spill porridge or wipe my hands on it when they were grubby, because I wanted to be a bit like Tom Whickham, all clean and tidy, but it quickly got as grubby as it usually does. When I got a huge ink blot on it only one week after the beginning of term, I just knew it wasn't worth bothering about. I know I'm never ever going to be as smart as him, so I may as well just accept it.

It was beginning to get dark then. Pugh finished his writing, slapped his diary shut and plonked it down loudly under his bed. And then it was absolutely quiet apart from the sound of the wind in the big trees outside and Lucky Lorrimer, who was snoring but not so loudly that we'd have to wake him up like we sometimes do.

I couldn't sleep, though. I was awake far into the night thinking about Mummy. I was wondering whether if she closed her eyes she might be able to see me lying in my bed so far away across the other side of the country from her, over the Cotswold Hills and across the wide river on the edge of Wales. If she could see me, that means she's with me all the time, and I'm not really away from her.

Suddenly I thought that I was glad I wasn't at home with her which frightened me because I love her and miss her so much, and I hate being here at school. I tried to push that idea far away and make it go out of the window to be caught by the wind and drowned in the river, but it wouldn't leave me alone. If I don't want to be here or with Mummy either, perhaps I don't want to be anywhere at all, just by myself, like a solitary squirrel in one of those nests in the trees outside being rocked to sleep in the wind. I put my hand under the bed and unzipped my bag and felt through the blue tee shirt Granny gave me till I found the tissue paper that I'd wrapped my clock in. It was still ticking away. I took it out and wound it up under the blankets very slowly so that no one could hear and then put it back at the very bottom of the bag. Then I found Jollo's paw and held it in the darkness till I fell asleep.

Miss Carson woke me up in the middle of the night like she normally does.

'Okay, Teasdale. Out you pop…'

'What time is it, Miss Carson?'

'Shush, shush—try not to wake the others. Nearly eleven o'clock. Hurry up now, there's a good boy.'

I always ask her what time it is when she wakes me, and I think that's what makes her smile because every night it's the same old question. I probably have a surprised look on my face because I've been asleep. It's very dark when she comes in and she has a torch so that she doesn't have to turn on the light.

Then I get out of bed and wee in the pot that she brings in with her.

Quite often, I don't really need to, and I have to do a tiny whistle to make myself go and that makes her smile again, and then I do a little giggle. Sometimes, when I'm finished, she rubs the back of my head for a second just before I get back into my bed.

I don't know why I wet the bed. I don't do it on purpose. It just happens.

That's my third big secret.

Sometimes I think it's an even bigger secret than the one about Mummy not being very well. I just have to make sure it doesn't get around the whole school. It would be dreadful if everybody knew, and it would be a major thing to bully me about. But it's very hard to keep such a big secret. Nicholas and Stuart Goodwin, who are brothers, both wet the bed, and everyone calls them the Pisspot Twins, though actually they're not twins at all. Nobody likes them because of it. Absolutely every single person in the school knows, and even Mrs. Marston said something about it to Goodwin Senior last term when he hadn't learnt all his dates. 'Too lazy to finish your work, Goodwin, and too lazy to get out of bed to go to the bathroom.' He's in my class and when she said that to him, it made me so frightened that she would do the same if she knew about me. It's the most shameful thing. Nicholas Goodwin doesn't seem to care very much about the bullying though. I would hate it more than anything in the entire world.

Actually, Miss Carson's really nice to me when she wakes me up. She looks a bit different in the night because she doesn't have her white coat on, and it's a bit like she's forgetting to be a matron. Probably she's been watching the telly and having a glass of sherry and a relax. I feel as though we're sharing a bit of a secret. The other boys don't usually wake up, but if they do they just look very puzzled with screwed up faces that I can't see in the dark, and they never remember a thing about it the next morning. I don't feel so bad about it now, but when I first had to tell her about it, and she said she was going to come in every night, it made me want to cry, especially when she told me there would have to be a rubber sheet under the sheet. I was very, very ashamed. At first she kept the pot under the bed. Then one morning after breakfast when we went up to make our beds, Theo started mucking around with it and put it on his head as though it was a helmet from the war; Fisheye was saying 'yuk' and 'disgusting.' I knew that was going to happen over and over again, so I plucked up the courage and went into Matron's surgery to ask her whether we could keep it somewhere else where the other boys wouldn't see it.

'Don't be ridiculous, Teasdale—I'm not carting a pot around with me on my eleven o'clock rounds...'

'Please, Matron. Please, please. I don't want the other boys to see it. They make fun of me because of it...'

She didn't say anything more then, because she was busy sorting out the socks that had come back from the school laundry, but when I went up to the dorm—I was in Somerset then—that same evening, the pot wasn't under my bed anymore. When she came round that night she had the pot with her, and when I saw the whiteness of it clinking against the torch in her hand, I was so grateful to her. After I had finished and I was getting back into bed, I took her hand just for a little moment and said 'Thank you so, so much.'

Mummy used to get upset about me wetting the bed because it meant there was more work to do like washing sheets and things. I hated it when she told my dad, and he would look at me with a cross, disappointed expression. I remember one day when Mummy was taking wet sheets off my bed. We were staying in England; if we'd been in Beirut, it would have been Miriam, my old nanny, who would have done it, and she never used to say anything about it apart from making a clucking sound with her mouth. But Mummy was very worried about what the people who owned the guesthouse where we were staying would think about the stain I'd made on the mattress. She was saying over and over again to me, 'What will they say—what on earth will they say?' I was sitting on a chair trying to learn how to do up my shoelaces to make up for it, and suddenly I was able to tie them. She looked up at me from the other side of my bed with all the sheets bunched up in her hands and said, 'Well at least that's something, I suppose.'

Quite soon after that, when I was about six, I must have stopped doing it because I don't remember Mummy being disappointed about it any longer.

But it started again right in the middle of my first term, which means that I must have been about to be nine. I woke up one morning just as the warm feeling was turning to cold. I didn't know what to do at first, and I lay there shaking and shaking. It was still dark and everyone else was fast asleep. I got out of bed and went to get my towel from the washstand, and I put it over the wet patch and then I got back into bed and took off my pajama bottoms under the covers and put them under the pillow. Then I put my head right under the blankets and prayed and prayed that my breath would make the bed as warm as possible so the dampness would dry by the morning. I cried too, because I couldn't believe that it had happened. Then I fell asleep for a bit although I was hoping that the morning would never ever come.

My bed did get dry. Nobody noticed when we got up although there was a stain on the sheet that got worse as it got drier. We all have to strip our beds back before we go down to breakfast, and we're supposed to leave them very tidy with the under sheet all straight and the top sheet and blankets perfectly folded back at the end of the bed to allow it all to air. We go back upstairs to the dorm after breakfast to make the beds properly before classes start.

That first time, after I'd folded the sheets back, I put my dressing gown over the stain and Langford, who was our dorm prefect and luckily not very bothered about tidiness, didn't seem to notice, although dressing gowns are meant to be left folded neatly over the bar at the end of the bed. It's quite a strict rule, actually.

After a few days, I thought that it might have just been that I had too much to drink at high tea. And so it was like a little bit of a warning not to drink too much near to bedtime.

But then it happened again, and this time it was even worse because I knew that it was going to happen over and over again, and that I would have to learn to hide it and even then people would probably find out. I had to start pretending that I wasn't a tidy person, which I am really. I was always the last one to go down to breakfast in the morning because I wanted to make sure that the patch on the bed was covered by my dressing gown or my towel. If I wet the bed quite soon after the sheets were changed or we had clean pajamas which happens every two weeks, I would be very worried about the smell which would be horribly bad if I wet the bed once or twice with the same sheets. I didn't want to be known as a smelly person, like everyone says the Goodwins are. I tried to be wearing my dressing gown as much as I possibly could whenever I was in my pajamas upstairs so no one would be able to smell them.

I knew that one day I would be found out, though. It was getting worse and worse and even when I went home for the Christmas holidays, it didn't stop. I didn't tell Mummy about it, though, and I've never ever told her, even now. I wanted nobody in the whole world to know about it. It was the deadliest, deepest secret.

On Boxing Day, when it was my first holiday at home and I was already dreading going back to school, my dad came into my bedroom before I had time to make my bed. I was sitting at my desk looking up in my old Gibbons catalogue some new stamps that Granny had sent me for Christmas. He opened the door and looked straight down at my bed. I just don't know why I had been so stupid and forgotten to cover it up, because I'm usually so careful.

'Oh, for heaven's sake, Ben...' he said very slowly and closed the door. He's never said anything more about it, though. I don't think he was so sure what to say.

I was in Somerset dorm when I came back from that Christmas holiday for my second term. It's just the same size as Dorset, which I'm in now, because it's directly underneath, but it doesn't have the sloping roof and the ceiling is much higher. Halford was the dorm prefect, and he's dead keen on tidiness, so it was much more difficult trying to arrange things to cover the stains before going down to breakfast. One day I was on table clearing duty and went back up to the dormitory after the other boys. When I got to just outside the door, I saw that everyone was leaning over my bed and Halford was holding my dressing gown. Then they all shot away as though they didn't want me to know that they had been looking, and Halford put my dressing gown back on the bed. I pretended that I hadn't seen anything, though I was shivering inside. I prayed and prayed that no one was going to say anything about it, and while I was making my bed no one did, though everyone kept looking at me in a funny way. But just as we were leaving to go downstairs, Halford said—in front of everybody—'got a slight problem here, have we, eh, Teasdale?' He sort of half pointed at my bed and I tried to look as though I didn't know what he was talking about, but I was blushing and my hands were shaking.

He didn't say anything more about it, and nobody else did either. I was so relieved, but then I was just waiting for the exact same thing to happen again another time.

It was just a few days later, and I wet the bed again very badly. I think it was just before we were going to get up and not the middle of the night so there was no time for the sheets to dry. When the morning bell went, I got out of bed and put my dressing gown over the wet patch and went to the washstand. There was snow on the ground outside, and it was icy cold in the dorm with the radiators only slightly lukewarm as usual. I was shivering. My pajama bottoms were completely wet and sticking to my legs, and I could see that Halford had noticed. He told me to put my dressing gown on like everyone else. I walked back to my bed ever so slowly and put it on. Then he looked at the damp patch where the dressing gown had been and told me to go and see Matron and tell her that I'd wet the bed.

Someone—I think it was Fisheye actually—said 'Oh, blimey, we've got a blooming bed wetter in the dorm,' and Theodorakis said 'l-l-lazy rat—can't you p-pee in the bog like e-everyone else?' and someone else—I think it might have been Reynolds—called me a cretin. I knew I'd been found out good and proper, and things would never be the same again.

I sat down on the edge of my bed and covered my face with my hands really tight, as though if I pressed hard enough it might all go away and I might be somewhere else or a different person.

'Please, please don't tell anyone else,' I said and I looked at everyone to see if there might be a possibility that they'd keep it a secret.

'It's alright, Teasdale,' said Halford, 'It's not such a big deal. Just go and tell Matron, and she'll sort something out.'

'But she'll be so cross with me...'

'No she won't. Just tell her the truth. It'll be okay.' And then he said, 'Listen everyone. Dorm secret. This doesn't go any further than here, okay?'

I didn't know why he'd done that. I thought perhaps it was because it's a bit shameful to have someone in the dorm who wets the bed. The best kept dorm on each floor is awarded school points once a week from Matron, and Halford was always pleased when Somerset won, which was very often, on account of him being such a tidy person. But actually, he left to go to Brecon School last summer, and then I heard someone saying that when he first came to Courtlands, he'd been a bed wetter too. I don't know if that's true, though. He didn't seem at all like a bed wetter to me.

I was ever so grateful to him. It meant that no one was talking about it, and I don't think even now most people in the school really know. Nick Gower doesn't know. I've never been in a dorm with him. Tom Whickham didn't know before, but he must now after two terms in the same dorm as me, though he's never said a word about it. I really wish he didn't have to know, though.

Every time I'm in a new dorm I get terribly worried about what people will say about Miss Carson waking me up in the middle of the night. That's why it's so important to me who's in the dorm and whether they're good at secrets, but I hardly wet the bed at all now that I'm weeing in the pot, so nobody's actually very bothered about it. Sometimes there's a tiny bit of an outbreak of teasing, though. At the beginning of this term I had an argument with Theo about a desk in our classroom. I'd bagged one of the new shiny light brown ones that everyone wants, and when he didn't manage to get one for himself, he started singing ever so softly, and without any bit of his stutter—'Make an umbrella, make an umbrella - out - of - Teasdale's - rubber - sheet!' No one in the form asked him what he meant, because, luckily, just then, Mr. England came in, and we all sat down for the beginning of term. I've still got that desk.

But I'm always worried about being properly found out, and everyone, including the teachers, going on at me like they do at the Goodwin Pisspot Twins.

—m—

The Headmaster's bell on Centre Table has just rung for silence. Lunch is finished, and I'm still here. Now they've all gone quiet, and Mr. Burston is going to say grace before everyone comes out and goes along the corridor again. He's got a very deep voice, so wherever he is in the school, you can hear him.

'For what we have just received, may the Lord make us truly grateful. Amen.'

What am I going to do? Mummy's not coming or she's had an accident, and absolutely nobody knows that I'm still waiting in this hall.

The thing is—anything could have happened to her. She might be asleep on the train and gone to Swansea, or she might have had a bad accident. She could have fallen over when she was getting off and banged her head like she did when she went to the Prestons' at the top of the road for dinner. That was the night that my dad had to carry her back. There was snow on the ground, and he slipped and fell all the way down the front steps with her. It was very late in the night, but I was worried and watching from my bedroom window. I didn't do anything about it, though. I pretended that it wasn't happening. In the end, my dad put her on the bed in the spare room and started shouting at her to pull herself together. I could hear from his voice that he might even start crying, and I pulled my pillow over my head to cover my ears.

They're coming out of the dining room now. I can hear all the feet on the wooden floor going past. When they get to the end of the corridor, Miss Newman will open the big door at the back. Then the chattering will start, and everyone will go outside for twenty minutes before the bell goes for afternoon classes.

I'm going to get a telling off when it's discovered that I'm still here. They'll think that I've just been sitting here enjoying not being in class. They don't know how I really feel about it.

Everyone's outside now; I can hear them in the distance. There's shouting about a game of football that's started.

I'm going to have to find someone in a minute and tell them that I'm still here. They'll be really shocked, and the matrons will talk more about Mummy and perhaps call a staff meeting to discuss it all.

When Mr. Burston told me she was coming, I pretended to look very pleased about it, but actually inside I felt horrid. Really horrid, because more and more Mummy can't cope by herself, and I don't know what to do about it. And if she does still come today and she's had too much sherry, where will we go, and what will people say if she's not walking properly? And what if she's in one of her really silly moods and doing stupid mad things like when the van from Harrods arrived at the house to deliver a cage with a huge red parrot inside it. I said 'I think there's been some mistake here'—just like my dad does—and the delivery man said it wasn't a mistake and showed us her funny scrawly signature to prove it.

'Heavens, Ben—you still here?'

It's Mr. England. I never heard him coming along the corridor. He wears very quiet Hush Puppy shoes. He's carrying a big tape recorder in his hands with a pile of books and tape reels on top of it.

'Hello, Mr. England.'

'You still waiting for your mother?'

'Yes, she's coming to take me out for lunch.'

'I know. We thought you'd gone ages ago.'

'She's just a bit late. She's probably been delayed or something.' I'm trying to make it sound like I really don't mind. Mr. England stops in the middle of the hall, and his floppy yellow hair moves because he's very slowly nodding his head. He looks away as though he's thinking about something and then he walks over to the big table on the other side and puts down the tape recorder.

'What time were you expecting her?' he says after quite a long time.

'Well sometime round just before lunch, I think. But sometimes that train can be a bit late, actually.'

'Yes, that does seem to happen quite a bit, doesn't it? Are you alright sitting here waiting? You've been here an awfully long time.'

'Oh yes. In fact I'm just learning some of my history dates. She'll be here in a minute, I expect.'

He's getting his music class ready. He teaches it in the front hall. It's a special event. You have to be invited, and it means you finish prep early and stay up late, too. It's one of my favourite things, because he plays us music, and then we answer questions about it. I'm always invited. I love it that he asks me more questions than practically anybody else. Once he played a tape of a man with a very deep singing voice, and I said that he sounded the same as someone who we once heard when we went to a concert in Gloucester Cathedral. Mr. England said he thought that I was a 'very clever young man' because in fact it was the same man! I think about that moment over and over again.

He's gone out again now to get more things for the class.

I want to tell him that I must find out about Mummy. I must tell someone, and he's the best one. He'll be back in a minute. I'll tell him as soon as he comes back. I'll say that we need to find out about the times of the trains. I'll say that sometimes, if you're not quick enough, it's difficult to get off that train at Chepstow. I'll say that perhaps we should telephone the station to ask if there's a lady stuck on the platform.

He's come back in with a long piece of wire with a plug on the end of it, and he's bending down trying to arrange the electricity.

'Mr. England...'

'Yes, Benjamin?'

'I am actually just wondering a little bit where my mother might be. She is quite late now, in fact.'

'Yes, Ben. I've just had a word about it to Mr. Burston. He's got it all in hand. Probably phoning Chepstow Station at this very minute.'

So they know now. They know she's not here. They know I've been waiting all this time. They'll be talking about me, and they'll be talking about Mummy. Miss Carson will be nodding her head at Mrs. Burston as if she can't believe there's trouble with Teasdale's mother again. They'll all be talking about how long I've been silently waiting in the hall for her, and they're going to be feeling sorry for me. I hate that.

Mummy's coming because it's one of her bad days, and that's very worrying. It means she could be terribly late, or get lost, or worst of all, hurt herself. If she's not on the train perhaps she's coming in a car with somebody else, like Caroline Dawson. She lives up by the golf club and is one of Mummy's old friends but likes a drink the same as Mummy does. If they're coming in her car they'll have an accident, because Caroline Dawson drives very badly. When she's leaving our house in the afternoon, she gets in her red sports car and revs up the engine till it's about to burst, and then she drives off right in the middle of the road with a lot of smoke coming out of the back. Perhaps Mummy's having a day out with those people from home, and when they open the front door Trotsky John will be swearing, Anna Maria will have a bottle with a napkin round it in her hand, and Caroline Dawson will be wearing her big scarf skew-whiff on her head and her bright red lipstick smudged all round her mouth.

I'm sure that my dad doesn't know, otherwise he would have been the one to phone to say that Mummy was coming. He might be abroad at the moment, and that would explain a lot, because when he's away, she's much more likely to be bad. When Mummy's had too much sherry at home my dad doesn't always seem to notice, or perhaps he pretends not to. I always know, though. But if she's had so much that she can't make the dinner, or she's in bed when he comes home, or she's wobbling a lot in the kitchen and not talking clearly with the radio on too loud, they might have a furious argument before he goes to his study. The thing is, he only shouts at her if she's really bad, and if she's just quite bad, he doesn't say anything. Mummy tries ever so hard to be a bit better if my dad's at home.

I never ever talk to him about it, and he doesn't talk to me about it. I wouldn't know what to say, and I'm certain he doesn't want me ever to mention it. It's a very strict rule in our house.

Mr. England's setting up his tape machine, and it's making squiggly backward noises while he's trying to find the beginning of the music. There's a loose bit of the tape poking out of the middle of the reel which is whizzing around, and it's hitting against the side of the machine making a clicking noise like a mad clock. Mr. England's trying hard to get it ready. I don't think it's the right time to interrupt him, but I want to tell him about my dad not knowing.

'Sir…? I wait for a little while. He doesn't say anything, and I think he didn't hear me.

'Sir…? I say it again and look at his face. He's biting his lip because he's concentrating so hard trying to find the right place to stop the tape, and then he says, 'Yes, Ben?' without looking at me.

'Actually, Sir… I think perhaps we should phone up my father. I think that probably it's best if he knows I'm waiting, because… because…'

'Because what, Ben?'

And then suddenly I'm talking so fast I can hardly keep up with myself.

'…because sometimes my mum isn't so well, and she does things that my dad doesn't always know about, and it could be that perhaps this is one of those times. I'm really not sure that he knows she's coming today, because he might be on one of his abroad trips and that means we couldn't talk to him anyway—and if Mummy's really bad today, I don't want to go out with her; I really don't. I just want it that we try and speak to him in his office in London to tell him, please, and—and actually I think it's best if I don't go out with her if possible...'

'Hold on, hold on. Calm down, Ben, it's all going to be alright. Listen, we've already thought of that, and the Headmaster has spoken to a nice lady at your father's office to let him know that your mother's been delayed, alright? He's out at a meeting at the moment, but he'll be phoning us back when he returns. I'm absolutely sure he knows exactly what's going on, though. Now just take a couple of deep breaths and try to relax.' Mr. England smiles at me, and I realise that my face must be red, and I'm clenching my hands, and my chest feels funny. Now he knows I'm upset. I hate that very much. But at the same time, I'm a bit relieved I've said it.

'Now—I'm going to fetch you a glass of water, and if you're still here in ten minutes or so, I think we ought to arrange a bite to eat for you. Do you think you need your inhaler? Do you know where it is?'

'I'm alright thank you, Sir. I know where it is, but I don't really need it.'

He goes out and comes back very quickly with water in one of those glasses from the dining room which the seniors have a joke about because it says 'Duralex' on the bottom. I take it from him with both hands and have a sip.

'Better now?'

'Yes, thank you, Sir.' It feels as though the water must be medicine or something, because I do feel a bit better and calmer now.

'I'm going into class now, Ben, but I'll pop out and see if you're still here in ten minutes or so, okay?'

'Thank you Mr. England, I'll be alright now. I'm sure she's going to be here any second, actually.'

The storm started on the same day Granny crashed her car. It was the Sunday of the first exeat of this term. Mr. Burston felt sorry for me, and secretly asked Alex Harman's mother and father if they would mind taking me out for the day. Probably he told them that I was disappointed and upset, though I made sure he hadn't seen that I was nearly crying when he told me in the study. Mr. Harman and Mr. Burston are old friends from University, and they were doing him a big favour by taking me with them.

I was sitting on the bench by the practise nets by myself after we'd all come back from church. I'd just been told about Granny not coming, and most of the boys had already gone. When I wasn't upset anymore, I was thinking that I liked the loneliness of it and was just beginning to plan what I might do all by myself for the day. Last time I was alone for a Sunday exeat, Miss Carson went out for lunch and let me watch the telly all afternoon in surgery. She left a Cornish pasty and a piece of lemon tart for my lunch from her own private fridge. I fetched my slippers from under my bed and watched a film with Bette Davis in it where she went away on a holiday ugly and came back a few months later beautiful. I'd had a lovely time all by myself, but just when I was thinking that it might happen again, Miss Carson came and sat on the bench next to me and said that Harman's parents were wondering whether I'd like to go out with them for the day.

I didn't want to go at all, because Harman isn't a friend of mine— in fact he's still a nip and that would make me look a bit of a spastic, really. But I could see from Miss Carson's face that I was meant to be awfully excited about it and it would be very rude to say no, so I said, 'that would be terribly nice,' in a surprised way and then made an expression as though I was dead pleased.

They were waiting in the hall for me. Everyone else had gone by then, and the whole school was really quiet. Usually you can hear at least something going on in the background, like cricket practise or tennis being played, or the lawn being mowed, or that fat Mrs. Ridgeley the cook dropping some pans in the kitchen, and the cleaning ladies chatting while they're mopping around—even teachers shouting in one of the classrooms. It was quiet enough to hear nothing except the big old clock, as though it was the loudest thing in all the world. I was walking along the corridor in a hurry because of knowing that the Harmans were waiting for me, trying to get my arms into my too small blazer, and holding my boater and wishing I wasn't going out. In the silence I could hear Harman talking to his mother.

'But Mummy—I don't want Teasdale to come with us—please...' He sounded as though he might start to cry at any moment, and I wondered what I should do.

'Now be nice, Bo-Bo. His Granny's just had an accident in her car, and he's very upset. Just think about how horrid it must be for him at the moment.'

'I don't care, and I just don't want him to come. I don't like him. I don't like him at all. I just want to be with you and Daddy. Please, please...'

'No, Bo-Bo—we've asked him and he's coming, and I want you to be nice to him.'

I thought it best to pretend that I'd not heard anything, and when I saw Mr. and Mrs. Harman I put out my hand and said, 'Hello. I'm Benjamin. Thank you ever so much for inviting me out.'

'Hello, there,' Mrs. Harman said, 'Lovely to have you with us— we're going to Speech House in the forest for lunch, and then we thought we might go on to Symond's Yat for a walk. I'm so sorry about your bad news, Ben, but Mr. Burston's told us your grandmother's not at all hurt, so no need to worry too much...' Mr. Harman had a pipe in his mouth and tapped me on the head with a rolled up paper as he was opening the front door for us all to go out.

Speech House is a posh hotel in the middle of the Forest of Dean, and we had roast beef and Yorkshire pudding in a very old dining room with walls made of dark wooden panels. The people who lived in the forest in the olden days used to go there for meetings, and once, Judge Jeffreys, who we've learned about in history, came and sentenced hundreds of people to be hanged for rebelling against the king. There was a picture of him on the wall, and another one of King Charles II who once went there for his lunch too. Alex Harman didn't speak to me all day. When we were in his dad's car, which was a Rolls Royce and should have been a bit of an adventure, he just folded his arms and made his lips all big with sulking and stared out of the window. After the roast beef, we had some scrunched up fruit in a jelly called 'summer pudding', and then Alex stopped talking even to his mother. In the end, she got up from the table, took him by the wrist out of the big door that went into the garden, and shouted at him.

'I'm not putting up with this behaviour, Bo-Bo. Benjamin's a charming boy with lovely manners. I don't think you realise what it must be like to have a mother who's not very well. You're behaving atrociously. I've had enough, I really have...'

'But I told you I didn't want him to come,' he shouted back, 'and the whole day's been ruined by it. And stop calling me Bo-Bo when he can hear it...' Mr. Harman who'd not being talking very much and was mostly smoking his pipe and reading his paper all day looked over at me across the table and said 'Sorry about that, old chap.'

I didn't blame Harman very much really. Who wants to go out for the day with someone from school when you just want to forget about it all for the day? Actually, I don't blame him for not liking me, because I've never been especially nice to him. He's got a lisp, and quite often I've joined in the teasing of him about it.

It had been really hot all day, sunny at first and then a sort of mist in the sky that meant you could look straight at the sun without hurting your eyes and see it was twice as big as usual. It was funny having roast beef when it was such a hot day, but Mrs. Harman said Speech House was famous for it. After we were finished, we went to Symond's Yat which is a beautiful high up place overlooking the river. Mr. Harman wanted to read his paper and sat on a bench with

Alex. Mrs. Harman was trying her very best to be extra polite to me to make up for Alex's bad behaviour, so we went for a walk and left them behind which was the best part of the day because she's quite a nice lady actually. Then, when we were having tea and scones and meringues at a café in Monmouth full of old ladies with hats on, Mr. Harman looked at his watch and said, 'What time are we meant to be getting these young gentlemen back to school?' Mrs. Harman answered 'Five-thirty,' and Mr. Harman said, 'Best get moving then,' and Mrs. Harman said 'Doesn't time fly?' with a big relieved smile on her face. We got back to school earlier than anybody else. I was ever so glad. I sat all by myself on the bench by the nets again waiting for everyone to get back wishing I'd been there all day.

The sky was a pinky grey colour by then, and the big sun had completely gone. The air was thick and hot and damp. Mrs. Burston sat on the balcony with baby Mark on her lap, fanning herself with the Sunday paper. She kept making a funny noise with her mouth trying to blow some sticky hair from her forehead. Mr. Burston came out with no jacket on and his shirt sleeves rolled up, which I've never seen before. He looked at the sky with his hands on his hips and said, 'It's going to be a big one when it arrives.'

On the other side of the river I could just make out ghostly trees with dogs barking underneath them. There were people on horses. The fogginess made them look as though they were in a black and white film except for their tops, half of them scarlet and half of them orange, shining through the distance. They were galloping around holding long sticks, and you could hear the sound of echoey clunking when they hit the ball on the ground, though you couldn't see it. It's a game called polio, I think.

There was no wind that day. Absolutely none, which just isn't normal for Saxham-on-Severn. Even the rooks in the big tree were silent for once. I thought I was going to have an asthma attack, which is something that I only have at home. Then I thought that it was just that there was no air to breathe, and everyone was probably feeling the same. I even started thinking nice things about the school swimming pool, which I hate because it's an indoor one with not the slightest little bit of heating. It's freezing even on the hottest day.

It was getting hotter and hotter although it was nearly evening and time for bed. When the other boys started to come back I saw that a lot of the fathers weren't wearing their jackets and had big wet patches under their arms. I heard Mrs. Theodorakis say 'Don't you find it unbelievably close?' to Mrs. Burston, who said 'Like being in a warm bath, isn't it?'

That night, when Miss Carson turned out the lights in the dorm, it went quite dark even though the curtains weren't drawn. We'd opened all the windows as wide as we could on account of it being so hot and uncomfortable and then, when Pugh took the blankets off his bed, we all copied him. The night was turning into a little bit of an adventure with no one being able to settle down and go to sleep—except for Lucky Lorrimer, of course. He was asleep straightaway. Lots of whispering started that turned to chatting which Pugh didn't try to stop, not even when Nick Earl, without asking my permission, stood on my bed with his grubby feet on my pillow so he could look out of the window.

'Very, very strange for late May, this…' he said, '… to be this hot. Quite extraordinary. Unusual.'

Miss Carson came in while he was still looking out and talking loudly about what he thought was going to happen. She told him to get back into bed and asked us all to settle down. But she wasn't using a cross voice at all, which made it feel that all the rules were being relaxed, just the same as when it's the last night of term. Everyone was excited—even Miss Carson. She got on my bed to look out of the window next to Earl, who hadn't gone back to his bed even after being told. Next, Theo came over and climbed on too. They were looking so hard that I decided that I needed to see out as well, and so I got up and squeezed in beside Theo. No one said anything for a while. It was so peculiar—the gloomy darkness, the scary silence and the stuffy heat. Suddenly, she clapped her hands together, which made me jump. 'Okay everyone. Back to bed. Just a storm brewing that'll pass over you all in the middle of the night. Come on—chop, chop.'

'Careful of that open window, Teasdale,' Henry Pugh said to me quite quietly after she'd gone out, 'If it pours in the middle of the night, your bed's going to be even wetter than it usually is.' I looked across at Tom Whickham, but I don't think he heard.

The flashes were lighting up the whole dormitory when Miss Carson came in and woke me for my wee. While I was kneeling down doing it, she moved around closing the windows and drawing the curtains. For a tiny moment every now and again, I could see her, bright as anything—but stuck as though she was in a photograph. Then there was blackness again, apart from her little torch, and a few seconds later she would be lit up again, but now stuck in a different place. The chamber pot was flashing a brilliant white, and my pee was frozen in space as though I might be doing it for the rest of my life, waiting for a spell to be broken in a fairytale.

'Why are there all these flashes but no thunder, Miss Carson?' I whispered.

'I'm not sure, but I think it's just that it's still so far away. It might not ever get to us.'

When she'd gone out, I got up to draw back the curtains of my window, and I decided to open it again. I put my pillow on the sill so that I could lean on it and get really comfortable for a long look out. The other boys were fast asleep, and it was lovely to wait for the storm to come in the middle of the night all by myself. Everybody but me was completely missing it. I prayed that the storm wouldn't pass us and go somewhere else. I wanted it to shock us and scare us and become a huge adventure that we could talk about for days and days.

Each time the flashes came, the river sparkled as though someone had thrown millions of diamonds into it. I could see right across to the flat plain on the other side and then up to the hills miles and miles from us, way in the distance. I saw tiny flying shapes close to the window, caught in the lightening. At first I thought they might be the house martins, but I think they were tucked up in their nests for the night trying to ignore it all. They're not the type of birds, like owls, who are flying about in the middle of the night, and they're so busy during the day it must be that they need to have a good long time of resting. I do know for a fact that there are bats who live up in the roof of the school; they are night time animals, so you never get to see them unless they're lit up by the lightening or passing a lamp on the street. I'm sure it was them flying around and getting excited. They probably like slightly scary things like storms, because they are slightly scary themselves.

I was straining to catch the sound of the thunder, but I couldn't. I listened to the river, gurgling and splashing away, and the three big trees where the rooks sit, which were just beginning to rustle a little because of a tiny bit of a wind that had started up. It was a gentle friendly little breeze, and it blew on my face and made me smile with the new coolness of it.

I was sleepy again after a while. The storm was going to take a long time to reach me if it came at all, and my eyes were beginning to close even though I was telling them not to. I put my pillow back on my bed and lay down to watch the patterns the flashes were making on the ceiling.

My face was wet when I woke up again. I thought I'd wet the bed, and the worry of that immediately made me wide awake. But my pajama bottoms were quite dry and something else was happening. Someone was screaming as loud as can be. The shadow of Henry Pugh was standing over me, wearing a huge billowing cloak that covered half my bed. He started to say something to me, but then there was the biggest bang I'd ever heard, and I pulled the sheet over my head. When I looked out again, I could see that it wasn't a cloak he was wearing but the curtains from my window that were wrapping themselves around him. It was the wind that was screaming, with massive claps of thunder in between.

'Help me close the window, Teasdale, before we all blooming drown...' he shouted. We had to lean right outside which was very frightening because the wind was so bad it could have picked us up and thrown us out, and I knew that at any time we might be struck by the lightening. There were great forks of it, some starting at the ground and some coming from the sky. The rain was not coming downwards like it usually does, but straight at us and a bit from below as if the river was being picked up and thrown into the dormitory. While Pugh and I were trying to close the window, I saw that there was someone else helping us and then, when there was a flash of lightening I saw that it was Tom Whickham. He was smiling and enjoying it all while I was thinking about how silly I'd been to want the terrible storm at all. Even when we'd closed the windows, it didn't seem to make much difference to the noise. They were rattling as though a giant was trying to get in, and the wind was so strong it was still coming through the sides so all the curtains were moving as though we were living in a haunted house. In the gaps between the thunder, I could hear things being blown along and banging and crashing into each other, and I thought about what we would all do if the massive trees were blown over and hit the side of the school.

I was wet through from leaning out of the window. So were Whickham and Pugh. They were a silvery colour from the rain when the lightening lit them up, as though they were eels that had come up from the river. Tom went to the light switch and tried to turn it on, but nothing happened. It seemed as though this was getting to be a more and more dangerous situation what with all the electricity having probably been sucked right up back into the sky. Tom was laughing out loud and shouting 'It's the end of the world—it's the end of the world!'

The flashes got closer and closer together, and I could see that Lucky Lorrimer had wound all his bedclothes around himself and was just one big lump on his bed. Simon Chirl was sitting dead upright with his sulky expression on which I think he also does when he's frightened. Nick Earl didn't seem to be at all worried and sat cross-legged on his bed with his arms folded just staring straight out of the window. I think he was making notes about it all in his head as though he was an explorer on an expedition who is used to frightening things happening all the time.

Theo knelt on the floor beside his bed, covering his face with his hands, and I think he was crying. I couldn't hear him properly, but it sounded like he was saying 'Get Matron, get Matron,' over and over again, and then, when there was the hugest clap of thunder, he screamed and scrambled right underneath the bed.

It seemed like the storm went on for ever such a long time, but actually it wasn't that long. After a while, the wind wasn't so bad, and the rain that had been bashing against the windows started to calm down. Then the noise of the thunder got a bit less, and there was a gap between the sound of it and the lightening. All of a sudden, it started to get lighter outside, and I realised that it wasn't the middle of the night but quite early in the morning. Then the lights flickered a bit and came back on, and I knew we were getting to be out of danger. Tom was still laughing about it all, and I started laughing with him. 'Wow! That was incredible! Truly incredible!' he kept saying.

'You can come out now, Theo,' I said to Theodorakis who was still hiding under his bed. 'The bogeyman's gone!'

I liked saying that to him. I think he's a person who might not be very good at keeping my secret, and now I have a bit of a secret about him being really scared during the storm when I wasn't the least bit. Well, I was a little, but I was the one who leaned right out of the window with Tom Whickham and Henry Pugh to close it and prevent further damage.

The storm was getting more distant and going off into Wales to frighten people and wake them up unexpectedly. If only they knew what a big shock they were in for!

After a few minutes, Miss Carson opened the door and came in holding Webster by the hand.

'Everyone alright?'

'Yes, thank you, Miss Carson,' we all said at the same time.

'Good. Nothing to worry about now; it's all over bar the shouting,' she said, and I wondered why someone was going to be shouting.

'Is Webster alright, Miss Carson?' I said, because I was remembering my promise to his mother.

'He's absolutely fine now, but he wasn't too fond of the storm, were you?'

'No,' he said very slowly in his tiny whispering voice.

Before she went out, Miss Carson told us it was only half past six, and there was going to be another hour before she rang the bell, but everyone was far too excited to go back to sleep.

I stood on my bed and tried to open the window. Water had come through the side because it's old and leaky and there was a puddle by my bed, which I thought might lead to a bit of teasing. When I was able to open it, another gush of water splattered onto the floor, and then the fresh air from outside came in.

It was like we were in a spaceship, opening the cabin door to peer outside at a new planet where no one had ever been before. Everything outside seemed different. The air smelt tangy and mouldy, and there was the sound of the water gushing from the roof where the gutters couldn't deal with all the rain and dripping from all the places where it had managed to get in. The sun was just beginning to come up from the other side of the river and shone on all the wetness, making it flash as brilliantly as the lightening, so that it was hard to look at anything without half closing my eyes.

The others were crowding onto my bed for a look, even Theo. There was a shed just by the river outside the school grounds that didn't have its roof on anymore, and great branches from the trees that had been snapped off and were lying on the tennis court and practise nets. A big bit of the fence that had been between them was lying on Mrs. Ridgeley's vegetable garden and had knocked down all her runner bean poles.

'Oh wow! Incredible!' Tom Whickham shouted when he looked

out of the window by the washstand. 'One of the trees isn't there anymore!'

I'd been worried about that very thing happening during the storm. But it hadn't bashed into the school like I thought it was going to. It had fallen the other way and was half drowned in the river. It was rocking to and fro in the big waves that the storm had made, and its branches were pointing up out of the water as though it was pleading to be saved. It was the saddest thing I'd ever seen. I thought about the squirrels and whether they'd been killed and also the rooks and where they would all go to now without their home. I wondered whether they could all squeeze up with their neighbours in the other two trees that were still there.

There was a massive gap because the tree that had fallen over was the biggest one, the one in the middle, and now there was a view from the window all the way down the river, right as far as the new suspension bridge at Chepstow, twenty miles away. It was like someone had taken down a pair of beautiful curtains, and now too much light was coming in. In the mornings when the other boys were still asleep, I used to like to watch the sun shining through the leaves of that tree. They'd be moving in the wind and sending patterns onto the wall on the other side of my bed, and I would watch them and get to be sleepy again. And now the tree has gone forever.

We're meant to be completely quiet when we're going down the stairs to breakfast, but everyone was talking about the storm, and the matrons didn't say a word to stop it because they were talking about it like everybody else. It was kippers for breakfast, and usually when I smell them I try my hardest to be standing next to Nick Gower. By the time we'd sat down and I knew what we were having, it was too late. But no one took any notice whatsoever that I wasn't eating the flipping thing, and that has never ever happened before.

There are three huge glass doors that open out from the dining room onto the balcony, which starts at one end of the school and goes right along to the other. They're called French windows. We're not allowed on that balcony. It's only for teachers and parents when they're here for Sports Day and Prize Giving so that they have a good view of the lawns and the river. The glass in one of the doors had a new crack in it that started down at the bottom and went right up to the top, and there was a little puddle of water where the rain had got in just the same as upstairs in our dorm.

There was a terrible mess on the balcony—lumps of mud, fresh green leaves, twigs and moss, and slate tiles from the roof. I wondered what would happen when it rained the next time because it seemed like half the roof had fallen off. Everyone was talking about it all so that even after grace was said and we're allowed to talk, Mr. Burston had to bang on the table and tell everyone to be a bit quieter.

I was the very first one to notice. I was sitting right by the window at the end of one of the long benches, staring out at how different it all looked outside. I was feeling so sad about it all, especially the big tree not being there anymore, and at the same time it was great that I wasn't having to eat the blooming kipper, and no one was taking any notice.

Suddenly I saw something moving in all the dirt on the balcony. At first I thought it was a little mouse or something, but I wasn't quite close enough to see properly and it was difficult anyway because the window was so dirtied up with splattered bits on it. And then, when I looked up at the sky, I could see all the house martins flying backwards and forwards and diving down towards the balcony and racing around as if they were in a panic. It was a bit odd because you don't usually see them so low. They like to be high up where their nests are, and they only dive down when they're by the river where they catch most of their food. Some of them were flying so close to the windows that they were hitting themselves on the glass, as though they didn't know that it was there. I was certain that they were going to be quite badly hurt.

When I looked down again at the balcony, I could see there were some dead ones there already, lying amongst all the mess. Then I knew that the big lumps of mud were the house martins' nests that had fallen all the way down from the eaves up by the dorm windows.

The little moving thing was a tiny chick that hadn't been killed when its home crashed down. There were two or three others in all the muck that must have been its brothers and sisters, but they weren't moving at all. They must have been killed when they fell all the way down with the nest.

But it wasn't the only survivor. When my eyes got used to what they were looking at, I could see that there were lots of them, slowly trying to move themselves away from the rubble of their homes.

'Look at all the chicks!' I said and stood up. I must have said it very loudly, because quite suddenly the whole dining room went quiet, and there was no noise at all apart from the sound of the house martins bumping into the glass at the windows and baby Mark banging his beaker on his high chair on the Headmaster's table.

The sun has travelled right over the roof and is trying to beam in through the top of the tall windows, which means that it really is the afternoon now, and I'm still waiting for Mummy. It's windy outside. It has been ever since the storm and that's nearly two weeks ago. It's making that whistling sound in the keyhole that I had to tell Webster not to take any notice of. I think that's the reason that some boys talk about this part of the school having a ghost. The key's hanging down just by the side on a chain, and there's enough wind coming through for it to be moving ever so slightly from side to side and clinking against the door frame. There are great grey clouds in the sky, rushing from England across into Wales and bringing showers with them. It's like the sun is in a battle with them, and sometimes it manages to charge through and shine like crazy for a little while before it's beaten back again. While I've been sitting here, the hall has gone very dark and then changed to light and then back to dark as though I've been sitting here through whole night times and day times.

Right now, the sun's shining onto the biggest print of them all, which is of King George IV at the battle of Waterloo. It's a made up picture because I know for a fact that the last king who was in a battle was George II. His face is all lit up, and he looks as though he's staring at the front door, waiting, just like I am for Mummy to arrive. There's a sword in his hand, which he's waving above his head. He's like one of those people who wave a flag at the end of a motor race, and when Mummy opens the door, he's going to swish his sword about to let everyone know that she's here.

That's if she ever comes, of course.

All my worry's come back. It's much more than ten minutes since Mr. England went to take his class. He's not been back to check on me like he said he would, and that means I'm all forgotten about again. I wish he'd come back and tell me what to do. I don't want Mr. Burston to come along and make me feel bad by saying those things he thinks are funny, but which actually means he's cross with me that I'm not gone even though it's not at all my fault.

It really is the oddest thing ever that Mummy's coming without my dad. It feels all wrong because she never really goes anywhere all by herself. The only time that ever happened—and then she did go away for ever such a long time—was nearly the whole of the summer term last year. It was when my dad had been away on a massively long business trip, and she didn't want to be alone at home. She loved the place she went to more than anywhere she'd ever been in her life. She told me she only came back because she wanted to see me when I came home for the summer holidays.

I was so excited when she told me about it because I could see that it made her happy, and I loved asking her questions and dreaming that one day we might really go there together.

It was an island in the Mediterranean, not so far away from Beirut where we used to live, and when she got there she met some Americans who were running away from the war in Vietnam and had become poets and musicians. They had long hair and stayed up all night drinking wine and dancing round the fires that they made on the beach, and when the people who lived in the village shouted at them to be quiet because of their guitars they'd laugh and stop playing for a bit and then carry on again. They made lovely jewellery that they sent home to be sold in their old colleges in America. They took Mummy with them to see ruined temples and talked all day long about how the ancients had lived and how they wanted to be free like them. Mummy told me that those people were hippies, just like the ones who live in San Francisco and have peace marches against the war. She would have stayed with them if she could have. But she said she loved me too much not to come home to me, her 'Only'.

She changed after that holiday. When she talks about that place, which was called Matala, her eyes fill up with tears, and her voice goes funny.

I used to imagine that one day we really might go there. But then I'd think of my dad and what he would say about it, and I know it's just never going to happen. Once, we were having dinner in the summer holidays when Mummy was still sad about having to come back. My dad had come in and sat at the table straight from work and wasn't talking very much because of a bad day at the office. Mummy said she'd love to have some real soft goat's cheese with juicy tomatoes and olive oil like they have in Matala, and my dad shouted at her, 'Oh for fuck's sake, Pamela, please let's not bloody start on the wonders of Crete!'

She was a bit drunk, but not so much more than usual that he would be cross about it, so it made me know not to talk about Mummy's long holiday when he was listening. It would have to be one of our secret conversations. That was the first time I'd ever heard my dad saying that swear word. It's usually only said by people who are very, very angry—apart from Trotsky John who uses it whether he's angry or not.

I liked it so much when Mummy talked to me about packing our bags and going to live in that beautiful place, but of course I knew

that we couldn't really go there. Even if my dad didn't mind us going, I know that Mummy's not well enough. I'd be alone with her
having to do all the arranging of things, and I'd start to get more
and more worried because the Americans have gone home to California by now. There wouldn't be anyone to show me how to light
the fire on the beach or teach me how to make beautiful jewellery
to sell in America, so we'd have no money. We'd get more and more
hungry and then the winter would come, and we'd get cold as well.
Anyway, there are soldiers in charge of Greece now. Trotsky John
told me it's a fascist country. They've booted out their king, they
don't like people sleeping on the beaches anymore, and they cut
your hair if it's too long. I've read about it in the newspapers, actually. It would be a hopeless situation even if we could go.

The sun's gone in again. Just a minute ago, it was shining straight
onto my face, but now it seems as though the whole world's turned
grey and ghostly.

There's a car coming down the hill outside, very slowly. They all
have to do that because it's so steep that no one can go fast. There's a
sign at the top, in the High Street, that warns drivers to go as slowly
as they possibly can. It's a very narrow street of tall houses on both
sides with their front doors right on the pavement and no space for
front gardens. You can hear the echo of the engine as the car comes
down right from the very top, getting louder and louder. Last term,
when I was in Northumberland, which looks down onto the street,
I would wake up when a car came along in the middle of the night
because it would be so loud that I thought it must be a tank from the
Second World War.

The car's gone past the front door. The noise of it is disappearing
quickly because the street gets wider after the school, and the cars
can begin to speed up. It's not Mummy arriving.

But there is someone at the door now, trying to get in. As I watch
it, the great brass doorknob is turning ever so slowly, first one way,
and then the other, and it's making a little clinking sound. The
double doors are shaking a bit because the person outside is pushing

them inwards, then trying to pull them outwards, and the wind's making them shudder a bit at the same time. But still they don't want to open. Then it happens all over again, but even slower this time. And now it's gone still again. I'm sitting up, waiting, staring at the door and clasping the arms of the chair as hard as hard can be, wondering what I should do. It's not my job to open the door, after all. I might get into trouble if it's a person who shouldn't be allowed in. Now it's gone dead quiet again, and the doorknob isn't moving. I think that whoever was there has given up and decided to go away, perhaps to the kitchen door. That's farther down the street. It's probably the grocery man who comes from Gloucester in his van bringing things for Mrs. Ridgeley, the fat old cook.

Suddenly the doorbell rings, and that's a huge clanging noise that sounds like an emergency as though the school might be burning down. It's got a stuttery sort of sound like a machine gun because I think you have to press it really hard to make it go. This bell is something I've only ever heard in the distance and even then not at all often because people just don't ring it on account of there being a big door knocker with a lion's head. But if you're right here in the hall like I am, it's one of the loudest things ever, and it makes me jump right out of the big chair. My boater and the empty Duralex glass fall off my lap onto the floor. The glass doesn't smash, because of being hard and unbreakable, and it rolls along the floorboards making a noise until it stops by the bookcase under the picture of King George IV.

So now I'm standing up and thinking I'll have to open the door quickly to stop the person who's doing the ringing. I take one step towards it, and then there's silence again. But everyone in the whole school must have heard the noise, people will be coming along any minute now, and they'll see me standing here and think how stupid I look.

It's gone quiet again, and I hope that the person has gone away.

A tiny chink of light comes through the bottom shutters which are meant to be closed tight but don't properly meet up because they're a bit wonky from old age. Through the gap, I can see the shadow of a person trying to look through. Now there's tapping on the window—not very loud at first, just like a polite question to find out if anyone's inside. Then there's a pause, and now it's louder, angry tapping because no one answered the first time. I wish this person would go away.

My heart beats really fast, and I tiptoe into the corridor and look through the gloom towards the Assembly Hall and then the other way down towards where the kitchen, dining room, and staff room are. There's no one coming along yet, but everyone in the whole school must have heard the terrible racket.

The doorknob's moving again but this time not so shyly, so I know the person's definitely wanting to come in, and I start to walk back into the hall and decide that it's best that I should go to the front door after all, before there's any chance of the bell ringing again.

But all of a sudden both doors open just the tiniest little bit and immediately the wind catches hold of them, and they swing wide open as though they've been hit by a battering ram. One door crashes into the wall and the other knocks over a stand which has lots of walking sticks and umbrellas in it and the noise it makes when they all spill onto the floorboards is even worse than the bell ringing.

At that very moment the sun comes out again from behind the clouds and shines straight in through the door, and the brightness and the wind rush into the hall at the same time. Mr. England's papers for his music class that are on the tape recorder swirl around in the air and then begin to settle on the ground like snow on a freezing cold day.

A dark silhouette of a person is in the doorway.

I know it's Mummy even though I can't see her properly. She's holding her arms out to the side and the palms of her hands are open as though she's saying 'Here I am at last.' The sun shines through her mass of curly hair blowing in the wind, and it looks as though she's got a halo. It makes me think of the picture of the Virgin Mary in the church hall where we go for choir practise. She looks ever so small in the big doorway just as though the wind has blown her in before she was properly ready. Now I'm getting used to the light and can see her better. She smiles at me, and we both look surprised as though we weren't expecting to see each other—even though I've been waiting for hours and hours and hours. I don't know what to say to her because I'm so worried about what is going to happen next, and I wonder when someone's going to come along from the staff room to see what was making all that noise.

—m—

Mr. Burston rang the bell at the end of the breakfast after the big storm, though he didn't really need to because after I'd shouted out about the chicks everything went ghostly silent, and no one was interested in eating anyway. He said grace and as soon as he'd finished, he left the table without saying 'Dismiss' to us. We were all left standing there not knowing what to do because usually we start filing out, table by table, to go upstairs to make our beds and get ready for Morning Assembly. Then Miss Carson and Miss Newman both sat down so everybody else did as well. All the talking started again, which is a thing that never happens after grace, but this was a very different day with no one telling us to be quiet. It was getting louder and louder and didn't even stop when Mr. Burston came back in.

He went straight to the windows and unlocked them with the key that he'd fetched from his study. When he pushed the first one open, he popped his head out and looked up and a bit of mud from the storm plopped onto his forehead. I had to put my hand over my mouth because I was smiling about it a bit.

By the time he opened the other two windows, everybody had completely shut up again. Mr. Tulley, the science master, had come in from the staff room to see what was going on, and he was the first one to step out onto the balcony. He teaches biology to the sixth form, and so the Headmaster thought he should be the one to have the first look. We all tried to get a better view and slowly we started moving forward bit by bit. Mr. Tulley beckoned to Henry Pugh and another prefect, and they stepped outside to join him. There was a great crowd of boys jostling round the windows until the ones at the front were nearly being pushed out.

'Prefects only on the balcony,' shouted Mr. Burston, 'Prefects only. Everybody else, upstairs to your dorms, please.' Then he looked at his watch and said, 'Morning Assembly in twenty minutes.'

There were eighteen chicks to start with; eighteen that hadn't died when they fell down from the nests. The five prefects who went out onto the balcony missed the Morning Assembly because they must have been making arrangements to look after them all with Mr. Tulley. The rest of us didn't get to hear about it until we were in the queue for milk during break, which is after French and history class on Mondays.

Mr. Tulley was sitting on the steps outside the Assembly Hall with a cup of coffee and a cigarette. He was being very chatty which is quite unusual.

'It's a fairly hopeless situation, I'm afraid. They need quite a speci-alised diet, you see,' he said, 'but there's no reason why you shouldn't try to save them, though I doubt you'll succeed.' When we were going into Scripture class after the break, Whickham said to me he thought Mr. Tulley was a bit like Pontius Pilate washing his hands of the whole thing. So then it was just up to us to do something about it because the teachers weren't interested.

It was Ford, the Head boy, and Henry Pugh who were the ones who decided who was going to have the chance to look after them, so they called a meeting just before high tea, and nearly every boy in the school turned up in the Assembly Hall. Everyone was there on account of the fact that there were no games that day because of the mess that the storm had made to the playing field. There was so much talking that you couldn't really hear what was being said. It's a very big echoey and noisy room in the annex built onto the side of the house when it became a school. It's got high ceilings and rafters where you can see lots of paper darts which have been stuck up there for years and years. Sometimes they fall down unexpectedly, like in the middle of our history exam last year when one came down and went straight into Mrs. Marston's hair. Theo and I laughed out loud and got a detention.

I'd already decided that I didn't really want to have a chick to look after for myself, because I wasn't sure I'd be very good at it. Really I'm quite squeamish about things, and I'd absolutely hate it if the one I had died. I thought I'd be more use if I helped someone who was doing the looking after. When they asked us to put our hands up if we wanted one, I kept mine down. So many hands went up, and there was such a lot of shouting that in the end Ford and the other prefects decided that it had to be turned into a proper debate and then the senior low and senior high formers—who've got their very own debating society—started using words like 'overruled' and 'motion carried' and 'committee' and stuff like that. Then a group from senior low started shouting out 'objection' over and over again, and it all began to get as unruly and rough as it was in the beginning before it was turned into a debate. Ford was shouting out 'Order! Order!' in quite a loud cross voice and banging the floor with the pole that's used to open the top of the tall windows.

In the end a motion was passed that said only senior high and senior low would be given chicks. They were made into 'guardians' and what they were doing was 'in loco parentis', which is Latin and means in the place of the chicks' mothers and fathers.

Giles Webster put his hand up right at the wrong moment, way after the voting had finished and when Ford was just about adjourning the meeting. He hushed everybody up and said, 'Yes, Webster— what is it?' and he said, 'Could I be a "local apprentice", please?' and there was a gale of laughter.

'No, Bat Boy, you're just a little too young, I'm afraid.' It's unfair that they call him 'Bat Boy' still, and anyway he hasn't really got the bat anymore. Hapgood has borrowed it for so long that he's just about started keeping it, if you ask me. Webster's too frightened to ask for it back, and I know I should do something about it soon, because I did give a promise to his mother.

The fourth form was given the job of finding the food for the chicks, which meant they had to go round collecting dead spiders and flies and other yucky stuff, and we in the third form were to bury all the birds that had died. When that was decided on, we had our own little meeting of 3a and 3b. Actually that's quite a lot of boys—about twenty, in fact—and that's when six of us were chosen to be the Graves Committee. I was made chairman on account of the fact that I had been the one to first notice the chicks on the balcony during breakfast. It was an 'honorary' position and quite important. Apart from me, there was Morrison from 3a who's very popular and always voted on to everything; Rooke from 3b who's top at art so was probably going to be good at making the graves look all nice; Fisheye because he spoke quite well at the meeting; Harvey Junior from 3a just because his brother's a strict prefect in senior high, and it's best that he's kept pleased; and Theodorakis. He's on because he was looking all upset when no one voted for him, and I said that I thought he'd be jolly useful. I'm influential on account of my being chairman, so he was voted on. That was quite nice of me actually, because I don't always get on with him, and it really was a bit of a favour. I think he's very grateful to me.

After prep finished and before bed, the Graves Committee went outside to look for dead birds. Fisheye didn't come, though. He'd liked all the debating about third formers' rights being taken into consideration and stuff like that, but now that the hard work of burying was starting, he was nowhere to be seen. That's typical of him.

We didn't have very long to search because it was quite late and at any minute the bell was going to be rung for bedtime, but we couldn't find very many birds because Mr. Benson, who's the odd job man and the husband of the lady in the laundry, had cleared most of them away when we were in class in the morning. During the day, he'd tidied up quite a lot of the damage from the storm, in fact. By the time we did the burying just on the other side of the cricket nets, most of the branches from the trees and other bits and pieces that had landed on the grass were being collected together for a big bonfire by Mrs. Ridgeley's silly old vegetable garden. He'd even started repairing some of the fences. There was a terrible noise going on while we were doing the burying because there were three or four workmen with Mr. Benson who were using machine saws cutting up some of the bigger branches that were scattered around.

We found thirteen dead house martins all together—eight chicks and five grown-ups. I didn't touch them, though. I don't like things like that, and I noticed that I wasn't the only squeamish one. Nobody wanted to do that. In the end, I went to get Chirl who was making a model battleship in the library. He came straight out with me and picked them all up. He used his bare hands to do it. He can do all that sort of thing on account of the fact that he's lived on a farm all his life. Once he told me that when they're going to eat a chicken at his house, he goes and finds a nice fat juicy one from the yard and wrings its neck. Can you believe it? I'd never be able to do anything like that! Anyway, he wrapped the dead house martins up in The Daily Telegraph from the library—without asking permission to use it—and brought them over to where the graves were going to be. Straightaway I put forward a motion to vote him onto the committee and to get rid of Fisheye. Theodorakis seconded it, and the motion was carried. It was a unanimous decision.

Mr. Benson allowed Morrison to borrow his spade to dig the graves, but the ground was very hard just there, and it took quite a long time before it was ready. We knew that we were going to have to go upstairs to bed at any minute, so we just had to get on with it and bury them and then make it look nice the next day. That often happens with real life graves, actually. You bury someone, and then when everything's settled down you go back and tidy it up and put a gravestone on it later.

Just as they were safely buried the bell went, and Morrison said that there had to be a prayer and that since I was the Honorary Chairman of the Graves Committee, it was my job. I didn't know what to say but decided to just do a quick one because we were in a hurry and anyway, it didn't really matter because the saws were making such a racket that I thought no one could hear me properly.

I said, 'For what we have just buried, may the Lord make us truly sorry, and may the Lord look after their mortal souls, for ever and ever, Amen.' The others nodded at me to show I'd done it right.

At Assembly the next morning, Mr. Burston was doing his funny singing—very loudly. Sometimes, in the middle of a hymn—we were doing Guide Me Oh Thou Great Redeemer—he starts singing something different to everyone else but using the same words. It sounds so funny that it's very difficult for me not to laugh and get told off. I'm not the only one. Even Mrs. Marston can't help smiling when that happens, and that's quite funny too, because she's standing right bang next to him for everybody to see. One time when he was doing it, loads of us couldn't help it and started giggling and after, we had to go to the study for a telling off. 'Haven't you ever heard of harmonising? Do you not know what a descant is?' he said to us. Sounds dead funny to me. When I asked Mr. England about it, he went red, put his head down, and was trying not to laugh himself. He is the school choirmaster and knows every single thing about music and singing so that just proves what Mr. Burston does is a bit odd.

Anyway, when we'd finished singing and Gibbs from 4b had read the lesson, Mr. Burston announced that the cricket match that was meant to be happening against St. Mark's School in Chepstow that afternoon was cancelled on account of the storm and there being measles there. Instead, everyone—the whole school—was going to go for a walk in the Forest of Dean. It was great news because cricket is the most boring thing in the world apart from rugby, and even better, our Graves Committee would be able to collect some stuff to make the graves nice, like some moss and smooth stones and twigs from the side of the road as we were walking along.

Doing the graves was going to be a bigger job than we first thought, because when the guardians went to their lockers straight after Assembly, they found that five of the chicks were dead, and another had gone missing. That was the one that Mackenzie was looking after. All of them were being kept in the games lockers downstairs in the changing room, locked up for the night which I think was a bit like keeping them in prison. I didn't say anything, though, because really I don't know anything about it. The missing one was found after a few days. There was a hole at the back of Mackenzie's locker and the poor little thing must have fallen through it to the locker underneath. It was only discovered much later when Lewis was putting on his cricket boot, and there it was, dead inside.

The fourth formers had collected loads of dead insects but when the guardians tried to feed the chicks they just wouldn't eat them. Just as the bell was going for maths class, I said to Pugh that perhaps they should try and give them some milk on account of them being babies. He called me a cretin for not knowing that birds never ever drink milk. 'Ever seen a house martin with bosoms, Teasdale?' he said. I was very cross about it because I think that some birds do drink milk, so during break when everyone was crowding around the lockers in the basement looking at the chicks, I went to the library because I once heard that a captive penguin sometimes has a saucer of milk, but I'm not sure about that now, since I couldn't find anything about it.

It was a stupid thing for Pugh to say anyway, because creatures that have milk don't necessarily have bosoms. I should have said to him, 'Ever seen a squirrel with bosoms?' That would have shut him up, because squirrels are mammals with no bosoms and certainly do have milk for their babies.

Another chick was dead by the end of break, and then there were only ten left.

I love it when we go for walks in the forest. Sometimes I pretend that I'm lost in it, even though you never truly are because you can always hear other boys shouting in the distance. Lost but not really lost. No one's ever that far away from you, but I like the feeling of being all alone. I like pretending that I'm not at school, that I live in the forest in a secret hideout that no one knows about.

One of the teachers is usually shouting to us to stay together, but it's quite easy in the forest not to take any notice for a little while.

Everything looked different that day, though, on account of the storm. There were trees that had been blown over, lying on their sides with their roots forced up into the open air leaving huge black holes in the ground where they'd been standing, like giant graves waiting for the poor sad victims of the storm to be buried. Fresh red mud had been flung about when they'd toppled over, and as far as you could see there were ripped off branches with new green leaves on them that were already wilting a bit in the sunshine. It must have been a dangerous place to be when the storm was on. Imagine if one of those trees or even one of the branches had landed on you!

It was difficult to recognise where you were with whole trees missing, huge branches lying across the paths, and a sea of green on the floor from blown away leaves as though it was some kind of strange early autumn. Instead of the deep dark of the forest and the echoing song of the birds high up in the trees, there were whole patches of bright sunlight and the noise of the chainsaws of the forest workers beginning to clear up.

I don't think there was a single bird singing that day. If you looked very hard you could see one or two sitting forlornly around in their strange new world looking puzzled and trying to understand all the changes. Perhaps they were thinking about their lost chicks and nests wondering how they would be able to start all over again. They'd become refugees in their very own forest. There was nothing we could do to help them, though. Back at school in the games lockers, half the house martin chicks were dead already. It doesn't make any difference to nature, because even when we're trying to help, we can't.

I felt very sad about what had happened to the forest, but I think

I was the only one. All the others were just excited about it, even the teachers. Mr. Tulley was talking loudly to a group of seniors about how the forest would regenerate itself and how the tree trunks would soon be colonised and become the homes of all sorts of creatures for years and years. The first and second formers aren't allowed to run around in the forest and Miss Carson was trying to keep them all together and losing her temper because they were all getting overexcited. We third and fourth formers are a bit more free and were clambering all over the fallen trees, turning them into rival forts that needed defending.

I'm not interested in games like that, so I started slowly walking away while no one was noticing. That's the same as I do when we're playing cricket. I try to get to be deeply fine leg—that's a fielding position so far away from the batting that sometimes I just start wandering off bit by bit until I'm no longer part of the match. Then I go into the long grass at the far end of the field and lie down to stare at the sky and think about things. No one in the team much notices because it's no use having me on your side anyway.

I was suddenly quite a long way from everybody, but I could still see some boys in the distance when I turned round for a look. Nick Gower was balancing on top of a massive fallen tree, one hand on his hip and the other clutching a large stick, looking all proud, like a sailor waiting to have his photo taken on top of a huge sperm whale that he'd just harpooned.

Then I walked away and was quite alone, and that always makes me so happy. After a little while I came to a dell that was down a steep slope. It was a place that I didn't know from when we'd been to the forest before. A magical, secret valley. Quite suddenly, I couldn't hear the others, even when I strained my ears, and then I thought perhaps I'd been transported back in time, or travelled a thousand miles to a different forest, and I was the only person in the world who knew about it. It was like the storm had never been there because the dell was in a bit of a valley and the wind must have gone straight over and not touched it. All the trees were still standing, and it was a shadowy, still place like the rest of the forest used to be. Right in the middle there was a silent pool with the clearest water and tiny fish that went dashing off to hide when I looked in. There were two squirrels chasing each other about going 'chic-a-chic-chic,' and high up above my head, a lonely blackbird was calling out questions to his wife who wasn't answering. It was as though he had no idea about the terrible storm that had wrecked the rest of the forest.

And then I saw it—a huge black glossy raven. It was resting on top of an old stump of a great big tree that must have been sawn down a long, long time ago, cut perfectly flat and smooth so you could easily have counted the rings to add up how old it was. The bird's wings were stretched out across the stump, his head to one side and his beak wide open. I moved very slowly towards him because I thought that perhaps he was asleep and would suddenly wake up with a start. When I dared to get up closer, I saw a little bit of black feather moving on top of his head, and I was sure that as soon as he saw me, he'd flap his wings and fly away with fright. But then I saw the blood on his beak and a crimson puddle that had collected under his head. He was dead. It was only the tiniest breeze that was ruffling his feathers.

I tiptoed ever so gently right up to him and bent down to look into his eyes. They were wide open, frightened and glistening, as if he was surprised to be dead. Then I saw the smallest round dark red hole in the back of his head and I knew that some cruel person had shot him, probably for no good reason but for the fun of it, and had splayed him out on the tree-trunk to mock him and boast to the forest of his power and his evil. The sight of it made me feel cold and shivery, and I turned to go away. When I looked back at him the little feathers on his head were still moving.

When I got back to where all the others were, Miss Carson was unpacking the hampers for tea, which everyone was very excited about. In fact it was the picnic that was meant for the cricket match, but now we were going to have it in the forest, and that had never happened before. There was orange squash, and jam, marmite and vegetable spread sandwiches. Then there were huge round dough-nuts, all sticky with sugar. They're one of my favourite things, but I just couldn't eat mine because of the little round hole in it, gooey with red jam, like the hole in the raven's head.

On the walk back, we started collecting all the stuff for the graves. Miss Carson let us borrow two of the tin trays that the sandwiches had come in. Mr. England was going to take them back to school, but I got a bit worried about getting too close to his car again, so when we'd collected all of the stuff we needed, I let the others in the committee take them to the car, and I just looked on from a distance.

Theo and I had a bit of an argument about what we should be collecting, because he wanted to pick daisies from the side of the road. I knew perfectly well that they would get dried out very quickly and then go all floppy and sad. He was beginning to annoy me a bit going on about it and trying to get his way, especially since it was only because of me that he was on the Graves Committee in the first place.

When we got back to school, there was quite a little time before prep started because we weren't going to have tea on account of having had the picnic in the forest, so we were able to start doing some of the work on the graves. I'd found some really nice pebbles on the way back and we started to make a little wall in the shape of a heart. We'd collected nearly enough moss to cover three quarters of the space leaving a little corner at the top right hand side for more graves because, actually, we all knew by then that every single one of the chicks was going to die. It was just a matter of time. Theo insisted that he put his daisies right in the middle.

'I think they look really spastic,' I said, 'and they'll all be dried up by the morning anyway. I'm vetoing them.' I gathered them up and put them on the other side of the little pebble wall. He went into a big old sulk about it, and I thought how stupid I was to have helped him get onto the committee.

It was looking as though there could easily be an argument about it, but just then I heard crying and then some shouting. Perrington came running over to tell me that Giles Webster had been standing in the wrong place and been hit by a cricket ball that had come out of the practise nets. I ran straight over to him because it is sort of my job to look after him. He was lying flat out on the ground, and when I moved his hand away from the side of his face I could see there was a big bump already coming up. I told Perrington to go and get Matron because after all I'm not a nurse. But I was able to cheer Webster up with a bit of a joke and by telling him that he was actually a rather brave boy and stuff like that. He stopped crying very quickly which means he probably is quite brave because it hurts a heck of a lot if ever you're hit by a cricket ball. The really peculiar thing is that it was Hapgood who hit the ball with Webster's own bat! I noticed that when Miss Carson arrived to look after Webster, he hid it under a bit of the net so that there'd be no chance of a discussion about him giving it back.

When I got back to the graves, Theo was standing with his arms folded looking all puffed up.

'Sorry, T-T-Teasdale. You're out.'

'What do you mean?' I said.

'You've been v-voted off the g-h-g-Graves Committee.'

'But that's not allowed. I'm the honorary chairman.'

'Sorry, T-Teasdale. M-M-Mh-Majority decision.' There was a pretend regretful look on his face, but I could see that he was trying not to smile.

'You can't do that. It's just not fair.'

'Majority decision, Teasdale,' he said again, very slowly and deliberately and not stuttering for once. 'There was a v-vote taken on it and you're out by a m-mh-m-majority decision, and that's the end of it, I'm af-f-fraid.'

I looked over to where Morrison was bending down rearranging some of the stones.

'Morrison,' I said, 'what's going on?' But he didn't even look up at me, and Rooke then started helping him so that he wouldn't have to talk to me either. When I looked at Chirl he just shrugged his shoulders as if to say there was nothing he could do about it. Harvey Junior wasn't there just then, but I knew there was no point talking to him because he just goes along with everything, and it was quite obvious that Theodorakis had turned them all against me.

He's a complete scumbag is Theodorakis. He wheedled his way onto the committee on account of my niceness, and then he got rid of me.

I didn't say anything after that, but I could feel that I was getting angry and upset, and so I decided to walk away quite quickly because I thought I might be about to cry.

I went straight to the library because I thought there'd be no one in there and plonked myself down on the battered old sofa. Then I saw that Fisheye was sitting at the big table, reading one of his books, and I wondered if he'd heard me saying to myself that I didn't care about the stupid graves anyway, and about how silly were they going to look in a day or two with Theodorakis's dead dried up old daisies on them.

'Theo is such a bugger, Fisheye,' I said to him after I'd sat there silently for a while. He put his finger on the sentence in the book where he was stopping and looked up at me. Then I started to tell him what had happened. Halfway through I remembered that I'd put forward the resolution to kick him off the committee when we were doing the burying, but the thing about Fisheye is that he's just not the sort of person who stays angry about anything. It's like he doesn't even remember. Instead of telling me it served me right he said, 'He's a right little Mussolini, that one—a real little dictator.' Then he looked down at the end of his finger and carried on reading.

'I quite agree,' I said and then told myself to look up 'Mussolini' in the Dictionary of Biography after we'd finished prep.

The next day, Mr. England never came into Morning Assembly. After the hymn there was a long silence before everyone realised that no one was going to read the lesson, because it's Mr. England who chooses who is going to do that straight after breakfast, which gives the person a little bit of time to practise and to ask about words that are difficult to pronounce. But Mr. England wasn't even in breakfast that morning, let alone Assembly, which means that he probably wasn't here during the night. That's not so unusual because his dad, who's a retired teacher, just moved to Monmouth all the way from Kent because his wife died not very long ago, and he wants to be closer to his son. Mr. England sometimes stays over at his dad's new house now, but it never happens that he's not here to give someone the lesson to read.

In the silence, Mr. Burston opened the Bible and looked around for someone to hand it to. I tried to pretend I was invisible because although I'm often chosen to read at Morning Assembly, I don't like to do it and need to have a good look at it first. In the end he gave it to Bryant, a sixth former who never ever reads the lesson, and then the funniest thing happened. There was a bit in the chapter where an old prophet had to saddle his ass. Bryant got it all wrong and said 'He saddled his arse and rode into Jericho.' Everyone started to giggle like mad, the Headmaster went very red and cross looking, but even Mrs. Marston was laughing, so he couldn't say anything about it at all except for 'Boys, boys—pay attention, please!' It really was the funniest thing.

Mr. Tulley was quite right about there not being much hope of saving the chicks. Just before Assembly, the guardians went to check on the lockers, and six more had died in the night. Only four more to go. I think we all knew then that none of them would be alive by Saturday. That meant there were more graves to be got ready, but that was none of my business any longer. By then I didn't care anymore, although I still was completely not talking to Theo.

Our first class after Assembly on Wednesdays is English, which is just about my favourite, actually. Mr. England never keeps us waiting like Mrs. Marston and the other teachers do. Usually he goes straight back to the staff room after Assembly, picks up his books and comes into class way before the other teachers. Sometimes long after we've settled down for our lesson we can hear the racket going on in the other classrooms because they're all still waiting for the teachers to arrive. Perhaps they're having a last cigarette and a cup of coffee and a chat before they get going.

But anyway, that day, he didn't come in. We were still waiting when all the classrooms had gone quiet, and we'd even stopped talking and running around because of the silence everywhere. I started to wonder whether we'd just been all forgotten about, and then just as Macer-Wright, who's class monitor, was saying that he would go along to the staff room to see what was happening, the door opened, and Mr. Burston came in.

'Quiet boys, please,' he said which was dead silly, really, because no one was saying anything at all.

'Mr. England's not going to be with us for the rest of the morning, so I want you to open your copybooks and write an essay which I'll be collecting from you in three quarters of an hour. I want about eight hundred words on the subject of our walk in the forest yesterday.'

'Where's Mr. England, Sir?' Theo said.

'He's had a slight bump in his car. Nothing very serious. He'll be in later on this morning. Now not a peep out of any of you, please. Macer-Wright, you're in charge, and I'm leaving the door open.'

I wrote my essay about the secret bit of the forest that I'd discovered, but I don't think it was very good because I couldn't help thinking all the time about what might have happened to Mr. England, and his car, and all the stuff that he keeps in it.

He was back by the time we went into lunch, and I made sure to sit right at the end of the bench next to his chair at the top of the table. He had a little plaster on his forehead and another on his hand.

'What happened, Sir?' I said.

'A little old lady not looking both ways properly, I'm afraid. She pulled out straight in front of me so I couldn't avoid hitting her.'

'How horrid…'

'Not to worry, Ben. These things happen. I've only a little scratch. Car's in a terrible state, though. I'll probably have to get a new one…'

'Where is it, Sir?' I said.

'What?'

'Your Mini. Where is it now?'

'They had to tow it away, I'm afraid. It's very badly damaged.'

'Are all your things still in there, then? All your books and other stuff?'

'Yes. I'll have to arrange a visit to the garage to collect it all, won't I?'

He didn't seem at all worried, so then I was thinking that he must have taken some stuff out of the car before the crash, because he couldn't just have forgotten about it.

But I knew it was still in there.

I'd seen it again the day before, when Miss Carson asked us to take the tin trays out of the car for the picnic. That's why I wanted to make sure I didn't get too close again. It was still in the back, mostly hidden under a pile of books—the blue folder, the same one that I'd seen the day we went to Bristol.

'My Only One! I've come for you…'

Mummy walks towards me very slowly and stretches her arms out as though she's feeling in the dark in case I'm not there. I put my arms around her. It's horrid that I didn't want her to come, and suddenly I'm trying not to cry because of it. She's as small and delicate as one of the baby house martins, and I think that I might crack her bones and squeeze the breath out of her unless I'm really careful. It's as though I'm holding her up. She is getting tinier and tinier. I notice it every time I've been away from her, and one day it might be that she could just about disappear forever.

'Hello, Mummy. I've been waiting ever such a long time for you. For ages and ages, actually...'

'I'm sorry, Sweetness. I got here far too early so I've been waiting in the King's Arms in the village.'

I can smell the peppermints but not too much of the sherry, so I don't think she's had enough to make her wobbly.

'You have come by yourself, haven't you, Mummy? Trotsky John's not outside, is he?'

'Just me, Darling. All by myself. And I've got a secret to tell you...'

'Okay, Mummy, but you can tell me about it after, when we've gone out.' I want to go before anyone comes along the corridor and starts talking, because sometimes Mummy likes to keep a conversation going on for ever and ever, especially when she's not very good.

And I really don't want anyone to see her. She's got on a blue dress and a white jacket both made out of something called cheese-cloth, which she's liked ever since she came back from Crete. She's wearing lots of her jangly bracelets and a huge pair of earrings made of tiny blue stones that are dangling right down nearly to her shoulders. She's got white slip-on shoes with great big yellow daisies on the strap, but at least there are no fishnet stockings today. She's put black rims round her eyes and smells of a perfume which is called 'patchouli'. I know that because Trotsky John gave it to her when he came the day after Boxing Day when my dad had gone back to work. Mummy winked and said, 'One of our secrets.'

She takes me by the hand, we walk straight out of the hall into the street, and it's a bit of a relief to be gone after all the waiting. But suddenly I remember I've left my boater on the floor by the big chair, and it's absolutely forbidden to go anywhere without it so I run back inside to get it. As we're walking away, I look back and see that the front door is still open, so I let go of her hand and rush back to close it, which is quite a struggle because the wind is so strong.

'Where are we going, Mummy?' I ask her when we start to walk along the road. She smiles at me and squeezes my hand one moment and holds it lightly the next. '…because I have to be back for high tea. I think the special concession only lasts till then. It's really nice of Mr. Burston to let me come out at all in the middle of lessons, actually. It's very unusual… But I must be back quite soon, Mummy.'

'You're not going back, My Only. Never. I'm taking you away…'

It must be one of Mummy's jokes. She doesn't have a suitcase or anything—not an umbrella or even a coat to keep her warm if it gets chilly in the night. All she's got is a bag with a long strap over her shoulder made out of jeans material without even a zip on it with probably only her sherry bottle with the peppermints, and a purse, and some cigarettes, and some tissues inside. And I've got nothing with me except my silly old boater, which is no use at all. I haven't got a pair of pajamas or a toothbrush, or clean underpants, or anything at all, and I don't like to go anywhere without Jollo anyway, and I think she must know that after all this time. It is a joke she's telling me. It must be.

When we lived in Beirut and travelled to England for the holidays, Mummy used to start packing days and days before we were going, and Aisha—who was her maid—and Miriam would empty drawers all over the house, washing and ironing, and folding things in tissue paper. The house had to be cleaned from the top to the bottom although it was just going to be nothing but an empty house when we'd gone. She would give tons of instructions to Abdul the gardener about making sure the geranium pots were watered every day. The pool was to be kept clean even though no one was going to swim in it till we came back; the well had to have its lid on so nothing could fall in, and the big garden door in the cherry orchard had to be kept bolted at night. Abdul was my grown-up friend when I was little, and it was silly telling him to remember all those things when he was so good at his job. On the way to the airport Mummy would ask my dad if he had the passports safe and he would say 'You've already asked me that,' but it wouldn't make any difference because she would very soon say again, 'Are you sure they're in your jacket pocket?' and he'd say 'Oh Pamela—for heaven's sake!' and carry on staring out of the window without even looking for them.

That must be where I got my worrying from. From Mummy. And now it's exactly this very same person who doesn't seem to be the least bit bothered about going away without any packing at all! That's how much she's changed.

When she says the thing about going away, I start walking a little bit quicker so after a bit I'm the one that's leading the way, although I don't even know where we're going. I'm trying to think whether I should say anything about her plan and really, I'm hoping that any minute she's going to start laughing and say, 'Only joking, Only One—had you worried, didn't I?' But I'm very worried about it now, and I think it's best not to mention it at all.

There's going to be another shower of rain. I can feel the first few drops even before the sun goes in again. There's a high garden wall that's got a door with its own little roof over it that we quickly run to for some shelter. Mummy laughs about it, but I don't see what's so funny, and I'm thinking about what I might say to stop her joke about going away, because I know she's going to talk about it again. Then there's a huge rainbow that I'm staring at while I'm thinking about it all, and suddenly Mummy giggles and kisses my forehead. I can smell the dampness of her hair when it touches my lips. She's loving the adventure as though she's a little girl.

She starts walking again as soon as the sun comes out but before the rain has properly stopped, and I'm worried that we're going to get completely soaked. I nearly have to run just to keep up with her.

'But where are we going now, Mummy? I mean right now this minute… Where are we walking to now?'

'To the park, My Only. We're going to the café in the park to watch the river for a little while and to enjoy the sun coming back out and to make a plan.'

This is the same street that we walk along nearly every day to get to the school playing field. There is a small park at the end when you get to the main road that goes to Gloucester. Right in the middle of the park there's a broken down old café where you can buy sandwiches and things and sit on picnic benches for a view of the river. Mr. England's told me that soon they're going to knock down the café and bulldoze the park away so you can see the river from your car without having to get out. I'm not surprised about that because no one has looked after it for a very long time.

I've been to the café before—one time when Mummy and my dad brought me back to school. I think it was one of the times when my asthma was so bad that I couldn't come back on the train. We stopped there because we were too early. It was raining that day, too, so we had to sit inside and my dad bought me a coke and a Mars bar as a special treat. I pretended to be pleased but it all got stuck in my throat. The bubbles went up my nose, and I just couldn't swallow the chocolate because my stomach was already full up of homesickness and worry.

When we get there, I push the door quite hard but it doesn't open and I think the café must be shut, although through the window I see that there's a man behind the counter and an old lady sitting at a table. She's leaning over a cup of tea and an iced bun with a cherry. I push the door again, although I don't want to go in, and I'm just about to say to Mummy 'Let's not bother with it' when the man sees me and makes a pushing sign with both his hands. So I push it hard with both my hands, and it opens and scrapes the floor with a terrible noise like Mrs. Marston using the chalk on the blackboard when she's in a temper with us. Then it gets stuck halfway, and I have to give it another big push before it opens properly, but it carries on making a juddering noise for a bit.

Inside, the café's hot and stuffy and smells of old cigarettes and the same disinfectant they use at school when someone's been sick. The man must have just mopped the floor. It's wet, and shiny, and sticky when we walk on it, and some of the chairs are already upside down on the tables. There's a poster stuck on the wall behind the counter of a lake with very blue water and very blue sky. It's got a rip in it that starts in the middle at the top, and another one which starts in the middle at the bottom and quite soon they are going to meet up and the poster will be in two pieces then. It says 'The Italian Lakes' in big white slanting letters. It's very bright in the café because there are neon lights on the ceiling.

It's the same man that was here when we came before, which was a long time ago. He looks fed up to see us and was probably expecting to go home because of the rain and the floor being clean, but instead we're here. He's got a bald head, a red nose with a small pair of glasses right at the end of it, and a thin moustache like the fat man in Laurel and Hardy. He's wearing a dirty white apron with his tummy resting on the counter, and there's a cigarette dangling out of his mouth. I don't want anything to eat here, not even an ice cream.

'Have an ice cream, Only One...' When she says that I know she's forgotten that I was waiting for her for so long that I haven't had any lunch. The thing is that although I haven't eaten anything since my breakfast, I'm completely not hungry, just like the last time I was here.

'No thank you, Mummy. I don't want anything. I'm really not hungry.'

Mummy orders two cups of tea and a piece of coffee cake for me even though I said I didn't want anything. The man picks up a massive teapot using a tea cloth that's even dirtier than his apron and begins to fill it with water from a great big urn. Then he swooshes it around and pours the tea into the cups as though he's watering two pot plants—back and forward, back and forward till they're both full up with a lot of it spilled. He's definitely fed up that we're here, but he's the one who told me to push the door to get in, so it's plain silly if he's angry, and anyway, the little old lady who's sat all by herself doesn't look as though she's nearly ready to leave because she's not even started on her bun. When I sit down she twists her head round very slowly to look at me without straightening it up so she must be seeing me half upside down. I smile at her, but she looks puzzled, and a bit cross, and turns away again and makes a 'tut-tut' noise.

I wonder why the man's wife hasn't told him that he looks like Oliver Hardy with that silly moustache. Perhaps he might be too stern to tell something like that to. He doesn't look as though he would ever find anything funny. I don't think he looks like someone who would like Laurel and Hardy, actually.

'Sugar?' the man calls out.

'Two for me please,' I say, 'but none for my mother. She doesn't take sugar in her tea.' He spoons the sugar in very quickly and stirs it so that it makes an angry clinking sound. He comes towards our table, shuffling along with a cup and saucer in each hand and balancing the cake plate on his wrist. He nods his head up and down when he gets to us; then he stops and waits. He nods his head up and down very quickly again, and I see that he wants me to move my boater that is taking up all the room because it's a small table. I say 'sorry,' and I put the boater on my lap.

Mummy must be about to say something because it's exactly the sort of tea that she would never ever drink at home. It's white from too much milk in it and not nearly strong enough. I get a bit worried because the fat man already looks like an angry enough person, and I don't think he'd like it one little bit if he's asked to take the tea back. How funny to have a job making tea all day long and to have years of practise and still make it so horrible!

But she doesn't say anything, thank goodness. I pick up my cup, but I don't like it that I didn't put my own sugar in. I think that it's unnecessary that he did it for me. There's a brown chip in the rim of it, and I think of the old lady at the next table with her scraggy wet lips. I put my bottom lip right over the edge of the cup so that I'm touching it as little as possible. It's a cold cup of tea as well as being too milky. Mummy picks hers up with both hands. I wait for her to say something, but she settles her elbows onto the table and holds it in front of herself. She takes a sip and closes her eyes all dreamy-like and smiles as though it's just the best cup of tea in the whole wide world. Then she looks out of the window.

'My God,' she whispers, 'the river! It's like something from a fairytale! Look at it, Only One! Oh my God!' She shakes her head from side to side. 'It has such an extraordinary, ethereal beauty... It's so, so beautiful.'

She turns round suddenly in her chair to face the man and forgets that she has the cup in her hands. The tea spills out onto the table and splashes her dress and some of it goes on my boater. She shouts, 'You're so lucky!' as if she's angry and jealous and then pulls a long sulky face as though she might do pretend crying. 'This beautiful view all day long. You lucky, lucky people. How can you bear it? How can you bear it?'

She puts her cup down and slowly stretches her arms out to the side, like you see ballerinas do when they're about to do their curtsey at the end of the show. She leaves them frozen like that for a long time, and I watch the man as he stares at her and then looks out of the window all puzzled as though he's never seen the view before. I look at the old lady at the next table. She puts her face even nearer to her cup of tea, and then she goes 'tut-tut' again.

I look out at the view too. The rain's running down the steamy window, and outside it's like one of my paintings in art class when I've mixed too much water in with the colours, the paper's got wet, and everything's blurring together. I can't see the river, just a flower bed with no flowers, long grass that hasn't been mowed, and a waste paper bin so full that it's overflowing with soaking rubbish covering the ground all around it. There's an old motor scooter that's fallen over and is rusting away. It reminds me of the pictures you see in the newspapers of dead cows turning into skeletons when there's a famine in Africa.

The Oliver Hardy man doesn't say anything, but he's staring at Mummy. His lips are moving ever so slightly like he's not very good at reading, and I know he's telling himself that there's something odd about her.

I put my hand on the window and wipe away the steaminess so

that I can see up towards the sky, and I pray there'll be the tiniest bit of blue so we can go out and sit on a bench overlooking the river even if it's still raining a bit. I want to get out of this café and away from the man with his dirty apron, and red nose, and horrid tea who's looking at Mummy and is right on the edge of deciding that she's a bit funny. If we go now, he'll stop thinking about it, and he'll have forgotten all about her in a few minutes.

'We're chained to such futile lives, you know. We never really, truly look at anything. Our eyes are closed to real beauty because of the banality of our existence…' Mummy's talking out loud like an actress in a Shakespeare play. Her arms are still up in the air, and she's moving them back and forward very slowly.

'Can we go and sit outside Mummy? It's not raining anymore…' There's a silence, and I wish the rain would stop hitting the window. She puts her arms down and stares at me as though she hadn't noticed I was there.

Her eyes have gone funny, like at home when my dad comes back for dinner and she's had too much sherry. I don't know what is going to happen next, but I'm very concerned about it.

'Can we, Mummy?'

'What, Darling?'

'Go outside? It's too stuffy in here for me. I think I feel a bit sick. I just want to sit outside for a bit…' She looks out of the window and then slowly back at me as though it's taking her eyes a bit of time to find out where I am, which is right in front of her.

'It's raining, Only One…'

'I know, Mummy, but not very hard and it's finishing now, and you don't mind the rain anyway… Let's just go outside. Please…?'

'It's far too wet out there, Darling.' Then there's a silence before she says, 'It's tipping down, and I don't want you wet through before we even start! We'll have to wait for a bit, I think…'

Then she looks all around the room as though she's searching for something. Suddenly she pushes the chair back from the table and stands up. I don't know where she's going, so I get up too, because I think we must be going out after all, and I put my boater on because there's no one here from school to see me. She sways a little but not so much that anyone but me might notice. But she goes up to the counter instead of to the door and leans right over as though she's going to tell the man a deadly secret and says in a whispery type of voice that's really quite loud, 'I say, would you mind awfully if I was to rob you of one of your ciggies?'

And then I know that this is a bad day, because Mummy never goes anywhere without her cigarettes. Either she's run out of them or she's left them in the pub.

The old lady who's still drinking her tea does another 'tut-tut' and the man says, 'Don't sell them here. You'll have to go back into the village for those...'

'No... No, I was just wondering if I might possibly pinch one of yours...'

I can see that he doesn't want to give her a cigarette, but Mummy isn't noticing and just waits.

'We can go and get them, Mummy,' I say. 'I know where they sell them, actually. I know that place very well...'

For a long time there's no sound apart from the rain and wind on the window and the hissing of the urn, and then the man does a big sigh, reaches behind himself without looking, and lands his hand on a packet of cigarettes. He flicks it open with his thumb and stretches it out towards Mummy. She slowly puts her fingers into the packet but doesn't seem to be able to get a cigarette out and does a funny little laugh. He sighs again and takes one out for her. 'You're so kind to me,' she says and then she does her little girl look. I hate it when she does that. I sit down again because I can see we're not going out yet, and I take off my boater. There's an old paper napkin scrunched up on the table and I pick it up to start trying to rub off the spots of the tea Mummy spilt on it, though it doesn't really matter because actually it's a good thing at school if your boater is a bit grubby.

Half way back to the table, Mummy stops and does another little giggle.

'Silly, silly me—nothing's going to happen without a light, is it?' Then she looks up towards the ceiling, closes her eyes, and laughs really loudly. She turns round to go back, but this time she puts her hand out and holds onto one of the tables because she's getting more wobbly. The man must know more and more that there's something wrong with her.

When she gets back to the counter, she holds onto it and leans over, with the cigarette in her mouth.

'Light, please?' She's still doing the funny voice a bit. The man leans over from his side, and his face is right up close to Mummy's. He stares at her without blinking once. I'm getting really very worried because I know that expression is the same one that some of the bullying boys at school use when they're going to be really nasty to someone.

'We've got a lighter in your bag, Mummy. You don't need a light,' I say, and I pick up her bag from the floor. I put it on my lap and rummage around past the sherry bottle, the tissues, the purse, the peppermints and a scarf, and then I pretend I've found it.

'Here it is, Mummy. No need to worry!' But just then, the man reaches out behind himself without looking again, and puts his hand on his lighter. By the time that he has it in front of Mummy, he's flicked it on. She tries to put the end of the cigarette in the flame, but can't find the right place. It's burning halfway along before the man grabs hold of her hand for a second to make it steady.

'Thank you so much,' she says.

There's another 'tut-tut' from the old lady as Mummy slowly comes back to the table and sits down. She smokes the cigarette and it looks as though she's enjoying it more than anything in her entire life. I can't wait to grow up and learn how to smoke a cigarette. Abdul let me have a puff of one of his cigarettes once, and it made me choke and my head spin round. I thought I was going to be sick, but I think it's just that you have to get used to it, and then it's a very pleasurable experience.

Mummy's not talking now. She's just enjoying the cigarette for a bit. Please let her not talk in that silly voice about the river again. The sun's going to come out in a minute, and we'll go outside away from the Oliver Hardy man and the tutting lady. When we leave here, we might be going in a taxi to the train at Chepstow, and then perhaps to an airport so that we can fly away to Greece, or back to our real home in Lebanon where everything used to be alright, and I'll see my friend Abdul again and my cat Nurbanu who I rescued from the street outside when she was a tiny sick kitten.

But it's not going to be like that. It can't be, and it's all just because Mummy's not well. I don't think she would remember how to get back to that place in Greece, and they wouldn't let us sleep on the beach anyway. We haven't got our house in Beirut anymore; it's all packed up. There must be someone else living there now, so if we were to go there, we would just be out in the street looking up at the old veranda outside the sitting room and knocking on the door with a maid we don't know answering it.

It might be that I'll just not get into the taxi when it comes, or I'll shout to one of the porters at the station that I'm being kidnapped, or perhaps I'll leave it till we get onto the airplane and tell one of the stewardesses. They might be thinking that something's not right already, of course, on account of the fact that we haven't got any luggage, and no one goes so far away without at least a few cases. Besides, my dad's finding out now because Mr. Burston's phoned him up. Then he just really will have to do something about Mummy now because this is the worst time. This is definitely the worst time of all.

But I'm most worried about what's happening to Mummy because, actually, I know perfectly well that we're not going anywhere at all. We can't, because she hasn't any tickets with her. Not for the train or the airplane, and no passports, and probably not even a single penny in her bag, not even enough for one packet of cigarettes. Perhaps what might be best is to tell this horrid man behind the counter so he can let someone know where we are.

But if I do that, I'll spoil the whole thing for Mummy, and it will be like I've given her away—betrayed her—and I'll be the one who's smashed up all our dreams. She'll never be able to look at me without being reminded of it, and it will be the most hurtful thing I've ever done.

She begins to put the cigarette out in the tin ashtray on the table even though she's not finished it properly. It takes her a long time of fiddling, and she carries on till there's not the slightest bit of glow or smoke. Then she stretches out her hand and strokes my cheek very gently and very slowly.

'More cake, Darling?'

'No, thank you, Mummy.'

'You sure? What did you have for lunch?'

'Mince.' I'm lying about that, of course, but I just really want to go outside.

'Oh good.'

And then she just stares at me for a bit and she says, 'I'm going to pop to the Ladies, and then we'll be off.'

'Mummy—where are we going? Where are we going in fact?'

'Away, My Only One. Just the two of us...' She gets up, walks toward the counter again, and I say, 'My mother would like to know where the Ladies is,' in a loud voice. I hope the man will look at me and not at Mummy while she's going out. 'Over there,' the man says and nods towards where the rotting scooter is. On the other side of it there's a small broken down building which has so much ivy growing over it that you can't really see what it is. The door, which is a bit ajar, is blowing about in the wind.

'Is it open?' I ask the man.

'Yea, yea—for the time being it is, yea.' Mummy's wobbling a bit. She gets to the door of the café and pulls the handle, but it's stuck. The old lady says 'tut-tut' again. I jump out of my seat, yank the door open for her, and then I see the rain's stopping.

'I'll wait for you outside, Mummy—the sun's going to come out in a minute, I think.' I close the difficult door and rush back to the table and grab my boater. Then I see that Mummy's left her bag, which is typical when she's not good, so I pick it up. I say to the man as I'm putting my boater back on and walking quickly to the door 'Thank you for the tea,' and he says, 'Three and six,' and I say, 'Pardon?' and he says, 'She hasn't paid.' The old lady goes 'tut-tut' again.

I do a little laugh as if to say 'How silly we forgot!' but I'm thinking that Mummy's probably not got three and six, and what am I going to do? I reach into her bag and find her blue purse, which I know very well, and take it out very slowly so as to take up as much time as possible. The man stares at me with a frown on his face, and he knows what I'm thinking. I put my mouth in the shape to do whistling because I'm trying to look as though this is just the first place that I'm beginning the search for the money, though it's probably somewhere else, but it's in here somewhere for sure. When I open the purse I can see there's lots of pennies and some threepenny pieces and one shilling but definitely no pound notes. I count it out with my heart beating. There's going to be enough after all. I'll give him the money, and then I will be getting out of here.

After I've laid out the shilling, some threepenny pieces, and loads of pennies on the table, I scoop it all up and walk over to the man with Mummy's bag under my arm. I open my hand and the coins clang onto the counter as I'm saying, 'I think that's right.'

The man checks the pennies as quick as a flash and flicks a three-penny piece back towards me with his finger because I've got it wrong. It rolls towards me so quickly that I don't have time to catch it, and it falls off the edge of the counter and onto my shoe. I bend down to pick it up. When I stand up again he's looking at me as if I've done something wrong, which I haven't.

'Goodbye,' I say. The man says nothing, and the little old lady is still stuck over her tea. I walk out into the wind, which is blowing like mad, and as I try to pull the noisy door shut behind me with all my might, my boater flies off and disappears round the corner. It's essential to get it back because I'll be in big trouble back at school without it. I run round the corner after it with Mummy's bag under my arm, and the wind's pinning my boater up against the side of a big bin and making it quiver like a frightened shivering animal.

I sit on one of the benches outside the café. There are lots of them, but they're mostly broken. This one's right underneath the café window, and it's the only one that's not so broken you can't sit on it, though it's not really very good because I can feel a bit of wetness from the rain coming through my pants. The man can see me sitting here, and I don't like that very much. At least the sun's shining for the moment, and I'm not in there with him and that funny old lady.

I can see the door of the Ladies. When Mummy comes out I'll run over to her, and we'll go away from here. My boater is jammed onto my head as hard as hard can be so the wind can't blow it off again, and I'm holding her bag, so we're ready to go to wherever we're going.

I look behind me through the window at the Oliver Hardy man. He's smoking a cigarette. I smile at him and nod, but he just looks at me. He's a frightening person, actually. I don't think he's going home yet after all because he's not putting any more chairs on the tables. The old tut-tutting lady is still having the same cup of tea and bun that she was having before. Perhaps he just didn't like the look of us and didn't want us inside his café.

I'm waiting for Mummy again—just like I have been for most of the day.

I know the man's watching me, and I try to look like I'm concentrating on the river and asking myself questions about it, which is dead silly because I see it everyday and I've got a much better view of it from my window in the dorm anyway. I try not to look the slightest bit worried about Mummy. The fact is we're just on a bit of a day out, and it's unfortunate about the rain, that's all. I don't want the man to be thinking that there's something wrong, and he's got to do something about it.

I bend over and pretend I've got to check something in Mummy's bag. I can see for absolute sure that there's no tickets and passports, and when I open her purse again I can see straightaway that there really is no sign of nearly enough money for anything. I pack it away at the bottom and fold my arms and look at the river with a smile on my face for the man to see, but inside I can feel every last bit of the coffee cake churning around. And when I have a quick peep round, the man's not taken his eyes off me for one single second, so I get up and pick up Mummy's bag. I pretend that I'm having a bit of a stroll around. I move farther along to a bench which is all broken up but isn't in front of the window and sit down again. I'm glad he can't see me, but I'm having to balance my bottom on the edge otherwise I'm going to be falling straight through because it doesn't have any seat left.

I start to wonder what must have happened to Mummy after all these minutes that she's been in the Ladies' loo. If she's much longer I'll have to go over and call out to her, and if she doesn't answer I might have to go in through the door even though it's the Ladies. I tell myself she must be having a drink of sherry but then remember that the bottle's in the bag, and I've got it here with me. That's the oddest thing because she never goes anywhere without it for even a few minutes. Even when we're at home she does that. We'll be watching the telly after dinner, and then she'll say, 'I'm just popping up to the loo,' and I'll hear the sherry in her bag when she picks it up. I know that sound ever so well. How silly is it to be taking your bag with you wherever you go, even in your own house? It's that sort of thing that makes me sometimes a bit angry with her, actually. My dad knows exactly what's going on too, but he never says anything about it, of course. Sometimes I look at him to see what he's thinking and wonder whether he might just quickly look at me so we know for each other what's going on, but he just stares at the telly and does a face that says 'We are strictly not going to talk about this.'

I look in the bag again just to make sure that the bottle really is there, and I feel it without taking it out just in case someone is look-ing. It's so light that I know there's only a drop of the sherry left, which means that quite soon there'll be none left, and Mummy will be thinking about that more than anything else, even more than about going away.

It's only the tiniest while that the sun has been shining again, and already there's another black cloud coming over from the other side of the river. When it gets here it's going to rain, and there's nowhere for me to shelter. I'll just have to sit here and get wet. It doesn't really matter as long as nobody knows. Hopefully, the man in the café will think that Mummy and I have gone away, now that he can't see me.

But Mummy's been in the Ladies for ever such a long time now, and I'm going to have to call through the door to see if she's alright. When I walk over there the man will see me again and wonder what on earth's going on with that boy's mother, and that makes me want to just stay sitting here for a bit longer. I think he should be minding his own business and not concerning himself with other people who he doesn't even know. That's what I think. I'm just on a day out with my mother who's come to visit. It's a shame about the rain, that's all, and he's no right to be staring at me. No right at all.

But the more I wait, the more worried I get. I can't think what Mummy could be doing in there all by herself without her sherry, and it looks the sort of place where there might be a tramp inside even though it's just meant for ladies, and perhaps he's trying to rob her or something. Anything could be happening, especially since Mummy's so bad today.

I'll just have to ignore the nosey fat old man. This is a serious situation after all, and I really must go and check that everything's alright. I pick her bag up just as the clouds are coming over again and walk across to the Ladies. It's not easy because the big slabs of pavement are all breaking up and have got mixed up with bits of shingle. There are old slippery leaves and weeds growing up and puddles from the rain that I have to jump over. Mummy's bag bangs against the ground because the strap's so long, and I'm worried that I might smash the bottle, so I pick it up and put it under my arm. Then all the things inside start moving around, and it feels like I'm holding a wild angry cat that's trying to get away.

Mummy certainly wouldn't be able to jump over these puddles because she's far too wobbly, and it's a wonder that she didn't fall over. Her feet are going to be soaking wet, and I'm going to get water in my shoes as well—which is just another problem to think about for later.

All the time I'm trying very hard not to look round at the man because I can feel that he's looking at me.

I walk past the old scooter and stand at the door to the Ladies' loo. The hinges are broken at the bottom so it's rocking to and fro, and quite soon the hinges at the top will break, and the whole door will fall right off. That probably started to happen during the big storm. It's extra dark inside, and I can just see a little high window with broken glass and ivy beginning to come through from outside. It's letting a bit of light through which is just as well because I can see that the electric bulb on the side of the wall is all smashed up and probably hasn't been working for a very long time. No one's going to put it right anyway because quite soon it's all going to be pulled down and made into a car park.

There's a smell of mould and mushy paper and wet wood. I can hear echoey water, which I think is from a broken tap or a cistern that's overflowing. I don't think that anyone uses this loo nowadays, but Mummy must be in here somewhere because I saw her going in, and she's not come out.

I call her ever so quietly from the door.

'Mummy? Mummy, are you there?' I wait for a little while and I'm listening for the slightest noise.

'Can you hear me Mummy? Are you alright?'

'Is that you, Ben?' She's talking in a very soft voice that I can hardly hear.

'Yes, Mummy. Are you alright? I was getting to be bit worried about you. You've been in there for ever such a long time.'

I hear her laughing a bit then, ever so softly.

'It's the funniest thing, Ben. I just sat down here for a second, and

I fell asleep. Isn't that the oddest thing?'

'Yes, Mummy. But I really think you should come out of there now. Let's go. Please, Mummy—I'm getting a bit fed up of this park actually...'

'Alright, Only One. I'm coming out right away—in just a minute...'

'Okay,' I say, 'but as soon as possible, because we've been here a long time now.'

'Two minutes, Darling. I'll be out in two minutes.' She doesn't sound to be so bad now, so perhaps everything is going to be alright after all.

When I step away from the door it's raining again, and there's nowhere for me to shelter unless I go right into the Ladies. But I don't want to. It's creepy. I think there are bats and mice in there, and it reminds me of scary places that I used to be frightened of, and anyway, it's the Ladies' lavatory.

'It's raining again, Mummy. I'll wait for you by the café, okay?'

I don't hear her answer, but I run across the broken slabs back to the café. I jump over the puddles and try to make sure I don't slip on the wet leaves and bits of rubbish. When I'm halfway across, something moves inside the bag, and I feel it slipping away before I can do anything about it. There's a huge crash because the sherry bottle has fallen right out. I stop and look down at tons of broken glass. The bottle's not a secret anymore. The man in the café's going to know that it's Mummy's sherry bottle, and she's drunk nearly the whole of it. That's the one thing that I didn't want him to know about. For a minute I just don't know what to do, and I stand still in the rain looking at the café to see if the man is watching, but I can't really see him through the steamy glass. At the same time I know that there's nothing I can do about it, and when I look at the smashed up glass again, I see that the sherry is slowly being washed away by the rain. I start running again, and I hope I'm not going to be in trouble with the man for not clearing up the mess, but now it's raining so hard that I'll just have to tell him that I'll do it later. I push myself up against the wall by the side of the café door. I'm hiding from the man and sheltering from the rain. I'm getting wet, though. The rain's not coming down straight; the wind is blowing it everywhere, and if Mummy's not very quick I'm going to be soaked through. I don't know what we will do then because for a start we're going to look very bedraggled when we walk back to Saxham. Everyone will be looking at us.

There's a screeching noise, and the door of the café is pulled open.

'Better come back in here, sonny. You're going to get wet through if you stay out there.' The Oliver Hardy man is leaning halfway out of the door.

'I'm waiting for my mother.'

'I know you are, but you may as well wait in the dry. In you come.'

I say 'Okay then,' and sit down at the table nearest to the door. As I wipe my forehead with my hand, I notice that I'm shaking a bit and hope the man doesn't see that. There are drips coming off the rim of my boater and bouncing on the table. The old lady says 'tut-tut' again. She must have seen the bottle breaking, but the man says 'That's enough, Nora,' as though he's talking to a dog that won't stop barking. Then I know that she can't help making the 'tut-tut' sound just like Hughes who keeps scrunching up his nose even though he doesn't want to, and the teachers tell him not to.

I look out of the misty window, staring at the broken door of the Ladies waiting to see if Mummy ever comes out.

'She alright?' The man's looking at me and doesn't seem so cross as he was before. He's got a cigarette in his mouth again, and he's drying teacups with the dirty cloth.

'I beg your pardon?'

'Your Mum—she alright?'

'Oh yes, she's fine, thank you very much. She's just tidying herself up a bit before we go.'

'I see...' There's a bit of a silence, and I'm back to just waiting.

Then the big fridge behind the counter turns itself on again with a loud whirr and he says, 'Where you going, then?' I look at him, and I think what to say for a bit.

'Back to school. I'm going back to school when she's ready. I'm just having a day out.'

I feel a bit cold which is funny really because it's not such a cold day. I fold my arms around the bag in front of myself and pull it tight towards me. It feels different without the bottle in it, empty and scrunched up. Then just as I look out of the window again at the broken door of the Ladies I see it swing open in the wind, and Mummy comes out. A bit of ivy hangs down over the doorway and begins to wrap itself around her. She throws her arms around so it looks as though she's having a battle with a whole swarm of bees. But then she's free of it, and I feel so relieved that she's out, and there's nothing wrong at all.

She walks ever so slowly towards the café as if she's not thinking of the rain, although now it's as heavy as can be. I pray that she won't start running because if she does she's going to fall over.

Then she stops. She stands still in the rain with her arms flopped down by her sides.

I stand up very slowly and can't take my eyes off her. All of a sudden everything is really not alright again—just when I was feeling relieved, so it just goes to show you never can tell with Mummy. I don't know what I'm supposed to do. I quickly look at the Oliver Hardy man, and his mouth is moving again to tell himself things about her. Then I look at the picture of the lakes in Italy and wish I was there and not here and pray that everything will be alright. It's only for a second, though, and I can't stop myself from looking out of the window again.

Mummy stares up at the sky for a bit as though she's got to make an important decision and starts to walk away from the café towards one of the flower beds. She kneels down even though she's right in the middle of a puddle, puts her hands round some old plants with dead flowers, pulls them out of the ground, and clutches them tightly. She's doing it quickly as though she's going to run out of time, but I can't see what she's thinking because she's facing away from me. The rain's pouring down more than ever. Her clothes stick to her as though they're her skin, and the curls are coming out of her hair which is flat against her back. She's getting to look tinier and tinier.

Very slowly I take my eyes off Mummy and look at the man even though I don't want to. He's stopped halfway through drying a cup, and he's completely still. He looks out of the window with his mouth open. The old lady's staring out sideways. There's a terrible silence for a while and then she does another 'tut-tut,' and the man says very slowly, 'Lord love a duck. She's away with the fairies, she is—away with the bloody fairies...'

Suddenly, an orange light flashes on the wet window, and I think it must be a reflection from behind the counter. But when I look round there's nothing there at all. It gets bigger and bigger. When I wipe the window with my hand I see it's coming from the top of a car stopped halfway up on the pavement of the road to Gloucester.

It's a police car.

There's a flashing light on top of it but no noise. Two policemen jump out and slam the doors so hard I can hear it even though I'm inside. They run along the road, and when they get to the little wall of the park they jump straight over and run through the flower bed on the other side. One of the policemen is very tall with his helmet clutched under his arm and lanky legs that are shooting out in front of him while he's running. The other one is smaller and a bit fat so he's having to use his legs very hard to keep up.

I know why they're here. They've come for me and Mummy. They're heading straight for her and are going to reach her ever so quickly. She hasn't noticed because she's far too busy pulling the old flower plants out of the ground, and now she's got a huge bunch that's nearly as big as she is. And then just before they get to her I see Mr. Burston who's huffing and puffing his way through the gates of the park with his big old Rover, parked right behind the police car. He's not running, but he's walking more quickly than I've ever seen before.

When the policemen reach Mummy, they stop for just a second as though they're going to catch their breath, and then the tall one puts his helmet on the ground, bends over and taps her shoulder. Not roughly. Not at all roughly—a bit as though you're gently trying to wake someone up. Then he starts talking to her with one hand on her elbow and the other on his knee. The other policeman folds his arms and stands up straight and looks around. Mr. Burston has stopped a little way off, probably not wanting to interfere. He's fiddling with his jacket and is just now beginning to notice that it's raining. Then he starts looking from side to side, and I realise that he's most probably wondering where I am.

I don't want him to see me. I'm just thinking that if there was another door at the back of the café I would like to go through it and run along the Gloucester road and then when I get to the school playing field I could run right across to the other side and over the stream into the Forest of Dean, and there I would shelter all by myself till everything is alright again.

Mummy suddenly looks up at the policeman, and it's as though she's had an electric shock because she lets go of all the old flowers and stands up. Straightaway she pushes the policeman in the chest, and even though she's so small, he goes quite wobbly. And then I can see that the two policemen who had started off trying to be as polite and nice as possible have now got a very difficult person to deal with. Mummy's starting to shout, but I can't hear what she's saying. Both of them grab her by the arms, and she's in between them and struggling to get away. It's like they're all doing a little dance, and the tall policeman accidentally kicks his helmet which he put on the ground into the flower bed. The fat one's helmet falls over the front of his face so he can't see for a bit; he looks like he's playing blind man's buff.

I run to the door of the café because now I've just got to go out and look after Mummy. I pull it so hard that it opens too suddenly and bangs me on the forehead, but I don't care. Just before I get to her, she sees me and looks at me as though she's forgotten that I was here in the first place.

'Leave me alone! Leave me alone!' she's shouting, 'Stop them, Ben—please stop them. You've no right to do this. You've no right to arrest me...'

'It's all right, Madam, we're not arresting you—we just want a little word,' says the tall policeman, and then Mummy manages to free her arm. Her hand goes up in a big circle and smacks him full in the face. And then both her arms are being held tight behind her back and the top buttons of her blouse are popping undone one by one. There's soaking wet mud from the plants all down her front, and it's hard to see that her jacket is meant to be white.

The shouting gets louder and louder. She's crying as well now and struggling as hard as ever, but the policemen have managed to get hold of her very firmly and are marching her along quite quickly towards their police car.

'Stop it! Stop it! Please let me go! Please, please let me go! Ben, do something—you must stop them...' The crying turns to scream-ing—terrible screaming like I've never heard in my life before. I put my arm over my face and my hand over my ear because I don't want to see it, and I don't want to hear it. But at the same time I walk be-hind the policemen and don't try to stop them, because I absolutely know that Mummy must go with them for her own good.

Then she turns her head to look at me, and I can see that it's not that she's angry but that she's frightened. It reminds me of a little girl who fell into our pool when she came to lunch with her mum and dad at our house in Beirut. Before we helped her out, when she was swallowing water and thought she was going to drown, she had exactly the same expression that Mummy's got on now.

'It's alright, Mummy—please don't be frightened. Actually, these policemen are here to help you really. Everything will be alright, and we'll phone Dad up in a bit. He'll sort it all out. Just be good and go with them, Mummy...' But she's screaming so much I don't think she can hear me. Then all of a sudden, the screaming turns to wailing like those Arab ladies do when they're going to a funeral. Mummy's legs stop working, and she goes all like a rag doll. The policemen drag her along with her feet following behind. When they get to the car, the tall policeman lets her go while he opens the door, and she slumps onto the ground. She's got a cut on her knee, and blood's starting to run down towards her ankle. The policeman puts his hands under her arms, picks her up, and just about throws her on the back seat. She lies down flat on it. While the fat police-man opens the driver's seat, the tall one looks over my shoulder and calls out, 'You alright with the young lad, Sir?' and then I see that Mr. Burston is right behind me. 'Yes—yes, absolutely,' he says. He's taking a big white handkerchief out of his pocket. The tall police-man goes round to the other side of the car, opens the door, and gets in beside Mummy. But I don't think he'll have to hold her because it doesn't look as though she's going to struggle anymore. I think she's going to go quietly after all.

Mr. Burston's suddenly dabbing the great white handkerchief on my forehead, and there are big red blobs on it.

'I think you've managed to cut yourself, young man. Nothing that Miss Carson can't patch up, though. Are you alright?'

'Yes, thank you, Sir—perfectly fine, thank you. Why have they arrested my mother, Sir? Where are they taking her?'

'They're not arresting her, Ben. They're just looking after her for a bit. We'll explain it all to you later when we get back to school.'

Mummy sits up and looks at me through the back window of the car. She's gone quiet, and there's no expression on her face. She's crying black mascara tears which are running down her face and onto her neck, and as the car turns onto the road, she puts the palm of her hand, all grazed and red raw, flat against the glass like a star-fish in a rock pool on the beach. She doesn't move, and she doesn't stop looking at me until the car turns the corner by the telephone exchange and is out of sight.

'Anything I can do, Mr. Burston?' The man from the café's stand-

140

ing at the door with his hands cupped to his mouth and the dirty tea towel over his shoulder.

'No thank you, Mr. Norton—you've been very helpful.' Then Mr. Burston looks at me sadly and says in a very gentle voice that I've never heard him using before, 'Come on, let's get you back to school for a tidy-up. Looks as though you could do with a nice hot bath. You're soaked through.' He puts his hand on my shoulder, and we start to walk towards his big Rover car.

And then I see it on the pavement. At first I think it's an injured bird, a white dove only a little bit conscious, with its feathers moving ever so slightly as the raindrops are hitting them. But when I look at it for a little bit longer, I realise it's one of Mummy's shoes with the plastic daisy on top. I run over and pick it up and hold it in both my hands.

'It's one of Mummy's shoes, Sir. She's left behind one of her shoes.' I can feel that I'm crying, and when I wipe my face with my sleeve I see that the tears have mixed with the rain and the blood from where I banged my head on the door of the café.

III.

Monday, 29 September, 2008

At the end of a narrow silver pathway, a pool of light shimmers where the sea meets the horizon. Above it floats an improbably large moon surrounded by an ostentatious display of stars.

I'd affected my usual air of casual disinterest walking past this little taverna before coming in, trying to decide whether it might be the right place for the first meal of my holiday. It's important that it's not so full that my lack of a dining partner makes me feel conspicuous, but neither must it be so empty that I'm in danger of being too fussed over by the staff. So, on a second or third look through the window, I decided that the Golden Hen—a brightly lit establishment perched directly above the sea on a little cliff in the centre of the village—fitted the bill. Three occupied tables—two couples and a singleton—perfect, and a vacant table waiting for me out on the balcony. I walked in, averting my eyes from the display cabinet occupied by a mini-holocaust of dead mullet glaring at me through outraged, accusing eyes. Dead fish. I'm funny about that.

I settled myself at a small table on the far side of the doors that open out onto the veranda, under an awning gently flapping in a warm evening breeze. So, I've chosen my taverna—I've had a nice dinner; it'll do me just fine. Once I'm on nodding terms with the proprietor, I'll stick with it, not bothering to venture farther afield.

It's quite odd really, knowing how uncertain I am about things, but I'm not really self-conscious about being alone on holiday. I know lots of people are—but it's just not one of my many, neurotic quirkinesses. I've grown used to travelling by myself, quite happily spending the early evening alone on the balcony of an apartment with a book and my iPod for company before venturing out after sunset for something to eat. I'm quite comfortable sitting alone at a table so long as I can bury my face in a book in order to discourage conversation with a stranger. I've often been away and realised at the end of my holiday that I've not had a real big fat conversation with anyone at all. In the old days, sometimes the most I'd ever utter would be an instruction to some waiter to fetch me yet another half carafe of wine. These days I don't even do that.

It's the way I like it—never having to be beholden to a holiday companion's whims. I do exactly what I please without having to compromise. No waiting while hair is dried before dinner, no endless splitting of bills at the end of each meal, no questions about whether I might have an idea as to whether the moussaka is better at this establishment rather than the one next door, no decisions about whether to go out now or later to replenish the bottled water, and no discussions as to which beach is to be preferred for the day on account of being too sandy or too pebbly, the water too smooth or too rough. I'm free of all that; I do exactly as I choose.

But to be really honest, there's something else, too. I've never been sure that I have the right to inflict the madness of my travel insecurities on other people. I really can't think that anyone would be able or willing to understand. I'd rather that no one's witness to such silliness.

I dozed fitfully for only two or three hours last night in my bed at home, waiting for the alarm to rattle me awake; now fatigue has caught up with me, and I'm gloriously sleepy. I'm looking forward to climbing the steep narrow lane edged by white-washed houses, back to the sparse little apartment where I unpacked my things earlier this evening, putting my stamp on the place that's going to be home for the next week. There are shutters at the large window just above the bed. I'll close them when I get in—lock out the night and consign myself to dreams till morning, and when I awake, I'll throw them open and treat myself to a view of the fishing boats bobbing up and down on the blue water in the harbour.

Jesus—I'm here! London in the early hours of this same day might be a month ago, and the trauma of travelling is receding. For a whole week, I can put behind me the ridiculous, paralyzing fears I experience when removing myself from one place to another, forget the endless unbuttoning and unzipping to check for documents, keys, money, and whatever else I always suspect I've mislaid somewhere along the way.

God almighty—me and airports. The worrying about being caught in a traffic jam on the way (even with the three hours put aside for the hour-long journey), tickets and euros, passports and window seats, labels for luggage and gates clanging closed because I didn't realise it was a twenty-minute walk to the departure point, and all the other bollocks. Pure nonsense. The shame of it all.

By far the most painful trick my mind plays on me when I'm in travel panic mode is the rock solid conviction that my luggage has been lost in transit. So there I was this morning at Mytelene airport, my heart thumping in my chest while my eyes searched desperately for the green ribbon I tie around the handle of my case for easy recognition, my mind in freefall panic as it struggled to decide who I might report to after I found myself left behind by my fellow passengers, staring at the empty, motionless carousel, giving up hope of retrieving luggage obviously well on its way to some other far off holiday destination.

Of course, I'd made preparations as I always do for that eventuality. My backpack contains a sort of emergency kit for a week's holiday with no luggage. My Ventolin inhaler, sun block, toothpaste and brush, Paracetamol in case I'm caught short by a migraine, Diocalm to be on the safe side, cold sore cream, dental glue to guard against a loose veneer, one pair of pants and shorts, a towel and trunks, though I'd be far too distressed without my luggage to even begin to think about swimming. Talk about abandoning oneself to the magic of the moment in the seat of the ancients! No chance. Play it safe. Best be prepared for calamity.

But I wonder if it might be that now I'm here, just beginning to relax, something at last will begin to shift in my mad head, and I'll dare to be free—free of the obsessive worry about the smallest, most pointless and unimportant of things?

'Anything else for you, my friend?' The owner, with his hand on the balcony door and a tea towel thrown insouciantly over his shoulder, speaks perfect English. He's pulled himself away from a flirtation with two German backpackers to attend to me, now the only other customer. 'Something to finish with, perhaps?' he says as he collects the plate that I've used bread to wipe clean of the last traces of an excellent moussaka.

'No, thank you very much. That was really lovely, though. I'll just have my bill if I may.' I look down at the plastic tablecloth at the breadcrumbs and three marooned broad beans lost overboard from a side dish, spilled in my enthusiasm to banish the hunger that had engulfed me once it had finally sunk in that I'd safely reached my destination.

'Thank you, Sir.'

I pull the half empty glass toward me; the bubbles are weakening, and I lift the glass to my lips, gulp down the remains and place it back on the table.

Water. It's water I drink with my meal these days. I might start with an orange juice, a diet coke or a tomato juice, but then I drink water—sometimes mineral water with a piece of lemon, sometimes straight from the tap, sometimes fizzy with clunking ice cubes.

And it's at times like this that I'm struck by the enormity of what I've done. I'm living a life without alcohol—and I really didn't know that was in the realm of the possible.

It's been nearly eighteen months, but the extraordinary novelty of it all seems fresh again in a new place. Another barrier is being crossed—my first holiday abroad since I stopped.

God knows how many evenings in years gone by I've spent at a table for one, just like this—overlooking the sea, a busy street or grand square—ordering a bottle and pretending to be taken by surprise when it seems to have emptied itself. How many hundreds of times have I found myself asking for a glass and then another after that, telling myself that my prodigious consumption was no one's business but my own? How often have I sat at a table like this and wondered how it's possible for the young lovers opposite to stretch out a miserly half bottle between them and even then to leave an inch or so of red wine at the bottom of a glass? And how many times, at the end of an evening just like this, have I become aware that although I'm the only diner left, it's absolutely essential that I have yet another nightcap? This, in spite of the obvious impatience of the waiters wanting to go home at the end of a long shift, too polite to ask me to leave and nonplussed that I've not seemed to notice the shouted 'goodnights' of the departing kitchen staff, the neat row of put-to-bed, polished glasses glinting from behind the darkened bar, and the upended chairs on tables stripped of their cloths.

———

It was never anywhere near to total chaos, my drinking. I've not lost teeth in ill-judged fights, never had to sell my house or wonder where the next penny was coming from; I was never hauled before human resources at work or sent warning letters because of repeated hangover absenteeism. I've never woken up on a park bench with the snow settling on my forehead, or, like someone I recently met in AA, gone to a party in Basingstoke and come to in a sleeping bag next to a stranger in the Mojave Desert. No friend ever cut me or sent a letter to inform me that my behaviour was beyond the pale and our relationship was at an end. I never had to struggle to keep my hands off a bottle in the early morning, and I wasn't ever reduced to having to carry the booze around with me because I needed topping up on an hourly basis; I never found myself having to make shamefaced phone calls to friends to find out what I might have said or done the previous evening; I've never experienced the shakes so badly that I had to lift a glass with both hands to quivering lips.

No, it wasn't like that. I'm much too much of a control freak for it to have slipped so far.

But my fall at Charing Cross for some reason was my 'rock bottom'. It turned out to be, with God's grace up till now, my last drunken evening. I don't exactly know why—it wasn't that much of a mishap. It's not as though I was mugged that night. I didn't fall into the river or assault a police officer and find myself in the cells for the night. I suppose I'd just had enough of it, that's all—a little moment of clarity in the middle of which it occurred to me that unless I did something about it, a path was being mapped out for the rest of my life—nothing would ever happen apart from an endless series of hangovers unsuccessfully treated with the two Paracetamol placed on the sink in the bathroom at the very beginning of each evening, ready to be swallowed in the fug of morning. Quite suddenly, that just wasn't enough.

There was fearfulness too, the dawning of the idea that I might be setting out on the same path as my mother—my dear, sweet fragile mother who'd so utterly lost her way, slipping in just a few short years into such a state of drunken unreality that she'd found herself alone, living a hopeless life far away from the people who'd loved and cared about her.

Tuesday, 4.00 pm

I doze on the strip of beach that rings this strange little town, still catching up on the sleep I was deprived of by my early morning start yesterday. I'm nearly alone, apart from two funny little dogs and a couple who have settled a little farther down the beach. They waved enthusiastically at me as they passed by ten minutes ago, remembering the camaraderie of our shared journey on the minibus from the airport yesterday afternoon. No one has yet been round to collect the two euros that a sign on the changing hut behind me says is due for the daily rental of my lounger, and it might be that it's so late in the season that it's not worth the owner's bother. There are only two other rather forlorn specimens on the beach, and they may well have been abandoned. The capricious little breeze I awoke to this morning that might be signaling the very beginning of autumn in these parts has given way to a perfect stillness; there's just the gentlest lapping where the lazy sea meets the beach. Two teenage lads are tearing up and down the lane above the shoreline on what is obviously a brand new motor bike, the one riding pillion holding onto his friend's waist as though his life depended on it. The engine cuts through the stillness of the afternoon, a rich, gravelly baritone as they approach the village, fading to an almost inaudible buzzing as they zigzag away up the hill, helmets glinting in the sunshine, throwing up a cloud of dust on the road that winds its way south out of the town. A donkey in a dried up field of brown grass on the far side of the road has wandered over to the wire fence, ceasing his braying to give full attention to the new machine as it comes and goes. Now and again the boys stop and disembark, the proud new owner taking a cloth from inside his denim jacket to dust the stridently red metal before standing back to admire the machine with his arms folded.

The noise doesn't disturb me. I must be already chilling out, slowly letting go. Let the boys enjoy their new toy. It's not for me to disapprove anyway. I am, after all, an intruder, a guest in their little corner of the world.

I've been adopted by the two dogs. They turned up quite un-invited at my apartment this morning just as I got back from my first visit to the town bakery with my croissants, jumping up at me and licking my heels while I attempted to eat breakfast at the little table outside my front door. For a while, I tried to pretend they weren't there, thinking they might move on if I studiously ignored them. Then I fancied that they amused me a little, and I deigned to stroke them both for a brief second in what for me was frankly a rather unusual gesture, probably brought about by the early morning sunshine, the deliciousness of the freshly baked croissants, and the resultant feeling of being at one with the world. It was a mistake. They've been following me around ever since. One of them is a grey, whippet-thin nervous creature with ears that point back as though he's expecting ill treatment at any time—and perhaps he is—and the other is a sort of King Charles Spaniel affair, small with a luscious long coat and much more indulged looking, though God knows if that's true, since he seems free to spend all his time with me. He does have a collar, though, unlike his friend. However, I managed to escape from them during my first walk along the southerly coast road, having dropped my slight feeling of indulgence towards them. We'd all set off together, my uninvited companions so close to my feet that I was struggling not to trip over them. I thought they'd get to the edge of town and then lose interest, but I couldn't have got it more wrong. It was soon apparent that they had every intention of following, wherever I might be going. 'Off! Off! Shoo!' I found myself saying while wagging my index finger at them and then pointing at the town, hoping that no one was witness to the scene of the determined dogs making a fool of the self-conscious Englishman. It had no effect whatsoever. Eventually, exasperation overcame my natural diffidence. I stamped my foot petulantly and shouted at them that I'd prefer to be alone, thank you very much, and I hadn't come all this way to be pursued by two fucking dogs with nothing better to do than ruin a man's holiday. Whippet immediately slunk off back towards the town, trailing his tail with an air of acceptance that implied that this was the way things usually ended up with most of the visitors they adopted. Charlie followed him, looking quite devastated at the rejection. As I hurried myself along the road, praying that they'd got the message but feeling slightly ashamed at my outburst, I kept turning back to make sure I was no longer being pursued. Charlie was reluctantly making his way back, pausing every now and again to turn around and watch me striding purposefully into the distance, perhaps in the hope that I might change my mind about the 'being alone' thing. I felt like a prize shit, though I don't know why I should bother to feel bad about it when I'm nowhere near to being any sort of a dog lover. But they were both sleeping in the shade cast by the table at my front door when I got back and woke to welcome me enthusiastically, my bad tempered rejection of them put to one side. I suppose I might get used to them—as long as I can dissuade them from accompanying me on my walks.

—m—

It's an odd sort of place I find myself in. I wasn't sure about it at first—this dusty, dried out, silent village at the end of the world, but I think I might be coming round to it now. I'd asked for quiet, and quiet is what I've got.

It was all a very last minute decision to come away. I got it into my head that I deserved a break in the sun before the long winter nights set in, as a reward for the last few months of trauma surrounding Pa's illness and his move from the old house into the nursing home. I couldn't have come away any time sooner, and even now, I'm being subjected to powerful pangs of guilt every time I think of having moved him and then left him. He's only been at Tree Tops for three weeks. But I've got to establish quite firmly and as soon as possible, that I'm not totally at his beck and call. That might be a hard lesson for him to learn, and I know it sounds selfish but that's the way it is. There's no point my being around him if I'm seething with resentment at the curtailment of the liberty I've grown so used to as a resolutely single person.

It's been utterly exhausting, too. The sale of the house fell through twice, and then things moved so quickly with the third and final lot of buyers—they'd behaved appallingly, threatening to withdraw unless I set a firm, and far too early, date for completion. In the end, that meant I was left with only two weeks to clear the entire house. I had to do the whole thing myself; Pa's not in a fit state—either physically or mentally, after the stroke—to have been any help, and I'd had to decide not to ask him his opinion about anything and to just get on with it. It felt horribly grown up—everything being down to me, having to own all the decisions, right or wrong. And it felt horribly grown up not to be drinking.

It would have been so easy to resort to a drink. Thank the fuck I didn't. I'd still be at it now, sitting around looking at displaced items of furniture in partly empty rooms with a glass in one hand and a corkscrew in the other, crying maudlin tears about not wanting to part with anything. Nothing would have been done, and I'd probably have lost the buyers into the bargain. I'm not sure how far away I was from slipping, but I did start hearing a little voice in my head that hinted in soothing suggestive tones that a little drink now and again would 'Surely be quite alright because aren't you really being rather hard on yourself seeing as what you've got on your plate at the moment, and don't you think you might be allowed a little something to get you through the next difficult few weeks and anyway, why not start afresh on this sobriety thing when everything has been well and properly settled—let's say sometime after Christmas or at the end of Lent, or, what the fuck, at the end of next summer when the whole of this moving and sorting out thing is well in the past and you're feeling better about life in general, eh?'

It's part and parcel of a middle-aged life, of course—having to make decisions not just about houses, but also about the aged parents who'd lived in them and can't manage on their own anymore. Anyway, who's to care what I decide to do about mere possessions— because that's what all the anguish was about; it all belongs to me now and who is there to admonish me for my quick-fire decisions about what to keep and what to sell? I've no siblings to argue with over the spoils, so it was mere sentimentality that threatened to get in the way. They were things that finally, and for totally practical reasons, had to be let go of, that's all.

Holy shit, it was difficult, though. I didn't seem to have much idea about how hard it would it be—the dissolution of our little family's possessions and history—and it took me by surprise. I had to decide to part with things that have been around me all my life, things familiar to me from the old days in Beirut and then all the stuff that came my way from Granny when we persuaded her that it wasn't safe for her to be alone in her house any longer. Now it's Pa's turn, and one day, I suppose, it will be mine—though who the hell's going to move me around, I've no idea.

With each decision to let something familiar from childhood go, I felt I was delivering a heartless rejection to a near-to-living thing, an object grown unfashionable that wouldn't sit well in my 'just-so' house, like a faithful old servant who's outgrown his usefulness, become a burden, and is to be disposed of without even the courtesy of a proper explanation or goodbye.

It put me in mind of something that Mummy once told me as we sat in the car together, waiting for Pa to complete some Saturday morning task in the centre of town. It must have been sometime in a school holiday, not long before her life, and mine, descended into chaos, just a little while before the days when the sherry bottle became her constant companion. We were talking, as we very often did, of the 'old days'—that's how we always referred to our lives in Beirut, the still fresh memories already turned to gold. I'd asked her what she thought our old servants, Abdul, Aisha and Miriam, might be doing now that they weren't looking after us any longer. 'I don't know, My Only—I really don't know, but I think so often of Miriam.' Then she told me that one of the greatest regrets of her life was her leave-taking of Miriam outside the front of the old house before we drove away forever.

I remember the scene with a crispness that is quite undiminished. Miriam, in floods of tears, holds open the car door, but it might as well be the door that is holding her, she's so upset. 'Goodbye, dear Miriam,' Mummy says, lowering herself elegantly into the car as she puts out one hand, the other sweeping under her skirt so as not to crease it against the seat. Miriam takes her hand and presses it hard against one wet cheek, and then the other, before covering it with kisses. She's speechless with grief. Mummy, quite gently but firmly, pulls her hand away. She's embarrassed. 'Thank you so very much for all your help with Benjamin. I'm sure he'll never forget you.'

'Why on earth couldn't I have put my arms around her and cried with her?' she said, eyes filling as she fixed her gaze on the parked car in front of us. She was talking to herself as much as to me. 'I missed her immediately, terribly. It was the unkindest thing I've ever done. She must have felt as though I just discarded her—she'd served her purpose, and I was moving on. But she was my best, my sweetest friend in Beirut. We didn't speak the same language, but somehow I was able to tell her everything, and she understood. She understood everything...' She was silent for a very long time before she said, very quietly, 'Do you know, I don't even have her address?'

I guess it was some sort of fucked up notion of propriety, of correct British reserve, and bizarre on that account, since she really wasn't at all like that.

Mummy's been around me in these past few weeks of packing up. She spent only a fraction of her life in the house, but three years to an eight-year-old child, the age I was when we moved in, would have seemed like a lifetime.

The house had been redecorated several times since she'd left us. Pa had seen to that. He'd obviously been restless with her memory but had only half-heartedly tried to erase it, like an artist painting over a work without ever having the nerve to chuck out the canvas and start afresh. He should have moved on years ago, given himself another chance with somebody else. It wouldn't have been that difficult; he was a good-looking man right up to recent times. But, after she left, he had lived on there for nearly thirty-five years, quite alone once I'd gone too. In some extraordinary way, though, Mummy continued to occupy it in a way that he never did, almost as though he might be there under sufferance, a guest in her house. It retained an essence of her that never faded, even when I last saw it, emptied of all the things that had connected her to the place.

Friday, 6.00 pm

I walked over the headland to the beach at Faneromeni this morning.

I've been almost completely alone all day on a two-mile stretch of sandy beach on an enchanted island in Greece. At midday, as I swam back towards the shore, I might have seen a young lad on a distant hillside rounding up goats, and much later, a couple emerged from a car they'd parked outside the tiny church that sits alone right at the water's edge in the middle of the bay. They could well have been creatures from another world, their figures fuzzy in the midday heat and far enough away so that the muffled sound of their car door slamming didn't reach me at other end of the beach for four or five seconds.

I got back just a few minutes ago, and I'm sitting at the little plastic table outside my door at the end of this God-given day. The wind that's blown all day has died, a half hour thunderstorm has had its moment and gone on its way, and the village has settled into the tranquility of a balmy late afternoon.

I've brewed a cup of tea in a pan since it appears that the use of a kettle and teapot is something that is reserved for the English alone, but that's not stopping my intense enjoyment of the two Assam teabags, brought from home, that I've stirred and coaxed into a rich brown nectar. Charlie Spaniel rests her head on the arch of my foot, eyes blissfully closed as she dozes in the warmth of the late afternoon sun. I'm intimate enough with her and her companion now to have noted the little line of teats under the belly that she presents for a gentle scratch whenever I can be persuaded, but at this rather late stage in our fast moving relationship, I've not bothered to give her a name more fitting to a lady. A discarded chocolate wrapper propelled more by a current of warm air than by the dying wind nonchalantly passes by on the path in front of us. Charlie opened one eye for a second to observe its progress, and I'd watched a plan of chase being considered for a moment before it was dismissed. Her eye closed, she'd smacked her lips together and rearranged her head, nestling deeper into the suntanned pillow of my foot, then a reluctant ear had made a half-hearted attempt to point upwards before falling ever so slowly back over my ankle as sleep took hold once again. Whippet hasn't stirred since he stilled himself after the effusive meeting that had greeted me on my return. He'd retreated to his favourite corner as soon as the excitement began to die down and has been lost to the world ever since.

I'm happy, really happy. The feeling took hold of me today while

I was swimming far out to sea at Faneromeni and has stayed with me; an almost tangible feeling of deep contentment that I don't think I've experienced since I stopped drinking. It fills me with hope. Might this just be the day that everything begins to change—the day when something in my head switches on, or off perhaps—and allows me to become the small cog I am rather than the very centre of my own egocentric universe? Might this be the day when I can begin to say to myself, 'It doesn't really matter what life throws at you. Don't bother wasting time being afraid of nothing?'

As I'd set off on the road north out of the town this morning, the chill wind I'd noticed while I ate my breakfast was stubbornly refusing to die down, and fierce little waves were slapping against the hulls of the fishing boats moored just a few feet out from the road, forcing them into a frenzied drunken dance as they threw themselves from side to side, while loose bottles and cans clunked noisily back and forth in their holds. I was sublimely alone but for the odd passing car; a man in a uniform driving a blue utilities van sent me up with a jolly salute, and then Felicity—our 'Shirley Valentine' travel rep—and her glamorous poet-fisherman husband raced by, she waving enthusiastically while he tooted the horn of their battered dusty open-topped Mercedes. The lad on his red bike that I remembered from the first afternoon nearly felled me as he turned a corner at breakneck speed, leaning so far into the bend that he was practically horizontal. 'Careful! Little sod!' I shouted at his receding back, beginning to raise my right hand into a v-sign before changing my mind and touching my fingers to my smiling lips. Jesus, one small week in paradise, and I'm blowing kisses to a youth I'd want hanged in Clapham!

Far out of town, I pass a lonely whitewashed farmhouse set among the olive groves where a vine grew over a shaded porch with an infant asleep in a pushchair. He was being watched over by his granny preparing vegetables for dinner, while his mother, granting me a distracted sideways nod, battled against the wind to hang disobedient flapping clothes on a washing line. In the adjacent scrubby fields, sheep with melancholy eyes stopped to stare at me for an instant before lowering their heads, bells clanging, to continue a search for morsels of nourishment among the dried up grass of late summer. Even farther along the road, the shuttered weekend houses of the nouveau riche of Mytelene, wind turbines hissing and solar panels reflecting back the sun into the cloudless sky, stood behind neat walls in oases of carefully tended green grass with blood-red geraniums in terracotta pots on white tiled patios. Huge threatening dogs with mad, angry eyes, impatient to move beyond the confines of their leashes, barked at me from behind ostentatious filigreed gates.

I walked the whole two-mile length of the deserted beach, singing Italian arias at the top of my voice, with my sandals in my hand, my feet sinking into the wet sand and surf while the wind howled around me and left speckles of white foam on my skin. After pulling on my tee shirt, I paused for a moment's lonely contemplation and lit a candle in the whitewashed interior of the silent church that smelt of sea salt and candle wax. When I reached the rocks at the far end of the bay, I took off my shorts and swam naked among tough little waves, bantam-weight fighters that playfully slapped and buffeted me, knocking me about as though I might be a child in a playground, trying to keep up with the too rough games of boys a class or two ahead of me. I climbed out of the water giggling at my ineptitude and fell asleep on my unfurled towel, my back to the sun and my toes buried in the sand. I ate my little packed lunch with my eyes fixed on the crisp straight line of the far away horizon where dark blue meets sky blue. Afterwards I swam again, sparring with the waves with a newfound confidence. And then I walked back along the beach, resuming my operatic performance for the delighted audience in my head.

Before heading for home, I swam again, far out to sea, until the chill of deep water eventually forced me back to dry land. Then, with a towel wrapped tightly around me, I sat on the beach and daydreamed in the weakening late afternoon sunshine. I don't know whether I shivered from cold or exhilaration.

I did more than swim with the fishes today. I flew again, like I remember I did in a far away, nearly forgotten childhood. I looked down at the dark seabed a hundred feet below the surface and kept my nerve. I spread my arms out across the water and dared to imagine they might be wings.

Vast black storm clouds, appearing from nowhere, began to gather far out to sea as I left the beach. Quickening my pace, I half hoped that I might be caught up in the excitement of a drenching thunderstorm.

It hit land like an invading Ottoman army as I reached the village. I half-heartedly ran towards the shelter of the church and then gave up, laughing to myself as I sat on a bench in the square and surrendered myself to the downpour. A troupe of little girls abandoned an after school game of hopscotch and ran home shouting in mock horror at the flashes of lightening and drum rolls of thunder; women hurried from their houses to snatch clothes from washing lines while others placed pots of geraniums in the way of the rain. A young waiter from the taverna in the square, momentarily stopping to take in the sight of the eccentric, grinning tourist sitting in the downpour, dashed from table to table collecting salt cellars, draping tablecloths over his arms while his white shirt turned transparent in the rain and stuck to his back. It grew dark as night as the winding streets between the houses became brown rivers, and the awnings over the tables in the square bulged, pregnant with the weight of the water.

And as quickly as it came, it went on its rumbling way, rolling over the mountains inland as the light returned, and the sun broke through again. I waited for a while and then waded through the middle of every brown puddle, stamping on the water with my sandals as though I was a naughty three-year-old with no one to tell me not to.

I stopped to look at the sad, unloved Turkish hammam just to the side of the church. It's slowly falling apart; ugly breeze blocks fill the elegantly arched doorway that faces the street. At the far end, the wall has collapsed, and the domed roof now leans precariously towards the centre which is filling with rubbish. Next to it stands an ancient Turkish house; its delicately latticed balcony, built to air the large room beyond with cooling winds from the sea, is beginning to disintegrate and fall into the unkempt garden below. Against the street wall, there's a long-dry fountain with a Turkish inscription. I took my little guidebook from my backpack and opened it to find out what it might tell me. 'With this delicious water, he satiated the spirit of those who thirst. Haci Osman Aga, counted among the pious, built this noble good work. The year of the hirja. 1319.' The Greeks obviously don't care for these signs of a gentler side of the old Turkish occupiers; there's too much history here, and not yet enough years in between for ancient injustices to be forgotten. Perhaps, if I come back here in a year or two, there'll be a bright new house with plumb-straight walls where the commander of the Ottoman castle that overlooks the village once entertained visiting naval captains and their officers with the delights of soap and steam and a vigorous rubdown.

Monday, 7.30 am

I'm ready to go. I've pulled on my jeans for the first time in a week, and they feel foreign against my sunburned legs grown used to the freedom of shorts. I've been up for ages, though I packed last night, of course. I wanted to be absolutely sure I'm not leaving anything behind. I've looked under the bed for the umpteenth time and slid open the drawers at the bottom of the wardrobe yet again to make sure there's not a recalcitrant pair of boxers hiding at the very back. When I checked the shower just now I found I'd left my bloody shampoo in there. I hate that. I don't want to leave anything behind, not even a more than half empty bottle of shower gel. It shows that I'm not really in control of things. Next, it'll be my passport that disappears because I haven't pushed it far enough into the pocket of my jacket.

The bats were still flying around outside while I made my mug of tea over an hour ago. I could see their silent silhouettes as they flew out of the inky-black early morning past the street lamp outside. It's just beginning to get light now, and in the last few minutes they've gone off to hang upside down somewhere till the dark returns. A pigeon coos on the roof, and it won't be long before all the other birds in the neighbourhood start up. I've folded back the shutters above the bed, and now there's just enough light for me to make out the shape of the two dogs asleep and huddled up together under the plastic table. They've quite obviously been there all night long. Perhaps they really don't belong to anyone.

There's a taxi coming for me at 8.00. I found a note from Felicity when I got back from the beach yesterday telling me that I was the only person leaving today, so I'm going alone to the airport. No jolly companions on a minibus. I'm panicked by it. I've got it into my head that the taxi driver won't be able to find the apartments, and I've already decided that he won't be the type to bother with a determined search for me. The taxi service operates from Kalloni which is miles away, so it's not as though he's familiar with this place. Even if he's a diligent, responsible type who'll bother to ring Felicity's mobile to enquire about my whereabouts, there's going to be time wasted before he's pointed in the right direction. And then it becomes quite possible that I'll miss my flight. I have a dreadful, crushing certainty that things are going to go wrong.

I wish I'd arranged with Felicity to meet the taxi outside her office—that would have made things so much easier. Perhaps I'll walk down there now, so that when and if the taxi driver gets here and can't find his way around, he'll put two and two together and know that I've been sensible enough to change our meeting point.

But then, on the other hand, if I take my case out of the apartment now and go round to the front of the building, I can keep an eye on the road and flag him down from a distance when I see him approaching. There'll be a pretty good chance he'll see me, too.

Oh Christ and Holy shit. Here I go again, doing my usual

nonsense.

So now I wait, sitting on my upended case by the side of the road with the dogs stretched out at my feet. My hands are shaking. There's five minutes to go before the taxi's meant to be here. I'm a man of fifty who's so terrified of something that hasn't yet happened that I feel as though the ground might open up beneath me and swallow me whole.

Nothing changes. My sweet day at Faneromeni was a false dawn. All that bollocks yesterday about flying, with joyful singing filling my head. I'm not free; I never have been, and I never will be. Somewhere along life's way, I've taken myself prisoner and thrown away the key to my cell. It's always going to be like this.

When the taxi turns the corner of the street and starts a precarious descent towards me with the pebbles of the unmade road scrunching under the braking tyres, I raise a hand to attract the driver's attention and manage to concoct a laid-back, 'ah-there-you-are' type expression followed by an unconcerned little smile of breathtaking dishonesty.

'You are Teasdale?' asks the young man with wrap-around sunglasses and dark curly hair who emerges from behind a tinted windscreen. He's already opening the boot without waiting for a reply.

'I most certainly am,' I say, trying not to grab the door handle too quickly. He swings my case into the air, catches it on his thigh and expertly directs it into the boot.

Charlie and Whippet sit side by side, watching me in the car as it backs into an alleyway to turn. They're wearing an expression of concern and disbelief, ears pricked as they listen to the familiar sounds of abandonment. As the taxi pulls away up the hill, I look back at them one last time and chide myself for not saying goodbye. I begin to raise my hand in a gesture of farewell, but let it fall back into my lap when I glimpse the young man pushing his sunglasses onto his head and observing me in the rearview mirror.

IV.

I've got three photos of Mummy with me at school. They're in my little blue album that I keep in the bag under my bed. It's only a small one for putting favourites in, probably for when you're going away. There's only room for about ten photos, and I've not even got that many. There's one that my dad took of me at the bottom of the stairs of the Boeing 707 when we were leaving Beirut, and another of my cat Nurbanu, looking out of the top of a flower pot and taken on the same day—the last one of her ever. I've got one of me on Abdul's shoulders and another one of Granny when she was young and had a sports car.

The first photo of Mummy is when she was a little girl, and it's so old now that it's gone quite brown. She's sitting on a little stool in a dark room, and her hair is very short and completely straight—not curly like it is now. I think she's only about four years old, but still, if you look closely, you can see that it's her.

Both the grown-up pictures of Mummy were taken when we lived in Beirut. All the best pictures are from Beirut, and the ones I've got with me are just one or two of them that I've chosen from my big album at home. The first one is of her on a balcony high up at the front of a beautiful house.

I remember that day. We drove high into the mountains where there were huge trees and it got cooler and cooler the farther up we went. My dad stopped the car at some massive iron gates that were opened by guards, and then we went up a long drive to a very big old house with flowers growing up the walls and windows in the shape of arches. A servant in a white jacket opened the car door for us. Then, a very tall man with a moustache came down the steps from the house and kissed Mummy's hand and spoke to her in French. Later she told me he was a sort of prince and the head of a very important tribe. He was so powerful that he could have people killed whenever he wanted, and however nice he was to us, he was also known to be 'very ruthless'. That's what Mummy said about him, but I don't know if that's true or not. He seemed ever such a nice man to me. There were two girls there who were his daughters and about the same age as me. To begin with they were very shy, but when I'd been with them for a while they started talking Arabic and French so I couldn't understand, but it didn't matter. They showed me all the rooms in their house—which was really a palace, Mummy said. There were rooms as high as the sky with beautiful Persian carpets and very low sofas and tables with great vases of flowers and bowls of sweets and fruit. In the garden there was a shady pond with a little fountain and some of the biggest fish I've ever seen in my life. We stayed there all day, for lunch and tea, and before we left we went onto the balcony so we could see all the way down the mountain. It must have been my dad again who took a photograph from the drive below. He took lots that day.

Mummy's very beautiful in it. She's got a black dress on and is wearing a shiny white scarf round her head and neck. One of her hands is resting on the railing, and the sun's shining off the rings on her fingers as she looks out into the distance. The Prince is next to her, and he's looking at her out of the corner of his eye. After we said goodbye to him and his daughters on the steps of their lovely house, we got into the car to drive away. Suddenly the Prince ran down the stairs and put his hand through the window to give Mummy something. It was a little black box. He put it into her hands and said 'This is something to remind you of the Cedars of Lebanon for the rest of your life,' and she said, 'Oh my dear, Prince, thank you so very, very much,' but she didn't dare open the box until we were quite far away down the road from his house. That's when she got the brooch that she loved best of all her things. All the way back home she just stared at it in its little box saying 'Oh my goodness' over and over again, and my dad kept saying, 'We'll have to return it, of course.'

The next photo must have been taken by my dad as well, and I think he was actually in the swimming pool at home when he took it. Some of it you can't see very well because there's a bit of dazzle on it and a splash of water as well. Mummy's sitting on a chair right by the side of the pool. She's wearing a white dress with huge blue spots on it called polka dot, I think, and her legs are crossed. One of her shoes is dangling off her foot. She's got her head thrown back and she's laughing and laughing. In one hand she's holding a glass, and you can see the ice in it, and the other hand is on the shoulder of a man who's in the seat next to her. He's leaning right forward and looking up at her with a beaming smile. It's him that's made her laugh. Jerry Paxwell. That was his name. He was always at our house. My dad used to joke to me about it and call him 'your mother's beau'. Mummy liked him because he made her laugh. But you can see from the photo that he was in love with her. That's what I think. Everybody loved her, though. He wasn't the only one by far.

That was in the olden days. When I close my eyes and think of Mummy, that's how I see her still. I wish, I wish we could just go back to our old life in Beirut. Everything would be alright if we could just go back. I know it would.

I'm in sickbay. I'm sitting up in bed, and I've been trying to read a book. It's Peter the Whaler which is one of my favourites, but it's not really going in very much so I'm looking at my little album instead. The thing is—I'm not really sick, so I'm feeling a bit silly about being in bed in the middle of the day when everyone else is in class.

When Mr. Burston brought me back from the park yesterday, Miss Carson and Miss Newman were both waiting for me in the hall. As I came through the door, I started to get all strange because suddenly I couldn't breathe and my hands went numb and there was blackness and stars in my eyes. I nearly fainted actually, and I could hear myself trying to breathe as if I was in the distance and not in my own body. I started to get more and more frightened because I was thinking that I was really ever so close to dying and my spirit going away from me. But it wasn't at all the same as when I get my asthma because there was no wheezing sound. Anyway, Miss Newman ran up the stairs to get my inhaler just in case, and I did do a puff of it.

They sat me down in the same big old chair that I was in when I was waiting for Mummy, and they made me put my head between my knees. After a bit I started to get my breath back, and I could see properly again. When I'd been sitting there for quite a long time, Miss Newman helped me up the stairs to surgery and sat me down with a glass of water. I can't remember it all so clearly, but when we got there Miss Carson was already talking to the doctor on the telephone. She was listening to what he was saying for quite a long time, nodding her head and tapping her pencil against the top of the table. Miss Newman had her hand on my shoulder and was moving her thumb up and down my neck very gently while she was listening to the conversation. They were being very kind to me so I knew they thought that I wasn't very well.

'He's fine now, Dr. Spears, much calmer. Much, much calmer.' When she put down the telephone, Miss Carson told me that I was to rest in sickbay till at least the next evening, and that the doctor was going to come and see me in the morning.

So that's why I'm here. I've never been ill enough to be in sickbay before, actually. It's my very first time in this room. It's very comfy. There are thick red curtains that go right down to the ground and don't let any light in whatsoever when they're drawn. So last night, after Miss Carson said goodnight and turned out the light, I lay in the bed with my eyes stretched wide open. For a while there wasn't the slightest bit of anything that I could see until I got used to it, and then only the tiniest bit where the curtain was moving in the wind. I like that, though. It's cosy, like the house martins' nests, or where the squirrels lived in the tree before it was blown down.

When they brought me here last night, I had a real surprise because guess what? Jollo was sitting up on the pillow waiting for me! At first I was a bit shocked because I don't really like people to know about him, and suddenly there he is right out in the open and sitting up all threadbare and tatty on the pillow! Then I was suddenly a bit worried about that because it means that they must have looked in my bag, and I'm not very sure that I like to have anyone at all see in there. But it wasn't actually till this morning that I discovered that not only was Jollo in the room but my whole blue bag was underneath the bed with my radio not confiscated or anything! And that means I was able to wind up my clock like I do every single morning, and it will still carry on its ticking that started at home.

There's a rug on the floor, a bit the same as the big one downstairs in the hall but with more colours in it, and a wicker chair in the corner by the window with a red cushion that matches the curtains. That must be for the visitors when they come to see you, and so that's probably where my dad will sit when he gets here. Miss Carson told me he was coming when she came to take my tray away after breakfast.

'Why's he coming to see me, Matron?'

'Because he's been worried about you, of course—like all of us.' I tried to tell her that I was quite sure I wasn't the least bit ill, and she said that was for the doctor to decide.

I think I was a bit rude to the doctor when he came after breakfast. I didn't want to talk to him. I didn't want to talk to anyone, actually. I think he was sitting in the wicker chair, but I'm not sure because I went under the sheets and turned my head away from him and was just looking at a little bit of the wall that I could see through the blanket all the time he was talking to me. I thought he was going to ask me some questions about Mummy, and I had told myself before that I just was not going to say anything at all about all the things that happened yesterday. He didn't ask me though, but I just wasn't in the mood for talking, that's all. He was asking me things about whether I was happy or not, or if I was worried. He was using a nice soft voice, but still I never looked at him once. When the room went all quiet and I heard the door closing, I pushed back the blanket to have a look, and he wasn't there anymore. He hadn't used his thermometer or stethoscope or tapped my chest or put the air pump thing round my arm or any of the usual things that happen when you go to the doctor. I thought Miss Carson would come in and tell me off for being rude, but she never did. I heard whispering voices outside the room, and when she opened the door to come in, I was able to see the back of the doctor walking away along the corridor carrying his black case. I think he was the same one who came to give us injections last term. I recognised him from his brown suit and wavy grey hair. Then Miss Carson told me in a very serious voice that the doctor had ordered 'complete rest for the whole of today and tomorrow.'

The funny thing is that he's not left me any medicine that I have to take, so I don't see what the point of me being here is. I've not been sick, and I haven't even got a temperature.

Everyone's in class now, and it's gone really quiet. Surgery's right at the other end of the corridor so I can't hear Miss Carson and Miss Newman talking, and this is a day when there's no cleaning going on in the school. It's a bit like I'm the only person in the whole wide world. I'm not sure what I'm supposed to be doing, though. Perhaps Mrs. Marston will come up and set some work for me or something. Probably I shouldn't be looking in my album. I should be doing some schoolwork instead of being treated as a sick person.

There's a knock on the door. Perhaps the doctor's come back with his stethoscope. I push the album away and quickly open Peter the Whaler. There's another knock, the door opens just a bit, and a head comes round. It's my dad.

'Hello, there, Ben...'

'Oh, hello, Dad,' I say in a surprised voice as though I didn't know I was expecting him. He comes into the room and closes the door with both hands so as not to make any sort of noise. He's got his briefcase under his arm, but he's not wearing his office clothes today.

'Well, I say! Look at you sat there in the lap of luxury. How are you feeling?'

'I'm fine, Dad. I'm not ill at all, actually. It's for just in case, I think.'

'Yes, that's what Mr. Burston's told me. Just had a cup of coffee with him. Quack's been to see you, I hear...'

'What?'

'Quack's been. The doctor?'

'Oh, yes. He said I was absolutely fine. There's no problem at all but just to stay here till tomorrow.'

'Good, good, good,' he says. He's nodding his head up and down and looking round the room. 'This really is rather nice, isn't it? I think you've fallen on your feet here, Ben.' Then there's a long pause, and I don't know what to say.

'I bought these for you,' he says and he opens his briefcase and takes out a brown paper bag. I can see into the opening. It's a packet of chocolate fingers. He stretches out his hand towards me. I stare at the packet for just a moment, but when I put my hand out to take it I'm just a bit too late because he's already putting them on the little side table next to the lamp and the jug of water that Matron left for me.

'You can enjoy those later.' he says.

'Thanks, Dad, I will,' I say, and I can feel that I'm beginning to blush a bit.

He walks over to the window and looks out. 'I say! What a splendid view of the river.'

'Yes, it's really nice, isn't it?' And then no one says anything again.

'Did you come in the car?' I say so that the silence will stop.

'Yep. Straight over the river. Marvelous, the suspension bridge, isn't it? Saves hours and hours.' He's still looking out of the window, and now he's put his hands in his pockets. There's another long silence.

'So, you're feeling okay then, are you?'

'Oh yes. Absolutely fine. Back to lessons tomorrow.'

He sits down in the wicker chair for visitors. His hands are still in his pockets, and he makes a sighing noise like you do when you first sit down to show you're quite comfortable. He's looking all around but there's not even one picture on the wall for him to talk about. I wonder what I should say now, because quite soon I'm going to have to ask him about yesterday.

'Sorry to hear about Granny's visit having to be cancelled. I hear you had a nice day out with the Harmans though. All worked out in the end...'

I know I'm supposed to talk about that day now, but I'm just not able to think about it quickly enough. Instead I say nothing, and the silence fills the room like a balloon that's filling up with far too much air and might be about to burst.

And then I say 'Dad...' and I know that I'm going to ask him about yesterday.

'Yes?' he says straightaway. Suddenly his face looks different. I open my mouth to speak again, but nothing comes out.

'Yes, Ben, what is it?' He takes his hands out of his pockets while he's sitting there and weaves his fingers together on his lap and starts twiddling them up and down, and his knuckles go white.

'Why did the police arrest Mummy? Where have they taken her?'

And then he tells me the story. I know he doesn't want to say any of it, but he just has to. It's like he's taken a huge breath and has got to say it once and for all. He doesn't take very long and starts to use that same voice he uses in the study at home when he's trying to get me to work harder. It's loud, and he's not looking at me while he's speaking. And then it feels so funny because we're talking about Mummy, and it's been a strict rule that we're never ever meant to.

My dad says Mummy hasn't been living at home since nearly the beginning of term, since just after I came back to school. He'd noticed some time ago that she really wasn't coping terribly well, and so he'd mentioned to her that it might be an idea for her to have a complete rest at a very nice sanatorium that Dr. Scott had told him about. She hadn't really wanted to go, but in the end he'd managed to persuade her. It's a place where they specifically deal with people who are 'emotionally exhausted'. Everything had been going fine, and she'd seemed much better when he saw her just a few days ago.

But yesterday morning, she'd just disappeared.

'She obviously decided she wanted to see you, Ben.' Dad's voice suddenly sounds different and softer, and he looks straight at me. 'She just walked out early yesterday morning without telling any of the staff. They thought she must have gone for a walk round the grounds, but they couldn't find her. The first thing I knew about it was when Headmaster phoned my secretary yesterday to say that she was due here to take you out for lunch.'

'But I don't understand why the policemen had to arrest her, Dad. She hasn't done anything wrong.'

'They didn't arrest her, Ben. It was to protect you both. She's been so unwell recently, you see. The police just needed to check that you were both alright.'

I look out of the window, and there's another silence but not a horrible one like it was before. And then I think about whether I'll ever get to see Mummy again.

'But where's she gone now, Dad? Where have they taken her?'

'She's back at the hospital. Safe and sound. Getting the best treatment there is for her sort of condition.'

He tells me I'm not to worry about it all, and everything's going to be just fine. Mummy's bound to be better and at home by the end of term, and everything will be back to normal. I wonder what normal would be like because Mummy's been bad for a long time now. She can only be better if she's not having so much sherry and starts to like tea again, and I honestly don't think that will be able to happen.

When my dad says he's going, he gets up from the wicker chair and comes and sits on the bed with me for a bit and takes hold of my hand which is very odd. I can see that he's not going to stop, so I don't try to take it away.

'I'll phone Headmaster to see how you're doing tomorrow, and I'm coming to take you away at half term. We'll go to visit Granny, and then we'll drive to the Brecon Beacons for the weekend. How would that be?'

I say, 'That would be great, Dad. Really great!' with a big smile on my face, but really I'm thinking what will there be to talk about for a whole of a weekend without Mummy there, and that is something that I would be quite worried about in fact.

Then he leans over and kisses my cheek, and that's never happened before. He gets up and opens the door. When he's halfway out he does his funny little wave and says 'Bye, Ben. See you in two weeks' time,' and he closes the door ever so carefully so it doesn't make a noise.

Perhaps Granny's car will be mended from her car crash by half term. I could write to her to say that if it's possible, I'd like to stay with her for the whole of half term, and I'll ask her to write to my dad to tell him not to bother about the Brecon Beacons.

After he's gone it's dead quiet again. I try to read more of Peter the Whaler, but not the slightest bit of it is going into my head. All I'm thinking about is how unhappy Mummy is, and that she came to see me, and I didn't want to go with her, and however horrible it was I was a bit pleased when the policemen came to take her away.

I told her to go with them.

Now she knows I didn't want to go away with her, and I feel so sad that I didn't pretend harder for her sake.

My hands won't keep still on my lap, and the book slides off the bed and whacks onto the floor so that I've lost my place. I open my little album again and stare at the pictures, trying to make them come alive so that Mummy might step out of the photographs, and I'll hear her laughing and being happy again. But all I can see is her eyes from yesterday looking at me, with the blackness running down her cheeks. I close the album and stare at the blue cover and tell myself it's the wide open sky, and I'm flying away. But it doesn't work because there's not the tiniest bit of room in my head which isn't full of the pictures and the noise that Mummy was making when she was being taken away.

Then I put my head under the blankets again, like when the doctor came, and try to make it as dark as I can so that I'm not in this bed in this room, and my name's not Ben, but I'm somebody else. Then I pray and pray that I might fall asleep and just be somewhere else for a little while till the noise and the pictures have gone away.

The door opens ever so gently, and Miss Carson says 'Teasdale?' I don't say anything because I'm pretending to be asleep. I can hear the clinking of a glass against a plate like a tiny alarm bell. She's got my lunch on a tray, but I just want to stay here in the dark, not eat anything and wait for the night to come and then the next day when I might feel not so bad.

'Ben? You awake?' I move a tiny bit when she says my proper name, and then I'm still again. There's a tiny pause, and I can feel her looking at the back of my head. Then I hear the door closing again, and I pull the blanket closer to my face and scrunch up my eyes so tight that I see dark red flames and stars.

'Ben? Hey, Ben, wake up!' A hand pulls back the blanket from my face and suddenly there's so much light it's like an explosion. There's breath on my cheek, and I see goofy teeth and a big clump of hair right up close. It's Nick Gower. My heart is beating like mad because I was so fast asleep and don't know where I am.

'Hello, Nick. I was asleep, I think. What time is it?'

'You lazy bum! It's nearly five o'clock. Miss Carson's sent me in to see you for a minute before High Tea.' He's looking at me with his face to one side. 'You been ill, then?'

'No, not really. I'm just under examination I think.'

'Blimey, hope it's not infectious. If you've got mumps, they'll send you home, you know. You'll be put in quarantine.' He quickly walks over to the wicker chair and sits down so that he's not so close to me.

'I'd love to be at home in quarantine doing just what I want all day long—but not with mumps,' he says. 'It makes your balls grow to five times their normal size, and it hurts like billy-oh. And after, when you grow up, it's very difficult to have children, and if you do, sometimes they're born inside out.'

'I've definitely not got that, Nick. I'm better from whatever it was though. I'll be back in class tomorrow. Doctor says I'm right as rain, actually.'

And then he's talking to me about what's going on at school as though I've been up here for weeks and weeks instead of since yesterday afternoon. He tells me that the school tennis tournament is between Henry Pugh and Tom Whickham, just the same as the table tennis last term and that we're all going to watch it on Sunday afternoon, and that Theo's making a right pest of himself on the Graves Committee trying to get all his own way so that all the others are getting fed up with him. When he tells me that I realise I really just don't care anymore. Then he sees the chocolate fingers on the table and asks if he can have one. When I say 'yes' he comes over and fetches them and goes back to the chair. He opens the packet very quickly without having to look what he's doing and starts eating them two at a time so that he's not talking so much, but I don't mind because it might be that if he finishes them he'll go away. Nick is my friend, but I'm not in the mood for seeing him today.

'Ford's house martin chick died in the night,' he says with his mouth full, 'so now there's only Gilligan's left. The only one of all those sixteen! What a shame. But guess what? He's just about flying! He sits on Gilligan's finger and buzzes his wings like a bumble bee, and this morning he did actually fly from Gilligan's blazer pocket to halfway across the games room. That's where he's living now, in Gilligan's blazer pocket. If he lives another day or two, he might just make it and fly away.'

'I don't think he's going to live, Nick. Why just him when all the others are dead?'

'Well Ford's and Gilligan's have lived much longer than all the others. There were four of them left the day of Mr. England's crash, then two were dead the next day, and that's a whole week ago. Two left up to last night and now just one. We're all praying like mad for him—Tom Thumb. That's what they're calling him now. Tom Thumb.'

Far away downstairs we can just about hear the sound of practise going on in the cricket nets and Theo playing the piano. The bell rings ever so faintly as though it comes from another world which means that Nick has to go for High Tea. When he gets to the door he suddenly stops and points towards my pillow. 'What's that?' he says and he's noticed Jollo who no one in the school has seen before because he lives in my bag. I turn red and say 'I don't know,' which is dead silly really because he's sitting up right next to me. Nick says 'Creepy. Really creepy,' in a deep slow voice and then, 'See you tomorrow' in a high voice with an American accent as he's closing the door.

Miss Carson comes in straight after he's gone and asks me if I'll have something for tea. I say I don't want anything, and she says I must eat something to keep my strength up.

'How about some nice tomato soup with bread and butter?' she says. I don't want it because I'm just not hungry but say 'Thank you very much that would be lovely,' and feel a bit embarrassed about her having to be so nice to me when I'm not really ill.

'Good, I'll bring it up for you after High Tea.'

Then there's silence again because everyone's in the dining room. I like it that I'm completely alone by myself right at the top of the school. I get out of the bed and look out of the window far across to the other side of the river. The tide's so low you can see a great stretch of yellow sand. There's a man walking alone along the shore. When I look really hard I can see he's got a walking stick and is wearing Wellington boots. Perhaps he lives all by himself in a little cottage and though he's not so very far away from me, it's miles and miles to get to where he is because you'd have to travel such a long way to find a bridge that he might as well be living in another country. I want to be him. I want to go from here and be grown up and have a new life, miles away on the other side of the river.

When Miss Carson brings the soup, I have it although I'm not the least bit hungry. I wipe the plate clean with the bread and butter so that she'll be pleased with me. When she comes back to get my tray she draws the curtains. As she's going out of the door, she tells me to have a good night's rest in a strict sort of voice, but I know she means it kindly. I lie back on the pillow for a while getting used to the darkness. Then I get up and tiptoe to the window and draw the curtain back to look out to see if the man with the Wellingtons is still there, but he's gone of course, and the sun's going down on the other side of the school. There's the shadow of the great big chimneys that are at either end of the building, stretching right across the cricket nets and the tennis court and touching the river like the fingers of a long ghostly hand. The colour of the sand on the far away side has changed from yellow to dark brown. I go back to bed and think about the long evening because I'm so far away from being sleepy. The pictures of Mummy and the noise she was making come back into my head, and I remember that I was dreaming about her when Nick woke me up.

It was a nightmare, really. I was in my bed at home in the middle of the night and heard a noise. When I looked out of the window, I saw Mummy in a white nightdress on the lawn in the moonlight. She was crying and saying that she had lost something and was sure she'd never be able to find it again and I must help her look, and so I went downstairs to cheer her up. I don't know where my dad was in the dream—probably on one of his foreign trips. When I asked her what we were looking for, she was crying so much that I wasn't able to understand her properly. But we looked anyway. We emptied all the drawers in her bedroom, and then we went through my dad's wardrobe looking in all the pockets in his jackets and trousers and leaving them all piled up in a mess on the bed. Then we went to the downstairs cloakroom and took the lid off the lavatory cistern to have a look in there, and we checked inside the oven and the ice compartment in the fridge with Mummy still crying but more softly now. She kept saying 'I must find it, I must find it,' over and over again. We let down the ladder that goes up into the attic where we keep my trunk when I'm on holiday, and Mummy climbed up while

I held her waist to make sure she didn't fall down. She shone a torch around, and still she was saying 'I must find it, I must find it,' and I think that's when Nick came in and woke me up.

—*m*—

'Pop your dressing gown and slippers on. We don't want you getting splinters from those stairs, do we?'

It's Mr. England. I'm not nearly asleep when he comes in. I'd just been thinking about trying to listen to Radio Luxembourg, but then I thought it really wasn't a very good idea because I don't want to be found out when everyone has been so nice to me. There was just a little knock on the door and then a pause so I knew it wasn't Miss Carson because she just comes straight in, and it wasn't going to be any of the boys because it's already after lights out.

'Special treat, Ben,' he says, 'Matron says you can come to my room and listen to some music for half an hour. Would you like that?'

It feels like I'm going on an adventure in the middle of the night, a bit like having a midnight feast.

I've been in his room before to listen to music, and it's really the most special treat. Last term when it snowed for a whole week and rugby was cancelled I went in there twice on games afternoons. The first time was with Theo and Glossop from the fifth form who's learning to play the violin and is probably going to be a musician. Theo probably won't ever be invited again, though, on account of falling asleep during the Vienna Boys' Choir. The next time it was me and Ford, who's the head boy, and another prefect called Johnson who goes to every single concert there is and has his own portable record player that the teachers let him have because he only ever plays classical music. So that's me in Mr. England's room with two prefects, and I'm just a third former!

To get to his room, you open a tiny door just outside surgery and then straight in front there are stairs that go steeply upwards almost like being on a ladder. You have to be quite careful not to bang your head, and it's a bit like climbing a tower in a medieval castle. I really don't know how Mr. England manages to get up and down, because it's difficult enough even for boys let alone when you're as tall as he is. When you reach the very last step, there's a door and that's where his room is. If you were inside and didn't know about the stairs, you'd open it and fall straight down to the bottom. 'Careful now, Ben,' he keeps saying. 'Watch where you're going. Sorry about the lack of light.'

But it's lovely inside the room when you get here, as cosy as anything. You can't get farther up than this. It's like it's nothing to do with the school, because everywhere else has bare floorboards and hardly any furniture and that horrid schooley smell of mouldy old games kit, dubbin and floor polish, and cooking smells from the kitchen. But Mr. England's room smells of his clean shirt for the morning that's hanging on a hook behind his door and of something nice that he puts on his face probably after he has his shave.

The ceiling slopes down on both sides, right from the very top to the bottom, like a triangle. There are two high up windows and a cosy gas fire at one end, which makes the room warm as toast in the winter with shelves on either side of it that he's made himself from bricks which are holding up planks of wood with rows and rows of records and books on them. The weight of it all is making them sag, and right in the middle of the bendiest bit, he's got his record player. One day I should think they're all going to fall down. His bed's very low down, behind the door with a tartan rug on it just like we have in our dorms. 'I've kept it since I was at school,' he told me when I saw it the first time, 'I'm very attached to it still.' Next to it, there's a big armchair—all sagging in the middle, like the shelves, and there's another rug thrown over it, and he's got a swivelly chair and a small desk with an electric typewriter on it. Next to the typewriter he's put a bunch of yellow roses which are getting old now, and some of the petals are falling onto the floor. Above the bed there's a huge picture of a sad looking clown and also a smaller one, which is a photograph of somewhere called King's College Cambridge where they have one of the very best choirs in all the world. He's got records of them singing that I've heard. He hasn't got the big light from the ceiling switched on, just two teeny lamps—one on his little bedside table and one on the floor by the fire.

It's very tidy, this room. Absolutely full up of things, but very tidy. It's not at all like his chaotic car.

I don't think the blue folder's in here. I wouldn't be able to see it even if it was, but I just don't think it's here. And it's probably not left in his crashed up car either, because he must have gone to get all the stuff out by now. I hope he's thrown it away. I really do, because I'm sure he knows it's not alright to have something like that in your car or in this nice room. Anyway, I'm not going to worry about it anymore. I'm just going to pretend that I never ever saw it. Whatever was in his blooming old car, Mr. England's still the best master in the school as far as I'm concerned. In fact, I just think it's possible that it wasn't anything to do with him in the first place, and he might not have known about it anyway.

He puts a pan of milk on the tiny gas stove and makes us a mug of cocoa. I'm sitting cross-legged on the bed holding it with both hands. There's a plate of digestive biscuits on the floor in front of me, and for the first time today I feel a bit hungry, but I'm being polite and trying not to eat them all in too much of a hurry.

'Listen to this, Ben...' He goes over to the saggy shelves and chooses a record, which he takes out of the cover ever so carefully, so he's just touching the edges. He breathes onto it as though it's a mirror, wipes it with a little yellow cloth and bends down to put it on the record player. Then he turns up the volume as he puts the needle on and just for a second there's a noisy silence before the music starts.

It's a cello and a piano and nothing else, and the sound of it fills up every bit of the room. The cello is terribly sad, and then the piano talks ever so gently back as though he's trying to cheer it up. I know that Mr. England has chosen it specially. Whenever he does that it's always something that I like, and this is one of the most beautiful pieces of music that I've ever heard. While it's playing, Mr. England sits in the big chair with his legs crossed and his hands tucked between his knees which is his usual position for listening to very lovely music. His eyes are closed. When the music finishes it's like he's been asleep, but then he's quickly wide awake and gets up to lift the needle off just as another piece is starting.

'What was that, Sir?'

'Brahms. The adagio affetuoso from his Cello Sonata No. 2. Did you like it?'

'Yes, I did, Sir, very much. I think he must have written it when he was feeling very sad about something.'

'Yes, and the thing is that bad, sad things happen to all of us now and again, and I think that the music is saying that it's alright to express those things, don't you think?'

'Yes, Sir. I think it is saying that.'

'I think it's time for a little Beethoven. How about the Violin Romances? They're two short pieces he wrote as a practise for his Violin Concerto. I've remembered how much you enjoyed that last term, Ben.'

I close my eyes to listen when it starts, just like Mr. England does. The music goes right inside me and warms my chest, and I hope that the feeling will stay in me forever and not seep out again after it's finished.

When I open my eyes, Mr. England is smiling at me. 'Do you think your mother's like you, Ben?'

'Yes, I think she is, really.'

'Then I think she must be a very sweet person.'

When he says that, I blush a bit and wonder if we're going to talk about Mummy and all the things that happened yesterday. But he doesn't say anything more about her after that. I think that if he knew her, he would in fact like her quite a lot, and they might even be good friends during the times when she's not drinking too much sherry.

Then there's a knock at the door. Mr. England leaps out of his chair and quickly turns the music right down. I don't think he's used to anyone coming up those funny stairs. He opens the door very carefully.

'Is Ben Teasdale with you, England?' It's Mr. Burston.

.z'Yes, but it's nearly ten o'clock.'

I can't see Mr. Burston, because he's hidden behind the door, but I can tell by his voice that he's trying not to be angry. 'I really think he ought to be in bed by now, don't you?'

'Gosh, is it really that late? I think we rather forgot about the time, didn't we, Ben?' Even though it's quite dark, I can see that Mr. England's face is turning red, and so is mine, because I'm listening to a master who's being told off. It's very embarrassing, and I think it's my fault.

'Come on young man, bed! Now! Immediately!' says Mr. Burston from behind the door.

I get off Mr. England's bed and put the empty cocoa mug on the little side table.

'Thank you for the lovely music, Sir,' I say to Mr. England who's got his back to me and is putting the record away in its sleeve. He doesn't say anything as I go out of the door. Mr. Burston's in the dark and all doubled up because of the low ceiling on the stairs; he pushes himself up against the wall to let me pass by. I can't see him properly except for his glasses that are catching the light from the inside of the room, and I feel scared by the look of him. He puts his hand on my back and pushes me a little so that just for a bit I think I'm going to fall down the deep dark stairs.

'Now straight back to sickbay, Teasdale,' he says, 'and I'll be down in a minute to check on you.'

As he's turning off the light after following me down, I say, 'Thank you for letting me listen to the music with Mr. England, Sir.' The room goes black. 'It was ever so nice…' I'm not sure if Mr. Burston hears me though, because he says nothing as the door is closing. I hope that it makes him less cross though, because I don't want Mr. England to be in trouble because of me when he was just being kind.

———

Mr. England's late again like he was the day of his accident, but we know he's here because he was in Assembly just now. He did a secret wink at me when he came into the hall with the other masters, so now I'm not worried about him being in trouble about me being up so late in his room last night.

It's Saturday, and it's my first lesson since I went to sickbay on Thursday afternoon. I had breakfast downstairs, and everyone's been asking what I was ill with. I'm saying that I had a tiny bit of a tummy ache and sickness and diarrhea, so I was in quarantine.

Saturday classes are different. They don't feel so strict because it's very nearly the weekend, and there are lessons only till lunchtime. I think the teachers feel that they're already on a bit of a weekend holiday and can't be bothered with us so much. I always look forward to Mr. England's classes anyway, but especially today because it's Scripture, and last week he said he was going to set up the tape recorder and tell us about gospel singing and Negro spirituals. We're going to hear a man with a very deep singing voice whose name is Paul Robeson. I've remembered that from last week.

We're not in our usual classroom. We're in the first formers' classroom on account of their not being here because they're too small for school on Saturdays. When Mr. England uses the tape recorder we're either in the entrance hall or up here away from all the other classrooms, so that the noise doesn't disturb the rest of the school. It used to be a dormitory, and it's right underneath Northumberland where I was last term. If ever we're in here I try to be the first in so that I can sit by one of the two big windows and look out up the hill to the village.

Everyone is chattering like mad because we're quite far away from the other classes, and there's no one to tell us to be quiet.

Macer-Wright keeps shouting, 'Keep it down, keep it down,' but no one's taking any notice. If it goes on much longer, I think that Miss Carson will come in because surgery's not so far away, and the noise will start disturbing her.

They're having a go at Bradshaw, one of the day boys. There are only three in the school, and they're always being teased. Bradshaw's got an accent like the people in the village, and so they pick on him and call him a peasant. His clothes are different from ours, too. His shirts are far too big for him, and his grey trousers are made of a different material from everybody else's. I don't think his parents bought all his clothes from the school shop. He loses his temper when people go on about it and then gets into fights, but he's no good at that so everybody tries to get him going so they can laugh at him.

I don't join in though. I just look out of the window. I don't want to have anyone asking me questions about going to lunch with Mummy and coming back ill. But actually, it doesn't seem that anyone is interested. No one from school saw me in the park except for Mr. Burston, and then only the matrons when we got back. All the masters must know, though. They'll have been talking about it in the common room for sure and feeling sorry for me.

Theo's got hold of Bradshaw's tie now and is dragging him round so that his face is going all red. Everybody's shouting, especially Macer-Wright who's telling everyone to 'Flipping shut up.' It gets noisier and noisier. I can't believe that no one has come in to tell us off.

I stare out of the window daydreaming about the man that I saw last night walking along far away on the other side of the river. Even though the window's open at the top, it's hot in here, and it's making me feel quite sleepy. My eyes are stuck on looking at some geraniums in a window box opposite the front door of the school, and I try to keep them open.

And then I see the car, right beside the geraniums. Just its roof at first, all lopsided, because the wheels must be up on the pavement. I'm wide awake in a second, and my heart is beating so hard and fast I think it's going to come out of my mouth. I push my face up against the window so I can see down into the street better.

It's a police car.

I know it, even though I can only see a bit of it. There's a light on the top, though it's not flashing. There's no one inside. It's just parked there, waiting.

It must be here because of me. Perhaps it's the very same car as Thursday with the very same policemen. They've come to ask me some questions, but I won't speak to them about Mummy, however much they want me to. I won't answer, just the same as I wouldn't answer the doctor.

I slip along the bench away from the window to the farthest end of the desk so that I can't see out anymore. Perhaps the car will go away in a minute. Perhaps the police have come to speak to the lady who has the geraniums. She's probably got a son who's a bit trouble-some and has been smashing window panes. They're not coming into the school. They're not here about me and Mummy. It can't be about her because she's back at the hospital safe and sound like my dad said she was.

I can't stay not looking out though, and I slide back along the desk to the window again, and I tell myself that there'll be no sign of the car now. I only saw it for a tiny moment, and I think that my eyes made it up because I was a bit sleepy for a while.

But when I look down again, it's still there, waiting.

My chest goes funny, like it did when I came back from the park, and I can hear myself breathing. It's a bit like I'm living under wa-ter, and the noise all around me sounds like bubbles. My hands are shaking, and suddenly I want to have a pee so badly that I can't stop myself. I can feel the warmth beginning to spread in my trousers and run down my leg. And then I'm by the door and open it. I pray with all my might that no one will notice that my pants are wet. I can hear Macer-Wright telling me in a surprised voice to come back and sit down, but I don't take any notice.

When I get to the lavatory I see the pee's all down my leg, but there's not so much coming through my trousers on account of them being shorts. For once I'm glad that my dad hasn't bought me long trousers yet. I unzip them and wipe my legs dry with loo paper. I feel a bit better as though I'm not in the water anymore although there's a ringing sound in my ears. When I look in the mirror my face is white and wet and I splash it with cold water from the tap. Then I splash my trousers and shirt, too, so that I can say that I got all faint and had to wash my face, and the water spilt all over my clothes.

I walk slowly back along the corridor wishing that I was never going to arrive at the classroom. I'm so worried about the questions that will be asked about the wetness, and it's just about possible that Theo might tell the whole of 3b about the bedwetting secret.

There's shouting and banging of desk lids coming from inside as I put my hand on the doorknob, but then, just as I'm opening it, I hear Cartwright shout 'Look!' and he's right by the window and pointing outside. Just for a second there's complete stillness and silence, followed by the noise of everyone rushing over to get a good view. The whole class is climbing on the desks and clambering over each other pushing and shoving; meanwhile no one says anything at all.

'It's Mr. England!' Theo says in a great loud whisper after a bit. I walk over to the window behind the first overcrowded one because I can see there's a little space to see out at the very bottom.

I'm just in time to see Mr. England is by the open door of the car and a tall policeman is holding his elbow just like the one the other day was holding Mummy's. The policeman lets him go, and Mr. England puts his hand on the roof above the door and bends his head to get in. But just before he does that, he runs his fingers through his hair like he always does and then looks behind himself and glances up at us for a tiny second. There's not the slightest expression on his face. Everybody ducks away from the window as though there might be a shot about to be fired. And then he disappears into the car.

When we look out again, it's just possible to hear the engine starting up. The police car drives away without being in a hurry and without the blue light going on. Then we're all left still staring at the empty space where the car was. Slowly by slowly we get down and go to our seats in silence because no one knows what to say.

'He's been arrested,' says Theo after quite a long time, 'Mr. England's been arrested!'

At lunch everyone talks about the arrest, of course. All of us boys, that is. It's a funny sort of talking that everyone's doing—fast and sort of whispery. No one wants the teachers to realise that we know about it, because they're not saying anything at all, and we just know not to ask them.

Mr. Burston eventually came into the classroom this morning and told us to be quiet, although by that time you could have heard a pin drop. He looked very, very worried. He never said a thing about Mr. England being indisposed or anything like that and straight-away told Macer-Wright to keep control, and then he set us an essay. The subject was 'The walk in the forest' which is the same as last week after Mr. England's accident. He's forgotten that, though. Mrs. Marston was going to take us for French after that, but she just never came in, so we continued to pretend writing the essay and began to whisper about what had happened.

Miss Carson is sitting at the top of my table. She's very quiet, but that's not so strange because sometimes she can be chatty and some-times not. Today, she's not. Mr. Tulley's on the next table reading his Daily Telegraph with his seat tilted back and the paper mostly hiding his face. He reads it in class sometimes when he's fed up with us but never ever at lunch. Mrs. Marston's on the seniors' table. It's a rule on Saturday lunchtimes that whichever table she sits at has to speak French, so that means it's mostly a silent lunch on that table, and I don't think the subject of Mr. England is going to come up.

When we were coming along the corridor to lunch just now, I

was at the end of the queue, and when it stopped for a bit by the Headmaster's study, I saw in because the door was open. Mr. Burston was standing beside his desk with the phone in his hand. Mrs. Burston was sitting in a chair leaning right forward rocking backwards and forwards with her elbows on her knees and her hands under her chin. When she saw us she quickly got up to close the door. They haven't come into lunch; that's very unusual.

—·—

We're having a game of cricket. My position is deeply fine leg which is miles away from where the batting is, so I'm lying in the long grass, which is just about my favourite place. I'm in Henry Pugh's team, but he's lenient about me not being interested, and they've forgotten about me. I think that's especially true today after what happened this morning.

Now, instead of seeing Mummy's face, I'm seeing Mr. England's when he was getting in the car. There's a picture in The National Geographic in the library of a cheetah holding a gazelle in its teeth, halfway through suffocating it, but there's no expression on the poor thing's face. You can't see if it's frightened, or in pain, or anything else—just staring eyes, waiting to be dead. That's what Mr. England looked like.

On the walk down here to the playing field I heard Walby and Jones from the sixth form talking about it all; I was just in front of them. They saw that I was listening and told me to scarper, but I managed to hear some of it. Apparently, there were two police cars. The second one came a bit later and was parked farther down the street by the kitchen door so it wasn't so noticeable. There was a detective that went up to Mr. England's room. Walby saw him by accident when he was just coming out of Matron's Surgery in the middle of the morning. He wasn't in class with everyone else because he's got a poisoned toe and had to have it cleaned out by Miss Carson.

There's all sorts of ideas going round about why Mr. England's been arrested. Theo says it's because he hated his mother, and he's murdered her and buried her in a wood in Kent. Now they've dug her up and discovered all about it. I think that's completely ridiculous. He's not anything like a murderer, and I've even heard him talking about his mother. It seems to me he liked her very much. Chirl says he's probably been committing embezzling because he needed some money to help his father buy his house in Monmouth. But most people in senior are saying it's because actually the car crash last week was really his fault, and he's not been telling the truth about it.

But I think it's because of the blue folder.

It's Sunday afternoon, and we're getting ready for the finals of the school tennis tournament. All the benches that are usually kept under the veranda have been brought right to the edge of the tennis court, and there are lots of chairs from inside the classrooms. It's really hot again, and so we've all been given permission to unbutton our shirtsleeves and roll them up.

The school tennis finals are really important. There's something that's always exciting about this day, just like a sort of mini Sports Day in fact. That doesn't happen till the very last day of term, but the tennis match usually means we're about halfway through the term, and sometimes everyone goes away straight after. That's not happening this time though because half term starts next week. But it still feels like a special day. We have tea outside to make it like a picnic, and it's all set out on the trestle tables under the veranda. The Tennis Gala Cup is in the middle of all the sandwiches, shining away ready to be presented by Mrs. Marston who was a junior champion player herself once. Henry Pugh's parents have come from Cardiff to watch him play, and they've brought his sister Isabelle, who's very beautiful. All the seniors are looking at her. Tom Whickham's parents aren't here, of course, because they live abroad in Hong Kong.

The Headmaster and Mrs. Burston are up on the veranda outside their sitting room with Miss Carson, and Miss Newman's there too, with baby Mark on her lap. Mr. Short, who takes us for geography, is sitting at the end of the row of benches with his wife who we haven't seen for a very long time because she's not been so well. She's in a wheelchair now, poor thing. The silly old cook's here in a big red frock with her husband who hasn't got any teeth at the front. Probably her horrid cooking has rotted them away. Mr. Benson the odd job man's looking very pleased because the Headmaster's just called down to congratulate him on getting the grass and fences nice and ready for today after the big storm. We did three cheers for him, and he blushed bright red. His wife from the laundry, who's got a hat on instead of her curlers, smiled and waved at everybody when she got here. I know it's a bit of an occasion, but who the blooming heck does she think she is—the Queen Mother?

Only Mr. England is missing. But I think he might be coming back tomorrow because on the way out of church this morning I heard Mr. Burston telling Ford that he was going to be reading the lesson in Morning Assembly, and Mr. England would give him the chapter straight after breakfast. So that must mean that the Headmaster knows he's coming back. It's the first time we've heard any of the staff talk about him; that's a very good thing. Probably the police have just told him off about something to do with his car, and it's nothing to do at all with the blue folder like I thought.

Mr. Tulley's going to be the umpire. He's already sat on the other side of the net in a high up chair smoking a pipe, which is what he does on important days instead of cigarettes. He's just told Whick-ham and Pugh to start warming up.

Mrs. Marston's sitting on the bench right in the middle facing Mr. Tulley. She loves anything to do with tennis, so she's in an especially good mood. She's changed out of the clothes she was wearing at church this morning, and now she's got on big sunglasses, red lip-stick, and a pair of slacks, which are showing her legs. All the seniors fancy her, and they're always talking about her, even more than they talk about Miss Newman's big bosoms. She's twenty-three years old. We know that because it came out in a French lesson when we were learning to say how old we are. She said 'j'ai vingt-trois ans,' and that's how we found out. Although that's quite old, it's younger than the other teachers apart from Miss Newman and Mr. England. Her husband works in Gloucester and sometimes comes to fetch her from school in his e-type Jaguar. He must be very rich to have such a snazzy car.

All Mrs. Marston's favourite seniors are around her, sucking up as usual. Johnson's on one side, Wallington's on the other, and Ford is right behind leaning over to tell her something. She likes Johnson on account of his being good at music, and he's got a real crush on her. He's holding an umbrella over her head to stop her getting sunburned. Ford's one of her favourites on account of the fact he's 'debonair'. That's what she says about him. It means he's carefree and gay—I looked it up in the dictionary. But Wallington's her real favourite. He's the best rugby player in the school and is going to Brecon College next term, even if he doesn't do so well in his common entrance, because he's so good at that game. He's a bit like a grown-up in a way. He had a broken voice and cubic hair by the time he was eleven, and he's very, very strong. Also, he's got the biggest willy in the whole school. I've seen it when he's been in the foot bath after games because he walks around without a towel round himself to show it off. He's as famous for his big willy as he is for the rugby. Lorrimer and Theo said that once when they were down at the playing field they saw him rolling around in the long grass kissing Mrs. Marston with his shirt all unbuttoned, but I'm not sure that can really be true, because I don't think a teacher would do that even with someone who's a senior and as grown up as Wallington. He's still only thirteen, after all. But she does seem to like him an awful lot.

Tom Whickham's won the first set. If he gets the next one, it means he's won the whole tournament and is the best player in the school both at tennis and at table tennis, and Pugh will be the second best. One day Tom Whickham will be Mrs. Marston's favourite because of being such a good player and so good looking at the same time.

I'm not really watching the tennis though, because I'm looking at Tom Thumb. I've managed to sit on the same bench as Gilligan, even though everybody else wanted to. It was just by accident really. I was already sitting down and he came along and sat beside me, so I've got the best view of his blazer pocket where Tom Thumb is living. He's poking his head out and looking around. Gilligan's all proud even though his face is wet with sweat from having to wear his blazer because of the pocket.

It's the strangest thing in the whole world that Gilligan's Tom Thumb is still alive when all the others have died. Theo's been keeping a little space in the graveyard especially for him, and now it might just be that he'll never have to be put there. Fancy Gilligan being the best at looking after his chick! You'd never think it was possible if you saw him. He's absolutely the clumsiest boy in the whole school. Last term he dropped a whole crate of milk that he was carrying in for milk break; I never saw Miss Carson so angry. Later on, when she'd calmed down, I heard her saying that he was just growing too fast. Sometimes his voice is all deep, then it suddenly goes squeaky, and he's getting very bad spots now. It's dead odd because although he's getting bigger all over, it looks as though his feet and hands are growing even faster than the rest of him. The funniest thing is when he's in the swimming pool. He tries so hard, but however much he kicks his legs, he moves just a very few inches with tons and tons of splashing. He's got a great big head and all the wet curls on it go from side to side with the spray making a mist, and his mouth's wide open with his eyes shut tight. You can't help but have a good laugh at him.

But with Tom Thumb, he's just somehow managed to do it alright. When he's feeding him, he'll be concentrating so hard that his tongue will come out with the effort of trying to get his great big fingers to do what he wants them to, and there's Tom Thumb, fluttering his wings like mad while he sits in the middle of Gilligan's palm, eating the spiders and things that are being put straight into his mouth. Then Gilligan sticks out one of his fingers, and Tom Thumb perches on it looking around at everything and taking it all in. Probably he's forgotten his parents by now. He must think he's a human being, and Gilligan is his dad. It's a really brilliant thing to watch actually, especially since he's been doing a bit of flying around the locker room and then coming back to Gilligan's hand.

Henry Pugh has managed to win the second set, which is a surprise because he wasn't looking so good after losing the first one. Everyone shouts encouragement because now it's a really exciting game that's going to go on for another whole set. Tom Whickham looks up at Mrs. Marston, trying to lip read what she's saying, which I can see is 'keep up close to the net!' You can see that she wants him to win.

Whickham's won the first game in the set after quite a bit of effort. The ball's been going back and forward for the longest time in the match and then Whickham, who's doing what Mrs. Marston told him to and is right up to the net, hits the ball so that it goes to the far corner of the court right behind Pugh to where he can't possibly hit it back. There's a huge cheer, and I can hear the Headmaster's booming voice shouting out, 'Jolly good rally!' Just at that moment, I look at Tom Thumb sitting in Gilligan's palm. I don't know whether it's because of the noise, but suddenly he flaps his wings and hovers in the air about six inches above Gilligan's hand. He stays like that for a second or two, like a hummingbird, and then he's on top of Gilligan's head, burying himself in his curly hair. I start to laugh and so does Gilligan. He's got a very loud laugh so that the whole school looks at him, and when they see what's happening, with Tom Thumb looking out from inside the curls, they start to laugh as well.

'Quiet, please,' says Mr. Tulley, 'Whickham leads in the final set by one game to nil. Two sets all. Resume play, please. Mr. Whickham to serve.'

Gilligan slowly puts his hand up towards his head so that Tom Thumb can sit in his palm again, and just as he gets it to his forehead, the chick half jumps and half flies back into his hand. He ruffles his feathers for a bit like birds do when they're having a bath and cocks his head to one side.

And then, Gilligan's palm is empty again. Tom Thumb swoops over the tennis court just as Whickham's about to throw the ball in the air to serve. Everyone breathes in with surprise, and I can hear Webster and the other small boys nearly screaming with excitement. Tom Thumb has reached right to the other side of the court, and he's sitting on the post that's holding up the fence behind Mr. Tulley. There's a second of silence and then another cheer. Tom Thumb rearranges his feathers as though he's showing off. Whickham smiles and lets the ball drop. He puts his hands on his hips while he stares at the little bird, and even Mr. Tulley who was trying to get them to restart the match has taken the pipe out of his mouth and swiveled round in his chair to look up at the post. Gilligan's got a smile on his face.

Tom Thumb looks different now. Just a minute ago he was a fluffy ball in Gilligan's palm. Now he's as sleek as though his feathers have been oiled, and he looks like all the other house martins that are flying around high up in the sky above us. He's not a chick anymore, and no one had noticed him changing. Perhaps it all happened right this very minute as he crossed the court.

He's flying again! He's swooping straight along the net, just like he did the first time, and everybody makes a whooping noise. Gilligan puts his hand in the air, and Tom Thumb heads straight for it. When he just about gets there, he hovers again, only an inch or two away as though he's trying to decide whether to land or not. Just for a single second, he touches Gilligan's fingers, though he never stops beating his wings.

Then he's off.

He flies back towards the post, a bit higher this time, and when he reaches it, he doesn't stop. He's past it and dipping down below the hedges that are on the river bank, and he's out of sight. When he comes back into view, he's over the water and getting higher and higher. I shield my eyes from the sun like everybody else and strain to look for him. Before long he's up nearly as high as the other house martins. For a moment, he turns and it seems he might be coming back, but he's still getting higher and higher, far away over the river and still climbing, doing loops and swirling round. Then I don't know which one is him because he's just the merest black dot amongst all the others.

He's gone. He's not coming back. Everybody knows it.

Ford, who's been leaning over Mrs. Marston's bench, stands up straight and looks at Gilligan. He puts his hands above his head and starts to clap. Then Wallington stands up and joins in, and it spreads to the whole school with everyone on their feet. Mr. Tulley gets down from his high up seat so he's standing as well, and Mrs. Marston joins in the clapping, though she doesn't stand up. Even the Headmaster's balcony has joined in with baby Mark clapping his little hands together while he's sitting on Miss Newman's lap.

'Well done, Flopsy,' shouts Ford, because that's what the seniors call Gilligan. He's the only one sitting down now, and I'm right beside him standing up and clapping with everybody else. When I look at his face I see there are huge tears rolling down his cheeks. They're falling on his great big clumsy hands that looked after Tom Thumb so well, and where he was sitting just a few moments ago before he flew away to freedom.

Mr. England's not come back after all. The whole of Monday morning has gone by, and he's still not here.

I knew it before everybody else. Mr. Short came into breakfast this morning and leaned over the prefects' table with a Bible open in his hand, so I knew he was setting the chapter for Ford to read in

Assembly. That's usually Mr. England's job. Mr. Short never usually comes into breakfast because he lives in the village with his wife in their own house, and the first we see of him is in Morning Assembly. And it's dead odd for him to set the lesson anyway. Mr. Burston does it when Mr. England's not here, and that hardly ever happens.

Now I'm absolutely sure that something terrible has happened because yesterday even Mr. Burston was expecting him back today. He told Ford that Mr. England would be setting the lesson. I thought everything would be back to normal, and I really hate it that it's not.

No one on my table seemed to notice Mr. Short coming into the dining room apart from me. None of the others mentioned it during the rest of breakfast, nor when we all went upstairs for bed making, and not even when we were queuing for Assembly. I kept my mouth shut. I didn't want to start a conversation about it because if I was to say it out loud and everyone started saying 'You're right, Teasdale. He's still not back,' it would feel as though it becomes the real proper truth. I didn't want that. I really didn't want that.

When I was making my bed I prayed so hard for it not to be true that Mr. England still wasn't here. We came downstairs, and I listened for his voice in the Common Room. While I was standing outside the door, Mr. Short opened it to come out. I wanted to peep in to see if the brown corduroy jacket was over the chair by his desk. But it wasn't. Before the Assembly bell, even though his Mini's wrecked and will never be there again, I went outside to look at the empty space by the kitchen where he used to park it.

After that I felt better for a bit because then I was thinking that even if he wasn't back it didn't necessarily mean it was anything at all to do with the police coming on Saturday. It was quite possible that he'd phoned to say that he was delayed because he was staying with his father and would be the tiniest bit late, because, after all, his arrangements must be different now that he doesn't have the car. When I told myself that, it worked in my head for a moment, and I was feeling quite a bit better about it. But it didn't last because there was immediately another voice in my head saying that Mr. England is never late whatever happens, so then I was worried again and searched every corner of my brain for a better explanation.

At Morning Assembly, when the door opened, we all stood up as usual. Mrs. Marston came in first, as she usually does because she's the only lady member of the teaching staff apart from Mrs. Agnes the art teacher, who's only here in the afternoons on account of looking after her little granddaughter in the mornings. The really strange thing is that it was as though I had x-ray eyes and could see who was in the corridor following her, and I absolutely knew that Mr. England was still not here. I was thinking so hard about it that just for a minute I didn't see that Mr. Burston was missing as well.

When the masters had reached their seats under the plaque with the names of all the old boys who died in the wars, Lucky Lorrimer, who was standing beside me, whispered, 'Mr. England's not back,' and then it was no good making up stories for myself anymore. That's when it really became the truth.

Mr. Short took Assembly because he is the Deputy Headmaster. It was ever so strange. It was the first time I've seen him do it. It felt all wrong. He doesn't have a loud voice like Mr. Burston, and it was sounding a bit wobbly, just the same as when I had to sing Once in Royal David's City at the carol concert last Christmas, and I got all nervous about it. But I don't really think he could have been that bothered because he is a grown-up and a teacher after all.

Assembly usually finishes straight after the hymn, and that's the time when Mr. Burston makes his announcements, like last week when we were all told off about how much lavatory paper the school was getting through, and he said that it wasn't necessary to use more than two or three pieces at a time. It was very embarrassing.

We all waited to see if Mr. Short would say anything after we finished singing, but he just picked up his prayer book and started to go towards the door. The other masters were following him and then, when he was opening the door, he paused very suddenly so that there was nearly a collision of masters behind him. He turned back to face us all and said, 'Mr. England and Mr. Burston are indisposed, probably for the rest of the day,' and then he went out.

That's all. So we still don't know what is going on. We've had French and English this morning with Mrs. Marston, and she's said nothing about it of course. And then, after milk break, we had Mr. Short for geography, which was a very boring lesson about all the steel they make in Sheffield, and still there's not the slightest clue about what's going on. It feels like an emergency is happening, and it's made worse by the fact that Mr. Burston isn't in class either. He is here though. I saw him during the break going from the entrance hall into his study. I can see by his face that there's something very, very wrong.

There's a very strange feeling all around the school—sort of silent and mysterious, and a bit spooky. When we went into lunch there wasn't the usual talking when we all sit down after grace. Mr. Burston came in specially to say it, because they hadn't remembered to appoint anyone, but the oddest thing is that he nearly forgot the words for a second, even though it's only one sentence without punctuation, and an 'amen' at the end. He said, 'For what we are about to receive…' and then there was a long pause before he carried on, and after that he went out again without having any lunch at all.

I don't know why I feel so worried about it all. I haven't done anything wrong. None of it is my fault. But I'm just waiting for something bad to happen. Just waiting, and I hate waiting more than anything.

—m—

After lunch I sit in Mrs. Agnes's art class in the library. I'm quite good at art, but I just can't concentrate at all today. She's telling us all about perspective, but it's not going into my head. Mrs. Agnes isn't in the school very much, and I'm not at all sure she knows about what's going on. She's just told us that she's going to take prep this evening because Mr. England isn't available today. I think Theo thought that he could find something out and asked her why he wasn't here, and she said 'I don't know' with a look on her face that proves she knows nothing about it. Probably the other masters haven't told her because I don't think they like her very much. She's not at all like the other members of the staff. I think she used to be a beatnik, actually. Her hair, which is very white, is up in a bun but with straggly bits all around, and she wears an artist's smock with paint all over it—even when she's not in class—and a blue denim skirt and sandals on her feet. She's got a badge on that says 'Ban the bomb,' and she votes for Harold Wilson. Last term when George Brown was in all the papers because he had an argument with Harold Wilson and got the sack, I heard Mrs. Marston saying to her 'No doubt you'll miss your friend Mr. Brown,' but she was frowning a bit when she said it. Mrs. Agnes just looked the other way.

Fisheye said to Chirl just now as we were coming into the library, 'It's all quite ominous, quite ominous...' I knew he was talking about Mr. England. I thought that perhaps he'd heard something new about the situation, so while the others were laying the big oil cloth on the library table and setting out the paints, I had a quick look in the dictionary. It said ominous means threatening, like a bad omen, and that means he used exactly the right word if you ask me.

The picture I'm doing isn't working. I'm trying to do a long street with some mountains at the end of it, but I've started it too low down, so now I've got far too much sky in it.

I put up my hand up, and Mrs. Agnes looks at me over her spectacles and smiles because I'm one of her favourites.

'Yes, Teasdale?'

'Could I start again, please, Mrs. Agnes? This has gone all wrong.'

Before she can say anything there's a knock at the door, and it opens as she says, 'Come in.'

It's Mr. Burston. 'Ah, Mrs. Agnes. Sorry to interrupt all your little Michelangelos.' He pauses and closes the door. He leans his back against it and uses his finger to count and check all the boys in the room, and then he says, 'Do we have young Mr. Teasdale here?'

I slowly put my hand up in the air and straightaway there's wetness dribbling down onto my fingers because the paintbrush is still in my hand, and all at the same time my chest is going a bit funny like I'm wearing something that's too tight.

'There you are!' he says, 'Just the fellow I want to see,' and then he's properly pointing at me and smiling.

We walk along the corridor towards his study, and his hand is on the back of my head, which I don't like because it feels as though he's pushing me along. He hasn't said anything to me about why he's come to take me out of the class, and I don't want to ask him. When we get to the door of his study, his hand goes down to my shoulder, and I stand there as though I'm at attention while he opens it.

There's a man sitting behind Mr. Burston's desk with his back to the window. At first I can't see him very clearly because of the light coming through. The rest of the room is ever so dark.

'Benjamin, this is Mr. Lightfoot. He wants to ask you one or two questions,' says Mr. Burston.

'What about, Sir? Have I done something wrong?'

I didn't want to say that. I really didn't, but it just came out before I could stop myself.

'Nothing at all, nothing at all,' he says back to me.

'Hello, Benny. How are you?' the man says.

That's not my name. I hate it when people call me that. He smiles and waits for me to say something.

'I'm very well, thank you.' The man's got long brown teeth and a big forehead with a few wisps of oily white hair all combed back and pressing against his scalp which looks pink and itchy.

'Sit down, Benjamin,' says Mr. Burston, and he pulls up a wicker chair the same as the one in sickbay. I do what he says and look at my hands on my lap, wondering what is going to happen and trying to think what the man might ask me, and what I might say. Then

I wonder if I can do the same as I did to the doctor and just not say anything at all. But I'm not in sickbay now, and I might be in quite a lot of trouble if I don't answer any questions.

The man has a pair of glasses that he's swinging in his fingers, and now and again he puts the bit that goes round his ear in his mouth. I can see even from here that it's quite chewed up. Then he puts them on and turns the pages of a notebook, writing things down and ticking away as though he might be a teacher marking an essay.

I wait for the questions to start, and nothing happens apart from the sound of the tick-tock of the clock on the mantlepiece and the creaking of the man's chair, and the turning of the pages of his notebook while he's writing his things down. It's like when you go to the doctor for one of those great big injections that goes right into your arm, and you've been dreading it, and now here you are waiting just before he does it to you. And the thing I most hate in all the world is waiting.

I look around the room and put an expression on my face to show that I don't know what is going on, which is the truth because I really don't know what is going to be asked. It might be about Mummy, and it might be about Mr. England. All the time I know they think I've done something wrong, and I haven't.

It's a horrid, gloomy unfriendly room this, half empty with nearly everything in it dark brown. Dark brown walls, dark brown leather chairs, and a dark brown rug on the dark brown wooden floor— even the pictures and the books on the shelves are dark brown. There would never be flowers in here like there are in Mr. England's room, not in a million years. We only ever come in here if we're in trouble, and now that I've got used to the light I can see the plimsol and the cane in the book cabinet next to the desk. It's as though they're waiting patiently for boys to come in, and actually, they never have to wait too long because Mr. Burston's always taking them out of the cabinet. Henry Pugh says he loves using them. He says he's a sadist, and if you look up what that means in the dictionary it says 'deriving pleasure from cruelty'. So that means there might be a properly nasty side to Mr. Burston. Nixon in 5b says he's more than a sadist. He says he's a member of the living dead, and that's why his study is so dark, and if the sunlight came in and touched him, he'd wither away to dust. He's sitting in the armchair underneath the cabinet. It's strange to see him actually in it because that chair is usually only used for caning people. Apparently, he makes you bend over it and hold onto one of the arms and then says 'Ready?' before whacking you as hard as hard can be.

After a long time the man, who's still writing things down, says, 'Benny, I want to ask you some questions about Mr. England.' Then he puts his pen down, folds his arms on the desk and leans forward. Now he's properly looking at me. 'Is that alright?'

So that's it. He's here to ask me questions about what I saw in the car. He's not going to ask me about Mummy. It's all about Mr. England. I look at Mr. Burston. He's sitting in the armchair crossing and uncrossing his legs and moving his arms into different positions. He nods at me to show that I should answer.

'Are you a policeman?' I ask the man.

The man chuckles a bit. 'Not really, Benny, no...' He's got a big Adam's apple, and there are some white hairs around it that move when he speaks, and I try not to stare because it's rude. Just then the door to the study opens, and when I turn round for a look, Mrs. Burston's standing there with baby Mark in her arms.

'Oh, I'm so sorry', she says, 'I thought you were doing this in the staff room.' She's really embarrassed, and baby Mark says 'Dada' when he sees Mr. Burston. She quickly goes out. There's a silence again, and I wonder if I'm meant to be the first one to say something.

It's the man that talks first, though. 'Now, Benny, I want to ask you just one or two questions about what happened the other night when you went to Mr. England's room.'

'About what happened, Sir? Nothing happened.'

And then he's asking me all sorts of questions like did Mr. England say to take off my dressing gown, and where was he sitting, and how far away from me was he, and when I say I was on the bed he asks me why, and I'm telling him that it was the cosiest place to be. He asks me why Mr. England said I was to go to his room, and I tell him 'It was just to listen to music, Sir. Just for music—that's all.'

'You like music, do you, Benny? That's nice. That's very nice...' He's writing, and then when he puts his pen down, looks at me again and smiles. I don't like it when this man smiles. It's like he's not smiling at all, but instead he's thinking that I'm lying which I'm not.

'What sort of music do you like to listen to then?' He's not looking at me when he asks me the question—just turning the pages of his copybook and moving his head from side to side as he reads things on different pages.

'All sorts, really...' He picks up the pen again and scribbles away, and I know he's not listening when I tell him about the Brahms and the Beethoven.

'Uh-huh... Good, good. That's very nice, isn't it...?' Then he lets the pen drop out of his fingers, and it plops onto the page. He stares hard at me again. 'Did Mr. England put his hand inside your pajama bottoms when you were on the bed?'

———

Monday is a games afternoon, but I've been left behind because the man's questions went on for such a long time that they've all gone to the playing field without me. When the man finished, Mr. Burston put his hand on my head again to lead me out of the room like I was a dog or something. When he opened the door he said, 'You're too late for games now. Get on with some revision instead— in the fresh air though. You can sit on a bench outside.'

I don't know what sort of revision I'm meant to be doing. There's no exams at the moment. There probably wasn't a spare member of staff to take me along the main road to the playing field, so he didn't really know what to do about me. He must think I'm the worst nuisance in the whole school what with the bed wetting, the trouble with Mummy, and then me being in the sickbay. And now all these questions about what I was doing in Mr. England's room. When the man was asking the questions, I kept looking at Mr. Burston in case I was able to see how to answer, but he was always just looking somewhere else. The only time I did catch his eye, he quickly looked out of the window. He's very fed up with me and all the trouble I'm causing.

I'm lying on the grass on the other side of the tennis court. We're absolutely forbidden on the river side of the tennis court fence, but nobody can see where I am from the school. There doesn't seem to be anyone around anyway because everyone's at the playing field. I'm by myself again. Completely by myself, and I wish it was always like this. I've got my history copybook with me, but I've not opened it once, and I'm not going to. I'm just looking straight up at the sky, just like I do when I'm deeply fine leg. The house martins are flying so high up they're just tiny dots. One of them is Tom Thumb. He only left yesterday, but I bet to him it feels like ages ago, a whole lifetime already. Now he's doing exactly what he wants, and I'm doing what I want, too. It feels like a new private place I've found here with bushes all around so I can't see the school. I'm going to come here again another time to get away and have some quietness—it's going to be my secret place.

The man in the Headmaster's study thinks I did something wrong with Mr. England. He doesn't believe me when I say that nothing happened. I said again and again it was just music and some cocoa and biscuits, but I know he doesn't believe me. That's why he said he might be coming back to ask me more questions. But it won't be more questions. It will be the same questions, and I'll have to give him the same answers—that is that nothing happened. The police must be asking Mr. England the same things, and I bet they don't believe him either.

The man never asked me anything about the blue folder. What would I have said about it if they'd asked me? What will I say about it when they come back? I don't want to get Mr. England into trouble and at the same time, I don't want to tell lies. Actually, I think that is the reason that they're asking these questions in the first place. Somebody at the repair garage has found something in the car, and that's made them wonder about lots of things to do with Mr. England. That's what I think.

The thing is that I knew about it and kept it a secret. Maybe that's a crime, and everyday I don't say something about it, the crime gets worse. If they discover it, I might be sent to a borstal—that's where there are truly horrible boys who are all delinquents growing up to be convicts. You get the cane there every single day, and I don't think I would be able to bear it. But I'm still not going to say—I just can't, because Mr. England is my friend, he's done nothing to hurt me, and he's always tried to look after me better than anyone else. Besides, I'm not at all sure that he knew anything about the blue folder himself. I really don't think he'd have something like that in his car on purpose. So it really does have to stay a complete secret.

I wish I'd never seen it. It was only by accident that I did, after all.

It was the day of the Vienna Boys' Choir concert last term. Mr. England was in the queue for all of our tickets, and he suddenly remembered that his ticket wasn't at the box office because it had been sent to him separately a long time before. He'd left it in the car. There wasn't very much time before we had to go inside the theatre, and he didn't want to lose his place.

'I'll go and get it, Sir—I know exactly where the car is!' I said. I wanted to show him how quick I could be.

'Can you really remember where it is, Ben?'

'Yes, it's at the very bottom of the hill, and there's a full up rubbish bin right beside it.'

'Okay, good boy. Quick as you can, though. We haven't much time before the performance starts. The ticket's in my blue folder on the front seat. Bring the whole thing if you're in any doubt.'

The next thing I'm running down the stairs out of the theatre, and he's calling me back because I haven't got the keys to the car. I said 'Silly me!' as he threw them in the air. I smiled when I caught them because I'm not usually very good at that.

I couldn't find it when I got there though. It wasn't on the front seat, of course, because I'd had to move everything onto the floor to make a space to sit down for the journey to Bristol. So I unlocked the boot and eventually found it right at the bottom of a whole load of books. The very last thing under a great pile of stuff.

But then I realised it wasn't the right blue folder almost as soon as I picked it up. I just hadn't looked properly at the front where Mr. England said it was. It was because I was in a muddle and a hurry to get back; I could just about imagine all the others getting to their seats except for Mr. England who'd be waiting by the programme seller with his arms folded and wiggling his fingers, which is a thing he does when things aren't quite right or time is running out. It made me clumsy; I wasn't holding the folder properly, and then suddenly everything inside came spilling out before I could stop it.

Just for a little my eyes got stuck on what I was seeing. Then I knew I had to do something about it before anyone was able to notice, so I started jamming the things back into the folder but they were just coming straight back out again because photography paper is so slippery. I just wanted to run away before anyone noticed. I felt I'd done something horribly wrong like I'd broken a jar and let a truly evil spirit loose. Most of the stuff had fallen back into the boot but some of it fell outside the car, and the next thing I knew I was scrabbling around underneath the wheels to gather it all back together. It was like collecting up shitty lavatory paper. It was dirty and poisonous, and I couldn't bear to touch it. But I had to. Every time I did my best to get it all back in, it would suddenly come gushing out again, so after a bit I told myself it would only stay in the folder if I did it more carefully. I started doing big breaths like I've been taught because of my asthma, and then I was able to put it all back in. I was a bit shaky but managed to lift all the heavy books and stuff with one hand while I was holding the folder tight closed in the other. Then I pushed it right down to the bottom, rearranged lots of things on top of it, and slammed down the boot as hard as I could. I turned the key so hard that it got stuck, and for a while I couldn't get it out.

I must have looked in the front again after that, but I don't remember it so clearly. I found the right folder in there anyway, and ran back to the theatre and up the stairs two at a time to where Mr. England was waiting for me alone with his arms crossed and his fingers going. All the audience had already gone in for the performance.

'Hurry, Ben. You're just in time! Well done.' I gave him the folder, and straightaway he opened it to find his ticket for the usher.

The lights were slowly being turned off when we walked down the aisle to our seats, and everything was going quiet, ready for the curtain to go up.

'Everything alright, Ben?' he whispered to me as we sat down, 'You look upset. Do you need your puffer?'

'I'm fine thank you, Sir,' I said, but I didn't look at his face when I said it.

—·—

He never put his hand inside my pajama bottoms. When the man asked me that question, I looked at Mr. Burston and for a bit I didn't understand what he could be meaning because it was such a terrible thing to say. Mr. Burston just looked away as though he wasn't listening, making sure not to catch my eye.

'What do you mean, Sir?' I said to the man. And then he asked me the same question again very slowly and firmly. The man was leaning right across the table, and his breath was blowing all over me, smelling of fruit pastels, which is a strange thing to be eating if you're a detective. I was getting angry and frightened all at the same time and was thinking how unfair it was that he thought I'd done that thing when I truly hadn't.

'He never did, Sir,' I said to Mr. Burston when he was closing the door of the study as I was going out.

'Who never did what, Teasdale?'

'Mr. England. He never did what that man said, Sir. It's the truth, Sir, I promise.'

They think that Mr. England's the same as Mr. Clarendon. He was Mrs. Burston's uncle who was the carpentry master up until last summer term, and he was definitely putting his hand in people's pajama bottoms.

Sometimes Miss Carson used to wake me up early to take Uncle Clary—that's what he told everyone to call him—a cup of tea in the morning just before the bell went. He always had boys in his room who had got up early, with some of them actually in the bed with him. He was giving them Maltesers and tickling them and stuff like that. But then it all stopped because the seniors who were leaving at the end of term had the pep talk from the Headmaster that he always gives to boys going to their new schools about not letting older boys do sex things to them. Right in the middle of it, they realised that Uncle Clary was doing the very same things that Mr. Burston was talking about, and they absolutely knew that he shouldn't be. Halford, who was my dorm prefect, decided to go and tell on him, which must have been very embarrassing seeing that Uncle Clary was Mrs. Burston's actual real-life uncle. I think it was a very grown-up thing to do, but Mr. Burston got really angry and said 'what a ludicrous and filthy little story' to him. But anyway, when we all came back to school for the winter term, and I went past Uncle Clary's room on the way to the dorm, I could see that it was completely empty with the wardrobe doors open. It was announced at the first Morning Assembly that he'd made the decision over the long holiday to retire from being the carpentry master and wasn't coming back. I'm sure it was on account of the Malteezer chocolates and the boys in his bed, though.

Halston told me all about it. I was very shocked because Uncle Clary seemed to be quite a nice old chap. I felt a bit guilty too, because just the day before, he'd tickled me a bit when I took him his tea, and then he gave me a bar of Cadbury's Whole Nut which I was going to save for a special occasion. I thought it was a bad thing to keep it since it was given to me by such a wicked person, so the next day straight after breakfast I fetched it from my locker and sneaked down below the tennis court where we're not allowed and threw it with all my might far away into the river.

———

I want to stay here on the grass forever. I'd like it if no one ever came back from the playing field, and I could just be so still that whole days and nights and weeks would go past. I would slowly change and start to become part of the ground, and then I wouldn't even be a human being anymore. I'd like it that oceans of time would go by, and I wouldn't mind it if the sun was baking hot, or the rain was beating down, or if there was six inches of snow on top of me. Just so long as I could be still and there was no noise in my head. If I was turned into Tom Thumb, I'd be high up in the sky. And if I was looking down at where I am now, I wouldn't even be able to see myself because I would have disappeared. Perhaps there'd be just the tiniest bump with grass growing over what used to be me.

'Teasdale, what on earth are you doing? We've blooming well had a search party out for you! You're in big trouble, you are…' It's Wallington, standing over me with one foot either side of my chest, and I'm thinking he's a giant house martin because he's all mixed up with the dream I've been having. He looks down at me with a red face and his hands on his hips.

'Sorry, Wallington. I think I was asleep.'

'You're for it, you are! Everyone has gone into High Tea. What on earth are you doing this side of the fence anyway? You know it's out of bounds, don't you?'

I don't say anything, but I'm getting up and brushing the grass off my back and trousers and legs.

'Headmaster will want to see you. Now! On the double!' We walk back towards the school with Wallington's hand on the back of my head like Mr. Burston was doing before, and it feels as though I'm a prisoner and being taken to a place for punishing. I suppose that really is the truth of what's happening. When we get to the dining room all the talking goes down a bit when I come through the door, and then I wait while Wallington whispers to Mr. Burston at the centre table who then beckons me over. I'm really frightened because I've made such a mistake.

'Sit down and have your tea, and then wait for me under the clock. I'll see you in my study straight after.' His face is red and when he looks like that I know he's doing his best not to be angry. He's probably saving it for later when he's going to take the plimsol out of the cupboard to whack me with it for the first time ever. I try to eat my tea, which is Welsh rarebit and usually one of my favourite things, but it's not going down and my throat is hot from doing my best not to cry. Theo's sitting next to me, and he says 'Where have you been?' in a telling-off sort of a way. When I say I was asleep on the grass on the other side of the tennis court fence he looks at me as though I'm so crazy that there's no point in talking to me anymore. Then he just stares at me for a bit, nodding his head from side to side to show how serious the whole thing is. He's really pleased that I'm in trouble, that's for sure.

The noises and pictures are back inside my head while I'm under the clock. I look at the big leather chair and remember the day last week when I was waiting for Mummy, and then I'm seeing the plimsol in the cupboard that's waiting for me and Mr. Burston's face red with anger. It's my own voice that's telling me I'm in trouble and I'm probably deserving it what with having left Mummy to fend for herself with the police and also being silly enough to fall asleep on the other side of the fence. And I'm thinking how mad is it that I've done that, because usually I never ever break school rules on account of the fact that I really don't like people to be at all angry with me, and I just couldn't bear to get the cane.

Mr. Burston opens the door of his study. His face isn't red anymore. 'Come along in, young man.' He's beckoning me with his finger, which he does to everyone who's in some sort of trouble, then his hand's on the back of my head again as we're walking across to his desk. This time he doesn't pull the wicker chair up for me, and I'm standing there with my hands behind my back twiddling my fingers. My knees are a bit wobbly, and my bum feels tingly where it's going to be whacked. He goes round the back of the desk and sits down. The study is even darker than it was this morning because the sun doesn't shine on this side of the school in the afternoon.

'It's out of bounds, Teasdale. No one but staff and prefects are allowed on the far side of the fence without my express permission.' He pauses and one of his eyebrows goes up. 'You know that perfectly well, don't you?' he says.

'Yes Sir I'm sorry Sir.'

He screws up his mouth to make his lips thinner while he's thinking about the punishment. I'm waiting for him to say whether it's going to be the cane or the plimsol.

'Don't let it happen again, please.'

'No Sir I won't Sir.'

'Off you go now.'

—⁓—

'I cannot believe that you didn't get a thrashing for that...' It's Theo, standing by the washstands in the dorm with toothpaste ready on his brush, but too disappointed and angry to be able to start brushing. I've been trying to keep out of his way since the end of prep, but now that we're upstairs getting ready for bed there's nothing I can do about it since he's in my blooming dorm. He's been going on and on. I came into prep quite a long time after it had started on account of standing under the clock, and when I sat down I could see him looking at me, desperate to know all about it. He threw me a little scrunched up note from his desk that said 'Did it hurt?' but I just ignored it. After that, he kept making little whistling sounds to attract my attention, but I just wouldn't look over to him. Then he threw a crayon at me that hit the side of my head and with my mouth I made the shape of the words 'bog off' to him. I was hoping that Mr. Tulley who was taking prep this evening would hear the whistling and the crayon sliding along the floor, and he'd get into trouble, but no such luck. As soon as prep was finished he came rushing up to me in the queue for cocoa to find out all about it. When I told him that not only had I not been beaten, but I hadn't even been punished he shouted 'You're fibbing! You've got to be fibbing!' and just wouldn't believe it.

Just as I'm bending over the washstand to wash my face with my pink flannel from home, my pajama bottoms are pulled right down to the floor. I drop the flannel and bend down to pull my pants up, but someone grabs me by the wrist and my head is being pushed down. Theo says 'Grab his other hand, Chirly. Grab his other hand, quick!' Then my other wrist is being held tight behind my back, and my head's being pushed down so I'm bent over with my pajama bottoms still round my ankles. I fall down right to the floor with my nose pressed against the floorboards, smelling the polish and the dust. 'Let me go! Please let me go,' I'm shouting, but none of the others come to help me. Theo's holding one wrist, and Chirl is holding the other behind my back and sitting on me, laughing and shouting, 'Look at his bum! Look at his bum! Has it got red marks on it?'

'I don't believe it!' Theo's shouting. 'There's not a scratch on him. Not a single mark.'

'Whack him with your slipper, Theo, quick...' Chirl says laughing, and the very next thing I'm feeling is my bottom being hit.

It doesn't hurt very much. But I want to pull my pants up. Everyone can see me, and I just hate to be bare.

'Please let me get up, please, Chirl. Why are you doing this?'

'It's time you got the slipper, that's why. Slipper on the bum for Stuart England's bum-boy...'

'What are you talking about? Why are you saying that? It's not true.'

'Oh come off it, Teasdale,' says Theo, 'Everybody knows what you've been up to. Piss-pot bum-boy.'

'Piss-pot bum-boy!' says Chirl. 'That's good. That's his name from now on!'

'Oh for heaven's sake, leave him alone, you spastoids,' Tom Whickham says very slowly as though he's bored with them being horrible. I turn my head and from the ground, looking under the beds past everyone's overnight bags, I can see his legs swinging backwards and forwards. He's sitting on the side of his bed, watching it all. And that's the worst part actually. I don't want Tom Whickham to see me like this. I don't even like it that he's said anything to Theo and Chirl. I don't want it that he's got to stick up for me.

And then they're getting off me very quickly and rushing over to their beds. Pugh's just come in the door.

'What on earth is going on in here?' he says. I've already mostly pulled my pajamas up though I'm still on the floor. 'Teasdale? What's going on?'

'Nothing, Pugh. I just slipped, that's all. I just slipped over a bit.'

'Okay, okay, wipe your nose, stop blubbing, and get into bed.' I hadn't even noticed that I'd started to cry. I get up and wipe my nose on the back of my pajama sleeve and get into my bed with everyone silently looking at me. Then I go under the sheets and stick my hand out to feel for my rug and pull it right up over my head so no one can see that I'm crying and to make it as dark as possible so I can think that I might be somewhere else.

I can hear Pugh talking very quietly as though I'm not here or at least I mustn't be hearing the conversation.

'What's been going on, Chirl? Theodorakis? What were you doing to him?'

'He slipped, that's all, just like he said. And Theo and I were trying to help him up,' says Chirl.

'Don't lie to me, you cretin. I want the truth. What were you doing?'

There's a long silence and Theo and Chirl are deciding whether to say or not and after a bit I know they're thinking it's best not to. Then Pugh says in a loud voice, 'I don't want bullying in my dorm. Is that understood?' There's a long pause. 'Is that understood?' he says again, nearly shouting. 'Pack it up, all of you. Get into bed. Now. I'm putting the lights out early, and I want silence—complete silence!'

'Yes, Pugh,' everyone says together, with Chirl and Theo being especially loud because they're pleased that they've not got into trouble after all.

In the blackness of my bed there's quiet for a while. After a bit, the door opens suddenly. I can't see him, but it must be Pugh who's been listening secretly outside. Without saying anything, he closes the door again.

The quiet goes on for a long time, and I'm thinking it might be the end of this horrid day with them all about to fall asleep, leaving me alone with the darkness. I hope I'm not going to start talking to myself inside my head and seeing pictures again.

'What's he done, anyway?' It's Lucky Lorrimer, who's usually the first asleep, whispering to someone very loudly.

Chirl's whispering back. 'Shut up, Lucky. Pugh'll come back in.'

'I just want to know what he's done, that's all.' I can hear the springs in his bed as he's getting out and crossing over to Chirl. I fold back my rug just a little so that I can hear what they're saying.

'Get back to bed, Lorrimer.'

'Not till you tell me what Teasdale's done.'

Chirl stops the whispering then, because he wants me to hear.

'Burston found him in Mr. England's bed.'

'What was he doing in there?'

'Oh, for heaven sake, Lucky, don't you know anything? It means Mr. England's a prevert.'

'Pervert, Chirl, you cretin,' says Nick Earl loudly, because he's forgotten about the whispering as well.

Then Theo starts up, even louder to make sure that I can definitely hear. 'It means Mr. England's been perving him up. Like what Digby and Forman do after lights out. Only when a master does it to you, it means he's a pervert. And that's a crime, which is why the police have been here.'

'Golly!' Lorrimer's thinking about what he's heard for a bit. 'What will happen to Mr. England then?'

'He's probably going to go to prison,' Theo says.

'Blimey!'

—⁘—

Way into the night, I peep out from under the covers, and it's as black as black can be. I wonder if it's ever happened before that I've been awake for as long as this. Lorrimer's snoring loudly, but it's not making any difference to the others in the dorm because they've all been asleep for hours and hours, too. About an hour ago I heard Pugh come in and take his clothes off in the dark. He splashed his face with water from his washstand and after, he came over to my bed and leaned over me, but it was dark enough so that he didn't see me go right back down under the blankets. I made a big breathing sound so that he'd think I was asleep and wouldn't ask me if I was alright. He got into his bed, and after a bit I could hear that he was asleep, too.

Now I'm all alone in the night again, and it's the strangest thing to be so awake even though I want very badly to be asleep. It's just too noisy in my head though, and it's making my heart beat which is a thing that keeps you awake even when you think of sheep jumping over hedges. That's a well known trick for wide awake people in the middle of the night, but it's not working on me. I keep forgetting to concentrate on them, and there's only about twenty jumping over before, without wanting it, I'm seeing pictures of Mr. England, and the folder, and Mummy in the park, and all the boys at the borstal where I might be sent.

I'm so awake that I hear Miss Carson walking along the corridor even before she opens the door. She's got the pot in one hand and the torch in the other which is shining and making circles on the floorboards as she comes towards my bed. I'm getting out even before she reaches me. I try to pee but I'm just not able to do it tonight. I don't ask her what time it is like I usually do because I only do that if I'm fast asleep and not thinking properly. I don't think she's used to me saying nothing at all.

'Everything alright, Teasdale?'

'Yes, thank you, Miss Carson.'

'You sure? Haven't you been sleeping?'

'Yes. Yes, I have. Right until just now, actually.'

When I get back into my bed, she tucks the blanket into the side which means her face is right down close to mine. From the light of the torch I can see her big eyes looking at me trying to discover if I'm alright, and so I do a little smile in case she might be able to see. Then she gently touches the top of my head. I think she's still being kind to me because of all the business with Mummy last week.

And then she's walking away, shining the torch on the door. She closes it behind her, and I hear her going along the corridor back into the night. The silence and the blackness come back again.

I try to make the hours pass by looking at the ceiling to see if the shadows and cracks might be able to tell me some stories, but really it's too dark for me to see anything properly.

And then I hear something and know it must be my clock ticking away in between Jollo's paws at the bottom of my blue bag. That's the strangest thing because I've never been able to hear it before. It's as though it's trying to catch my attention to let me know that it urgently needs winding because I'm on the edge of forgetting. That's how it really is, too. I was on the edge of forgetting all my things from home—my clock, my album, Granny's blue tee shirt, and the scarf that's got Mummy's smell on it. And Jollo. He's the best friend I've ever had in all my life. He knows everything about me whether it's good or bad. He knows if I'm frightened or sad or angry without my having to say anything at all. He just automatically knows. If ever I'm not alright, I can feel he's under the bed in the blue bag knowing all about it, and his friend the clock is in between his paws, wrapped up in tissue paper and ticking merrily away. Jollo's always looked after me, ever since before Beirut. Ever since before I can remember. Actually, he looks after me much better than I look after him. And here we all are, far away from home, just a foot away from each other.

I lean out of the bed and wave my hand about underneath till it bangs into the bag. I pull it towards me and unzip it very slowly. I put my hand in and feel something soft and cool and slippery, and I know it's Mummy's silk scarf that I took from the drawer in her bedroom. I pull it out and hear the whispering swish of it unraveling, and then I weave it in and out of my fingers and kiss the smell of Mummy's perfume. I think of her far away in a strange bed where she doesn't want to be and wonder whether she might be awake in the middle of the night, too, thinking about me. After a while, I tuck the scarf under my pillow, though I know I mustn't forget to put it back because I don't want anyone to see it in the morning. Then I put my hand back into the bag and feel a small box. I can't think straightaway what it is. There's a little knob on the side, and I press it. All of a sudden, there's a mixture of music and foreign talking, and I know it's my little radio I've accidentally switched on, so quick as a flash I turn it off and snatch my hand out of the case. I lie as still as still can be, holding my breath and listening for any sign of one of the others waking up because of it. No one stirs though, and I let out my breath as quietly as I can. Slowly my hand creeps back into the bag, past the radio, the stamp album, the blue photo album, the tee shirt Granny gave me, and deeper down to where I feel the crinkly tissue paper that my clock is wrapped in. I feel Jollo's paw for a second to say hello, lift out the clock, and put it right by the side of my cheek on the pillow. Very carefully I unwrap the paper as if the clock might be asleep and I'm not to disturb it even though I'm winding it up—it's a bit like a father who's got to take a small sleeping baby out of the car after a long journey and put it in its cot upstairs. I pull the rug up over my head and hear my breath and the ticking, and I see the green luminous time that shines for a few inches all around and tells me it's 12.30, and I'm in another day. My lips touch the glass at the front and ever so gently I wind the clock and hold the little hammer thing between the two bells so it won't make a noise. I'm going to make sure to keep the ticking from home alive before I give it back to Jollo to look after.

And then there's a cracking, twanging sound. Something hard pings against my cheek. Just for a single second I'm sure it must be Chirl flicking something with an elastic band from the other side of the dorm. But I'm underneath the blankets. I put my head out, but there's nothing to see or hear apart from Lucky Lorrimer snoring quietly. I go back under to try and work out what's going on, and it's then that I know that the clock in my hand is in two separate pieces because the glass front has come off. I search around with my fingers to see if it will screw back on and then I feel that the back is half off as well, and there's something sharp poking out. While I'm holding it, more of it comes out from inside. It's uncoiling itself and growing bigger.

The clock has stopped its ticking. The spring and all the insides are bursting out, and I know it means that my little clock is broken forever. I lie still with it all in my hands thinking about what I should do. Then I lean over and put my hand deep inside my bag and feel for Jollo and the old towel from the garage at home, and I pull them into the bed with me. I sit up, flatten the tissue paper on my pillow, and then collect up all the bits and pieces of my clock and put them in the middle. I fold the four corners over until it's wrapped up as best as I can do in the dark. It doesn't want to stay like that though, on account of the spring, which is beginning to tear the paper, so next I unfold the towel, put the little bundle in the centre, and roll it up into a sort of ball. I get out of bed and kneel on the floor beside my bag and then, ever so gently I put the towel with the dead clock right down far into the bottom where it will stay till

I can get it home.

When I get back into bed after quite a long time of sitting think-ing by my bag, I wrap Jollo up in Mummy's scarf until just his head is poking out so he's like one of those babies you see from the Middle Ages. Then I go back under the blankets and put him close up to my face just the same as I did with my clock. I tell him that the clock has gone forever, and that we'll always remember him from the days when we were all in Beirut, where he lived on my pillow and the clock ticked away on my little side table.

I start to cry. I cry so hard that after a bit I worry that someone might wake up, so I go farther underneath the sheets and allow my-self to cry even though I usually don't like to do that. It's just that I really can't stop myself.

'Teasdale?' It's Pugh's voice. I'm frozen in my bed.

'Teasdale, is that you blubbing?' He's sitting up.

I'm praying with all my might that he won't get out of bed and come over.

'Teasdale?' His voice isn't so loud now. Perhaps he's thinking he just imagined it. I hear the sound of his bedsprings as he settles himself down again. I wait for a little bit and by the time I hear he's asleep again, I'm finished with the crying.

I think I'm getting a bit sleepy now. I come up from deep inside the bed and put my head on the pillow. Then I roll on top of Jollo so he's underneath my chest. I'm hoping that in the morning every-thing will be back to normal, and we both might be just a little bit better.

———

I was dreaming then. A really horrid dream. I was outside by the house martins' graves, kneeling down in the mud. It was raining hard, and I was wet right through. It was a bit like I'd turned into Mummy in the park with all her soaking clothes clinging to her. My broken clock wrapped up in the tissue paper was in the hole that Theo had got ready for Tom Thumb that didn't have to be used. I put some daisies on top of the paper for remembrance. Then I was trying to put Jollo in the hole as well, but he was screaming to me that he wasn't dead and I wasn't to leave him alone buried in the ground. But I was telling him that it really was time for him to be going, and I forced him in and covered the hole with soil until there was not the slightest sign of him. I was crying out loud and that was alright because there was no one to hear me on account of it being in the darkest middle of the night.

But I'm awake again now.

And I'm wet. I'm really wet.

I'm wet from my knees right up to my neck. My pajamas are clutching me tight. I stretch my hands out, and it's wet and cold right to the edge of the bed. I'm shivering, and my teeth are chattering.

I cover my face with my hands and plead that when I open my eyes again this will just be another terrible dream. 'Please, please, please, God, make this not be true,' but when I take my hands away and open my eyes, the wet and cold are still there.

The day is just beginning outside. I stretch my hand up above me to where the curtain is, and when I move it I can see that the sky straight above is no longer black but the darkest blue.

I push back all the wet bedclothes and stand up on my bed to draw the curtains back. The house martins are already out of their nests flying around. When they dive down towards the invisible river I'm able to see them for a second against the blue and yellow light that's just beginning to come up from behind the shadow of the far away hills.

I put my hands up to the collar of my pajamas and undo the buttons all the way down ever so slowly until my top slides off my shoulders and falls on the bed. It feels so lovely when the warm dry air touches my skin. Then I pull the cord of my pajama bottoms, and it gets stuck in a wet knot. But I quickly unpick it, and they fall down to my ankles, all heavy as though they can't wait to be away from me. I step out of them, free of the wetness, and it's like the truth of what's happened has been thrown away. I lean towards the window and grab hold of the latch. When I pull it down it doesn't budge for a bit because ever since the big storm it's not been working so well. But I push it down again as hard as can be, and it goes 'crack!' and half the window is swinging open so fast I have to catch it in my hand to stop it making a noise. There's a reflection of myself for a single second passing by in the glass, and I see that I'm smiling. The freshness of the outside touches the dampness on my chest and sends a little shiver through me.

Then I turn away from the window to look into the dark gloom of the dormitory; no one's been woken up by the noise of the latch. I look down at my pajamas, and I feel like a snake that has come out of its useless old skin.

Jollo's lying in the bed where it sinks in the middle, crushed by my lying on him. I bend down and pick him up. He's wet through so his head is lolling about, and the fur on his face is all flat and Mummy's scarf is sticking to him. He looks like a mangy homeless dog that's been caught in a storm. I get off the bed and delve in the darkness under it for the bag. I open it and press my lips up against Jollo's ear and whisper, 'I love you, Jollo. I love you. I'll see you another time, I promise.' Then I put him right at the bottom, next to the towel where the body of our old clock is. I straighten him out so he'll be comfortable, and I squeeze his paw to say goodbye.

I'm standing on the bed again. My hand is on the little bolt that's keeping the other side of the window from opening. I flick it up with my fingers, it clicks, and when I push, it swings open gently. I look up, over to the hills, and see that already, in just a few seconds, it's grown lighter. There's the very first sound of birds calling out to each other, and the dip in the hills with the yellow and blue sky coming through looks like a giant smile. The river below is tinkling like it's playing a pretty song on the piano, and everything's telling me that it's a good thing for me to go and be free, away from the darkness of the dorm and the wetness of my bed. I'm going to be brave, and do what I know is right because it might be my very last chance.

I put my hands on the top of each side of the open windows and my foot on the window ledge and straighten my legs. I stand up, leaning out towards the river like a carved figure you sometimes see pictures of on the prow of an old wooden battleship.

I'm outside. I'm in the light. I'm right between my old life and a brand new one. I fill up my chest with fresh air and look straight above into the sky. My smile is getting bigger and bigger, and it's spreading to the whole of my body. I really don't know why, but suddenly I'm nearly giggling, but I know I mustn't because I've got to be silent for a bit longer.

I turn back and bend my head for a look into the dorm before leaving for the last time. It's too dark to see properly, but I can hear Lucky Lorrimer snoring gently, and I can just see the shape of Henry Pugh's dark head on his white pillow.

I pull myself up so that I'm sitting right on the very top of one side of the window, and for just a tiny second I'm wobbling like mad because it's moving underneath me. I have to steady myself by grabbing hold of the gutter beside my head to stop from falling. I hold it with both hands and twist round. I lift my foot up to the top of the window, push with all my might, stretch myself out, and be-fore I know it I'm lying on top of the tiles which are cold and damp underneath my bare tummy. I can't see it, but I hear the window that's been pushed by my foot swinging away and clattering closed. There's no way now to go back. I'm a bit frightened, but at the same time I love it that I'm free. I'm frozen to the spot for a bit, not daring to take the slightest breath and not daring to look around. I stare at the silvery dew on the grey blackness of the tile that's right in front of my eyes.

But suddenly, I'm slipping and sliding downwards. Tiles are pass-ing by my eyes, and I'm crazily moving my arms and legs around like Flopsy Gilligan in the swimming pool, trying to find something to grab hold of. Bright green bits of moss that have come unstuck start to roll downwards. My fingers and toes join in till my feet find the gutter. I wedge my toes in, and the slipping stops. I still don't dare to look around but my hands travel ever so carefully, feeling up along the tiles of the little roof of the window until they come to the very top where it goes over. I hold on tight and pull myself up.

I look over the top at the big trees that you can see from the window in the dormitory by the washstands. I twist my head round ever so carefully because the slightest movement might make me start slipping again, and I look out towards the river. I'm so high up it sends shivers right through me, and my willy feels tingly from the danger of it all. I laugh a little bit because I know no one can hear me now, and there's nothing that anyone in the whole world can do about it.

I want to be even higher. I want to be higher than the squirrels' nests, higher than the very top of the trees. I want to be so high that I might know just what it's like to be a house martin. I want to climb up onto the big roof, the one that covers the whole school. I'm going to go right to the very top, right up to where the chimneys are.

But it's like the side of a mountain—a dangerous, steep, cruel mountain. One of those mountains that you read about in the papers that some brave person has tried to climb but has never come back from because they've slipped and crashed down all the way to the bottom, or got mangled up by a very powerful avalanche, or fallen into an icy pitch-black crevice where they've had to wait forever with a broken ankle and no food until they've died of the cold and the loneliness.

So I've got to be careful, because I can't fly. But one thing's for certain—I'm never going back down to underneath this roof.

It's best not to look down. I know that. And not to keep looking up, either, because if I do, all the time I'll be knowing just how far I've got to go. I'll go slowly, doing it one teensy-weensy bit at a time.

I'm moving again now, like a sea lion who's clumsy and heavy on the beach. With my hands still on top of the baby roof of the window, I flop myself sideways till I'm right up against the big roof. Then I take really big breaths and concentrate on the first few rows of tiles just like Marlowe in seniors' does when he's about to start the run up to the high jump on Sports Day.

And then I'm off. The first thing I notice is that once I'm actually on it, the roof's not so steep as I thought. Like I promised myself, I don't look down, and I don't look so far up that it gets to be really frightening. I just look at the bit right in front of me. At first I move gingerly, thinking about every tile that passes by, but quite soon I start to go quicker.

I'm not like a sea lion at all, now. More like a sleek lizard, moving my hips from side to side, slithering upwards on my tummy. It's just once or twice that I quickly look up for the direction of the chimney. It gets closer and closer, and it's standing there waiting for me right at the summit of this mountain, growing bigger and bigger till it's the same as a huge cliff coming straight out of the water like you see in Cornwall.

I'm there. I'm at the very top, where the roof goes over to the other side. I reach out and touch the chimney like it's a game of tag and no one can get me now because I'm home and dry. I put my leg over and straddle the centre of the roof with my arms down on either side as though I'm hugging the back of an enormous whale. My ear's against the tiles, and I listen to the silence of the sleeping school.

I close my eyes tight and pull myself up, holding onto the chimney. Very carefully I turn myself round, making sure not to lose my balance, till I'm sitting with my legs dangling down on either side, with my back up against the bricks of the chimney. There's been just enough light from the sun to warm them up a little, and it feels good against my skin. My eyes are still closed tight, partly because I'm frightened and partly because I want the surprise when I open them, like on Christmas day when you first see the big pile of presents under the tree.

Something slips away underneath my foot, and I open my eyes automatically just in time to see a tile coming loose. I watch it slide down the roof, faster and faster, skimming across the other tiles like a flat round stone thrown between the waves on the beach and making a noise like Theo practising his scales on the piano when he goes from the top notes to the bottom. It reaches the gutter by the window where I've just come from and disappears over the edge. There's a silence and a tiny while later a big crashing sound when it smashes onto the balcony far away down below.

I don't close my eyes again. I can't. There's too much to see, and I hold my breath with the surprise of it all. The whole of Saxham's underneath me, roofs and chimneys, and narrow lanes, and far away in the distance the beginning of the hills where the forest starts. The whole world's changed into doll's houses and dinky-toy gardens, tiny red telephone boxes, midget cars and make believe doll's clothes on washing lines. I look the other way, past Mrs. Ridgeley's vegetable garden and the paths in the school grounds that lead down towards the water. I'm so high up I might as well be floating above the river itself like Aladdin on a magic flying carpet. I push my back up against the chimney for safety's sake and hold on tight as tight can be to the row of red tiles that run along the very top of the roof. And then I'm thinking how would it be to let go? It might feel as though I'm really, truly flying! My hands dare to hold on less tightly. Just for a teeny while I loosen my grip to see what it's like, and then I'm holding on again with all my strength because I'm not quite ready yet. I take a long deep breath in again and let go, and my hands hover for an instant just an inch or two above the tiles. They're trembling, testing to see if it's safe for me to balance.

And then I lift my hands in the air and stretch out my arms as though they might be wings. I tilt my head right back so I'm looking far above myself until I see nothing but the sky. Nothing at all but the sky and the house martins. I'm not on a magic carpet at all, but flying with the birds. We're swooping and swirling around, and I laugh out loud because I'm happy and I'm free. I've travelled a million miles away from my old life, and I'm never going back.

I've got wings now. I'm with Tom Thumb. I'm flying with the house martins.

V.

January, 1969. Seven months later.

It's Swedish Lena, the au pair, who's going to take me to the station today. That's ever so silly; I've been there millions of times, and she's never been once in her whole life, so what's the point of her taking me? I'll be in charge anyway. I've even got the keys to the front door in my own pocket. But my dad says I'm not to go by myself. One of these days, probably quite soon, I certainly will go all by myself.

So here I am waiting for the taxi again, like I do at the beginning of every single term, sitting on the sofa with my cap and navy blue coat on. Lena's in the armchair with Mrs. Hamilton standing by the door with the lemon drops that she always gives me when I'm leaving; we're all listening out for the car coming up the road, and as usual I want it to come because I don't want to be late, and I don't want it to come because I don't want to go. The only different thing is that I'm not having a glass of sherry like I used to have with Mummy, because she's not here.

I packed my blue bag last night, and I'm pretty sure I've got everything I need—my stamp collection, my new Stanley Gibbons catalogue that my dad gave me for Christmas, the big wooly jumper from Granny—on account of the new rule allowing us to wear things from home on Sundays after church—my wash bag with the new toothbrush, and my new alarm clock that I'd specially asked Granny for at Christmas. It's ticking away like my old one from Rome airport, but it doesn't really feel the same. I took one of Mummy's perfumy scarves from the wardrobe in the bedroom while my dad was out for his walk yesterday. Then I thought he might just possibly see that it had gone missing so I sneaked it back in there this morning after he'd gone to work. I just completely hope he doesn't notice it's been moved around, and actually that really is a bit of a worry. The thing is, I don't need to have the scarf anyway. Not really.

Jollo's not inside the bag. I don't know what's happened to him. He's disappeared. I didn't notice when he first went missing what with the muddle of everything that happened. When the blue bag—the same one that I'm holding the handle of right now—came back, he just wasn't in there, neither was my broken clock. They must have taken them both out. I think Jollo's been thrown away. They probably thought he was just a bit of old smelly rubbish. And that means I've broken my promise to him, because I remember the last thing I said to him was that I would see him again. I think of him every day though, and I want him back so, so much. But there's nothing I can do about it. I'll just have to grow out of missing him.

The next thing I really properly remember after being on the roof is sitting in the garden at home. I was looking down at my knees at the books that they had sent from school so that I didn't get behind with all the work, but the sun was shining so brightly on the pages that I couldn't see to read. That's when my memory started up again.

I was being treated as if I was properly ill, although I wasn't really, except for everything being a bit of a blur in my head as though I was dreaming and not knowing what's real and what's not real. There was Lucozade in a glass, rice pudding, thermometers always being put in my mouth, and a blanket over my legs even though it was really, really hot. It was as though I was slowly going to die like Beth does in that film of Little Women when she's staring out of the window of her bedroom looking at a robin one second and then dead the next.

It was Granny that was doing all that. She turned herself into Florence Nightingale, though probably a bit stricter, actually. I'm not sure how long she'd been with us on account of nothing being very clear, but I do remember her arriving. My dad and I were watching the telly all about poor Robert Kennedy who'd been shot dead in the kitchen of a hotel in America, and just as the programme was finishing we heard the car outside scrunching on the gravel. My dad jumped to his feet and rushed to the front door looking ever so relieved. When he was taking her suitcase up the stairs to the spare room, he kept saying to her, 'Fantastically good to see you, Sylvia,' and all night long 'Marvelous to have you here with us,' over and over again until it was quite embarrassing. He's never been bothered about her before, actually. I've even heard him saying some quite horrid things about her to Mummy. That might be because he thinks that she wasn't very nice to her when she was a little girl, and that's why Mummy's become such a worried sort of a person. But anyway, he was probably just fantastically pleased that he didn't have to look after me all by himself and could concentrate on the office again.

Before that day in the garden, everything is sort of misty and chopped up. There was a white room with one of those long extra-bright lights and a fan on the high up ceiling that never turned and had cobwebs on it, and there were shadows and cracks that sometimes turned into scary faces that were staring down at me. There were bars from top to bottom on the windows which had no curtains and no view whatsoever to the outside because of a frosty type of glass, and bare floorboards brimming full of splinters that made me stay on the high up bed as though I was marooned on a desert island. There were stiff white sheets on the bed and a stiff white hat on a nurse who never smiled, and big pills that arrived on a trolley clinking with bottles that you could hear coming down the long corridor forever before it arrived. And there were pitch-black nights of no sleeping with total silence and mornings of staring at the doorknob waiting for it to move so someone would come in and see me. I don't know if I was there for just one day, or one week, or one month. It might be that I made it all up in my head. It could have been a dream. I just can't remember about it.

It may have been the same place that Granny took me to three or four times on the train a little bit later on, not very far from our house, but I'm really not sure. The first time we went there we walked holding hands down a long unkempt driveway with lots of weeds growing up through the gravel until we got to a red-bricked building with huge chimneys that reminded me a little bit of school. At first I thought perhaps we were going to see Mummy, and it was all meant to be a surprise for me. When I dared to ask Granny if that was true, she looked all surprised and told me that the visit was for me and that I was going to speak to a special doctor. Nobody had told me anything about it and I knew that I didn't need to see a doctor because I wasn't the slightest bit ill.

When we got to the big building, there was moss growing up the walls from where the gutters were leaking, big rusty fire escapes zig-zagged all over the place, and signs pointing everywhere with med-ical-type words on them. Just in front of the steps that went into the main building there was a bit of a parched lawn, and standing on it was a very tall stooping-over man. He had an awfully big wet open mouth, no teeth, and he was using a rake on the same bit of yellow grass over and over again. A lady in a big winter coat past her knees held a hanky up to her mouth and did a funny little dance because she was trying to keep her hand in the man's jacket pocket while he went back and forward, back and forward with his raking. It was very difficult not to stare at them. There was a bench right next to them with a fat lady with a shiny white jacket on, chewing gum and staring into the distance, so I think she was looking after them with-out bothering too much. Right beside her was a not very old man with a too-big head who was swaying from side to side as though he was listening to some music that nobody else could hear.

Inside we walked along a corridor that was especially dark after the sunshine outside and smelled of disinfectant and burnt toast. Some of the doors were open and you could see into the rooms, all big with not much furniture and glossy white where the sun was coming in, reflecting off the walls. Just for a second you couldn't help but see even when you knew you shouldn't be looking at the poor people inside on account of it being rude to stare. I saw a lady in a grubby old nightdress with the straps falling down over her shoulders. She was sitting on the side of her bed swinging her feet to and fro while someone was feeding her with a spoon, like Worgan at school rubbing his legs with his hands when he's eating his porridge to try to help it go down. Then in another room I saw a man in his vest and pants and long tangled hair with wide-open eyes turning his head from side to side while he was lying on a bed with a doctor person and a nurse holding him down. In the next room a huge round man with a red scarf and a cap and trousers right up to his chest was jabbing his finger in the air, talking loudly like you see politicians sometimes doing to a crowd of people, except he was doing it to nobody at all.

When we got to the end of the corridor, we sat together on a wooden bench outside a door, and I could hear someone inside crying in the distance, as though the room was very big and they were far over by the window. After quite a long time, an old man with a strict expression and his glasses in his hand opened the door. He was wearing a white coat just the same as everyone in charge at that place. 'Mr. Teasdale?' he said, not looking at us even though we were the only people there. I didn't think I should say anything back because I was waiting for the crying person to come out and because 'Mr. Teasdale' is my dad—not me.

'Ben Teasdale?' he said again after a bit.

'Yes, yes, that's me.'

He put his glasses on and beckoned me into the room at the same time as he was walking back in. Granny put her hand on my back and did a little push and a pat, and I got up and followed the man who hadn't even looked at me once.

I can't remember anything that was said in that room. Not from that first time or the other times that I went there. It might be that I sat there saying nothing at all, or perhaps I told the unfriendly man in a great big babble all the things that had happened at school. I don't know if he said some things to cheer me up or if he made me talk or anything. It's really just a big blank, actually. I think I just sat there and stared out of the window behind his head at all the silent people under the trees who were rocking back and forward, like the Israeli soldiers did when they got to that wall in Jerusalem in the war with the Arabs last year.

—⁓—

'We'll get you some long trousers for next term, Ben.'

That was my dad's way of telling me that I was going to go back to Courtlands for the winter term. Granny was serving out our dinner, and I could see him looking at my face to work out what I was thinking about it. I don't think I was very surprised because I had overheard him having conversations with Mr. Burston on the telephone in his study, and he had been forgetting to whisper about it.

'I'll send you the report I've had from Dr. Carstairs, Headmaster. It's really *most* encouraging.' He was talking in a sort of sucking up voice, which is why he was forgetting to be quiet about it. He must have been worried that Mr. Burston wouldn't let me go back, and then what would he do about it all, what with no Mummy being at home and Granny probably not wanting to stay with us for ever and ever.

Nothing was being talked about in our house. Granny treated me as if I was ever so ill, and I'd only get better if there was as much fuss as possible. But not ever, not once, did she talk to me about the roof business at school or anything about Mummy. In fact, she didn't even ever say her name out loud. Just like my dad. Exactly the same. I knew it was a rule in the house, but I don't know how Granny did without being told. So she just fussed over me instead. Fuss, fuss, and more fuss. Whenever we left that horrid old loony bin after seeing Dr. Carstairs, we'd get on the train, and she'd ask me if I was hungry, or thirsty, or too hot, or too cold, and even if I didn't answer, she'd poke around in her bag to find a banana, or some squash, or a Mars bar. Then I'd have to take my jacket off or put it on, and she'd wipe my forehead with a hanky that she'd poured some eau de cologne on, and the smell would fill up the whole carriage so that people would begin to look at us. I'd get annoyed because I thought they must all be wondering if there was something wrong with me, like the poor people who were living at the hospital.

It was getting to be more and more silent at home. My dad stopped saying 'Marvelous to have you here, Sylvia,' and when he came in from work he'd go straight to his study till dinner was ready because he said there was work to be caught up with. Then after the silence at the table, Granny and I would do the washing up together, and he would be back in the study with the door closed and his horrible Wagner records blaring out.

And then finally, after such a long time, Mummy came home. It was in the middle of August, not very long before I was going to go back to school.

I woke up in the morning and could hear two ladies' voices in the kitchen, one of which I knew was Granny's, and the other just the same but a little bit younger sounding, more like a girl's. At first I hid my head in the pillow to think about it for a bit because it was too good to believe, but then, when I heard her laughing, I knew it was true that she'd come back.

I jumped down the stairs three or four steps at a time and rushed into the kitchen. 'I knew you'd come back, Mummy—I just absolutely knew it!' As soon as I saw her, I knew she was better because of her smiling and what her eyes looked like, and she wasn't so very, very tiny any longer like when I last saw her. I wrapped my arms right around her, and she put both her hands in my hair and kissed my ear over and over again, and we both had tears in our eyes.

Granny drove away the next day in her car that she'd never used once since she'd arrived. She's a bit more nervous of driving since she got it back after they repaired the accident damage. She must have been very happy after such a long time in such a silent house to go back to all the things she does at home, like playing bridge with posh Mrs. Coleridge next door, her Woman's Institute meetings, and her visit to the hairdresser's to have her hair made blue again and the curls put back in.

And then I had whole days of Mummy to myself. There she was, sitting in her usual place in the armchair by the fireside, which was all filled up with bowls of roses from the garden with the petals falling around and filling the sitting room with beautiful smells. It was just lovely to sit on the sofa and watch her slowly smoking a cigarette with her legs all curled up, twizzling her hair with her fingers while she was doing the crossword puzzle from the paper. My dad had brought some new books back from London for her that she'd specially asked for, and right on top of the little pile was her teacup, which I made sure was never ever empty. It was just like the old days before the sherry.

'My constant companions, Only One! You and my books. It's all I need.' I can remember those books. There was a book of short stories by Somerset Maugham. I read one of them about a man in the South Pacific who waded into the water because he was bored and his wife didn't love him anymore, and he got eaten by a shark. Then there was another book about a man called Lytton Strachey who was an intellectual at the beginning of the century and another about the life of Tolstoy. The one at the very bottom of the pile was Anna Karenina, one of Mummy's favourites of all time. She wanted to read it again after she'd finished the one about Tolstoy so that she would understand it better.

She opened the study door and played records very loudly of Maria Callas singing Verdi and Puccini, and concertos by Elgar and Beethoven, and then some songs by Elvis Presley, The Mamas and Papas, and Joan Baez. The sound of it all filled the house right up to the attic and floated out of the open windows into the garden and down the street. At first she did a little bit of dusting round the house, but I don't think she's so bothered about that sort of thing and isn't very good at it, so she decided to stop and dead-headed the roses in the sunshine instead. After that we took all the silver in the house out onto the steps by the front door and slowly by slowly cleaned every last bit of it together. She said we were doing it because it was 'therapeutic'—that means 'treating or curing of disease' in the dictionary, and the funny thing is I think that's just what was happening because everything was getting happier and happier and better and better. My dad started talking and smiling again and shouting out 'I'm home, Pammy' when he came in the door from the station after work. Mummy was laying the table again and making nice things for our supper, and there were lots of conversations when we were eating, instead of the silence. They talked about all sorts of different things, like how the neighbours were putting up a new shed all wrong, the one way system in the town, how ugly the new cathedral in Guildford is, and lots of other really interesting political things that I didn't completely understand but were still nice to listen to. And after dinner was finished, Dad wasn't going into his study all by himself anymore. In fact, he started helping with the washing up which has never happened before. Then, best of all, the rule about me being in bed by nine o'clock was suddenly completely forgotten about and just for the very end of the holiday I was practically going to bed at any time I liked!

One day when Mummy had been back with us for about a week, I came downstairs for my breakfast and there she was in the kitchen with the tiny transistor radio from the bathroom pushed up against her ear. You could just about hear some voices very faintly coming through as though they were trying to speak above the noise of a hurricane. Now and again it would fade away completely, and then the voices would slowly come back again.

'What are you listening to, Mummy?'

'The most terrible thing, Darling. The Soviet Union is invading Czechoslovakia. I'm listening to a radio station they haven't taken over yet.'

That afternoon we got on the train together and went to London to the Czechoslovakian Embassy which is a massive grey building. When we got there we joined hundreds of other people, and we shouted and shouted 'Dubcek, Svoboda, Dubcek, Svoboda' who were the rulers of Czechoslovakia that the Russians wanted to get rid of. There was a huge crush of people in the crowd, and Mummy was explaining to me who they all were—there were old gentlemen in army uniforms with lots of medals waving little paper flags who were probably exiles from their country since the end of the war, people from universities who looked like hippies and had tied bandanas round their foreheads, big burly men from trades unions in Fleet Street and from the docks, teachers and professors, and a load of people with black flags who charged at the police even though they were on horses. Then there were others with red flags who were shouting, 'Down with Stalinism, no to state capitalism,' and carrying banners with drawings of the people in the Kremlin with their trousers down and tanks coming out of their bottoms. It was terribly exciting and actually quite dangerous. But it was very important to go. 'We have to take a stand,' Mummy kept saying to me.

I don't know whether she'd actually arranged to meet Trotsky John there, but when I turned round to see who was patting my head in the crowd, there he was with his beard all stained with the smoke from his cigarettes and his beret lopsided on his head. 'Hello, young man,' he said to me, and then he put his arm round Mummy's waist. I could tell that she didn't want to catch my eye when that happened, and actually, for a bit I didn't feel like talking to her anymore. I didn't want to see Trotsky John; he made me feel as though everything might go wrong again.

We went for tea in a café after the demonstration finished. It was crowded out with demonstrators all sitting around, some on the chairs, some on the tables and some even on the floor, with their rolled up banners and flags leaning up against the walls and ashtrays and cups falling off the tables when somebody's bottom sent them flying, and the ground all littered with thrown away pamphlets.

There wasn't any room for me to sit down at our table, and before I knew it, I was yanked up onto Trotsky John's lap like I was a three-year-old, which was very embarrassing. I'm ten years' old for heaven's sake! I picked up some of the pamphlets and started to read them so I didn't once have to talk to him. They were all about solidarity with the people in Prague and Vietnam, the students who have been rioting in Paris, and the editors of the newspapers in Athens who have been put in prison by the colonels who rule that country. Trotsky John was talking loudly which meant that he was blowing smoky breath and beer fumes over me because he was drinking some cans of that instead of the tea in the café; then he was calling out to people he knew and introducing them all to Mummy, but no one seemed to be very interested because they were all talking about the demonstration and couldn't hear anything anyway.

After a bit, Mummy whispered in my ear, 'Time to go, Only One. Dad will be waiting for his dinner.' I was ever so pleased. I was glad that we went to shout at the embassy, but I also wanted to go home to get far away from Trotsky John.

'You're not leaving us already!' he said, looking all surprised.

'We've got to, John. Adrian's expecting us back,' she said while I was getting off his knee and she was finding her bag under his chair.

'I see. Going back to your bourgeois little existence with your bourgeois little bank manager then.'

'He's not a bank manager, John.'

'I feel sorry for you, Pammo—really sorry for you,' he called out to us as we were going towards the door through all the people. It was lovely to get outside away from the crush and the noise and the smoke. We started walking along the pavement to the tube station and after just a few steps, Mummy suddenly stopped. When I looked up at her she was just staring at me with her head on one side.

'Gosh, Ben. Look at you standing there! As tall as me now.' She stared again and very slowly smiled as though she hadn't seen me for a long time. Then she bent her head down and gave me a kiss on the cheek.

—*m*—

The next Saturday, Mummy and my dad and me went to Bognor Regis for the day in the car. It was sunny and windy and rainy all at the same time, so there weren't very many people on the beach. Mummy and I went paddling and were running backwards and forwards away from the sea, screaming and pretending to be frightened of the huge waves that the wind was making. My dad skimmed stones and laughed at our game. Then we had tea and scones with strawberry jam and cream at a place with pink tablecloths and cups and saucers with roses on. I was laughing because Mummy had told me before we went into the café that a wave had wet her knickers, and she wanted to take them off. When she sat down she was making funny faces and crossing her eyes, and I got the giggles so badly I couldn't stop. The waitress joined in the laughter, though she didn't know the reason, and later she brought another huge extra dollop of cream as a special treat. Mummy was holding her cup up to her face with both hands like she does when she's really enjoying her tea. The day at the park in Saxham when the sherry bottle got smashed seemed as though it could have been ages and ages ago.

Afterwards, we paddled in the sea again while we walked back to the car at the other end of the beach. I smiled when I looked at Mummy and my dad away in the distance in front of me. He had his trousers wet up to his knees, and she had her dress all tucked up in her belt. They were holding hands tightly and every now and again they leant towards each other, and I bet they must have been thinking that now things had gone back to being as nice as the days when we lived in Beirut.

—*m*—

Just a few days after that I went back to school. This time when Mummy took me to the station I wasn't having to remember any of those things like I had to before, like the keys, the money, and checking for her half-finished mints. There wasn't the slightest sign of the sherry bottle in her bag, and she didn't cry when the train came. Instead she smiled at me and held my face in her hands and kissed me on both cheeks through the window of the train and said, 'I love you, Only One,' with just a slight shakiness in her voice. I think she was on some sort of best behaviour so that I'd know that everything was going to be alright from now on. 'I'll see you at half term,' she said.

I dreaded getting back to school even more than usual, and I was also a bit upset that my long trousers hadn't arrived from the school shop. But most of all I was worried that everyone was bound to be talking about what happened to me last term and why I'd done it, so I was having to plot like mad what I was going to say.

But no one was talking about it. I began to think that it must have been a rule that everyone had been told about 'not to say anything to Teasdale about being on the roof.' Only Theo properly mentioned it, and when he did he was whispering and looking around as though he was breaking the rules and might get into trouble for it. That was typical of course, knowing him. Nosey old cretin. I think they've made sure not to put him in the same dorm as me again, which is a jolly good thing if you ask me.

'Why d-did yh-yh-you do it?' he whispered to me when we were all going up the stairs to our new dorms on the first night.

'What?'

'C-climb onto the roof.'

'I don't know...'

'Oh c-c-come on, 'course y-yh-you do.'

'I wanted to see the view.' A bit of me wanted to say it was because he was so nasty and pulled down my pajama bottoms, but I never did say that in the end.

But it might have been because of Mr. England that no one was really talking very much about the roof. I think people were already getting a bit used to the idea of what I'd done, and it was quite a long time ago so they were forgetting it a bit. But the Mr. England news had happened during the holidays so everyone wanted to catch up about it.

Mummy told me the afternoon after our day in Bognor Regis. I was sitting on the steps outside the front door with her, and when Women's Hour finished on the radio, she moved up close to me and put her arm around me.

'Darling, there's something I've got to tell you.' She was stubbing her cigarette out on the step and taking a long time about it and flicking her hair away from her face which is a thing she does when she's a bit worried.

'It's horrid news, and I want you to be brave about it.' She was holding me very tight, and I started to get quite frightened during the pause. I knew I didn't want to hear what she was going to say.

'What, Mummy? What is it?'

'It's about Mr. England...'

'What about him, Mummy? What's happened?'

And then she told me he was dead.

She told me he'd been swimming in the sea and had got caught in a really strong current that had taken him right out to sea.

'When, Mummy? When did it happen?'

'At the beginning of the summer holidays, Darling. While you and I weren't very well. Daddy and I've not wanted to tell you about it till you were feeling a bit stronger.'

After she'd told me, I went upstairs to my room and lay in the quiet. Mummy came up to see me after a while and sat on the side of the bed. She never said anything but stroked my hair and my face with the tips of her fingers. Then when my dad came in from the office I heard them tiptoeing and whispering about it outside my bedroom door as though I might not be very well again.

'Have you told him?'

'Yes,' Mummy said.

'How did he take it?'

'He's okay. He's okay.'

When I went down for supper, no one talked about it. Mummy

kept smiling at me and stroking my face, knowing that there was no point in mentioning it all, and my dad was just silent about it so that it would soon be something that could be all forgotten about.

—⁓—

Actually, after a bit, I liked it—everybody at school knowing about the roof business but not daring to ask me any questions. Perhaps they thought that I was a bit of a mad person and the next time I got upset I might throw myself into the river or take too many headache pills like Marilyn Monroe or something. Sometimes I felt as though I might be a bit of a mysterious person, like somebody who's been sneaked over from an orphanage in Puerto Rico or Albania, or a prince who's mum and dad had been killed in a revolution, and if anyone was daring to ask me any questions about anything that I didn't like, I would just have to turn away looking sad and lost and far away as if I was someone a bit special with a tragic sort of a history.

In the first lesson of the term, when we were learning about the Tudors—we were just getting up to the dissolution of the monasteries and Henry VIII and the beheaded wives and everything—I looked up suddenly to see Mrs. Marston staring at me. She turned away very quickly, but I knew she was having a good old look and thinking about me. And at first, she'd been using a sort of slightly different voice when she was talking to me. She's probably been telling her friends outside of the school all about what I did. Actually, I'd probably become quite famous with it all—probably the most famous person in the school, in fact.

But that was only at the beginning of term. After a few weeks, Mrs. Marston one day asked us in class who we thought had given the Statue of Liberty to the people in the United States. I put my hand up and said 'The Anglo-Saxons, Mrs. Marston,' and she said in a not very nice sort of voice '...and when do you imagine that would have been?' and I said 'Just a little bit before the time of the Battle of

237

Hastings,' and then she looked at the ceiling for a bit and said 'Lord grant me the strength to carry on,' and I knew everything was back to normal then. My adventure was forgotten about. I wasn't famous anymore, not even for wetting the bed, thank God, on account of Miss Carson still waking me up every night for a wee.

'Mummy will not be here when you come home for the Christmas holidays. Instead, we have a nice girl from Sweden called Lena staying with us who will be helping around the house during the Christmas break.'

That's what my dad's letter said. That's not how it started, because he began it like he usually does, going on about hoping I was working hard and enjoying a good game of rugby—in other words forgetting all over again that it's football we play in the winter term and not rugby till the Easter one.

I knew there was something wrong even before that though, because suddenly there was not a single letter from Mummy, and he was writing every week instead, which is a thing that had never happened before. Usually it was just a small note he'd put at the end of Mummy's letter, after her hugs and kisses. So actually, when the one came about Swedish Lena, I wasn't completely surprised, but just very, very upset to think everything had gone wrong again. Then at half term, instead of going home like Mummy had absolutely promised at the station, I had to go to stay with Granny, which was worse than just staying at the school by myself, because Granny is quite forgetful about things now and keeps saying all the same stuff over and over again. She takes ages putting her blooming hat and coat on if we're going out, and always there's so much time that has to be spent looking for her purse and car keys and checking the back door's locked, and then when we're in the car, it's really quite frightening. When she was driving us to church, my side of the car went right up onto the pavement for quite a long time as we were going along, and I don't think she even noticed, even when an old man banged the car with his walking stick and shouted out 'Silly old biddy—you're a bloody menace, you are!'

'Damned cheek!' she said as though she hadn't done anything wrong. I didn't say anything, of course.

There wasn't so much talking that weekend, actually. Certainly not about Mummy. Not one bit about her, in fact—just like it was before she came back from that place where she'd been to get better from the sherry and stuff. I knew I wasn't meant to ask about it.

—◊—

It's been a really horrible Christmas, the worst one ever. Nearly as bad as the ones when Mummy had too much sherry. We didn't have a tree or any decorations, and my dad didn't put a single card on top of the mantelpiece or on the bookshelves. He just opened them up when we were having dinner, had a quick look at them and then put them in a big pile, all still closed up. When the fire in the sitting room was just about to go out the day before yesterday, he threw the whole lot of them onto it and then put some coal on top of them and said, 'There we are!' and that was the very end of this Christmas. I've just been locked away in my room everyday all by myself waiting for Children's Hour to start and trying to arrange my stamps and reading some history books. Lena was here for a few days at the beginning, then she went back to Sweden for her own Christmas, and I suppose she thinks this is how all Christmases are if you come to England. I bet she was really pleased to get away. She's come back now, but I don't know what she'll be doing after I've gone back to school. Probably she's going to iron some of my dad's shirts and things like that. I wonder if she'll still be here when I come back for the Easter holidays?

Granny came to stay again just as Lena was going to Heathrow Airport. She drove up when there was a huge hail storm going on and when I went down the front door steps to help her with her bag,

I saw that there was a big dent at the front side of her car. She hadn't even noticed, so that just proves how bad her driving is now. When I asked her about it later she said that perhaps she did remember a bit of a bang when she was round about Cirencester.

When we ate the Christmas dinner after we'd opened our presents, the potatoes were all burned, the turkey was pink inside and far too chewy, the peas were still a bit icy, and Granny even completely forgot about the gravy, so that means that she can't really cook anymore. At least we had the telly on after, before the mince pies, so Granny was a bit quieter and not saying the same things over and over again which is very annoying and worrying at the same time, because I always think my dad is just about to say 'Oh for heaven's sake!' or something rude and upsetting. It was me who put the mince pies in the oven to heat up, just in case of a Granny burning accident. I made the tea, too, because I'm an expert at that, cut the Christmas cake up into sensible portions, and put it all on the trolley for the sitting room to have while Moira Anderson and Jimmy Steward were on with their Scottish singing and dancing. The only good thing about this Christmas was that at long, long last my long trousers came as one of the presents—thank God! Also, my dad did get me the Stanley Gibbons stamp catalogue which is a very good thing.

It was ever such a big surprise when my dad asked me on Boxing Day if I wanted to go and stay with Mummy in London for the New Year. No one had said the slightest thing about her so I didn't even know where she was until he said it. It was such a relief thinking that Mummy wasn't ill again, and perhaps in fact they were just going to be having a divorce. There are lots of those happening all the time, after all, even with boys at school, and that's not really so bad. I'm sure I could begin to get used to it, and then I might live in two different houses at the same time.

My dad was sad and worried about it, though. When he asked me if I wanted to go, he started it with a little cough, went a bit red, and wasn't looking at me. I knew it was just best to say yes and then not talk about it anymore. But inside I was so happy—I just absolutely couldn't wait to see Mummy again.

My dad drove me to the station and took me onto the platform. It was very strange because usually when we're at stations he's talking about school and stuff. It's very difficult to think of the right things to say, especially when he's not saying anything himself. I was ever so pleased when the train came quite quickly.

At first I couldn't see that it was Mummy waiting for me under the same clock at Waterloo where my dad usually meets me. She looked so different. She wasn't wearing a coat, just a very big thin jacket made from jeans material. She had her arms wrapped round herself and was shaking like a leaf in the cold. Her eyes were black with makeup, and her hair was pulled back in a very tight ponytail so you could see the veins on her temples. When I put my arms around her, she didn't put hers round me. I think she was a bit too cold to let go of herself.

It was a horrible house that we went to, in a place called Finsbury Park. Really, really horrible. It was cold and damp and smelly and under a noisy old railway bridge that made the whole house shudder like mad when a train went by. There was hardly any furniture in there, just mattresses on the floors, hard old armchairs, and a sofa covered with a smelly blanket in the sitting room that went right down in the middle when you sat on it. There was a nailed up sheet instead of curtains on the landing, old wallpaper that was peeling off, a rickety banister with a part of it missing, bulbs with no lampshades and light switches hanging out of the walls ready to give you an electric shock. The loo was black inside with newspaper instead of toilet roll, a tap dripped all day in the kitchen with old dirty dishes stacked up and no one doing the washing up, and everywhere there were full-up ashtrays and mugs with bits of old coffee and wine at the bottom. There was only a bit of hot water in the taps now and again, and it was freezing, freezing cold with a fire in the sitting room that didn't make any difference but blew out black smoke that went up the stairs leaving the smell of burning. There was a very skinny cat with no tail and a stuck together eye, a dead pigeon on an outside windowsill, and in the kitchen a tail of something disappearing underneath the fridge, which I'm really sure was a big mouse.

It was the worst house I was ever in. It was called a squat. That's what Trotsky John said. He said it had been 'requisitioned on behalf of the working people.' But I don't think that any of the people living in that house had jobs.

I wasn't at all surprised to see Trotsky John was there. I was sitting on the sofa talking to Mummy when he came in and said 'Hi there, Ben,' and ruffled my hair which I completely hate. Mummy didn't say anything about it of course, because she knows I don't like him.

I never found out how many people were there because some of them were just staying in their rooms. Sometimes I heard the floorboards creaking, records playing, and the odd bit of coughing. Nobody spoke to me. Not even Mummy, really. Not properly. I sat trying to read my book in the sitting room with Mummy and Trotsky John and a lady with short blonde-hair and bony fingers with rings on who kept sniffing and wiping her nose on her sleeve. A man who was her boyfriend, with a droopy moustache and curly hair nearly as long as Mummy's, was rolling up big white cigarettes on the cover of a Led Zeppelin LP. He was passing them round the room and everyone was having a go of it. When the blonde-haired lady pretended to pass one to me everyone had a laugh about it. I didn't smoke any of it, of course, because I'm far too young. Mummy wasn't smoking the cigarettes, either. She was just having her wine which she kept going to the kitchen for, though she never got so terribly wobbly with it like I've seen her sometimes; she was just a bit not alright all the time, in fact.

The worst thing of all was that she just wasn't really talking to me. That was the very reason I'd come to see her, to talk to her all day long and have a lovely time with her.

In the evening, Trotsky John went out and came back with fish and chips for everyone. I went to the kitchen to see if I could make Mummy a cup of tea to have with it, although she'd said she didn't want one. 'I'll stick to my wine, Only One, thank you.' Anyway, there wasn't any tea at all in the kitchen that I could find.

I didn't like it there. Not one little bit. I think that everybody in that house just thought it was one big nuisance that I was there, so all I was doing in the end was sitting in the kitchen reading my book and wondering if the mouse would come back. Later on, when I was going back into the room where they all were, Trotsky John shouted at the lady with the blonde hair 'Not in front of the nipper, Skegs,' and she shouted back at him 'Jesus Christ, what the fuck's he doing here anyway? This is no place for a kid,' and then she was pushing something under the sofa so that I couldn't see it.

When it was nighttime, I was awake way past my usual bedtime and actually beginning to fall asleep on the carpet. After a very, very long time of no one talking, they all got up and went out of the room. It must have been the middle of the night by that time. Then Mummy came back with a quilt and a pillow. She did kiss me good-night though, and then I wrapped the quilt round myself and tried to fall asleep on the sofa, but something hard was poking through the cushions, and I was freezing cold although I had all my clothes on. I took all the cushions off the sofa and made a small bed in front of the fire that was just about going out, and then I found a newspaper that I scrunched up and put onto the last red bits of the coal to keep the warm going a bit longer. When the room was in complete blackness and cold, I suddenly remembered I hadn't brushed my teeth, so I had to get up and feel for the light switch by the door so that I could look in the bag my dad had packed for me. I thought my toothbrush might be underneath my pajamas that I wasn't wearing on account of perhaps someone coming in while I was undressing and it being too cold anyway. That's when I discovered that he'd completely forgotten to put it in, and anyway, when I went in the dark to the bathroom up the stairs and past the landing, there was not so much as any toothpaste in there to put on my finger even, and just then I really, really wanted so much to go home and felt right on the edge of crying about it.

In the morning of the next day—which was actually New Year's Eve—I asked Mummy if I could go out to the shops for a bar of chocolate. I went straight to a telephone box to phone up my dad. I prayed and prayed that he'd just this once pick up the phone and could hardly believe it when he did.

'I just need to come home, Dad.'

'Is everything alright?'

'Yes, but I just need to come home. I think I really need to concentrate on a little bit more of my homework before next term, and I've forgotten to bring my books with me.'

'Are you sure you're...'

'Please, Dad. Please, please. I need to come home. I really need to come home. Can you come and get me today...?'

Then I was sitting on a chair in the kitchen with my bag ready and my coat on, just looking along the hallway to where the front door was, trying to see through a broken bit of glass ready to catch sight of his brown coat when he got there.

It didn't take him very long, actually. When I saw there was somebody outside, I rushed along the corridor and opened the door and threw my arms around him because it was so great that he'd arrived at last. After just the littlest bit of time when he wasn't sure what to do about it, he put his arms around me, and pulled me to him really tight and put his cheek by my ear.

'It's alright, Ben. Everything's going to be alright. We're going home. We're going home...' That's what he kept on saying while he was stroking my hair.

Mummy stood at the doorway as we were driving away with Trotsky John behind her in the gloominess of that horrid house. I can't remember for absolute sure, but I don't think I said goodbye to her. I actually don't think I ever did say goodbye to her.

The taxi'll be here any second now. I hope it's not going to be late, but in fact we've still got plenty of time. I just wish Swedish Lena wasn't coming with me. I'm better going on my own. My dad will be meeting me as usual under the clock at Waterloo, and that's not necessary either, because I know how to go on the Bakerloo underground line. I know how to get all the way to the right platform at Paddington just as much as him, in fact, but he's insisting on coming too.

It might be only me, Fisheye, and Giles Webster catching the train this term. Nick Gower's going in his father's Jaguar car, I think.

I don't want to see Webster's mum. I'm embarrassed about it, on account of her asking me to look after him and then me not being alright during the summer and forgetting all about him. Perhaps it's best not to say the slightest thing about it if she's there.

It might be Mr. Burston who's coming to get us, or just as likely Miss Carson now that Miss Newman's left.

It would have been Mr. England if he wasn't dead. In the old days, it would have been him coming to see us back to school.

I dream about him. Sometimes just daydreaming while I'm looking out of the window at school when I should be concentrating on my work, or upstairs in my bedroom here at home lying on my bed, reading a book and suddenly not seeing the words anymore because he's there instead. Very often, he's in my actual dreams during the night, too. Mostly it's the same story over and over again, the story of what really happened that we all now know about at school but have to pretend that we don't.

The usual dream is of him in his Mini, which is a wrong thing, of course, because it had been completely ruined in the car crash with the-not-looking-properly lady. But that's what I see, and it never changes. I haven't told anyone about it in case they think I'm all upset still, and there's just no point because I'm better now. I'm quite alright again. Mummy's not here and neither is Mr. England,

and we've all just got to get used to it.

In the dream, he drives over the Cotswold Hills, through Reading, passing by quite close to our house here, and then he gets to the City of London and goes past the banks which are all shut up with no one in the streets on account of it being the very middle of the night. Then he crosses Tower Bridge, drives along the river past the Cutty Sark, up hill in Greenwich Park, and through the countryside of Kent. He clutches the steering wheel tightly with no expression on his face as he looks at the road in front of him. He gets to the Cathedral at Canterbury and then carries right on until he reaches where he used to live as a little boy with his mum and dad before they sold their house there, right by the English Channel. He parks his car next to the pebbles on the beach, and while he sits there in the silence with the engine off, doing nothing at all but staring at the waves, he sees the light beginning to come up because it's a new day.

He gets out of the car, locks the door very carefully, and goes onto the beach. Very slowly he takes all his clothes off apart from his underpants and folds everything ever so neatly before putting them in a pile on the pebbles with the car keys and his watch right on the very top. After that he climbs up to the top of the pebbles even though it hurts his feet, stops for a tiny bit, and breathes deeply, trying to be brave. Then he rushes forward just like those men you see pictures of in the First World War when they're going over the top of the trenches, and he's down the slope and splashing into the sea and just for a bit goes right under. When he comes up again, with his yellow hair flat against his head, he swims, and swims, and swims without ever stopping or looking back at the beach in case he suddenly loses his bravery. He keeps on going until his head is the tiniest white dot, far out to sea. And slowly by slowly, when he's about halfway to France, never once thinking of coming back, he gets sleepier and sleepier and begins to sink down farther into the waves until at last, he disappears forever.

I've still got the little prayer that he wrote down on the piece of paper for me. It's folded up in the front of my Bible. I don't have to look at it anymore because I know it off by heart now.

'Remember not the sins and offences of my youth; but according to thy mercy, think thou upon me, Oh Lord, for thy forgiveness...'

I say it to him, out loud if I'm all alone and silently in my head if it's in the middle of the night. I know it's a prayer about forgiving people. But he doesn't need forgiveness because he never ever did anything wrong, which I know for certain is the absolute truth. But he gave it to me, and I say it just for him. Wherever he is now, I hope he might be able to hear my voice in the far off distance.

VI.

Whitchurch School, September, 1973

'Travels! Get your head down and do some work!'

Bloody Portman, throwing his weight around just because he's been made prep prefect. It's none of his business whether I'm working or looking out of the window, and it drives me nuts being called 'Travels.' I can't stand it, but everyone's picked it up now. It's going to stick, I know it. A nickname always does if it's been used for a whole term or more.

I sort of asked for it, though. It's the stupidest thing ever. I'd be laughing about it too if it had happened to someone else, that's for sure.

It all started because I'm so in love with my stamps. For the last one or two years I've been completely obsessed with them—even down to dreaming about them. Big ones, small ones, triangular ones, first day covers, Penny Blacks, British Guiana 1c magentas; last week, I had an incredibly real dream about finding a US Graf Zeppelin in a bag of assorted stamps from Woolworths that only cost 25p. Can you imagine?

If I close my eyes right now I can smell that stamp shop on The Strand in London—all the musty old catalogues, the stamp glue, and the owner's cigars mixed up with his assistant's awful BO. My most recent dream was just last night, in fact, about managing to get hold of a whole sheet of England Winners, unfranked, in totally mint condition from the World Cup Final in 1966 from someone who hadn't a clue that he was selling something special. Bit of a laugh that I can't bear football but would murder to get hold of those! I think stamp collecting's absolutely the best hobby ever, but I suppose it's really hard for most people to understand that. It's probably something to do with the fact I like modern history so much. Perhaps it's the other way round, though—if you get to know about a country's stamps, you automatically know about its politics, and then it's just like being hooked on The Archers or Coronation Street, because you just have to know what's going to happen next. It was my stamps that got me so interested in what's going on in the world. I suppose I'm a bit of a freak, really. I dream about stamps while everybody else in the dorm dreams about tits and fannies and listens to Jimmy Hendrix, Pink Floyd, and David Bowie being Ziggy Stardust.

Anyway, this whole bloody nickname thing began last term when Sheldrake and Mossiman told me that a stamp dealing shop had opened up on the Monmouth Road, and I should get along there quick because there were a couple of absolute bargains going. That was silly enough by itself, because I'd never talked to those two about stamps before. I know perfectly well they're not collectors, so I should have known straightaway that something was up, but I suppose I just got overexcited about it. I think they'd heard me saying to Hillman, who's a collector from Dyfed House, that I was especially interested in stamps of the boy kings from the Balkans—King Michael of Romania, King Simeon of Bulgaria, and King Peter of Yugoslavia. Mossiman started by telling me all about this new place when we were going over to Friday breakfast, and once he could see I'd got really excited about it, he said, 'Did I hear you saying something to Hillman about Michael of Ruritania?'

'You mean Michael of Romania?'

'Yea, that's the one.'

'What about him?'

'Well, they've got a whole lot of stamps of him.'

'Really? Are you sure? They're quite rare, you know.'

'Yep. Seen them myself.'

So the next day, Saturday after games, I walked all along the Monmouth Road right into the country following exactly the directions Sheldrake had written down. Eventually I came to a track with a big sign saying 'Malpas Farm' and just by the side of it, right in the middle of the field, was this big hut which was what the piece of paper said was the stamp place. I went across the field, which was incredibly muddy and boggy and opened the door with a shove. Inside there was a terrific noise of saws cutting planks, with inches and inches of wood shavings on the floor and stuff. When the two men in there stopped the machines and took off their masks to see what I wanted, I asked in the silence, 'Is this the stamp shop?' and they looked at each other and then one of them said, 'Piss off, you twat.'

Just as I got back to the gate, wondering about what had happened, bloody Mossiman and Sheldrake and Charlton jumped out from behind a hedge and started laughing so much they were actually bending over and holding their stomachs. Then all the way back to school they were hitting the back of my head and throwing my cap around, calling me names, and telling me that I'm the most gullible person in the school. That's when the 'Travels' business started, right then, and they've told absolutely everybody. First it was 'Gullible.' That changed to 'Gully' quite quickly. Then it went to 'Gulliver' for a while, and now it's 'Travels' because of Gulliver's Travels. 'Travels Teasdale.' That's my full blooming name now. Even some of the masters are saying it in class. I'll just have to put up with it, I suppose. But really, how stupid could I get? A stamp shop in the middle of a field, for God's sake...

But it's the business of Mummy's letters that's really getting to me at the moment. I'm so worried about it I can hardly concentrate on breathing in and out, let alone doing the bloody homework we've been set for tomorrow, and there's literally hours of work to do. I haven't even started, and we're already nearly halfway through prep. It'll be cocoa break in a minute, and I've done sod all so far. Typical that the most difficult night of prep we've had for yonks is when I'm feeling this bad. I just can't concentrate on anything; I'm daydreaming, looking out the window, thinking about my own stuff, worrying myself into a frenzy. Everyone else is hunched over their desks, writing away like mad, and I'm staring out of the window at the starlings clattering around in the trees getting ready to fly away for the winter. I haven't got a hope in hell of finishing what's been set. That's a horrible vicious circle, because I can already feel myself getting worried about time rushing by, let alone the panic about the letters. And still I'm not getting on with it.

Wittenberg. That's the name of the place where Martin Luther nailed his ninety-five theses to the door of the church. Wittenberg. But can I remember it—get it into my thick skull for the test tomorrow afternoon? No, however much I blooming-well try. So half an hour ago I took a break from the The Reformation text book to see if the French translation old Miller set us might come a bit easier. That's for tomorrow morning, and I'm the sucker who's meant to be reading it out in class. I've got to translate the first scene of the second act of Les Mains Sales by Sartre. It's only two pages, but it starts with some chap called Ivan saying 'Dis!' That's his first word! What the hell does 'Dis' mean? It's not even in the dictionary for God's sake… Actually, I think Miller's losing it; I really do. I think it's possible he's set an 'A' level test for his 'O' level class. I bet Les Mains Sales is part of the 'A' level syllabus for this year, and the silly old bugger has got it all mixed up. It's way beyond our level. We've just moved up from the fourth to the fifth form for God's sake, and we're only three weeks into the new year.

Nothing's going to be alright until I solve the problem of the letters, but the plain fact is I can't do anything about it until I go home at half term, and it's not even certain that I can get there then. Pa hasn't said yes to it yet, anyway. I've told him I want to go to a meeting in Red Lion Square about the coup in Chile, and it is true that I really need to be there, but the absolute priority is to put the letters back in the suitcase. The thing is, I don't even know for sure there is a Chile meeting the weekend of half term, but that's the excuse I'm going to use. He knows how passionate I am about what happened, so I really think he might let me go home if I tell him there's some sort of meeting going on. He laughs at me a bit about my being so interested in all my political stuff, but he likes it really. He likes it that I know more about it than he does now, so he'll probably say yes as long as he's not doing one of his foreign trips that weekend. Please, God, he lets me go home and doesn't do a search of the attic before I get there.

The worry of it is making everything worse at the moment—especially this thing I've started about feeling sick. I've no idea why that's happening; all I know is that it's certainly getting worse and worse. Morning Assembly's the hardest time. I try to get there before most of the others so that I'm never in the middle of a row. If I'm at all held up—like I have been this week because I've been Basement-floor Cleaning Monitor in the House—I don't have a choice as to where I sit. Yesterday, one of the plugholes in the shower room was totally bunged up with hair and stuff, and I couldn't just leave it, so I was really late getting into the hall and ended up right bang in the middle of a row. It's not a small Assembly like the one we used to have at Courtlands. Here at Whitchurch it's in the main hall and goes on for ages—with the whole school there of course, all five hundred of us. It's a huge room. But even so we're jam-packed in like sardines, and it's always hot and stuffy.

I've started to do this completely mad thing now where I hear my own voice out of the blue saying bonkers things like, 'Oh shit, you're going to be sick,' and then it all starts happening. Suddenly I'm sweating and woozy and thinking I'm going to throw up. When it first started I thought I had flu or something, but the sick feeling went away nearly as soon as we got out of Assembly to go into class. When it happened again the next week and just a few days after that yet again, I knew it wasn't really because I was properly ill. I haven't told a single soul about it, not even Taff, my best friend here. Now it sometimes happens in other places too, like Mr. Sander's ghastly maths class. Once or twice in the middle of lunch I've been on the edge of it. I nearly had to leave the refectory yesterday, but did my best to stay sitting there until I started to feel a bit better, because I really don't want people to catch on to it. It's just the most important thing that no one finds out.

The first time I properly felt it was in the middle of last term during our fourth form outing. That was 4b and 4c's trip to the theatre in Bristol—to the very same theatre where we used to go from Courtlands for the Vienna Boys' Choir. We went to see The

Seagull by Chekhov, which was great at first but about halfway through, just at the bit when a chap called Konstantin is having his play performed in the garden of his mum's house, I suddenly felt horribly sick. I think that perhaps it was because I felt sorry for him or something—his Mum was being so awful about his play, not listening properly, and sending him up and making jokes about it to her boyfriend. Anyway, I felt so bad that I just had no choice but to get out and had to disturb the whole of the row in the dark, with everyone tutting and moving their knees to the side to let me through. Cooper at the end of the row whispered loudly at me, 'Oh for heaven's sake, Travels!' I went into the foyer and sat on the steps till the interval doing deep breathing the same as my old asthma exercises. It was horrible, that first one. But if anything, it's worse now. In fact, it's got to the point where I worry about being anywhere with too many people jam-packed in.

I'm not sure what to do about it. I've been determined not to tell anyone, though I suppose I might eventually have to talk to Senior Matron about it. But I'm going to see if it might just go away by itself, first. Perhaps it will just get better if I try not to think about it and concentrate on other things.

The thing is it feels a bit like my old bed wetting secret at Courtlands. I feel dead ashamed of it. Taff would probably understand, though. I might dare to tell him—as long as I can keep a straight face when I next see him. He looks so funny at the moment. He was being teased, as usual, about being ugly and fat with lanky hair last week. So, hey presto, he goes and gets a short back and sides done this morning. Now he looks like a member of the Gestapo! But in fact he's the kindest person in the whole school, though nobody realises it apart from me. The best time to talk to him would be next Sunday before tea down at the pavilion after we've finished listening to Pick of the Pops on the radio. He'll be there for sure because we never miss that. I can have a good old think about what to say before I see him.

This whole thing about the letters really started last Easter hols when Pa said out of the blue that he was thinking of selling the house. Even though he'd changed his mind about it by the time I left for the beginning of term, it somehow just got me thinking about everything.

Mummy chose it for us; that's why. In a sort of way it's her house. It feels as though it still is, even now after all this time of her being gone.

I remember her leaving us in Beirut because she was coming back to England to search for it. She came to my room to say goodbye. I was in bed in the dark, and she bent over to kiss me, all smelling of perfume and leaving a big smear of lipstick on my cheek that I didn't see till the morning. She told me she was flying back to England to do some house-hunting, and that she'd see me in a week, after she'd found a lovely place with high ceilings, lots of fireplaces and roses in the garden.

She did find the perfect house, and was incredibly clever at making it nice for us, with all the big sofas with shiny colourful cushions and Persian things—carpets, and brass lamps, and coffee pots everywhere. She covered the walls with lovely pictures and rugs from all the places she'd been to in the Middle East, and some of those things are still at home now. It didn't look like anybody else's house that we knew. She loved old things, even if they were quite tatty, like the curtains that were in the sitting room when we first moved in. They'd been left behind by the old lady who lived there before us, and Mummy wanted to keep them. They were yellow and shiny, hanging right down to the ground, but they had big rips in because they'd been rotted by the sunlight. Pa absolutely put his foot down and insisted that they had to be thrown away. 'Pam, no! It's ludicrous,' he said to her. 'They're falling apart in front of our eyes!' It was a terrible pity, because I thought they were lovely too. There were already lots of roses in the garden, but she bought more and planted hundreds of daffodil bulbs under the lawn that still come up every spring. She kept hostas in huge pots and, until she was ill, always remembered to search for the slugs that would come out to eat their leaves after it rained.

A lot of those beautiful things disappeared from the house when she wasn't well, round about the time of the roof business at Court-lands. She was probably selling them so that she had money for her sherry. There was a painting her dad had left her in his will that Granny brought to the house in her car soon after he died. It was a picture of a field of poppies, a bit like the famous ones that Monet did. I'm not sure that it was anything absolutely special, but it was gone one day when I came back for a holiday. I really adored that picture. I never asked about it, of course. Nothing like that was to be mentioned in front of Pa for a start, and that's still absolutely the way it is now. We don't talk at all about those things. We don't talk about Mummy or anything the least to do with her—ever. In fact, I think it's quite possible that we've never really mentioned her from the moment all the guests left the house after the funeral.

So that's why I need to get the letters back in the case. It would just be the worst thing in the world if Pa knew I had them here with me. Worse than anything. Nearly as bad as if he opened the door of my bedroom without knocking and found me doing something.

—⁊⁊—

I've always known about the case in the attic full of Mummy's things. There's some sort of faded memory I have about it, even though I'm not meant to know. Pa must have packed it and put it up there during that horrible muddled time after she went away, and I wasn't clear about anything.

I had to go up there once, ages ago. There was a damp patch on the ceiling of my bedroom, then a proper leak coming into the far corner, and Pa asked me to have a look in the attic. I was still quite small at that time and could squeeze into the space behind the water tank. I climbed up first while he stood on the ladder so his head was just popping up above the loft hatch. From there, he shone the torch where he wanted me to look. Just after I discovered where the problem was—I think there was a tile missing on the outside—his hand must have slipped. The light went all berserk and shot around the place so that just for a moment we could see all sorts of things that were stored up there, like the box of Christmas decorations, all the things we got from Granny when we had to move her to the nursing home after she went doo-lally—her old cracked everyday plates, all Granddad's history books about Napoleon's wars in Spain, his ancient encyclopedias stacked up against the telly we couldn't get to work, and the upside down piano stool Granny said had belonged to the Empress Eugenie but definitely hadn't, of course. Right at the end, when Pa stopped slipping or whatever he was doing, the torch was left lighting up the suitcase. He whisked it away again ever so quickly when he realised. I never said anything about it, naturally, and was quite clever in talking immediately in a concerned voice about the water coming in, as though I hadn't noticed.

That was the last time I saw the case until five weeks ago.

I needed to have a look. I needed to from the moment that Pa said we might be moving, and even when he changed his mind, the thought just never went away all through last term. So I made up my mind that during the summer holidays, as soon as he went on one of his foreign trips, which he was bound to do sooner or later, and only Lena—who came back for the third time this summer because of her policeman boyfriend in Guildford—and I were in the house, I was going to take the case down from the attic. It felt like the wickedest plan ever, as though I was being a traitor to Pa, but I just absolutely had to do it. In the end, I had to wait right till the last week of the holiday before Pa was away for two days, and Lena was out of the house at her English class, then the pictures, and not back till late. She only agreed to stay out after I promised her that I'd never tell Pa that she wasn't back to make my dinner, but in fact she knew very well that I wouldn't say anything about it because I hate being mollycoddled anyway. I'm quite capable of getting my own blooming food. It's ridiculous having an au pair in the first place. I'm fifteen for God's sake.

I didn't climb up into the attic as soon as Lena went out in the morning like I'd made up my mind to. I was going to do it before I ate the sandwiches she left me but got really nervous and just couldn't get myself to start. But sitting in the kitchen after lunch thinking about it, I took three deep breaths and said, 'Pull yourself together—one, two, three!' and ran up the stairs.

It was terribly difficult yanking the pulley to get the loft ladder down by myself. It just wouldn't slide down—I suppose because it's hardly ever used—but once I'd managed it, I went straight up into the gloom and felt my way very carefully over to where I remembered the case was. I had to make absolute sure I was putting my feet down in the right place on the rafters because it's incredibly easy to fall all the way through and land up in a bedroom or something. After I got used to the dark, enough light came through the hatch for me to be able to just make out the ghostly shape of the case, leaning up against the chimney breast.

It was a hell of a struggle getting it down because I'm not that strong, really, and a bit lanky and clumsy. I only just managed to squeeze it through the loft hole for a start, and then halfway down, while holding it with both hands and trying not to lose my balance, I wobbled and had to let go of one hand to grab the ladder to stop from falling, and then scraped my knee quite badly on the metal because I was coming down very much faster than I wanted to.

The next thing I know, coughing and spluttering, I've carried the case down to the hall and plonked it by the front door. I stare at it through a great cloud of dust, hardly able to believe what I've done. It feels as though it's staring back at me too, squinting after years in the dark and every bit as shocked as I am. It's a battered old thing, still covered with the labels from all the places it had been to and all the airlines that Mummy and Pa had travelled with in the old days— Sabena, KLM, BOAC, BEA, MEA, Lufthansa, Olympic Airways. I just love those old names; they bring back such exciting memories.

I had to open the front door because there was so much dust, and then I decided the best thing was to lug it all the way back up the stairs to open it in the privacy of my bedroom, just in case Mrs. Hamilton came from next door with a bit of pie or something, like she often does when Pa's away. I took hold of the handle of the case and had just started to lift it when 'whrrrrrrrrr....', the two leather straps are flying through the buckles, and the lid hits the floor with a smack with everything spilling out as though it's an animal that's been slaughtered, and all its innards are coming out. I nearly fell over because the heavy case was suddenly empty in my hand.

There was a great splash of colour spreading out and sliding around on the shiny tiles, then a tinkling sound, and a whole load of beads began to pour out of the corner of a knotted up red and blue scarf in the middle of the pile. They flew across the floor, bouncing off the skirting boards and rolling all over the place.

I didn't know what to do. I froze to the spot for a bit, standing there with my mouth open, still holding the handle. All the things from inside were still moving around, and twitching, and unwrapping themselves on the floor just as though they might have been prisoners who've broken out and can't believe their luck that they're suddenly free.

I absolutely had to put everything back, and I was telling myself to scoop all the things up into my arms and push them into the case as quickly as I could. I'd have to hunt for the beads so that Pa would never find even a single one, then pack the case up right away, and pull the leather buckles tight again to stop this adventure and put the whole damn thing back in the attic exactly where I'd found it and never be stupid enough to disturb it again. I shut my eyes as tight as could be, bent down and grabbed a whole pile of the things from the floor.

But then suddenly my eyes were wide open again, and I was gasping for breath as though I might be going to have one of my old asthma attacks.

It was the smell. Mummy's smell. The smell that was always with her wherever she went in the old days before she was ill. The smell of her in Beirut. The smell of her blouses, her nightdresses, her pillowcases, the smell from the drawers of her dressing table, and her bathroom—even from the glove compartment beside the driver's seat in the car. That same perfume that was on her scarves I used to take back to Courtlands with me to breathe in during the middle of the night if I couldn't sleep. After all this time, here it was again.

'Mummy?'

I only thought she was there for a tiniest moment. Just for a split second, that's all.

Then I let go of the things I was holding in my hands. They dropped back onto the floor, and I sank right down until I was kneeling in the middle of all her clothes.

I don't really know how long I was there, but it must have been ages. I was just thinking about it all, I suppose, about everything that had happened.

A long time later, I heard one or two of the last of the beads coming out of the scarf and plink-plonking onto the floor, and I sort of came round. By that time the sun was getting quite low outside and shining through the glass around the front door, which was still open. There was a breeze coming in, and all the dust from the case had blown away and settled.

I put everything back. Very slowly, not pushing and shoving in a panic to get it done, but just as carefully and calmly as I wanted, looking at all the things and trying to see if I remembered any of them, not caring about the time passing by. There were white gloves for the evening which I wrapped up in the tissue paper that they'd fallen out of, skirts with pleats, silky under slips, a cardboard-stiff swimsuit covered with huge red roses, a white jacket with big square crimson buttons down the front like a military uniform, a small handbag made out of crocodile skin, and a pair of dainty light blue sandals. I found a very wide black belt with a red buckle the shape of a heart and an empty perfume bottle that said 'Chanel No. 5', with its head newly snapped off at its neck when it had fallen out of the case. It had gone all these years being an empty bottle from the past, hidden away, and now it was broken. There were white blouses with sleeves down to the elbows, a brown paper bag with hair grips inside, and rolled up ribbons, and a girl's Alice band, which could easily have been from when Mummy was little. I didn't remember any of the things, although everything did completely remind me of her. There was a blue satiny dressing gown right at the bottom of the pile, and when I picked it up to fold it away, a book without its cover fell out of the pocket and all the yellowy pages scattered when it hit the floor. It was The Ballad of Reading Gaol, which in fact I do remember her reading and quoting bits from. I wanted to keep it out, but I knew that everything had to go back, so I collected up the pages and tried to put them in some sort of order before I put it all back into the dressing gown pocket.

The very last thing was another scarf with knotted corners like the one the beads had come out of. When I untied it for a look inside, I found a whole treasure trove of sparkly jewels—earrings, brooches, chunky rings, necklaces, and bracelets that jangled together when I picked them up, and right in the middle of the bunch, all knotted up in another string of beads was a very large brooch of ruby red stones on swirly gold leaves with very delicate veins showing through. I turned it over and over in my hands, trying to see if it might be the sort of thing Mummy could have been wearing when she was going out to dinner and came to my bedroom to say goodnight to me.

It was all stuff from the old days in Beirut. Pa must have packed it away when he knew for sure that Mummy was never coming back, and he'd only put things in that were about good memories. Perhaps he thought he might like to go up to the attic and have a look now and again—just to be reminded of how things had been before everything went wrong. Just for his own memories, that's all.

It was after I'd done up the leather straps of the case and was standing there holding the handle again, thinking about how on earth I was going to get the great weight of it back up the ladder, that it happened. I took a step and something flicked off my shoe and shot out of the open front door. At first I thought it was a black ball — something like a cricket ball but just a tiny bit smaller. I watched as it rolled down the steps into the garden and stopped in one of the clumps of little white flowers that grow along the edge of the path.

It must have come out of the case with all the other stuff and landed on one of the black tiles so that I couldn't really see it. I'd missed it altogether. I put the case down and went out of the front door to get it back, and as I was going down the steps, I suddenly knew exactly what it was. I remembered it perfectly. I remembered the silence and the feeling of excitement whenever Pa unlocked the little drawer in his dressing room in Beirut and took it out to put it on Mummy's dressing table while she was getting ready. Whenever the little black box came out, it meant that they were going somewhere completely special, and if there was any talking at all, it would be whispers, as though the thing in the box was having a long sleep and must only be woken up incredibly gently. It was always Pa that opened it and took the brooch out. Then there'd be another silence before more whispers about exactly where it was going to be pinned on the dress, and it was always Pa who did that too. And I think that at the same time we'd be remembering the man who'd run down the steps from his big house in the mountains to give it to Mummy just as we were about to drive away.

I don't think I'd seen it since we'd come back to England. I'd thought about it a lot, but I was just so sure that it must have gone ages ago at the time when Mummy was at her worst and lots of things were steadily disappearing; all the rings and bracelets made of gold, and the real pearls that she got when her great-aunt died, and then even the silver box that they all used to be kept in. But the brooch from Beirut was my favourite thing because I was there when she was given it. I'd never said anything about not seeing it, of course. It was just one of those lovely things from our old life that I thought was nothing but a memory now.

Walking down the steps, I told myself that it was very probably only the box that was there. I picked it out of the flower bed and tried to prize it open before I saw that the tiny clutch in the shape of an 'S' on the side was still closed. But even when I'd undone it, the box didn't really want to open—as though it was struggling to keep its secrets—so I sat down on the bottom step and very slowly tried again. It was a bit like opening an oyster shell. I had to put both my thumbs into the little gap that I managed to make and wiggle them around. Then suddenly, the box gave up the fight and twanged all the way open, as though it had changed its mind and was now going to show off instead.

Inside, peeping out of a little grey cushion just like a tiny cloud, was the brooch in the shape of a tree, just exactly as I remembered it from the past, with its trunk all encrusted with minuscule white diamonds, and above it, the pale green branches of emeralds shimmering in the last bit of the evening sunshine coming through the old apple tree.

I couldn't stare at it for too long because time was rushing by, and I knew I had ever such a hard battle coming up to put the case back in the attic before Lena came back. So I closed the box, went back into the hall and undid the straps of the case to pack it away, being clever enough to think that since it had rolled out and not been buried by the other things, it must have been near the bottom, so that's where it had to go now.

I'd finished putting it in its place and was just about to close the lid of the case when I decided I wanted to have just one last look, in case I never saw it again. I felt under the clothes, took the box out, and forced it open again. The letters had been folded up really tight and pushed into the top part of the box and now, with another jolt of the lid opening, they fell out onto the floor.

—⁂—

I think Pa was right never to talk about Mummy after she'd left us. From the moment we got into the car at Finsbury Park, I just automatically understood why he'd never said before. That had always been Pa's rule, and then it became my rule as well. I didn't want to talk about it either. Not ever, not to anyone. Mummy had gone and wasn't coming back, and I had to get used to it. I truthfully don't know why she didn't want to see me, but I think when you like drinking, probably your whole mind is affected, and all the things you used to like, even your own children, suddenly don't matter to you very much. She was ill, in fact. I've read some things about alcoholics now—there was a long article about it in the Sunday Times Magazine during the summer that Pa left out by accident. It said that until the person wants to stop drinking there's nothing you can do about it, and they'll always let you down—stuff like that which makes quite a lot of sense, in fact.

But just because I didn't talk about it all didn't mean I wasn't thinking about her, and I was still hoping she'd come home—and actually, she did for a bit. I can't remember how I know that, but she was at home for a little while during the summer term after that horrible Christmas. I didn't see her because I was at school, of course. But she didn't stay long before she went back to Trotsky John again. She never once wrote to me, or anything. By the time I went home for the summer holidays, she'd gone forever.

It's a blur, all that time right until I left Courtlands to come here to Whitchurch. I get things mixed up and in the wrong order, especially to do with being at home, and trying to remember things like all the au pairs who came to stay. There are only one or two things that stick in my mind to do with Mummy.

I remember a letter on the doormat once when I came down to breakfast after Pa had left for work, and the au pair was hoovering in the sitting room. It was addressed to Mummy. I think it was from her old school friend Sheila who lived in Ipswich, and I decided to send it on to the house in Finsbury Park. I looked up the road in Pa's A-Z in his study to get the postal district, though I wasn't at all sure of the house number and prayed that I'd got it right. I just hoped that if it got to her, and she saw my writing she might decide to write back to me. After I'd put it in the postbox at the end of our road and was walking back home, I started wishing that I'd written a little note on the back for her, just something to say I was missing her like, 'It would be lovely to see you,' 'Please write to me' or 'I send you my love, Mummy.' It didn't matter anyway, because a little while later it came back and was lying on the mat again one morning. Pa wasn't even at home that day, but all the same, I was really worried about it being there at all, so I picked it up and shoved it into my pocket in a panic. When I went upstairs to my room and took it out for a look, I could see my words had been scratched out and there was new black, angry sort of writing in capital letters. 'Pamela Teasdale has not lived here for many months. Address unknown. Suggest return to sender. John O'Brien.' John O'Brien—that must have been Trotsky John's real name.

I kept the letter in my room that night, but it felt strange, as though I was breaking the agreement I had with Pa. When he had gone to work the next day, I took it up to the top of the garden with a box of matches and burned it in the long grass and then stamped the ashes into the ground.

Some time later, two policemen came to the front door very early on a Saturday morning. It must have been in the Easter half term break because I can remember looking at the daffodils on the lawn behind them from where I was at the top of the banisters. They were talking in hush-hush voices that I couldn't hear all that well although I was doing my best to, even though it might be something awful they were saying.

'We're here on behalf of Medway police, Sir,' I heard. '…warrant for the arrest of Pamela Teasdale… charged with shoplifting… non-appearance at court…' I think they were talking like that, sort of low and respectfully, because they were surprised to be looking for a criminal in such a nice area. It must have felt all wrong.

'My wife has not lived here for some time, officer. I have no contact with her whatsoever—and so I'm afraid I'm quite unable to help you…' That's what Pa said back to them, nearly as quietly as they'd been talking. I think he didn't want me to hear.

I crept back to my room on tiptoe and closed the door as slowly and silently as possible. Then I climbed back into bed and pulled the blankets over my head and told myself I'd not heard anything at all.

I've always dreaded anything to do with the police, ever since the business in the park at Saxham. They are a bad omen, like ravens, or black cats, or smashed mirrors. I suppose a bad omen's just about exactly what they were at the end, the very last time they came back. Again I wasn't there, which Pa must have been very relieved about, because he would certainly have wanted me to know as little about it as possible. I don't know for sure if it was the police who came to tell him, but I bet it was. Naturally, we've never talked about it.

I did find out some of the details of what had happened, though. Quite soon after, I was having supper with the Hamiltons next door because Pa had a business trip and very often they invite me, even now, and I go along although I'd really rather not. Right in the middle of when we were eating, Pa phoned from somewhere abroad to check on me; Mrs. Hamilton answered and then told me to have a word with him in the study. Right on top of all Dr. Hamilton's untidiness on his desk, I saw a piece of paper with Mummy's name on it. I tried not to look, but couldn't really stop myself. I certainly didn't pick it up, but I've got very good eyesight and was able to read a whole chunk of it while Pa was talking. He kept saying 'Ben? Ben? Are you there?' because I could hardly take in anything he was saying. It was the weirdest thing—to be talking to him and reading about Mummy all at the same time. He'd absolutely have hated to know that I'd found anything out. I really don't know why the Hamiltons had that stuff in their house. Perhaps anyone is allowed to see a report like that, the same as you can read anyone's will if you ask to. When I went back to the dinner table my knife and fork were shaking in my hand so that I couldn't eat anymore, but the Hamiltons didn't seem to notice. It was only a few weeks after the funeral, and of course no one had told me any of the details. I wasn't meant to know any of it.

It was my last term at Courtlands when it happened, which is over three years ago now, but like I'm always saying, it's somehow a bit of a blur, those Courtland days.

In my head, it's sometimes the policemen who came to the house about the shoplifting, and sometimes it's the policemen from the park in Saxham, knocking on the door early in the morning. Then Pa is standing there with his arms down by his sides, and they're talking to him in those same quiet voices while they tell him the dreadful news.

Perhaps he told them again that it was nothing to do with him. Perhaps afterwards he went into his study and read his Daily Telegraph with a cup of coffee. Perhaps a few days later he went into the attic and undid the case and picked up Mummy's things and put them against his cheek just like I did a few weeks ago.

It's that same bit of the M2 motorway I always see when I think of Mr. England in his Mini, driving to Deal for the very last time. The bit that goes down to the big bridge that crosses the Medway where all the little boats lie on their sides in the mud when the tide is out. That's where I see him looking straight ahead with no expression on his face and his hands gripping the steering wheel. And that's where I see the doctor in his car who had to go to the coroner's court about Mummy.

It was very early in the morning, and he was on his way to see a lady who had phoned to say that she thought her old Mum had pneumonia. While he was driving along in the rain and semi-darkness, he saw what he thought was 'just a clump of old clothes' on the other side of the road. 'I don't really know what drew my eye to it,' he said, 'because it looked really quite insignificant. I can't begin to tell you why, but I felt compelled to take a closer look.'

The doctor turned his car round, although that meant going quite far out of his way, and went back. Just when he was drawing up close and slowing his car down, he saw it wasn't a bundle of clothes; for a moment he thought it might possibly be a shop window dummy, with the legs and arms at funny angles and a mass of red hair stretched out across a raincoat that was draped along the metal barrier on the side of the road. But once he'd got out and was walking back to have a proper look, he realised what he was actually looking at.

—⁓—

Not long ago, when Pa and I were driving to London to go to the cinema, we were waiting at a red light by a closed-up charity shop—I think in Clapham Junction—and against the padlocked shutters a torn bag with old rags falling out had been dumped. A pigeon was pecking at something inside, then a dog came along, and when the bird flew off, he cocked his leg against the bundle. It made me think of all the people who might be so poor they'd have to buy the rotten clothes, not knowing that they came from a heap of worthless old rubbish that had soaked up the dirty drizzle, dog's pee, and pigeon shit. 'Just a clump of old clothes…'

—⁓—

I didn't put the letters back inside the box. I kept them out. I wanted to read them slowly, over and over again to work it all out.

I was thinking I might put them back later, then something in my mind told me that Pa would never know I had them, and, in fact, he probably didn't know they existed at all. Mummy had put the letters inside the box herself, and he'd never noticed. I hadn't noticed myself, after all, when I first I opened it in the garden. They're written on air-mail paper, as thin and light as tracing paper, just tiny wisps of words on four pages folded over and over again till they're just the size of a few stamps.

When it became time to put them back, just before I was leaving for school, I didn't want to do it. I hadn't finished looking at them, even though I'd copied all the words out and can read them whenever I like. I just so wanted to have the actual letters for a bit. Besides, Pa was back from his trip and too much around for me to do anything about it. I just couldn't think of the business of bringing the case down again. It was such an unbelievable struggle to put it back up there, and I'd been so careful to make sure it was in exactly the same place as I'd found it. Before I pushed the ladder back up, I'd gone into the garden shed with a dustpan and brush and a cloth to gather up as much dust as possible to take back up into the attic to shake over my fingerprints on the case. I sneezed for absolute ages, and when Lena did come back from the pictures she thought I must have got flu or something.

So I put the four pages into the back of my stamp album and brought them back to school with me.

But I'm in a complete panic about it now. I just think that Pa does know about them. Perhaps he put them in the box himself? What on earth will he be thinking if he goes up there for old memories sake and they're not in there? Everything will be just as it was except for no letters anymore, as though they've been spirited away. It was none of my business to take them. Please, please let it be that I've got the chance to go home this half term and put them back. Please let that happen.

---

11 January, 1968
My dearest Pamela,

How wonderful it was to hear from you after all this time, and how would it be possible for me to have forgotten the pleasure I found in your company? Of course I remember you! Indeed, I ask your forgiveness for this late reply—I would have wanted that your letter be answered by return of post, but as you see I am in my apartment in Paris for a few days with my eldest daughter who is enrolling in a Parisian school, and your letter reaches me via my staff in Beirut.

It is of course quite impossible that I should want to receive back from you the brooch that I gave to you on our very first meeting; it was signifying nothing more than a joy at having made your acquaintance and for you to remember the sweetness of that day. It was quite—as I think you say in English—'a spur in the moment' decision to present it to you, and sincerely I tell you that you owe me nothing for this gift. I would obviously wish that you might keep it forever to remind you not only of that first meeting, but also our dinners together under the stars on the Beirut Corniche and by the beach at Juniyah. They were wonderful times, don't you think?

How is your son Benjamin that my daughters have fallen in love with on your visit to our house? And your husband is in good health too, I hope?

Pamela, it is quite possible for me to meet you as I am sometimes in London for my business, and it would be a delightful pleasure to dine with you again. I return to Lebanon next week and then have plans to be in London at the end of next month for a few days.

It is truly wonderful to hear again from you. Do not hesitate to contact me and to let me know if it might be possible to meet when I come to London— the address of my Secretariat in Tabaris Square, Achafria, is the same but recently I have moved to the 9th floor.

I send to you my very fondest greetings, dear Pamela,
Ramzai

15 September, 1968
My dear Pamela,

I am so very relieved to have word from you again after such a long time of silence that has so greatly perplexed me, but of course, I am also very concerned at the news that you have suffered such a terrible illness since our wonderful meetings last March. I do now understand why it has not been possible for you to answer my letters, and perhaps you have not been able to receive them? However, I am so pleased that the doctors at the sanatorium have now judged that you are well enough to have returned home, and I pray that your recovery is continuing.

I am too shy to ask you directly what the trouble has been, my dear Pamela, but may I say that when you are returned to full health that you might think over once again the sincere offer that I made to you in London in April. I wish that you might fully consider it without haste over the next few months. You know very well that I have all the time to wait for your reply.

I am most concerned that you need to rest further, and I would like to suggest to you that now Benjamin has returned to school, you might consider that you stay at my apartment in Paris for a few weeks? You will be quite alone and unmolested there since I have business that keeps me in the Middle East for at least the next month. You have only to say the word and my staff will make the necessary arrangements for your visit. The Grand Salon of the apartment overlooks the Jardin de Luxembourg which is glorious in these autumn days and is now returned to tranquility after the events of the students' disturbances in the earlier part of this summer—the trees are changing colour and the fruits in the horticulturists' area are ready to be picked! It is truly the most ideal time to be in Paris. Might you consider this visit? I know it will do you so much good. Contact me as soon as you are able. I am sending you all my love,

Ramzai

My dear Ramzai,

Thank you so very much for your letter and once again, please forgive me for not having been able to contact you over the summer. I can't express to you how terribly touched I've been by your letters expressing such concern, but I do really seem to be on the mend now after two or three very difficult months.

You've no need to feel shy—as you so sweetly put it—about asking what the problem with my health has been, but in fact, no one has really been able to tell me, even after many exhaustive tests. They begin to think that I suffered some sort of allergic reaction that had the effect of making me terribly weak and anaemic, but even now they are very far from certain. But the wonderful news is that every day I seem to be getting stronger and stronger. I say let it remain a mystery as long as I am better!

How incredibly kind of you to offer to open up the apartment in Paris for me. I have wonderful memories of the Jardin de Luxembourg from when I was very small, just before the war. I was there for a few days with my father, and it must have been just this time of year, since I remember quite clearly an area of the park where they grew all sorts of varieties of peaches and apples—I even seem to recall beekeepers dressed in funny mesh hats collecting honey from hives. I had a falling out with Papa when there wasn't time for him to keep his promise to let me have a ride on one of the donkeys because we had spent too long looking at the huge grey fish in the round pond in front of the Palais! I have been back since, but nothing touches you like your first memories of something, don't you think?

I cannot thank you enough for your generous offer, Ramzai, but I'm fine now and really feel that I need to be at home for a while. Ben will be coming back for his half term break in a few weeks, and I must be here. I think he was quite badly affected by my illness and then by my absence through most of his summer holidays, and it is very important to me that he sees that everything *is now returning to normal. He is a very sensitive boy, and though he tries to keep himself to himself and struggles to pretend to be grown up, I'm aware that he has been suffering. He became terribly stressed during the summer which led to a dreadful incident at school and as a result, he had to miss nearly half of the term while he recuperated at home with his father, who is a truly good man, but not—as you know from our conversations—the most patient of people. I desperately need to spend some time with him to reassure him that everything has returned to normal.*

Ramzai—this now brings me to the real point of this letter. I can't begin to tell you how difficult it is for me to write this, but I cannot leave Adrian. It would break his heart, and I do not think I could ever bear the guilt of that. But above all things, I cannot abandon my son. He's everything to me, and as I've tried to explain, I need to be at home to look after him and to try to repair some of the damage of the last few months.

I am so very sorry, especially when you are offering so much, and, in spite of what my heart would have me do, I have to listen to my conscience. Please believe me when I say that I'll never forget the sweetness of our few days together in London, and your extraordinary kindness and generosity. They meant the world to me.

I'm praying that eventually, however hurt you are by my refusal, you'll be able to understand because of your own feelings for Leila and Fareeda, who have so recently had to come to terms with losing their mother. Above all, they now need the constant, loving comfort and support of their father, just as Benjamin needs that of his mother. You, above all people, have such a feeling for…

She never finished writing that letter—and she never sent it because I think she couldn't really make up her mind where she wanted to be.

In the end, she didn't want to be with Pa, she didn't want to be with Trotsky John, she didn't want to be with Ramzai Abu'ilam, and she didn't want to be with me. What she says in the letter about looking after me just wasn't true.

I'm like her. Just exactly the same. I see her every single time I look in the mirror. I've even got a small mole underneath my collarbone, just like she had. My hair's just about the same colour, I've got her eyes and the same nose, and when I see something squeamish, my mouth turns down at the ends just like hers used to. When I'm reading a good book, I automatically curl my legs up underneath me on the sofa and start to twizzle a bit of my fringe round my fingers just like she used to, and when I do it, the boys in the library ask me why I'm so girly. I'm not particularly, I don't think. It's just that I'm the same as Mummy, that's all. I laugh at silly jokes too loudly, just like her, and if I'm gullible, so was she for sure. Once, when I was still quite small, I hid behind the sofa and dropped a huge black rubber spider into her lap. She screamed and screamed, and then saw the funny side, and we both became ill with laughing about it.

She was a dreamer, just like I am, always closing her eyes and thinking of lovely memories and being somewhere else with her music and her books. I think she just wanted to go back to her old life, but in the end she knew it was too late for that and was trapped; the dreams were too big, and the drinking more important than any other thing in her life, including me.

VII.

December, 2008

'Pa?'

He's sitting in his armchair as I open the door, the back of his head framed within the vast, distorting screen of the television he's far too close to. I'm not sure it's him for an instant—his hair's been cut, and it looks as though it might have been blow-dried. The oil that he's massaged into his scalp to tame his hair ever since I can remember has not been applied; now there's a white halo of soft down with a just-left-of-centre parting where there's never been one before. I struggle to check a giggle. It's Thomas's doing. He's the immensely warm and personable young man from Zimbabwe who's doing an IT course during the evenings and managing to persuade truculent old folks to do things they don't want to during the day, and he's been making a few alterations to 'Mr. Adrian's' appearance. The hair's the most recent and certainly the most alarming, but other revolutionary changes have been introduced, like the successful binning of an ancient pair of monogrammed slippers, which had earned me a stinging rebuke when I'd surreptitiously placed them outside the back door of the house with all the other rubbish on the day of the big move. He's forgetful about most things these days, and I thought I'd got away with their removal. But it hadn't passed him by, and they had to be retrieved from a black plastic bag complete with a couple of old tea bags that had found their way into an already darkly stained interior. Now, fingernails are regularly cut and cleaned, a shower-time rather than a bath-time has been introduced and declared 'a real time and effort saver' by the very same person who, in spite of a well established difficulty getting in and out of the tub, has refused to countenance just such a change for the past five or so years. I've just paid a bill for desperately needed new underwear from Marks and Spencer's—my gentle blandishments to encourage an updating of his socks and pants drawer have always been dismissed with a testy 'who's to see my bloody pants anyway? None of their business.' It's quite remarkable that Pa seems to be going along with it all, only very infrequently putting his foot down—the last time about being forced into a short-sleeve shirt that he'd insisted, quite rightly, was not his own. 'I know it's not mine because I haven't worn one since I came back from the Middle East!' On a quick visit before my recent holiday, unable to find him in his room, I'd ventured along to the communal sitting room to find him not only happily ensconced in the wheelchair he swore he'd never use—with Thomas standing behind him with a proprietorial hand on his shoulder—but also clapping his hands with gusto, slightly off the beat, to a rendition of Doing the Lambeth Walk. It was being performed by a large blonde lady dressed as a pearly queen, holding a microphone attached to a portable speaker on wheels. Gone are the days, apparently, when he looked down on me for enjoying the 'trite and vulgar' Tchaikovsky. I guess the simple truth is that it's not that he's growing more amenable, just less inclined to put up a struggle. It's probably a sign of closing down, a waning spirit of defiance, more than anything else.

Today the room's stiflingly hot, with the curtains at the closed French windows that lead onto a concrete patio half drawn against the sun's rays. On the bed next to his chair, there's a tray with an abandoned lunch—two thin sausages adrift in a sea of congealing gravy on a white plate. A segment of pallid tinned peach like a dead goldfish is lying in a saucer full of milky tea with the cup upside down beside it. Next to it, a digestive biscuit is breaking down into a brown putty in a small, not quite empty glass of orange juice balanced precariously at the very edge of the tray.

'How are you doing?' I say as I settle a hand on his shoulder and my head comes round to break his view of the omnibus version of Eastenders. He's never shown the slightest interest in the goings on at Albert Square in the past, but the sideways jerk of his head informs me of a frisson of annoyance at the interruption.

'Pa? It's me. Ben.'

'Oh! Hello there, old chap. How are you? How was your Greek trip?' The watery blue eyes behind the glasses light up with recognition. It's one of his better days.

'It was fine, Pa. But I've seen you since I got back, of course.'

'Of course. Of course,' he says, nodding his head and failing in an attempt not to look puzzled.

'Take a glass of port...' A finger is wagged in the general direction of the chest of drawers.

'Thanks, Pa, but I don't drink, remember,' I tell him, 'Nearly two years now.' His eyes settle on the television again. I move the tray on the bed towards the bank of pillows to make a space and hoist myself onto the bed. There's a pristine copy of the Sunday Telegraph at the foot of the bed that I stealthily reach for, momentarily feeling guilty at my never-ending urge for information of the outside world, before I remember that the rules of engagement round here have been changing swiftly recently, and that Pa is now quite content for me to be with him without the necessity of any verbal communication at all. But still, I find myself reading with care, letting gravity gently and silently coax each turning page from perpendicular to horizontal, glancing up from the paper every now and again just in case I might be under some unspoken obligation to follow what's unfolding on the screen. I let my hand rest on top of his on the arm of the chair. It's his good, right, side. The fingers of his left hand are constantly moving; sometimes a small ripple travels up his arm turning into a wave that engulfs his shoulder before travelling through his torso to his left leg and down to his foot that then erupts into a series of short spasms.

He's wearing a pair of brown corduroys I don't recognise. The turn-ups are adrift around his white calves and a morsel of scrambled egg from breakfast has made a home for itself in the folds round his crotch.

'Thomas's day off today, then Pa?' I ask, as the credits begin to roll on the television.

'What?'

'Thomas not here to help you today?'

'No.'

'I'll open the door for a tiny while, shall I?' I say, my voice rising above the theme tune that's still holding his attention, 'It's quite stuffy in here, you know.'

'Yes, if you want.' When I turn the key in the door, a seal of dried condensation, dust and fraying paint around the frame succumbs to my push, and it opens with an indignant crack.

'There we are. That's better, isn't it?' A tingling freshness sweeps into the room like a bossy housekeeper. I go back towards the bed, sit down and take his hand in mine again. I give it a squeeze as I look round his new home. I'm glad of the few things that I'd arranged to be brought from the house to accompany him—the early Victorian mahogany chest of drawers with the bowed front, and the bracket clock inherited from his father that sits on top of it, together with his prized first edition of Winston Churchill's History of the English Speaking Peoples next to the unopened bottle of port. Hanging too high above the clock on the freshly painted white wall is the passably good copy of Millais' Ophelia that had belonged to my mother and that Pa had rather unexpectedly insisted should come with him. When I was small, I was convinced that the hapless young woman floating in the clear, deep stream, with the open eyes and supplicatory palms turned upwards to the sky was a representation of her. It frightened me, made me fearful for her, and I'd do my best to avoid setting eyes on it where it hung in her room next to the dressing table in the house in Beirut.

There's a suitcase that sits above the utilitarian wardrobe opposite the bed; it overhangs the top, inviting attention, as though impatient to be taken down and repacked for the resumption of some interrupted journey. It invests the room with a feeling of impermanence, as though the occupant may be staying only temporarily.

'When are we going home?'

'What do you mean, Pa?'

'When are we going home?' he repeats slowly, insistently, and with more than a hint of impatience, 'I've had enough of the sea-side. I've not swum once—not once. It's too cold, and I'd like to go home. I've been here too long now.'

Not such a good day after all. I walk over to the door and close it again, mapping out my words for the forthcoming struggle. 'We're not at the seaside, Pa. We're in Weybridge, remember? We've left the house. This is where you live now.'

'I've not been told this,' he says, indignation rising in his voice, 'I don't know anything about this.'

'Pa, come on, now. Of course you do.'

'I'll pop in to see you tomorrow on my way back from my trip,' I tell him a few minutes later when the surprise at the news of his move has somewhat abated. I've not bothered to tell him that it's Saxham I'm visiting. I'm not sure that he'd process that information at the moment, and anyway, a new found interest in a very loud game of snooker on the television means he's not paying me the slightest attention.

'In the suitcase…' he says suddenly as I open the door to go. He's twisted himself round in the chair to see me better.

'What, Pa?'

'You must get it from the suitcase, Ben.'

'There's nothing in your suitcase, Pa.'

'No, not mine,' he says waving the finger of his right hand, 'Your mother's. Your mother's suitcase in the attic. The brooch—it's still up there. You know the one—the Prince chappy gave it to her, re-member? I've kept it there—always kept it there. Should be in the bank, you know. It really should be in the bank.'

'Yes, Pa. I know. I found it. I've got it.' It's the first time any mention of the suitcase has passed between us. It's as though light has streamed in through an opened window to expose our secret to harsh daylight, illuminating it for a second before it cracks and crumbles to dust.

'You could give it to your daughter. When you have a daughter, you could give it to her.'

'Yes, I suppose I could.' I immediately see an image of a young girl on a swing, the Teasdale heiress, demanding to be pushed harder and higher by a bemused middle-aged 'confirmed bachelor' who's asking himself how on earth it came to be that he finds himself with a young daughter.

I walk back across to the silent old man who's studying me from his chair. 'It's safe and sound with me, Pa,' I say as I put my hand on the back of his head. 'Safe and sound with me,' I repeat softly as slowly and deliberately I lower my head and place a firm kiss on his cheek.

—∿∿—

I haven't been back here to Saxham since the day I left nearly four decades ago. Not once. Until my recent holiday in Lesbos, I truly thought I'd not the slightest interest in seeing the old place again. Less than the slightest interest, in fact. Whenever the subject of schooldays has come up in conversation, I've heard myself boasting that I've spent nearly forty years successfully erasing it from my consciousness.

But now that I'm here, once again descending the steep lane that leads from the church down to the river bank and the old school house, it's an extraordinary revelation to discover what my mind has decided to pack away in its box of memories and what it has totally discarded.

I do remember the hill being this steep. Our little crocodile of boys, making its way back down the street towards the school after the Sunday morning service in the church, was always being forcefully reminded to stay on the pavement, even when that meant having to resort to a malformed, hand-in-hand single file. Step off the narrow band that hugged the houses on either side and onto the cobbled street, and you were likely to slip, especially if there was a late autumn deposit of rotting leaves or a stubborn ground frost resisting the anaemic mid-winter rays of the sun.

So I'm sticking to the pavement as though I've obediently fallen back into line. But it's also common sense. Physically, I'm in good enough shape, but a tumble onto the already complaining knees of a man just on the wrong side of fifty might be a deal more complicated than it would be for a ten-year-old who risks nothing more than a bruise and a scab and the joshing of his crocodile contemporaries. Besides, I've done enough falling around. Those days are over forever, I hope.

My box of memories contains no recollection at all of the warehouse that looms above the street on my left at the beginning of my descent. It must have been there in the sixties—fading rust-red letters on the wall proclaim it as the work premises of one long gone 'Arthur Readham, purveyor of plumbing equipment since 1887.' However, the red pillar box I've just passed outside the entrance to the churchyard is emblazoned on my memory. I leant my sweat-pricked brow against it early one Sunday morning when the smell of incense and an empty stomach combined to envelop me in a nauseous darkness. 'Deep breaths, now, Teasdale. There's a good boy.' Miss Carson's voice echoes down the decades as she cups my forehead in the palm of her hand after my flight through the church from the choir stalls. As I'd retched unproductively, my eye had fixed on the embossed 'VR' on the side of the box, which forever after alluded to my 'very' sick Sunday.

The view over the river is just as I remember it, though. Towards the bottom of the street, the terrace on the right stops abruptly and gives way to a sloping patch of vegetable allotments eerily unchanged by the passing years. Now in deep sleep for the winter, shriveled brown leaves cling to bamboo poles and wire where three months ago there were bright red tomatoes and fat runner beans. One yellow-brown marrow lies alone, split from one end to the other, slowly returning to earth like an unburied corpse on a battlefield. The stone wall that I'd buffet my hand along in celebration of our return to school after the end of the vicar's interminable sermon is exactly as I remember it, still protecting the street from the abundance of midsummer vegetables that always threatened to engulf it. Towards the middle of the descent, the wall lowers enough to allow a picture-postcard view of the wide river estuary as it makes its way southward to become the Bristol Channel. There are fewer trees down by the river's edge now, a sparse collection of oak and elm that has been pruned hard since my time, either by husbandry or punishing winter winds. It's no longer the thick, secret forest that allowed my ten-year-old's imagination to people it with Angles and Saxons who, under its cover, stole ashore from their longboats a millennium and a half ago.

There's really not much I recognise of the old street now. The sharply descending terrace of houses on the left that might have been the subject of a preservation order had it survived demolition just a while longer, has been replaced by neat, copycat red-brick houses with squat square windows and front doors so small I'm unable to figure out how even a small sofa might be accommodated. There's a break in the line of the new terrace halfway down that allows for the entrance to a courtyard for parking at the back where once there were kitchen gardens and outside loos.

It's a bright, early winter's morning. The permanent winter fog of the old days, permeated by the tangy smell of burning logs and coal from hundreds of chimneys, has long gone, replaced with the merest passing hint of carbon monoxide expelled from efficient new boiler systems. The smell is quickly dispersed by the sprightly breeze that hurries up the street, and my scarf, carelessly donned in the warmth of the guest house where I stayed last night, is snagged and playfully unwrapped by its pull. I stop to pay attention to its reapplication, suddenly aware of the chill, and it dawns on me that I'm taking my time, slowly fastening the buttons of my duffle coat and fussing the scarf back round my neck as though I might be a reluctant knight buckling on a suit of armour before riding into battle. The steep incline is leveling out—a few more steps will find me at the bottom of the street, and a sharp turn to the left will reveal the old school.

And now, quite out of the blue, I realise I don't know whether I want the information or not. What if it's no longer there, gone the way of the little terrace in a quest for nineteen-seventies' modernisation?

I can turn around if I want, remount the hill, climb into the car that I've parked next to the War Memorial, and drive away. I don't have to be here. My little trip into the past now seems ridiculous, foolish almost; I'm beginning to lose sight of the reason why I came.

—⁂—

It was at the end of my Greek holiday, while I was sitting in the taxi on the way to the airport in Mytelene, that the idea came to me to come back to Saxham.

The young taxi driver was showing off, driving like the devil possessed along narrow mountain roads with sheer, willy-tingling drops on either side threatening us like the wide open jaws of an alligator patiently awaiting a momentary miscalculation. Now and again, I'd catch his twinkling eyes observing me in the rearview mirror, thrilled at the discomfort of his nervous passenger experiencing the joyride from hell. Eventually, I'd plucked up the courage to ask him, in my own roundabout way, to slow down. 'Too much time at airport,' I said, 'We arrive too early. I like to see your island out of the window, slowly—slowly. More slowly...' By the time I'd realised that I might just be delivered to the airport in one piece—a good hour before check in—I was practically moving myself to tears with the imagined eulogies of my broken-hearted loved ones at a standing room only funeral.

As the taxi emerged out of the mountains, hurtling towards the airport on the last lap of the journey, the image of a skinny naked child, high up on a roof with his arms outstretched like wings, came back to me out of nowhere.

It struck me with the force of a slap across the face with an open palm, as though I might be a fainting heroine in a forties' film needing a shock to bring her out of some panic-induced reverie. It did just that, and I knew at that moment that as soon as I possibly could, the first available weekend, I'd come back to Saxham, walk down this very road towards the old school, and once again stare up at the window where the boy that I'd once been had found the spirit and mad courage to make a break for freedom and had climbed out of a dormitory window onto the roof.

I've left it a little while, though. My resolution faltered once I got home and back into the routine of work and the promise of lazy weekends doing fuck all. In the end, there's been some sort of resistance to the visit that I've not examined too closely, and for a while, it had allowed me not to bother to book a room at the only guest house I'd been able to find on-line in Saxham. I had a good enough excuse to postpone, too; Pa had another stroke, the week after my return—only a small one, but there's a pattern being set now, and it certainly won't be the last. In fact they suspect he's had at least another tiny one since then. He's alright—'coming out on top,' as he puts it, but I can see the inevitable direction we're heading in.

But last night, two months later than I intended, I went for it. I decided I'd pop down to visit Pa in Weybridge and then carry on West along the M4 rather than returning home. I'd spend Sunday afternoon and most of Monday in Saxham.

—⁓—

It was already growing dark when I arrived last night. I took my time after leaving the nursing home, determined to put a step on it, to get to Saxham and have a good nosey around before the light failed. But I found myself dawdling along the first stretch of the motorway, slowing the car from my customary eighty-five miles an hour to a sedate sixty-five, suddenly wondering what on earth I might do with an evening in a strange place.

A bank of grey clouds, heavy with rain, had been gathering over to the west as I set off from Weybridge and reached me an hour later as I stopped for a late lunch. I stared out of the window of the service station at the driving rain, taking my time over a lunch that resolutely conspired against me; the ham salad sandwich, extracted with exasperation from a cellophane package that wasn't prepared to give it up without a fight, was just old enough to be hinting at day old scraps in a kitchen bin on a warm day, and the cup of tea I'd bought to accompany it contained a tea bag that resolutely refused to part with any of the English Breakfast flavour that the label promised.

Just an hour or so later, sipping yet another cup of tea at the next service station, I try to bury my head in the Sunday Times. But now and again I find myself raising my eyes to look out onto the vast frame of the suspension bridge that lifts the road from England into the sky and deposits it on the far side of the river in Wales; the very same bridge that, years before, I'd wake early to stare at in the far distance from the window of the dorm.

I hadn't intended to stop. The outline of the bridge can be seen from many miles away as you approach it along the M4. I thought I'd take my reintroduction to it in my stride. I was coming at it from an unfamiliar direction, from the east, and besides, I imagined that any memory I might have had of it was well buried. But when it presented itself to me again in all its magnificence, its pillars like giant rugby posts disappearing into the low clouds above, it seemed to me to be entirely, shockingly familiar, concertinaing time and unexpectedly filling me with foreboding. Instead of just asking myself what I might do to pass the time on a rainy night in Saxham, I began to battle with the idea that I might not want to go any farther.

I read every last bit of the paper, including the sports section that usually finds itself sorted straight into the recycling bin at home; then I drank more tea and ate an unnecessary Danish pastry in a quest to delay my journey. I even toyed with the idea of tossing a coin to break my indecision—'Heads I go on, tails I turn back.' I left it so long that the bridge had turned white and red with the lights of the non-ending stream of traffic leaving England and arriving from

Wales. But as evening began to obscure the structure, slowly turning it into an unfamiliar stranger, I rose from the table by the vast plate-glass window on the cliff overlooking the estuary, went back to the car, queued at the tollbooth and crossed the river.

—⁓—

'It's a lovely place you have here,' I said last night to Mrs. Sheringham, stepping out of the rain into the warmly lit entrance hall of her guest house.

'Yes, it is a beautiful old house, isn't it? One of the oldest in the village, actually. Georgian front but Elizabethan behind,' she said to me as I signed the visitor's book placed next to a terracotta bust of Nelson and an arrangement of dried flowers on a mahogany side table. Huge black and white prints covered the walls and climbed the staircase of the wood-paneled hall.

'Wonderful mezzotints,' I said, glancing up from the page where a departing Mr. and Mrs. Shultz from Escondido, California, had signed their names above mine. ('We loved our stay and sure plan to come back some day. Great breakfast!')

'Aren't they grand?' replied the petite figure in the neat check trouser-suit—more legal secretary than landlady, I thought to myself. 'We inherited them when we took over the house last year from the previous owners. They bought them for next to nothing when the contents of the old prep school down by the river were auctioned off.'

'Courtlands?'

'That's it,' she said, looking surprised. 'You know of it?'

'Yes, I'm an old boy, actually. And I think I remember the prints; they were in the entrance hall.'

She showed me up to a room at the back of the house where chintz curtains, heavy with colourful birds of paradise and already drawn against the night, pooled extravagantly onto the floor. On the walls were more prints in faded gold frames—a series of eigh-

teenth-century aristocratic beauties in ancient Greek costume looking sultry while leaning against urns and playing lyres. The duvet
was folded back invitingly to reveal off-white cotton sheets, and
on the bedside table, under a lamp with a pleated shade, there was
a little basket of potpourri and tissues in a silver dispenser. On a
low oak chest of drawers opposite the bed, a large glass jar of what
looked like homemade cookies had been placed next to a kettle, a
white porcelain teapot and two matching cups.

'You've done a wonderful job with the house. It's really beautiful—quite different,' I said. 'You've not been here long?'

'Just under a year. We're refugees from the Square Mile; we'd
had enough of the rat race and decided we wanted to be able to
spend more time together as a family.'

'Excellent.'

'I'll leave you to settle. Will you be staying with us for dinner?'
she said as her hand played with the single strand of pearls at her
neck.

'No, thank you very much, Mrs. Sheringham. I'm off to meet
friends,' I lied.

I wasn't sure about sitting in a small dining room with one or
two other guests whilst feeling obliged to indulge in a little polite,
strained conversation over soup. I imagined that I might find a window seat at a table laid for one in a busy little bistro in the village,
where I'd be able to bury myself in my book and take in the sur-
roundings.

It wasn't to be, though. A walk up the damp and windy high
street quickly confirmed that Saxham had failed to be colonized
even by the ubiquitous Indian takeaway. There was a chemist's, a
hardware store, a Spar convenience shop, a post office—all in darkness except for an outfit that flattered itself with the name 'Jo's An-
tiques and Bric a Brac'. When I cupped my hands above my forehead
and pressed my face up against the window to see what might be

inside, the cavernous space, lit by a single bulb, was nearly empty but for three or four pine fire surrounds to the side of the window, leaning up against each other and anchored against the wall by a vast brass bedstead in several pieces. In the centre of the shop was a rusting neo-Victorian iron garden table with four chairs. On a trestle table in front of them a large string puppet with a dejected look on his face—perhaps because he was missing a leg—was propped up against a bread bin next to a collection of tin tea caddies and two dusty fifties' decanters with tarnished 'whiskey' and 'gin' dog tags round their necks.

So I got back into the car and drove too fast through the silent, dark, rain-soaked villages that border the river on the way to Gloucester, where I was sure that I'd find some lively little joint in which I'd be an inconspicuous stranger. But when I got there, it didn't exist—at least not on a rainy Sunday evening in early December. I drove round the wet, deserted streets lit by half-hearted Christmas lights, and got caught up in a one way system that refused to release me from its clutches till I'd completed three or four turns of the inner city. Finally, I abandoned the car in a side street and walked into the windswept, pedestrianised and empty centre, losing my temper with my disobedient brolly that was trying to turn itself inside out with all the determination of a toddler embarking on a tantrum.

In desperation, I became the last customer in a McDonald's on the point of closing for the night, sitting on a plastic-backed chair in the hard, unforgiving light that sucked the little colour from the face that was reflected back at me from the mirrored wall opposite. The only other customers—two teenage boys eating with their mouths open and flicking each other's wrists with elastic bands—argued loudly over the results of some local football match, while a spotty, morose girl mopped ineffectively round my feet, the sweet, sickly smell of the disinfectant catching in my throat while I thought of the dinner I'd passed up back in Saxham.

—*m*—

'You've come to visit the grave?' Mrs. Sheringham was wiping her hands on a tea towel as she stood at the doorway that led from the dining room into the kitchen. She'd collected my empty plate, asked if I'd like a fresh pot of tea which I readily accepted, and had then allowed herself to relax into a conversation with me, her last remaining customer.

I'd dawdled in my room this morning, watching the nine o'clock news on the television until I supposed that most of the other guests had finished their breakfasts, and then made my way down to the dining room along corridors that smelt of fresh paint, the newly laid carpets muffling the creaking floorboards under my feet. Gloss-white fire doors opened and swung shut behind me, radiators hummed, and filling cisterns whistled somewhere above my head. A hint of soap, aftershave, and toothpaste emanated from behind closed doors where commercial travelers readied themselves for the day. I seated myself at a table on the opposite side of the room to an elderly couple muttering to each other under their breaths about whether it might be alright to ask for another round of toast and just a little more water in their pot before coming to a joint decision that there really wasn't time since 'We're supposed to be at Doreen's in three quarters of an hour from right now.'

'I'll expect you back for dinner, then,' Mrs. Sheringham had said to them as they rose from the table. While the old gentleman fussed about under his shirtsleeve to consult his watch, his wife steadied herself on the back of her chair before retrieving a walking stick from the nearby corner. 'Yes, yes, we'll be looking forward to that by then—won't be much of a spread at Doreen's, I shouldn't think,' she added, muttering to herself.

'The grave? I'm sorry?' I said.

'Freddie Burston's—Courtlands old Headmaster?' she replied,

looking perplexed.

'No, no, in fact I'd no idea he'd died,' I said, recalling the tall ungainly man with the loud voice that we'd all been so wary of. 'I've not had any sort of contact with the school for many years to tell you the truth. But I am so sorry to hear that. When did he die?'

'Oh I do apologize. I was just assuming it was the reason for your visit. We've had one or two old boys turn up since the funeral, actually. It was about three or four weeks ago, now, I think.' She turned her head back towards the kitchen where a shadowy figure was bent over an open dishwasher, noisily stacking plates.

'Martha!' she said, raising her voice as though addressing someone a little hard of hearing, 'Old Freddie Burston from Courtlands—how long's he been dead?' There was a pause while a large old lady with a wisp of white beard and wearing a plastic orange apron shuffled into view and leant against the doorframe. She slowly folded her arms across an enormous bosom, settling herself into a comfortable position from which to indulge in the welcome opportunity of a break from her duties for a little gossip with her boss and the visitor finishing a late breakfast. Then she cast her eyes upwards and narrowed them, as though the answer to the enquiry might be written in small print on the ceiling. 'Oh, must be more than a month, now, at least a month. They've put him next to his wife and son up there. Lovely view of the river they've got, too,' she said in the Gloucestershire accent that I remember had always presented schoolboys with an opportunity for a tease. 'You going visiting, then?'

'Yes. Yes, I'll be going up there, I should think. Gosh, I'd no idea—little Mark's dead too?' I said, remembering the toddler that I'd encouraged to walk all those years ago, '...and Mrs. Burston? How terribly sad. She can't have been terribly old.'

'When were you at the school?' asked Mrs. Sheringham.

'Oh golly! Eons and eons ago,' I replied with a smile, 'In the dark ages. The sixties, actually, end of the sixties. It's sheer curiosity that brings me back. I really just wanted to see if I remember any of it at all. Tell me, what on earth did little Mark die of?'

The thing is, I really don't know how much I truly remember.

I know I was on the roof. I know that it happened, but it might be that I'm recalling no more than split second flashbacks of that morning, as though they're the last surviving fragments of some ancient fresco that I've later subjected to an over-zealous restoration, applying too-vibrant colours onto damp pink plaster. At first, my efforts had sat uneasily with the original, but the passing decades have tempered the brash unsubtlety of the fresh paint strokes; they've faded and mellowed a little, returning a unity and truthfulness to the piece. And so it no longer matters if my mind has invented the early morning sky as it begins to lighten, the vast canopy of the trees with the rooks' nests and the squirrels' drays, the fallen elm that opens up the view down the river to the majestic suspension bridge and farther on still to the far off towers of the power station, the chilled dew on the tiles that dampen my stomach, the scratch of the rough red bricks of the chimney against my bare back, the smile that I can't suppress as I climb towards my destination, the joy of being free, and the sight of the house martins wheeling high above my head.

It might well be that it's the clearest memories of that morning that are the most unreliable. There's the milkman far below on his early morning round shielding his eyes against the rising sun, not able to believe what he's seeing; the monotone claxon call as he presses the horn of his van till outraged hands unlock doors, and windows clatter open in complaint; the pointing fingers of the gathering crowd in their dressing gowns in the narrow street, hands holding faces in horror; the boys from school spilling out onto the tennis court before they can be stopped and then being ushered back inside by Miss Carson and Miss Newman with flailing arms as though they might be marshalling a flock of geese, the far away sound of sirens approaching along the road from Gloucester, the giant red monsters that block the street with busy purring engines directing their swaying clanking ladders into the sky, the firemen slowly working their way towards me, their determined faces with puckered brows under the helmets that glint in the morning sun, the tangy smell of nervous sweat permeating the rough, serge uniforms that prickle against my naked body when strong, no nonsense arms crudely pluck me, uncomplaining, from my refuge.

But it's not just that immediate time that I have such difficulty remembering clearly. It's also the following weeks and months from which I seem to have been cut adrift. It's like a very small child's mixed up recall of events, with its inconsistencies and contradictions, its made-up scenes observed from others' viewpoints, its treasured anecdotes adopted from nursery-school friends and siblings who then object to the purloining of their personal memories. 'No, it's me that happened to, stupid. You weren't even born then!'

I was talking about it to Val Lorrimer recently on his most recent trip to London. We've become fast friends. I sought him out once I stopped drinking, initially because I wanted to spend time with people for whom alcohol wasn't important, and then because his self-deprecating humour made me laugh. It hadn't been difficult to pass on the corrected number of my mobile to the secretary of The old Breconians and within a day or two, he'd made contact with me. I encourage him to stay with me now and again, and he's been the grateful recipient of a key to my front door. I love to hear him sending himself up about his tireless efforts to make amorous conquests in various bars that I no longer frequent, and I'll take a vicarious pleasure in the day that he fixes himself up with someone special.

'Don't you just hate all the rejection, though, Val?' I asked him last week, 'I'd find it rather hard to bear.'

'Listen, Ben, how many passes have you made in the last six months?'

'God, Val. I don't know. I'm rather out of practise actually, and not that bothered either. To tell you the truth the whole sex thing seems horribly daunting without a skinful. In the old days, the two rather went together, really. There was a very half-hearted attempt a month or two ago, and I was rebuffed, too. Actually, I was horrified at being turned down and at the same time quite pathetically relieved not to have to do anything about it. Don't think I'll be repeating the experience in the near future.'

'Well I've made hundreds of passes and been "rebuffed", as you put it, by ninety-eight percent. But the remaining two percent means I'm getting a hell of a lot more sex than most. I feel as though I'm making up for lost time really—years and years of lost time.'

Val tells me he remembers practically nothing of that summer term either—except for the fruitcake on the roof, of course. 'If you're in trauma, your mind will jettison the memory, Ben. You weren't just sitting on a roof looking at the view, you know. You were having a nervous breakdown! Of course you don't remember it clearly, our little hero of the rooftops! Likewise me. My parents were going through the muckiest divorce in history, and I remember nothing about it, about them, about school, about the ghastly court cases for custody. Nothing. Fuck all. Just you on the roof—and Wallington's enormous dick.'

Lt. Mark Burston. Beloved son of Frederick and Mary. Saxham, 1966 - Balleygawley, Northern Ireland, 1988. So cruelly taken from us. RIP.

Mary Enid Burston. 1931-1989. Beloved and devoted mother and wife. Requiescat in pace.

Three graves. The last in the neat little row has heaped, newly turned earth with a small wooden cross with no name. It's too early for a gravestone.

I'd signed the visitor's book, paid, and said my thank yous to Mrs. Sheringham, taken my overnight bag to the car in preparation of a hurried departure should I lose my nerve, and then walked straight over to the church where I'd found the graves bathed in winter sunshine under the stained glass window of the high altar.

He was their only child. And now there's no one left to clear away the rain-smudged messages of commiseration for his father.

They are still attached to the skeletal wire frames of decomposing wreathes and soggy, browning bouquets wrapped in cellophane that rustles plaintively in the chill wind. There's no one to make the decision that the time has come to collect the decaying bunches and respectfully place them on the compost heap at the far side of the graveyard. The family will lie together through summers and winters and the day will arrive when no one comes to visit, and no one remembers them. The headstones will begin to lean with the weight of the passing years, swallowed up by the long grass until the fading, mossy lettering on the grey granite stones might as well say 'forgotten'. In the bare, swaying branches above my head, the rooks caw loudly, taking exception to the presence of a lone stranger, as though they might be the self-appointed guardians of the graves of the Headmaster, his wife, and their son.

I've left them behind where they lie together high above the river and walked down the hill towards the old school. I take a long deep breath and turn the corner at the bottom to confront my memories.

—m—

I'm standing in the road in front of the great door with its massive fanlight. It's no longer a dull green, but a brilliant white that matches the row of tall windows high above and to either side. When I cross the road into the freezing shadow cast by the building to look closely at the lion's head knocker, I see an array of brass doorbells set into the side of the doorframe with little engraved plaques that spell out the names of the inhabitants of the luxury flats within. I walk back across the road and lean against the wall of the house opposite, squinting in the low sunlight. The brickwork, once the colour of red-raw chilblains, has been scrubbed clean and repointed; now, in the sunshine that's battling its way through the icy mist over the river, it's a welcoming salmon pink. The assembly hall, the gym, and kitchens that stretched along the street on either side of the main building have gone. Shorn of its clumsy limbs, the old school reaches for the sky like a Scottish tower house. In the windows to one side of the still shuttered hall, there's a smart kitchen with halogen spots shining onto a dark marble worktop. It's in the large room that I think I remember used to contain the footbath where I dreaded taking off my unmuddied kit after games. As I creep round the side of the building, my view into the interior is obstructed by heavy blinds with tassels and voluptuously swagged curtains. Audis and soft-top Mercedes wait on reserved, herringbone-brick parking spaces where the Assembly hall once stood, ready to whisk their owners into the offices of service industries relocated from London to converted riverside warehouses in Gloucester.

I ignore the sign that informs me that this is private property, step over the low chain that connects the bollards separating the parking spaces from the pavement, and walk cautiously round the side of the building. There's a manicured lawn where the tennis court and the cook's vegetable garden used to be, an ocean of green touched by frosty white fingers. Now, it's unencumbered by the wire fences that penned generations of small boys. It sweeps down towards the river, interrupted in the very middle by an elegant flight of curving stone steps with two vast urns on either side before the descent.

I can't stay for long. I'm trespassing after all. I expect to be told off at any minute, waiting for a window to open, for a polite but slightly threatening enquiry about whether I need any help.

The great slate balcony along the upper ground floor still runs the length of the building. I half close my eyes and try to imagine a view of parents, prefects and staff ranged along it for Sports Day, little Mark in his mother's arms as he imitates the boys below, clapping at a high jump victor.

I look up, high above to the row of dormer windows that face out over the river. My eye starts at one end and travels along to the other. It comes to rest on the last one, the most southerly. It's a window no different to all the others; it's closed tight against the biting wind.

I try to manufacture an image. But I can't get one to appear—my imagination uncharacteristically failing me. There's no window being flung open, no skinny naked child emerging into the half-light, no belly-sliding ascent to the cliff face of the chimney, no swooping house martins celebrating a boy's escape.

And what did I think was going to happen if I could summon him up? Was his ghostly image going to bring about some almighty change in me, some earth shattering epiphany that explained and changed everything; a rebirth that banished fear, turned me whole, explained and laid the past to rest?

I wanted to be reacquainted with his spirit, to let it touch and change me. But no miracle's been brought about by my being here; there's to be no damascene conversion to a life of calm, peace and security, free of useless fretting.

But I am glad I'm here. I'm glad I've come back to be reminded of his joy and the determination that came to him from nowhere. And perhaps the spirit of that brave little boy is not dead. It's just a question of finding it—a spark, a tiny flame that still burns somewhere deep inside me, waiting patiently for rediscovery.

There's wire netting around the eaves under the dormer windows. The new occupants obviously don't want the mess that the house martins would make on the balcony while they're building their nests and feeding their young.

But now that I step farther away from the old school, bravely trespassing onto the lawn to give myself a view right up to the chimney that grows out of the roof, I can see that under the cornice at the very top, just below the tall chimney pots, there are the obstinate remnants of last year's nests, enduring battering winds and rains while they wait for the return of the birds from their winter homes in Africa.

The house martins will come back in the spring to rebuild them, to raise their young as they have done for generation upon generation. And Tom Thumb's descendents will be amongst them. They have lived through times of lean and plenty, through storms, searing heat and bitter cold, falling prey to cats on the ground and hawks on the wing, bullied by crows and hungry magpies who covet their eggs. But they take life as it comes, and in the spring they'll return to glide and dive, climb and stall, to spiral upwards on kind thermals that will gently lift them into the sky. They'll be back, in just a few months' time, once again to fly high and free above the river.

William Parker was born in Newport, Wales, and spent his early childhood in the Middle East. He attended schools in Gloucestershire and Wales before studying drama at the Guildford School of Acting. William spent 20 years acting, including a season at The Royal National Theatre, two national tours of *Peter Pan*, a production of *Hair* at Her Majesty's Theatre, Haymarket in the West End, in addition to three seasons in repertory theatre and many supporting roles in TV and film. He is now happily settled into a part time job—off stage—with Andrew Lloyd Webber's Really Useful Group, which gives him time to pursue his interest in writing. He has a nine-year-old son and lives in London.

Printed in Great Britain
by Amazon